Praise for Carol Smith

Double Exposure
'Totally fascinating' *Express on Sunday*

'A hugely enjoyable book' *Woman & Home*

Hidden Agenda
'Both a thriller – I was hooked by the very first page – and a gripping story about the power of female friendships. A winning combination!' Marika Cobbold

'A gripping and beautifully constructed story' Elizabeth Buchan

'Carol Smith has done it again, an unput-down-able thriller with a twist . . . Smith holds the reader in her grasp from start to finish, and gives us compelling psychological insights on the way' Julia Neuberger

Grandmother's Footsteps
'*Grandmother's Footsteps* . . . will keep you entertained, reading and guessing all the way to the end' *Crime Time*

Unfinished Business
'If a pacy thriller is your thing, *Unfinished Business* will suit you to perfection . . . an addictive read' *Sunday Express*

'A thriller which certainly keeps you turning those pages . . . gripping right to the end' *Daily Mail*

Family Reuni
'A gripping r

'Full of actio spense story
offers a fascin es'
Good Housekee

CAROL SMITH

Double Exposure

sphere

SPHERE

First published in Great Britain in 1998
by Little, Brown and Company
Published by Warner Books in 1998
Reprinted 1999 (three times)
Reissued by Sphere in 2006
Reprinted 2006, 2007, 2008 (twice)

A CIP catalogue record for this book
is available from the British Library.

ISBN 978-0-7515-3880-9

Typeset by Palimpsest Book Production Limited,
Polmont, Stirlingshire
Printed and bound in Great Britain by
Clays Ltd, St Ives plc

Sphere
An imprint of
Little, Brown Book Group
100 Victoria Embankment
London EC4Y 0DY

An Hachette Livre UK Company
www.hachettelivre.co.uk

www.littlebrown.co.uk

For Petra Lewis and Zoe Waldie—
comrades at arms

Acknowledgements

My thanks once more to my agent, Sarah Molloy; my editors, Imogen Taylor and Rebecca Kerby, and their brilliant sales and marketing colleagues at Little, Brown/Warner. And a special thank you to Ian Blackburn of the Royal Albert Hall who enabled me to go where few have trod.

DOUBLE EXPOSURE

'the deliberate superimposition of a second image on an exposure already made'

OED

Prologue

*T*hey'll be down on the beach waiting for the mystical green flash, thinks the judge, as the dying sun hits the water and extinguishes itself for another twelve hours. He surveys his carefully set scene, unaccustomedly alone, this time having to cope for himself. One final polish to the row of borrowed highball glasses, a check that the ice bucket is full and the mixers standing coolly in the bathroom sink. God, how he misses Vincent, now almost more than ever, but this is a ritual that has to be got through, practically a sacrament after all the years he has been performing it. They are late but there's so much to think about he doesn't mind, scrambling to get his thoughts in order before he has to face them all again.

To begin with, there's the guilt. At not having been more vigilant, at taking far too much for granted. At lowering his guard and allowing strangers to come too close. And then for not having worked it out earlier, with all that evidence spread before him and the main players performing right in front of his

1

nose. *Shame on him, once the youngest member of the US judiciary system. And the camera, Vincent's camera, lying there all those months unlooked at, the film still in it waiting to be developed. Evidence so obvious it took a senior law enforcer to ignore it. Let his colleagues at the Bar never hear about* that.

But they're here now and he goes to greet them, gaunter than last year but still austerely handsome in conservative chinos and a buttoned-down Brooks Brothers shirt. There are a lot of grim truths to get through this evening but first things first. Once he's made them comfortable, each with a glass in hand, he proposes a toast.

'*To my dearest friends and surrogate family . . . and to many, many more holidays like this.*'

They raise their glasses in heartfelt agreement.

'*To friendship.*'

1

It was hot on the feet but Jo was too anxious to reach the water to have bothered to pause first and dig out her flip-flops. She *had* had the forethought to remove her lenses and leave them safely in her room but now her prescription dark glasses lay abandoned on top of her towel and Jo was alone in an unfamiliar world of scorching sunlight, silver sand and a tantalisingly beckoning blue sea. The Caribbean was all it was cracked up to be and more, though she'd not yet had a chance to absorb it properly. As she cut through the water with her neat, economical crawl, she drew in great lungfuls of healing ozone and screwed her mind's eye as tight as she could in an effort to eclipse the dying child's horrifically damaged face.

Fifty yards out the diving-raft bobbed at the top of its anchoring chain and, viewed from this vantage point in the water, through bleary, half-focused eyes, appeared to be blissfully empty, a natural haven to one in flight from chaos. She reached its side and hauled herself up the slimy steps, only to discover herself disappointingly wrong. In the very centre of the weathered boards lay a couple entwined – a lithe young man in the briefest of bathing trunks, with a pale-skinned mermaid on top of him, apparently lost in the grip of greedy passion, practically smothering him with her thick, wet hair. *Oops, sorry.* Silently Jo retraced her steps and slithered off backwards into the welcoming water, as keen not to be seen as they obviously were to be with one another.

As she swam swiftly back to the beach and the safety of her recliner she couldn't help observing that one thing better than a holiday alone in a tropical paradise must be to share it with someone you so ardently desired. Well, if ninety-five plus was all she could notch up this time, she was still doing far better than those other poor suckers left behind in London in the rain and flu germs of pre-Christmas frenzy.

'Whatever you do,' said Sebastian, as he watched Jo pack in her tiny Chelsea flat, 'don't let on what you do for a living. That's crucial.'

'Why's that?' Shorts, Jo was thinking, and T-shirts, loads of them. And a couple of denim shirts filched from Sebastian, and her own white trousers, fresh back from the laundry. And suntan lotion. And mosquito repellent. And something from the pharmacist in case she got a gippy tummy. It was ages since she'd last had a holiday, a proper one like this, and until this evening, on the brink of departure, she'd been far too preoccupied to give it more than a thought.

'Elementary,' said Sebastian, switching from Bach to Haydn, 'it's a matter of simple psychology. What else do the *hoi polloi* obsess about, once they've dragged their fat bums to some sunny shore and plonked them in deck chairs, but their health? Their general hypochondria and tedious little ailments; their bowels and bunions, heat-stroke and insomnia.'

'Cynic.'

'It's true. If you don't believe me, suck it and see. I'm just protecting your quality time . . . since you're mean enough not to wait till I'm free to come with you.'

'Oh, sweetie, you know that's not the case.'

She turned and looked at him but his smile was intact, his eyes observing her with lazy fondness. She went across and put her arms around him.

'I'm sorry. But you know I can't get time off in the New Year and, besides, after all that studying I'm totally knackered.'

'I know.' He kissed her lightly on the nose. 'Which is all the more reason to keep your mouth shut. Don't let the buggers know your secret or you'll get no peace.'

'OK, Doc. Message received, over and out. Now how's about one final American Hot before I finish this, for tomorrow night, if I'm not mistaken, I'll be feasting on flying fish and sweet potatoes.'

That and masses more, Jo saw, as she strolled past the burgeoning buffet table and into the bar for an early evening aperitif. Taking her seat at a corner table, on a white wicker armchair beneath a potted palm, she smoothed down her neat linen skirt and waited for one of the handsome black waiters to catch her eye. This was the bit she hated most about travelling alone; no matter how emancipated she liked to feel she was, she still had inhibitions about entering a bar and ordering a drink on her own.

'Hello there!' The greeting came from just behind her and

Jo looked up, startled, to find the bluest, friendliest eyes imaginable beaming down into hers, for all the world as if they'd met already.

'Mind if we join you?' And before she could respond, he was pulling up another two chairs to her low, glass table and beckoning to his friend at the bar to join them.

'Vincent van der Voorst,' said the Dutchman, extending his hand, 'and this is my venerable friend, the judge. But out here you may simply call him Lowell Brooks.'

'Pardon the intrusion,' said the older man, with a slight smile. 'Vincent does get carried away at times and you're doubtless waiting for friends.' He didn't take a seat, just stood there hovering, tall and elegant in blazer and immaculate flannels, with an Ivy League accent and hair just touched with silver.

'Absolute nonsense!' said Vincent energetically, signalling to the waiter and moving closer to Jo. 'You know what they say, the more the merrier, and this young lady was clearly waiting for us. Am I not right?'

Jo laughed. In the face of such flagrant charm she had no defence; besides, they both looked friendly and accessible, a welcome relief from what she had been dreading. They sat and Vincent brushed aside her suggestion of a white wine spritzer and instead ordered vodka gimlets all round.

'Start as you mean to go on,' he instructed, 'and if you're vacationing with us, you'll need to develop a good head.'

'He's not kidding,' said the American. 'My dear, we are delighted to know you and please don't stand for any of Vincent's nonsense.'

Lowell was from Boston, Vincent from Amsterdam. They had both arrived an hour ago, and were here for ten days.

'We come every year,' they told her. 'We've worked our

6

way through most of the Caribbean, and Antigua comes out tops in our book, especially this hotel.'

This Jo was pleased to hear. She had taken potluck with Thomas Cook's computer and now realised how lucky she was to have landed so quickly on her feet. With such entertaining company on tap as well. Better than she would have dared dream of; wait till she let Sebastian know.

'My boyfriend warned me about travelling alone,' she said. 'Thank you for being so welcoming. I had no idea what to expect.'

'Don't worry about a thing,' said Vincent, handing her the peanuts and toasting her with his glass. 'Now you've got us to fight your corner you can relax with confidence. Pretty soon you'll meet the rest of the gang and they'll tell you.'

Jo turned her eyes to Lowell for reassurance but all he did was laugh apologetically and shrug.

'He's right, I'm afraid,' he affirmed in his soft, New England accent. 'You're stuck with us now. At least for ten days.'

Two people were already seated at the table when Vincent ushered Jo through an archway and into the spacious dining room, one side dramatically open to the elements.

'We always make a point of bagging the best table,' explained Vincent, 'the minute we arrive and have seen our room. Not too close to the band, that's essential, but situated where we can keep an eye on all the various comings and goings.'

'Now meet the other half of our team,' said Lowell, pulling out a chair so that Jo could sit.

Cora Louise Ravenel extended one tiny, exquisite, heavily bejewelled hand and nodded graciously in response to Lowell's introduction, while her daughter, Fontaine, archly stretched up her powdered cheek to receive his kiss.

'Well, how *are* y'all after all this time?' she beamed with delight, taking his hand in both of hers, eyes brilliant with happiness, head thrown back in a glory of auburn curls. Lowell took the seat the other side of her and immediately the two were in close conversation as Vincent explained Jo's presence to the older woman.

'We found her abandoned like some poor, lost seabird on the shore.'

'Y'all going to like it here,' said Cora Louise confidentially, patting Jo's knee. 'Goodness knows, we've been coming here for years – mainly with these two dear boys – and just can't get enough of it. Is that not so?'

She wore navy silk, tied with a pussycat bow, and her hair was drawn back sleekly from her face into a chignon as tight and polished as a hazelnut. Real diamonds glistened at her delicate ears, matching the rows of them on her doll-like hands. Tiny but perfect, thought Jo with appreciation. What a knockout she must have been as a young girl. Both ladies were from Charleston, South Carolina, and had arrived mid-afternoon by prior arrangement with Vincent and Lowell.

'But wait till you hear the news,' she exclaimed, tapping her daughter's hand to draw her back into the general conversation.

'What say? Oh yes,' cried Fontaine with animation. 'So exciting! There was a truly terrible drama just this afternoon, we gather, minutes before we arrived.'

They'd heard it from the head waiter when they went to announce their return. An English tourist, from a hotel just down the coast, had drowned while out snorkelling on his own. A freak accident, unknown in these parts where the

8

water was so clear you could easily see the sea creatures fifty feet down.

'Poor soul,' said Fontaine, 'what a way to start a vacation.' Then broke into helpless peals of laughter as she realised how odd that sounded.

Where exactly had it happened, Lowell wanted to know, but the Ravenels had no further information. There were three hundred and sixty-five beaches on this island, one for each day of the year. But, as Cora Louise had said, the Caribbean was renowned for its calmness, particularly at this time of year when scarcely a ripple disturbed its surface.

'Except,' she said darkly, 'when the Lord is feeling wrathful. We certainly know all about that, don't we, mah dear? After what Hugo did to Charleston just three years back.'

Jo nodded and smiled in sympathy. Even she had heard of the terrible devastation Hurricane Hugo had caused when it bowled in from the Caribbean in 1989 and struck the Southern States head on.

'Did you suffer any damage yourselves?' she asked politely. She had read in the papers that they'd virtually had to rebuild the town. Cora Louise clasped her hands theatrically and raised her eyes to the heavens.

'Thankfully we were spared,' she said, 'but only by a whisker. Our poor old house was so badly shook, it's a miracle we got out alive.'

A steel band struck up on the beach outside and the chefs, in their tall, white hats, began to serve as the diners fell into line at the central table and piled their plates with sumptuous food. Jo kicked off her sandals and let the cooling sand pour through her sun-starved toes. Less than twelve hours from a London winter and already she was into a bright new world. Things were looking promising.

That night, when she'd brushed her teeth and slipped into one of Sebastian's worn old T-shirts, she slid apart the doors out on to her veranda and stood in the darkness listening to the languorous movement of the waves. All along the water's edge were flashes of sulphur which created an eerie effect. She breathed in the health-giving salt air and thanked her stars, one more time, that she'd taken this precipitous step and come on holiday on her own. She fell asleep almost instantly that night; a dreamless sleep, for once uninterrupted by the terrible grimaces of that dying child.

'Sleep well?' Vincent was already up and about when Jo went down to breakfast, his hands filled with exotic blooms carefully culled from the hotel's abundant gardens. 'Just let me put these in water,' he said, 'and I'll join you in the dining room.'

He'd eaten already, after his morning swim at some unearthly hour, but Lowell was still lingering and the ladies had just arrived. It was not quite nine, a civilised hour for a holiday, Jo thought. This morning both Ravenels were casually yet strikingly dressed, Cora Louise in beige, her more flamboyant daughter in flame-red linen which contrasted effectively with her glorious hair. She wore huge tortoiseshell sunspecs which half eclipsed her face and was chatting animatedly to an attentive Lowell, as suave and dapper as last night. They greeted Jo with genuine warmth and moved around to make room for her.

'What's happened to the weather?' asked Jo, peering out. This morning there was no sign of the sun; the sky was a uniform, overcast grey with occasional spots of rain in the air.

'Don't worry,' said Cora Louise, 'this happens. Part of the glory of the Caribbean climate is its variability. Just when

10

it's getting uncomfortably hot, the clouds roll in. A short, sharp storm then all is clear again. You'll see. By the time you've eaten your breakfast you'll find you need to sit in the shade.'

'Which is why,' said Lowell, 'your chair already awaits.' He nodded towards the beach where a row of recliners were grouped together beneath a clump of palm trees, secured from invaders by pristine yellow towels.

'All part of the service,' he said, when Jo expressed her thanks. 'Vincent and I have been up for hours, getting the beach habitable for you ladies.'

Jo was digging into fresh pineapple and coffee when Vincent returned from his wanderings with another lost soul in tow.

'Meet Merrily Morgenstern,' he announced. 'Fresh in from New York last night where she tells me the weather is truly atrocious.'

The new arrival was petite and svelte, in an apple-green smock of such superlative cut it instantly made Fontaine appear blowsy and overdone. Her glossy black hair was woven into an intricate French plait and she surveyed the group appraisingly with frank grey eyes and no smile. *Oh dear*, thought Jo with a slightly sinking heart. She'd met this type before; they were invariably trouble.

'Hi,' said Merrily, in response to their greetings, sinking into the vacant chair and scrabbling in her raffia hold-all for her cigarettes.

'So what's with this fucking weather?' she asked, lighting up, and everyone watched her in silence. Jo, seated next to Cora Louise, was aware of a sharply in-drawn breath, so she covered up by smiling brightly and asking about the new guest's journey.

'Shit,' said Merrily, in one expressive word. Then: 'Eggs,'

to the waiter, 'lightly done. Sunny side up and hold the salt.'

Then began a chapter of complaints which drove the levity right out of the party and had them leaving, one by one, on suddenly remembered errands that could not wait. The flight, she said, had been a nightmare: three hours late leaving Kennedy because of snow and then an unscheduled stopover in Miami due to engine trouble or some such damn thing. She puffed hard at her cigarette, shedding ash into her eggs. Jo watched silently in distaste, the last of the group to linger at the table yet too polite to leave the newcomer alone.

Merrily was quite startlingly pretty but her permanent scowl made this less apparent. And then, she continued, when she'd finally got here it was the middle of the night and the water wasn't hot. And now, just look at the weather; could you believe it? All this distance for an overcast sky.

'I might as well have stayed in Manhattan,' she complained. 'And holed up there for ten days watching *I Love Lucy* re-runs.'

Damn, thought Jo to herself as she made her own excuses and hurried away, *who does this pushy New York think she is, butting in like this and spoiling our fun?*

Vincent was standing by the chairs beneath the palm trees, smooth-skinned and well-muscled in the briefest of trunks, listening to his personal stereo and dancing on the sand. His face lit up when Jo approached and he removed his earphones.

'What are you listening to?'

'*Aspects of Love*. Now, quickly, grab this chair next to me and let me rub oil on your back.' He glanced at the sky. 'It's already beginning to clear. Any minute now the sun will appear and you can't risk getting caught in it without protection. Not with skin as pale as yours.'

'Where's Lowell?'

'Out there.' He pointed into the middle distance where a head was just visible, cleaving through the waves. 'The moment he gets back, it's time for a Planter's Punch.' He saw Jo's incredulous look and laughed. 'Over here we start early. You'll soon adjust. After all, we're here to enjoy ourselves and there isn't a lot else to do.'

Jo obediently lay face-down on her towel while Vincent pulled off his heavy signet ring and dropped it into her hand for safekeeping, then, with firm, practised fingers, smoothed oil into her back and shoulders as well as the backs of her thighs for good measure.

'That ought to do it. Ten minutes in the sun for starters, then move into the shade.' He wagged one finger at her sternly. 'You may look at me like that now, my dear, but you'll thank me later, when you don't get a burn.'

Jo handed back the ring. It was solid gold and heavily ornate with a stone as milky blue as Vincent's eyes.

'That's some ring. I'm surprised you risk wearing it on the beach.'

He laughed and slipped it back on to his finger. 'I've had it so long, it's part of me,' he said. 'Fifteenth century, school of Cellini. There's quite a story attached to it which I'll tell you some time.'

Then he peered at her more closely as she removed her dark glasses in readiness for her swim.

'My goodness, your eyes are different colours. How truly remarkable. I swear I've never seen that before.'

Jo was used to it; she grinned. 'Just an accident of birth,' she said. 'And at least it makes a talking point in an otherwise uneventful life.'

The morning progressed and Jo lay back in her chair to dry off, a hefty cocktail placed in one hand by Vincent, the comforting buzz of muted conversation from all sides. Though by no means crowded, the private beach was dotted with hotel guests, most of them returnees who greeted each other with pleasure. There was a family of affluent Canadians from Vancouver and a couple from Manchester who strolled over for a chat.

'Meet Donald and Marjorie Barlow,' said Vincent, one arm slung matily around each of their necks, prodding Jo into wakefulness with his toe. 'This is our new discovery,' he explained. 'Joanna Lyndhurst, all the way from London. It's her first time here but we're going to make sure it's not the last.'

He smiled his infectious smile and ruffled Jo's wet hair. His tan was already developing, making his remarkably blue eyes seem even more startling. Marjorie, a slender, well-cared-for woman in her fifties, perched on the edge of Jo's recliner while Vincent fetched her a drink from the nearby beach bar. After he'd ordered Jo in from the sun and brought her a dry towel to cover her legs.

'Vincent and Lowell are the dearest men imaginable,' she said. 'We've been meeting them here for years now, and they feel like family. They even visit us when they come to England. You are lucky to have fallen in with them, particularly since you're on your own.'

She glanced pointedly at Jo's empty ring finger but made no further comment. Jo smiled inwardly. People were so curious; she'd come across this so many times. *What's a nice girl like you doing travelling on your own?* she knew they wanted to ask. *Pushing thirty and yet with no man in sight.* It was all so patronising and out-of-date. She would do what she wanted to do, as she always had. Which was why she continued to live alone despite Sebastian's occasional suggestions of a shared life together.

'It was a last-minute decision,' she explained. 'I'd just finished exams and felt I deserved a break.' *And my boyfriend couldn't get the time off*, she nearly added but didn't. It was none of Marjorie's business; let her just wonder. As it was, Vincent and Lowell were already on to her case, probing in the nicest possible way but definitely keen to winkle out her secrets. Marjorie, however, like most people, seemed far more concerned with talking about herself. Donald was a scientist, affiliated to the cotton trade, with a large house in the Wirral which Marjorie was all too keen to describe.

'It's taken me years to get it exactly right,' she sighed. 'And now the glossy magazines are beating our door down, keen to take photographs because they've heard how good it looks. Isn't that right?'

Vincent had returned, with two more Planter's Punches, and he nodded agreement as Marjorie described her home. Definitely worth a visit, he confirmed; as spectacular as any of the stately homes. Then he winked at Jo and moved off round the group.

'Never still for a minute is Vincent,' said Marjorie approvingly. 'Just like a will-o'-the-wisp, he is, and so kind-hearted.'

Merrily appeared shortly before lunch and tiptoed towards them over the sand in impractical strappy sandals which displayed to perfection her immaculate, pedicured feet. Vincent found her another recliner and dragged it next to Jo's without a word. *Thanks a bunch*, Jo thought silently, as she saw the wickedness gleaming in his eyes. And resignedly put aside her book, raised the back of the recliner two notches and prepared to entertain her malcontent new acquaintance from New York.

And actually, once she'd slathered her nose with Ambre Solaire, fidgeted with her recliner until she had found the best angle, sent back her Planter's Punch because she preferred a Bloody Mary, smoked two cigarettes in rapid succession – lighting one from the other – and complained about the sand flies and the fact that her digestive system was playing up after the change of time zone, she wasn't entirely bad company and even had Jo laughing once or twice. She was, it turned out, a Personnel Officer with the Chase Manhattan Bank.

'Wow!' said Jo, genuinely impressed. 'That sounds high-powered.'

'You better believe it. I work my ass off fifty weeks in the year and they still complain when I decide I need a break. Like two weeks before Christmas, when half the work-force is out of the office sick, the others bunking off.' Out came the Camels again, as Merrily warmed to her subject, and Jo – in order not to seem unfriendly – resisted an urge to wave away the smoke. Smokers, more than anyone, were selfish these days. It seemed not to occur to the American to ask if Jo minded.

But it was good to lie here in the sun and just schmooze. After the hospital and her recent nightmare experience, pretty near anything would have to be an improvement.

And so the days slid by – indolent, dreamy, seamlessly merging from morning to night, then back to bright morning again. The group stayed together in their charmed circle under the palms, while Vincent danced attendance on them and played the fool and Lowell entertained them on a slightly more serious level with anecdotes from the law courts and his vast experience as a New England judge. Jo noticed with approval how the passing of the days was beginning to make him relax.

'He seems young to be a judge,' she remarked to Cora Louise who nodded enthusiastically, as though he were in some way a credit to her, and said he'd held that honour for the past ten years.

'Since he just turned forty, in fact,' she said. 'My, but he's smart, though far too modest to show it.' She turned her bright chipmunk eyes to where Lowell was sitting, calm and elegant even on the beach, with an air of lazy indulgence as he listened to Fontaine's prattle. Fontaine, spilling out of a lime-green swimsuit, was waving her arms around with animation. You didn't have to be much of a sleuth to detect her fixation with the handsome Bostonian. And Cora Louise, seeing the direction of Jo's gaze, picked up on her thoughts and echoed them proudly.

'Don't they just make the handsomest pair?' she glowed. 'My daughter could have anyone she wanted in Charleston, but there's always been that extra special something with Lowell. Right from the moment they met, I can tell you. Pity he lives so far away and is always so busy, though these days you can fly direct. So I'm told.'

Sweet, thought Jo benevolently, stealing another look, but Vincent had just joined them and was joshing the judge as he perched on the edge of his chair. She glanced once more at Fontaine. For a woman in her forties, she must be remarkably determined if she hadn't picked up on that special something between the two men which surely went beyond ordinary friendship. Either that, or incredibly naïve. But what the hell, on holiday anything goes. And if they saw each other for only ten days each year, where possibly could be the harm?

Halfway through the week, Vincent returned from one of his mid-morning rambles, triumphantly towing another trophy. He grew restless just lounging and liked to do the rounds, seeing how the other guests were faring and catching up on the gossip. He'd encountered this young woman lurking in the lobby and immediately brought her out to join the group. Jessica Sutherland, she introduced herself; newly arrived from England and on her own. She looked all right, thought Jo idly, as she reached across to shake the newcomer's hand; reed-thin with colourless, almost transparent skin, made up for by marvellous, sandy, almost marmalade-coloured hair which was certainly her crowning glory. The sun shot darts of pure gold from its depths and caused her to screw up her eyes in the bright light. As with Jo, she told them, this holiday had been an impulse. Overworked and underpaid and all that, she had suddenly decided she needed a break. Her nose was slightly red, as if she had a cold, and there were unhealthy mauvish shadows under her eyes.

'So I just hopped on a plane and here I am,' she said cheerfully, 'more or less in the clothes I stand up in.'

Merrily tipped down her Jackie Onassis dark glasses and studied the new arrival critically for a second or two.

'So what does this broad think she's doing butting in on us?' she muttered. 'And do we need another woman tagging along?' She meant it, too. Luckily the others hadn't heard so Jo said nothing. Just grinned and shrugged and dipped back into her book. From the way the New Yorker sized up each new arrival, it was clear where her own motivation lay. *It just needs someone even halfway eligible to appear*, thought Jo, *and she'd drop the rest of us like hot potatoes*.

Jessica worked in the music business, as an arts festival organiser, currently based in Cheltenham. It was her first time to the islands, she said; a blessed change from the rigours and damp of a small English town in winter.

'But you've got a bit of a wind burn already,' said Marjorie.

'That's from riding my bike through all kinds of weather. And going out without an umbrella.'

Lowell was particularly fascinated to hear more about her job. A keen music-lover himself, he had a season ticket to the Boston Symphony. Along with his mother, though he didn't mention that. He warmed instinctively to this new arrival and looked forward to getting to know her better. Apparently more benign than the spiky Merrily, though also slightly jumpier than the serene Jo. An interesting mix; one of the reasons he so much enjoyed these winter holidays.

'If you ever hit Boston,' he said politely, 'you must allow me to take you there as my guest.'

Jo saw a flash of alarm cross Fontaine's face but Jessica simply smiled and said she'd love that. It was hard work, she confirmed, but all she'd ever wanted to do.

'I suppose I was born with music in my blood. Which is about all I did get so I have to count my blessings.' When she smiled, it transformed her and made her finely boned face almost pretty. Jo decided she liked her. Approximately her own age and presumably also single. A nice new friend, as her mother would say. Well, they'd see about that once the holiday was over. Certainly Sebastian would approve of Jessica's musical connections.

The company was so congenial, Jo was shocked to find how

rapidly time flew. She'd been here seven days already; soon it would be time to go home. It was amazing how busy a person could be, just lolling indolently on the beach, with the occasional foray into St John's in Lowell and Vincent's rented Jeep. There wasn't a lot to do there, but it made a change from all that sun. And she enjoyed their spirited company so much, it was fun just to tag along. Vincent was an art dealer with a passion for taking photographs. He was always looking at new, more powerful lenses and clicking his shutter, wherever they were, with the speed of a practised paparazzo.

'My problem,' said Jo, as they pored over newer and better cameras in one of the island's duty free shops, 'is that I never get round to looking at snaps again, once I've taken a film and had it developed.'

Lowell laughed in sympathy. 'I know the feeling. One look and you throw them into a drawer and forget all about them. I'm like that myself.'

'Philistines,' said Vincent. 'It's art in the making. An immediate record of contemporary life, as valid as the gossip on the beach.'

'I rest my case,' said the judge with a laugh.

I'm really going to miss those guys, Jo told herself on their last night, as she smoothed a touch of bronze make-up on to her flaking nose and tried to do something reasonable with her hair. Lowell was a dream of an escort – handsome, urbane, eternally interesting – while Vincent kept them all in stitches with his antics as well as dancing like Fred Astaire. With each of them in turn, what's more; amongst this group he appeared to have no favourite.

Even Merrily had lowered her frosty guard and was keeping them amused with her whiplash wisecracks. When she laughed she revealed her startling beauty. In less than a week,

Jo found she had really warmed to her and was pleased to see Merrily doing herself justice. It was a cliché to suppose she might be shy but it seemed to apply to Merrily.

'We will keep in touch?' she said to her anxiously.

'You better believe it,' said Merrily gaily. 'Just try and get rid of me now, doll, and you're dead!'

Then they all hugged and swapped addresses, and made impossible promises and vowed to meet again next year. And Jo found her eyes unaccountably misting and turned away quickly to hide her emotion.

Only later on the plane, a gin and tonic in hand and Jessica nodding off in the seat beside her, did three things occur to Jo. They'd heard no more about the poor drowned Englishman. Her secret had remained intact despite the probing. And, in the whole ten days since she'd met her new friends, she hadn't thought once about the dying child.

2

With Christmas safely out of the way, Jo started the new job with optimism, keen to get back to work after the break. It was only a short five minutes' walk to the Chelsea practice from Elm Park Mansions, about the same distance as the hospital, in fact, though the two jobs were certainly worlds apart. Chelsea and Westminster was a first-rate training ground but that final year in Casualty had almost finished Jo off. It was not something she was proud of; a case, in fact, of staying out of the kitchen if you can't stand the heat. But when Sebastian, with his customary diplomacy, had hinted that she might be more suited to general practice, where she could involve herself in all levels of healing, Jo had leapt at it. Anything to get away from the trauma of dealing on a daily basis with accident victims. She had, after all, chosen medicine in the first place because she wanted to do some good in the world, not just mop up the mess. Her father was inclined to laugh at her and call her his little Mother Teresa, but Jo stuck firmly to her guns and silenced him effectively by passing her MRCGP with flying colours while she was still under thirty. And now she had the job of her dreams, working in an NHS practice at the shabby end of the King's Road, and could hardly wait to get stuck in.

Sebastian, too, was moving on to new things. His application to study psychiatry had been accepted and he was due to start his training at the Tavistock Clinic right away. He had always been fascinated by the vagaries of the sick mind, right from that first year of medical school when he had grown so absorbed in the teachings of Jung and Freud. They were like two school kids, embarking on the new term with shiny new satchels, sharpened pencils and renewed ambition for the future.

'The problem is,' said Sebastian ruefully, holding her closer when the alarm went off, 'that I won't see nearly as much of you now you're escaping from the hospital. And my sight.'

'You should have thought of that when you suggested it,' said Jo, rolling back for a final squeeze. 'In any case, what with your studies and your music, I bet you'll have forgotten all about me in a matter of days.'

'Fat chance,' he said mock seriously and for the next few minutes kept her occupied until she squealed for mercy.

'Unhand me, villain! I'll be late on my first day.'

'And that would never do, Little Miss Squeaky Clean.' But he released her and she made a dash for the shower ahead of him. Whole new beginnings, she thought, as hot water hammered into her face; the end of a chapter, maybe, but also the exciting start of the rest of her life.

Steps led down to the basement surgery on the edge of a

housing estate close to the World's End, and patients were already beginning to arrive when Jo shot in at ten to eight after a hearty sprint from Park Walk.

'Sorry,' she gasped to the receptionist, exactly like a child on its first day at school, but the girl's dusky face lit up with an indulgent smile and she nodded towards the anxious Asian mother, waiting with her small brood for a doctor's attention. Start as you mean to go on; Vincent's words echoed through Jo's head as she preceded the small flock into a shabby examination room, tugging her freshly laundered white coat from her briefcase as she went. *I could certainly use one of his Planter's Punches right now*, she thought, then settled behind the desk and gave her full attention to the poor woman's concerns.

And the morning went by like lightning. Jo could scarcely believe it when she glanced at her watch and found it was already ten past one and time to leave the surgery and embark on her house calls. She hoped she wouldn't have to make much use of her car since she really enjoyed being able to walk to work. Luckily today she was only needed on the abutting housing estate.

It was late and she was exhausted by the time she made it home, and the final gruelling climb up five flights of stairs to her top-floor flat put Jo in mind of one of those commercials promoting the joys of support hose. She grinned as she put her key in the lock. Thirty going on fifty-five was how she felt right now, with the grim realisation that her fridge was virtually bare and her stomach rumbling after a lunchless day. The glamour of being a doctor, she reflected, as she flicked through her mail and dropped most of it into the bin. If only these drug companies would cut down on advertising, her poorer patients might be in less need.

The light on her answering machine was flashing but it was only Sebastian, enquiring after her day, so she left a suitable rejoinder on his own magnetic tape and reflected that in future this was how they were fated to communicate. What with his extra studies, not to mention that damned flute and those incessant rehearsals; and she with a back-breaking new commitment that both fired her determination and daunted her with its scope. She sank on to the lumpy sofa and sat there, dejectedly sipping a glass of wine, waiting for the juices to seep back into her brain and her feet to recover from their pavement pounding. Then she glanced at the clock, realised the corner shop would shortly be closing, and dragged herself off again to collect some vital supplies. Beans on toast it would have to be again tonight. She simply hadn't the energy for anything more elaborate.

She saw the child's face again that night, as she lay on her back with her head on her hands and waited for sleep. There had been a small patient in the surgery with those same small simian features and look of baffled terror as she'd tried to coax him on to her knee and smooth away the pain. But this one's mother had been alert and at his side and the anguish he was feeling could be dispatched with a short course of pills, a soft voice and a cooling hand. While that other one . . . she shook her head hard to dispel the image, then gave in to tension and went in search of an aspirin. Jo hated the idea of unnecessary tranquillisers, yet knew she needed to be alert for the next day's heavy workload. This was one job at which you dared not slack. When she first embarked on a medical training she had not appreciated that the slog to pass exams was only the start of a lifetime's commitment. Now she knew.

After a couple of weeks of early starts and shortened nights of patchy sleep, Jo could feel all the benefits of the holiday draining away. Added to which, London was gripped in a savage burst of freezing January weather which had her scrabbling through her underwear drawer for a long-discarded vest, and pulling on tights considerably thicker than the ones she had so much scorned at school. If only Sebastian could see her now, but there was little likelihood of that. He was really getting into this psychiatry kick and his musical activities took up most of his rare spare time. They had had, Jo reflected, probably the best of it in the eleven years they had been together since that first term at Cambridge when they fallen so comfortably into love. So long ago.

Maybe that was all love was, she pondered; the guileless dreaming of untutored souls before they embarked on real life. She thought of the grievously injured child and the look of anguish on the mother's face; of the scabies and tumours and raw running sores she was encountering now, in the course of her daily work. Learning, moreover, to take it without flinching, part of a reality she was having to come to grips with.

When they did talk, they were both preoccupied. And when they got together, usually at weekends, there was something lacking in the fervour of their love-making. In just a few weeks Jo felt they had grown apart. Which was hardly surprising, considering how their lives were diverging. After so long together, most couples by now would be married or split, but permanence had never really been on the cards for them. Jo had her own agenda while all Sebastian could talk about was music and bloody Freud. A... on the occasions they went out with other friends, they found themselves quarrelling because their thoughts were no longer in tandem. Scary, really, if either had had the time to reflect.

One dismal Sunday in early March, Jo decided she needed to clear her head. Sebastian, as ever, was stuck into his books so she telephoned Shona from the surgery and the two of them drove to Chiswick for an afternoon walk along the river. It was a chill, bracing day with few people around except couples with dogs and a solitary oarsman sculling along on the dark, oily water of the Thames. As the sky grew overcast and the sun prepared to set, they wandered along Chiswick Mall, admiring the elegant houses and dreaming of a time when they too might be able to afford to live in such splendour.

'Small hope,' laughed Shona, who shared with two others in Acton. 'The best you can hope for on a GP's pay is a two-up, two-down in West Kensington. Especially if you plan to start a family.'

'Which I don't.'

'Not now, maybe. Wait till that old biological clock starts to tick.' Shona was two years younger and laughing. She didn't have a regular boyfriend but that appeared not to worry her. She was dark and gorgeous and came from Mauritius. Jo often envied her casual approach to life.

From one of the Queen Anne houses at the end of the row, music was spilling and the two of them paused in the fading sunlight to gaze at the river and listen. A soft Chopin nocturne, emotive and melancholic, played with such feeling and subtlety of touch that Jo simply had to sneak a look. After so many years with a music fanatic, she recognised virtuoso playing. The man in the bay window at the Steinway grand piano was tall and sternly handsome with gold-rimmed spectacles and a fine patrician nose which mysteriously sent a tingle down Jo's spine, though she kept the feeling to herself.

'Boy,' hissed Shona with simulated reverence, unknowingly echoing Jo's own thoughts. 'I wouldn't half mind a go at that.'

'Out of your league, dear.' Jo was looking around. The house was in tiptop condition, the wrought-iron railings freshly painted, the roses pruned and cared for. Opposite the gate, on the far side of the narrow footpath, a flight of wooden steps led steeply down to the river where a dinghy was moored, its sails still on board as if waiting to be launched. Jo could imagine the picnic hamper safely stowed, the chilled bottles of champagne cooling in the icebox. And herself about to step aboard in a floating, flowery dress. As if.

'Oh Lord,' groaned Shona, clutching her side in mock agony. 'This is altogether too much. The house, the boat, the man. I think I am going to throw up.' She clutched at Jo and rocked with mirth but Jo's eyes were back on the pianist in the window, so calm, so involved, so locked into his music as though nothing outside his special world could touch him.

Shona was only larking around but something deep within Jo was responding seriously. This was the most beautiful man she felt she had ever seen and the music, the gentle dolour of the afternoon, the smart little sailboat all combined within her heart to strike a chord that was not going to stop resounding.

It's about time I fell in love again, thought Jo, startled by the realisation but immediately convinced of its accuracy. She risked another peek. He hadn't even glanced up as they hovered so rudely beyond his hedge. Eyes down, hands elegantly in motion, he reached the final bars of the piece, paused for a while, then gently closed the piano lid, rose and stretched. And that night it was not the dying child who haunted Jo's dreams but the aristocratic face of the romantic stranger, standing there in the peace of his own home, his hair lightly touched by the last rays of the sun.

In April, the postcards began to arrive. From Vincent and Lowell in Cannes for a spring vacation. From Cora Louise and Fontaine on a coach tour of the Low Countries, where they had managed to spend time with Vincent and even been treated to a tour of his gallery. From Jessica in Cheltenham, run ragged by the festival organisation and dying for a break when she could slip away to London. Jo sympathised. Her own feet had scarcely touched the ground all year, plus she was suffering from a recurring sore throat, brought on by regular contact with so many snivelling kids. Any tan she might have had was long gone; she longed for the sun and the feel of salt air on her skin. No chance of another holiday this summer, however; she was still too new in the practice. Besides, she couldn't afford one. She flicked through the calendar and marked off the days and started to save for another visit to her winter paradise.

There was no point in even mentioning it to Sebastian; he was already muttering about joining some orchestra for a Scottish tour. And Shona, fun though she was, simply didn't have the necessary money since her number one priority right now was a new car. Once again, she'd just have to go on her own but that was all right with Jo. Her heart warmed at the prospect of seeing her new friends again and she gazed at the kitchen calendar wistfully, willing away the months until she could see them again.

*   *   *

When the phone rang late one evening Jo almost didn't recognise the throaty drawl. The atmospherics on the line made it sound as if it was snowing heavily but then the crackling ceased and Merrily came through loud and clear.

'Hi there, doll! How goes it?'

'You!' Jo was startled and delighted. She realised how much she had missed her new friend; simply hearing her strident tones now made her smile.

'Not so bad. How's yourself? What's the weather like in the Big Apple?'

'Hot. Sixty degrees and still rising. They say we'll have a heat wave by the weekend which is just what I need at this time of year. Imagine. All my lightweight suits still in store and the temperature heading towards the nineties.'

Jo laughed. Merrily didn't change.

'How's life?'

'The same. Shitty, as always. So what else is new? Too much work, too little dough, and not a decent, red-blooded man to be found this side of Kansas City. How's yourself?'

'Ticking along. Hectic but I can't complain.'

She never had told them what she did for a living but, then, they'd never asked. Merrily, more than the rest of them, was pretty much self-fixated, preferring always to hold centre stage. Besides, her glamorous New York life sounded so much more exciting than Jo's. You could hardly compare the life of a high-flying Manhattan socialite to that of a humble National Health GP.

'How's Chase?'

'The pits.' Merrily made a spitting noise which made Jo laugh. 'There's talk of a sellout to Chemical and that will undoubtedly mean more job losses. You know how it is. The bigger the corporation, the less secure the employees.

And when the shit does finally hit the fan, you also know whose job it will be to clear it up.' She was laughing too but with an edge to her voice which underlined her seriousness.

'But *your* job's safe?'

'As safe as anyone's. Mother Chase won't let us down. At least, that's the company line. Can only wait and see.'

'And your love life?'

'Zilch. They're either gay or impotent, take your pick. Or else irrevocably married. There was this one guy I picked up at the health club. Hung like a horse, with muscles to match. Took him to Michaels and it cost me two hundred bucks just to soften him up. And when I got him into the sack, guess what? Couldn't perform, just lay there whimpering. Said he was in awe of me, or some such dreck. Pathetic! I tell you, there aren't any real men left in New York City. Don't know where they went but I've half a mind to hitch a ride back to the islands and find me a black.'

'Well, we're halfway there already. Only seven more months to go.'

'If I can hang on that long. Half a year's a helluva long time. Or it is in the banking business.' A terrible forlornness became evident in her voice. Jo heard the clink of ice against glass.

'What time is it?' Here it was almost midnight; she'd forgotten the five-hour difference.

'Seven-ish, I guess. Who's counting? I'm supposed to meet a couple of guys I work with in the Village but can't face it. They're so full of gloom and doom these days, it'd ruin my weekend. Thought I'd just stay right where I am and get smashed, here in the office alone. Let Mother Chase pick up the tab for once. She certainly owes me.' Her voice was beginning to sound blurry; Jo was concerned.

'Don't you think you'd do better to get off home and have

something to eat?' She knew it sounded priggish but it was out before she could stop herself. She was, after all, a doctor even if Merrily didn't know it. And she was fond of her friend who suddenly sounded so blue.

Merrily laughed, a hollow, metallic sound. Jo could just imagine the disdain on her beautiful face.

'So who's a little party pooper?' she sneered. 'Trust a Brit to try and spoil the fun.'

'Sorry,' said Jo meekly. 'I know it's none of my business.' She'd gone and put her foot in it when Merrily was only trying to be friendly. She felt wretched and wished they weren't so far apart. All she could hear now was the gurgling of liquor on to ice.

'Well, anyhow,' said Merrily briskly after a while. 'I just wanted to catch up with you and see how you're getting along.'

'It was great of you to call,' said Jo. 'Shall I see you in Antigua in December? I'm going if I can possibly afford it.'

'Why not. I guess so. That's still a while away.' Merrily paused and Jo could hear the sharp intake of smoke. 'You know something?' said Merrily, with unaccustomed emotion. 'I really miss you.'

'I miss you, too,' said Jo, meaning it. And when she hung up she found her eyes were damp.

3

Chase Manhattan Plaza was deserted so Merrily hailed an uptown cab on Pearl and headed home. No point tracking down Ed and Stanley while they were still in such a nihilistic mood. She knew how they must be feeling and also that they were bound to blame her initially and would only succeed in making her feel lousier than she already did. She sympathised, of course she did, but what could she do to help them now? If Mother Chase – in the person of Byron Kaminsky – was hellbent on deracination, Merrily's own best course of action was surely to keep her head down and do her darnedest to guard her own back. Which was only common sense, after all, as she was sure they'd appreciate once they'd had a chance to cool off and think things over rationally.

She told the driver to drop her at *Il Toscana*. It was friendly and informal and close to home and Luigi was always good for a little light flirtation, with a sympathetic ear if ever she found she needed one. Talking to Jo today had slightly unsettled her. Life in the fast lane was famously lonely and growing more so by the minute; that was the least of what she had learned these past twelve months.

After greeting her effusively and kissing her on both cheeks, Luigi led her to her favourite corner booth and whisked a perfect martini, stirred not shaken, on to the table without waiting to be asked. That's what Merrily called service. She could use him at Chase if ever his fortunes should change. Her spirits began to revive and she glanced round the half-full trattoria for a familiar face. But tonight she was out of luck. She drank another martini and a glass of the house red, ate her fettucine in silence and headed home.

'*Ciao!*' she called as she collected her briefcase.

'*Ciao, signora.* See you again very soon, I hope.'

The apartment was still and as silent as she had left it, the morning mail strewn across the breakfast counter but no friendly message light winking to welcome her home. She slid out of her suit in the pristine bedroom and into a loose T-shirt to match the muggy evening. It was still quite early so she poured herself a cognac, then switched on the NBC news. What sort of a life was this, working all hours yet with nothing to come home to? The icebox was empty apart from mineral water, mixers and a sealed packet of Colombian coffee. Her wine-rack was full but, after all she had drunk so far this evening, of little comfort to her now. The decor was perfect yet impersonal, done as part of a job-lot by a fashionable designer, with no real place where she could relax and feel comfortable apart from the bedroom, which resembled a hotel suite. Merrily stood in the doorway, glass in hand, and felt distaste. All of a sudden, she thought of her folks in Dayton, Ohio and longed to go home.

That, however, was the one thing she could never do. Not in her present mood, in a spirit of defeat, but only ever when she was really riding high again, in control of her career or with a smart new husband to flaunt.

Weekends were something of a wasteland to Merrily unless she had activated herself during the week and organised some diversion to see her through the barren hours. This one was no exception; she'd just been too busy. She slept in late on Saturday, emerging at noon for a quick coffee at Barneys, then took herself across to Fifth Avenue for the ritual trawl of Bendels and Saks before getting herself a manicure and her hair washed and trimmed at Richard Stein's Madison Avenue salon.

'Long face,' he remarked when she sloped in. 'Plans for tonight? I certainly hope so.'

Merrily pulled a face. 'Give me a break. What's there to do in this godforsaken city if you're single and unattached and over the hill?'

He laughed; he'd known her for years and she didn't change.

'My dear,' he said, in his best mock-English accent. 'This is the Big Apple, don't you know; the most thrilling city in the world. There's a new exhibition just opened at the Met. Why not mosey on up there when we've done with you here and have yourself a wander and a glass of wine. Who knows what you might find, if you keep your eyes properly skinned.'

She was looking particularly good this afternoon, despite the air of gloom. She had the sort of exotic beauty that only improved with the years, provided she kept the weight off, which she would.

Merrily thought about it but decided against. Ordinarily she liked the easy camaraderie of those social Saturday evenings at the museum but today she just simply was not in the mood. She thought about telling Richard what had been going on in the office, then decided against it. It was far too depressing to share with another and would only make her feel even more glum.

'Guess I'll just stay home,' she said, 'and catch the late-night movie.' Then nodded at her reflection as he wielded his mirror and groped for her purse to settle up. She wished she didn't feel quite so treacherous; company policy was beyond her control. But try telling that to the workers each time another list was posted and she had to stay hidden inside her office while they raged and argued round the water-cooler.

Talking to Jo last night had unsettled her. She realised how much she missed the Antigua gang and a great wave of melancholy swept up and engulfed her as she passed through her elaborate lobby and took the elevator to the fourteenth floor. Sure, living in this city was a gas provided you had the money and the guts. She had her plush apartment, her health club, and unlimited money to shop. But no Significant Other in whom to confide and nowhere to go on a Saturday night. Which wasn't much of a deal when you were divorced, under pressure and pushing thirty-six.

Michael Morgenstern, Merrily's father, believed in the family and putting down roots. Having married late himself, after a traumatic war spent racing across occupied Europe with Hitler at his heels, he had passed his first fifteen years as a US citizen establishing a bespoke tailoring business in the prosperous mid-West. That done, he sought around for a suitable life partner and settled down to raise children in an attempt to replicate the family he had lost. Sadly, the only one he'd achieved was Merrily; she had been bearing the brunt of his disappointment ever since.

It wasn't that she hadn't tried – far from it. From being Dayton's Homecoming Queen in 1974, she had raced ahead to dazzle them all at Smith and grab herself a husband ahead of the pack, the best-looking hockey player on the team and Phi Beta Kappa to boot. Not a Jew, as it happened, but you couldn't have everything and he was a dream to look at with a future in finance. Even Michael Morgenstern might have come to accept him, if only Phil had not had such an eye for the ladies. Merrily caught him *in flagrante* one time too many, threw him out of the rented apartment and changed the locks, finding herself alone again in a city she scarcely knew, one foot on the lowest rung of a steep corporate ladder, scared out of her wits and barely twenty-six. But she'd persevered and eventually won through.

Byron Kaminsky always claimed to have had one of his brighter moments of intuition when he first welcomed Merrily into Chase, not – as he regularly assured his colleagues – because of the neat figure and those lustrous grey eyes, but for the pure, dogged determination he saw in them which meant she'd fight every step of the way to the top. And how right he had been. Just nine years after joining the bank, here she still was – head of her department and still rising fast – with a condo on Madison and 62nd, stock options, pension funds and a salary commensurate with that of any of her male colleagues. More than anything, a secure future. Even Michael Morgenstern would have to be impressed.

But Chase wasn't the bank it once had been, nor did banking generally any longer offer safe tenure. It had been run in such a hierarchical way that senior management had kept its head in the sand long after other industries were watching the danger signs of a changing economy and America was beginning to be gripped by a terror word that refused to go away. Downsizing. As technology improved and performance grew more sluggish, even Mother Chase began eliminating jobs – and Merrily Morgenstern, as head of New York personnel, was quite literally right there in the firing-line.

Not a comfortable place to be. And at times like this, on a dateless weekend, when two of her closest work associates had just been axed, she wished she might be almost anywhere else in the world. She thought longingly of Jo in London whose life seemed so serene and uneventful. She wasn't entirely sure what it was Jo did – something, perhaps, to do with the social services – but since she'd never heard her complain, it was doubtless one of those mindless occupations where Jo just clocked in, worked a minimum of uneventful hours, then took the money and ran. Lucky Jo. She with a steady boyfriend too; what a lot Merrily would give right now for that.

Her thoughts led her on, quite naturally, to the rest of the Antiguan group and she smiled when she remembered the kooky mother and daughter, with their flamboyant dress-sense and sweeping, grandiloquent gestures. There was that about the Southern States which set them apart from the rest of America. Probably something to do with the heat, mused Merrily, who'd never actually been down there. Which might account for that crazy lady and her all-too-obvious pash on Lowell Brooks.

Merrily's bitter heart softened as she thought of those two great guys, Lowell and Vincent. Now *they* were both genuine life-enhancers, no question of it. Merrily didn't often encounter gay people but those two had stolen her heart. Sondheim had it right, she pondered, as she pottered around the apartment achieving very little. How odd that it should take a man of the opposite persuasion to see so clearly into the female heart. And what a tragedy for the rest of her sex. And on that philosophical note, since there was nothing worth watching on any of the other channels, Merrily poured herself a hefty nightcap and took herself off to bed.

On Sunday she rose early too and went into the office. There wasn't a lot else to do and she knew she'd left her desk chaotic. After last week's various crises, a lot of her time had been distracted and she longed for the peace of a silent Sunday to sort out her papers and generally catch up. It was a warm, bright morning but she couldn't be bothered to dress up, so slid into jeans and a T-shirt instead, topping it all with her ankle-length camel coat. Her thick, black hair she pulled back into a severe plait and she wore dark glasses because she was too lazy to make up her eyes. With luck she'd be out of there by early afternoon and then she'd treat herself to brunch at the Carlyle, where she could relax in peace and read the Sunday papers.

Sunday in Manhattan was something special and even Merrily, preoccupied as she was, couldn't help pausing on the sidewalk to inhale the smells of a city teeming with activity, the traffic almost as heavy as normal, a stream of yellow cabs bumping and swaying as they raced uptown as if life depended upon it. One of the reasons she remained living right here, bang in the centre of the affluent East Side, with its shops and restaurants and galleries and *life* was just that. Madison in the Sixties was where it was happening. You didn't get where Merrily was going without being aware of that. One block over, the park would be alive with joggers, horse-riders and people exercising their dogs. It had often been suggested to her, as she shot up the income scale, that she might consider re-locating to Long Island or Connecticut, even newly fashionable Brooklyn with its spacious houses and cleaner air. Who were they kidding? Much of the point of inhabiting one of the world's pulse points was the sheer excitement of being at the seismic centre. Where the action was and the buzz kept you motivated, even if you didn't have time for anything but work. Quality of company over quality of air-space. Merrily stepped out into the street and snapped her fingers for a cab.

The doorman greeted her as if it were a regular working day and she took the car to the twenty-second floor. There was no sign of life as she slid her electronic key into the slot and punched in the code to admit her to her suite. The flicker of computer terminals punctuated the landscape but no one was about with a conscience as keen as hers. Merrily dawdled along the silent corridor, enjoying the unfamiliar sensation of being there alone, then swung round the corner to her own executive office to find the door ajar. Caution prompted her not to make a sound, though she knew it was unlikely that an intruder could get past the doorman. Glad of her trainers, Merrily moved slowly forward, her heart beating in frenzied alarm as she reached her door and slowly pushed it open.

There in her seat, impervious to being detected, sat Byron Kaminsky at her computer terminal, peacefully scrolling his way through her private files.

4

Even this early it was almost too hot to sit out but Fontaine crossed the kitchen floor on bare feet, poured herself a cup of strong, black coffee from the chipped enamelled pot on the stove, and carried it out on to the porch to assemble her thoughts before the day really got going. Cora Louise had taken her headache to bed in the early evening, miffed – as she was too often these days – at another imaginary slight from someone in the town. Best to let her sleep it off; she would undoubtedly rise thoroughly restored, happy as a lark again, the cloud dispersed as though it had never existed.

'Mornin', Miss Fontaine.'

Old Silas, their loyal odd-job man, was clipping the grass in his customary leisurely fashion, straw hat pulled low over shrewd brown eyes, white wool undershirt tucked into the sagging pants. It was a fact that Fontaine had slowly grown to realise: at this time in the morning the faces you saw up and about on the street were mainly black. Other than a handful of pale-faced joggers around White Point Gardens – and they were undoubtedly tourists or upwardly mobile executives from out of town. Most other honest citizens were still in their beds like Cora Louise or else preserving their privacy – some might say modesty too – within the shuttered sanctum of their private front parlours. Which was, to Fontaine's impatient mind, nothing more than outdated bunkum, as so much about Charleston was these days, though Mama steadfastly refused to acknowledge it.

'Morning, Silas.'

This afternoon, she only now recalled, they had ladies in for a hand or two of gin rummy so she'd best shape up and check that Angelina had something in mind to feed them on, or else that would be another scandal to cause her poor mother to hide her head in shame. It would mean a drive over to the Piggly Wiggly to stock up, something she really hated to do. Fontaine heaved a great sigh. Living here, in this small privileged town, ought by rights to be so tranquil but was, in fact, such a minefield of dangers of decorum, you were obliged to keep your wits about you for fear of one exploding in your face. Which is why, she supposed, they were driven to travel so much these last few years. That, and the heat which right now, in midsummer, was pretty near impossible to live with anyhow. Especially when Mama was feeling vaporous like yesterday.

The mailman's van was progressing slowly along Tradd Street and Fontaine drew her wrapper around her and went to sit on the edge of the porch, holding her breath that there might be something for her today from the boys. Most particularly, from Lowell. They'd spent time with Vincent in Amsterdam just a few weeks previously but she hadn't seen hide nor hair of the judge since Antigua, though she did have plenty of Vincent's amusingly captioned snaps with which to fuel her fire. Plus the rare snatched conversation on the phone when she managed occasionally to catch him at home. Which, as Mama was fond of repeating, was surely no way to conduct a courtship, but what else was a gal to do? If only he might be persuaded to come down here and visit with them awhile, but lately he had grown so big in Boston judiciary circles; was even considering running for Congress, so Vincent said. Which was all very well, and a real feather in his cap, but how would that affect things between the two of them with him being that much busier? Excepting, as Mama had so happily pointed out, a man in that position would most certainly require a wife. It was all most perplexing and occupied Fontaine's mind far more than she knew was healthy but there wasn't a lot else to think about in this small, stagnant town where the biggest excitement in years had been Hurricane Hugo. Four years later they were still repairing the damage.

The mailman was passing their house now, with nothing more than a nod and a friendly wave, whereupon Cora Louise's shocked voice came hissing from the dim parlour behind her.

'Why, child, what ever are you doing out there like that? Showing all you've got for the whole wide world to see, I do declare. Come right on in now, before the neighbours see you.' As if letting the mailman catch a glimpse of her peignoir weren't shame enough already.

Reluctantly Fontaine rose from her perch, picked up her discarded cup and did her mother's bidding. It was always easier to comply than to argue, though she'd like to know who there was to see her at this time in the morning except for old Silas, and he was near-sighted. *And* he'd known her right from when she was nothing more than a bitty child and ran around near naked in the water sprinkler. Lord Almighty, when was she ever going to be allowed to grow up, escape from this stifling town and get to live a proper life?

The thing about Jo and Merrily – Jessica too – that most attracted Fontaine, as well as inspiring her envy, was their independence and cheerful acceptance of the fact that they had to work and stand on their own feet. All three of these enterprising young women appeared to have cracked the secret of personal fulfilment and were streaking along in their chosen careers, totally committed and absorbed by what they did, without so much as the traditional accoutrement of a husband to give moral support or help foot the bills. Which, in these modern times, was absolutely as it should be; what, in fact, a whole generation of doughty grandmothers had devoted their lives to making possible. Everywhere, it seemed, except in the American South, where time moved at a slower rate and the ghosts of an earlier era still stalked the cobbled streets and held political sway in City Hall. It was positively shame-making, really, to be halfway through your life still shackled to a parent. Fontaine's normally equable soul mutinied at this one inescapable fact.

It wasn't that Cora Louise was any sort of a burden. She was an utter darling almost all of the time and the two of them got along just dandy. It was more that Fontaine badly missed male company and was getting less and less of it as the years rolled by which, to a feisty gal in the tiptop prime of her life, was very contrary indeed. To put it at its least aggressive. Sure, she'd had her admirers over the years. There were even, on two occasions, out-of-towners passing through, who had taken to her mightily well and been prepared to linger and make an honest woman of her or else, better still, take her along with them. But something had always happened to spoil it, some busybody with a far too active tongue, so that both young men had gone sadly on their way without ever knowing precisely how wronged she had been, how entirely innocent of any slur that might ever have tarnished the Ravenel name.

Lowell Brooks was a different kettle of fish entirely and acted always with such refinement that both mother and daughter had simultaneously sat up and taken notice, silently saluting this new ray of hope on their threshold. Not to mention his diverting Dutch friend whom Mama had hailed as a distant family connection since the Charleston Vandervoorsts were amongst the most prominent of the old families, no matter how much Vincent might laugh it off and protest that no relative of his had ever, to his knowledge, set foot in the New World.

Lowell, however, was a pedigreed New Englander, a scholar and gentleman – there was no gainsaying that. Plus he was handsome and distinguished, a member of the Boston bar, with a mother known throughout Massachussetts as a doyenne of style and refinement. In the years they'd been acquainted with him and Vincent, the Ravenel ladies had learned a lot about Augusta Prentice Brooks and Fontaine's secret dream, devoutly shared by her mother, was one day to meet her and be invited to her home. It could surely only be a matter of time. And then let those old witches of downtown Charleston watch out.

'I'm sure I don't know,' Louella Petigru was saying, as she stacked the cards, 'what things in this town of ours are coming to, I surely don't.'

Louella possessed the kind of porcelain beauty, untouched

by earthquakes, hurricanes or scandal, that had scarcely diminished in sixty-two years, embellished only by a glazed patina that looked likely to crack should she ever be rash enough to smile. But that was unthinkable in this pillar of Charleston propriety; the whole town south of Broad Street hung on her words and quaked if anything was ever done to incur her displeasure. Cora Louise well remembered that time, way back in the sixties, when desegregation was first mooted and the church elders of St Michael's posited the unheard-of suggestion that black people be allowed to worship alongside white. No one could be more vehemently opposed than Louella.

'It's just not natural, not at all what our Lord intended,' she pronounced.

'But, Mrs Petigru,' said the Reverend cautiously in those far less tolerant days, knowing he trod on insecure ground yet for once not prepared to back down when a cause he had fought for so vehemently and so long was hovering on the brink of victory. 'Look at it this way. If Our Saviour were alive today, what do you suppose He would have to say about this matter?'

Nothing could ruffle Louella Petigru. Her ancestors had held sway here since the early antebellum days; like Cora Louise herself, she was a proud Daughter of the Revolution.

'I know full well what Our Lord would say,' she pronounced with fierce confidence, eyeing all around her with a peacock's icy stare and daring each to challenge her. 'But the fact remains, Our Lord would be wrong. Black and white were never intended to mingle. It just ain't natural, not natural at all.'

And there the matter was obliged to rest. Occasionally Silas and a few of his braver confrères might be observed during the service standing silently at the rear of St Michael's, heads dutifully bowed, but they would always have vanished by the end of the final hymn, and if Mrs Petigru ever glimpsed them as she processed back down the aisle, then she certainly never let on. What the eye did not see need no longer be contended but the fact remained that Louella's own household staff were still confined to an outhouse behind the garage and the maid who opened the door to visitors wore a neat black uniform with starched white pinny. And would sometimes even bob a curtsey, depending on the visitor's rank, even to this day in the 1990s.

Right now Louella was holding forth on the subject of homosexuality and Cora Louise was doing her level best to head her off. As usual, with little success.

'It just ain't natural.' Louella recited her mantra as she dealt the cards with her customary briskness, thin, taloned fingers flicking down the cards as if chastising them. They had been discussing this year's Spoleto Festival and the fact that an all-male dancing troupe from San Francisco was pulling record audiences in the North Charleston coliseum. 'They should all, by rights, be strung up, every last one of them, for going against Nature's intention. That's what they'd have done in my Daddy's day and good riddance, I say.'

I'll bet. Whilst wearing white hoods, thought Fontaine grimly, excusing herself from the repugnant presence and stepping out on to the porch for a breath of sultry late-afternoon air. Ye Gods, how she hated that woman, not just for her bigoted, archaic attitudes, but mainly for the soulless way she toyed with Cora Louise, batting her around with those cruel paws and playing on each one of her mother's sensibilities.

The crepe myrtles were in full flower and Tradd Street was awash with pink and white blossom. Fontaine leaned on the rotting railing and inhaled their powerful scent. Much as she loved this picturesque old town, she could scarcely wait to see the back of it – yet where was she ever going to go? After a lifetime alone together, fighting a private battle, she and her mother were virtually joined at the hip. It was far too late now, Fontaine feared, to sever the umbilical cord. Unless, by some stroke of unforseen magic, her prince should one day actually turn up. But even in that unlikely event, what in the world was she to do with Mama?

'The truth is, Louella dear,' Cora Louise was saying diplomatically as Fontaine re-entered the room, 'I've never actually been acquainted with a gentleman of that persuasion but I can't believe that they're not nice people. They are usually quite artistic, I believe, with a flair for colour and interior design. And such nice manners, so I'm told. The music world is full of them. Just look at those dancers.' Cora Louise had been quite bowled over by the Bolshoi Ballet; this latest local spectacular had left her reeling.

Louella tutted in disagreement, then glanced at her minuscule diamond watch and said she had to be going. Whereupon the other ladies murmured in unison and set about obediently gathering up their purses and helping Fontaine to stack the china.

'Tell Mrs Petigru about your recipe book, Mama,' tactfully prompted Fontaine. The Charleston Symphony was heading towards its sixtieth anniversary and the League, of which Cora Louise was a founder member, was putting together a commemorative book. Nice and homey was what they were aiming for, with well-tried recipes, simple to cook, contributed by musicians and adjuncts of the orchestra. Cora Louise had already donated her own many-times-tested secret formula for She-Crab soup, something of a sacrifice since it had been handed down from Great-grandmother Bee.

'Why, Louella, what an excellent idea,' beamed Cora Louise, delicately dabbing her mouth with lace-edged linen and eyeing her warily. 'Fontaine is entirely right, of course. Your mother's Shoo-fly Pie would exactly do the trick. Goodness knows, we've all of us enjoyed it so many times over the years.'

But Louella Petigru was never one for sharing. It just wasn't natural.

'That recipe has been in mah family these two hundred years,' she said severely. 'You surely don't imagine I want y'all knowing its secret ingredients.'

'Not even for charity, to help the Symphony?'

'Especially not for that.' Louella sniffed. 'Your nancified friends with their fancy manners should pull themselves together and learn to put in an honest day's work like the rest of us.'

And with that triumphant riposte she picked up her purse and swept on out to her waiting car. Set and match.

Much later, when the heat was a tad less ferocious and her mother had withdrawn to her canopied bed with a box of candy, a trashy paperback and a handkerchief soaked in lavender water, Fontaine changed out of her good afternoon dress and into the dungarees and T-shirt in which she felt more comfortable. Virtually everyone she saw on the street these days wore shorts but Fontaine just hadn't the figure for that and, besides, she knew the town would be scandalised. Her butt was way too large, though that seemed no deterrent to the tourists of all ages and sizes who strutted around so shamelessly, looking like goodness knows what. But her legs were still shapely and her ankles neat, so she compromised with these denim dungarees which her mother said, disapprovingly, made her look like some out-of-town hayseed.

She slipped out of the house, taking care not to bang the mosquito door, and headed towards Market Street where the action was. The streets around Market Hall, even at this hour, were still bright and colourful and swarming with life. In Charleston the tourist season was virtually unending so that, even in the height of summer when it hurt to open your mouth for fear of scorching your lungs, small town America flocked south towards the coast and it was hard to rent a room for the night for love or money. Cora Louise and her contemporaries despised this influx of marauding strangers but Fontaine fairly thrived on it and longed to get more involved.

Market Hall itself was still thronging with browsers, fingering their way among the rolls of cheap fabric, the gewgaw jewellery, the tacky souvenirs endemic to street markets all over the world, while the Gullah-speaking stall-holders chanted the attractions of spices and pulses with that special low-country flavour: black bean chili mix, fiery hot sauces and japone peppers of all degrees of heat. Fontaine adored it for its very vulgarity and came here as often as she could just to mingle and imagine herself a traveller in transit, with a choice of places to which she might move on. Pathetic really but, at forty-four, there was not a lot else she could do but dream.

Forty-four – even now she could scarcely believe it. Fontaine took a corner table at the popular Wild Wings and sat there with a beer, watching the world and its wife at play. The ceiling fans were steadily working and a silent baseball game went through its paces on the ceiling-mounted TV. While all around her sat clusters of like-minded folks: a cooing young couple with a delicious baby in a stroller, a group of youths in the regulation T-shirt and shorts, surrounded by bright and voluble young women with shiny hair, bragging about their jobs, their pay and how they intended to shake off the dust of this moribund town the very first moment they feasibly could. And outside roller-bladers coasting along the street on this hot and humid July night, plus cart-loads of tourists in endless horse-drawn carriages, still working the sights circuit as the lights dimmed and the mosquitoes flocked into their own.

Jesus, thought Fontaine savagely, gulping down her beer. *This fucking town is nothing more than a glorified wax museum. With me, if they only knew it, one of its most typical exhibits.*

Shit, she thought ten minutes later, as she finished her barbecued chicken and wiped the grease from her chin, *I'd best settle up and get going or I'll not be home in time for* Murphy Brown. And that, depressing as it was, more or less summed up her meaningless life.

Impulsively, Fontaine took a right off Church Street and rattled the rusty gate of the old Huguenot churchyard. Slightly to her surprise, she found it unlocked so followed the familiar, grass-edged path down between squeezed-together, bleached-by-the-sun monuments, beneath sepulchral banners of floating Spanish moss, to the one spot on earth that unfailingly drew her back, time after time, relentless as a magnet. For a while now Fontaine had filled some of her empty hours conducting a popular Ghost Tour round the old town which fairly pulsated with spectres, not all of them dead. It never failed to thrill her, the thought of these doomed spirits chained to their origins eternally, even more irrevocably than she was herself.

Dusk was creeping up behind her and the silence was interrupted only by the whirring of cicadas which switched on and off abruptly like the motor of a gigantic mowing-machine.

The sickly sweetness of the magnolias combined with that of the dying wreaths and she enjoyed a frisson of pure infantile terror at the thought of what might be silently lurking among those trees. Not a place to linger and Candice Bergen would be waiting for her at home but there was one thing she had to do before she left, a reverse sort of homage she regularly paid to the man she hated more than any other, the one who had so effectively ruined her life.

Close to the church, in the pre-emptive position, surrounded by a barrier of rusted railings, lay a stone. Flat and white in the paleness of the rising moon, she had to narrow her eyes and peer to make out the faintly etched inscription. Not that she needed to; those letters were engraved on her heart. *Paul Huger*, it said, *1795–1861*.

Fontaine Ravenel, Charleston debutante and daughter of a Daughter of the Revolution, gazed down at the grave of her illustrious ancestor and spat.

5

Vincent van der Voorst was laughing. Tears of pure merriment swamped the sapphire eyes as he stood before the wide bay window of his elegant first-floor apartment and hugged himself with glee. Below, on the Regularsgracht, glass-topped canal boats, conveying the last of the out-of-season tourists, glided by, slowing their motors at the junction with the Kaizersgracht to allow passengers to admire the symmetry of the famed six bridges, while the dusty golden leaves of early October fluttered carelessly to the ground.

'And the priceless thing is I swear she actually believes it!' he spluttered. 'That a simple Dutch boy such as I, with barely a second pair of clogs to his name, might actually be related to the cream of Charleston society. Is that not a hoot?'

'But all too typical of poor Cora Louise, I'm afraid, who seems to get nuttier by the minute. There are times I fear she is finally losing her marbles.'

Lowell Brooks was laughing too. He lay relaxed on Vincent's mustard Regency chaise-longue and squinted at the delicate tracery on the eighteenth-century wineglass in his hand. Yet, if he were fair, the delicious little Southern belle was not entirely off her trolley. For one thing was certain about his friend: it took considerably more than just inspired taste and a lifetime of relentless collecting to furnish a lifestyle this elegant.

Lowell's personal inclination was more to the austere, as befitted the way he had been raised. His bachelor chambers in Boston were in the style of a nineteenth-century gentleman's club: frugal, discreet, even a little fusty, appropriate to a man of his professional calling. Whereas this spacious apartment was an Aladdin's cave of quite outrageous splendour, chock-full of priceless collectibles and furniture that would not be out of place in a museum. Small wonder then that the divine Mrs Ravenel, that delicious air-head of muddled reason and inapposite conclusion, should have added it up so meticulously only to get it wrong. But that was all part of the fun.

'It's great to be back,' he said softly, extending one hand and feeling the weight of years beginning to shift.

'Good to have you here, old boy.' Vincent levered himself upright and slapped the proferred palm as he crossed to the hi-fi to change the disc. It was four o'clock on a Thursday afternoon and for once he was playing hookey in order to act host to his friend. Three glorious days spread in front of them before Lowell would have to return to the strictures and confinements of his ordered New England life. Jacket off, feet comfortable in monogrammed velvet slippers, he was content just to lie back quietly and feel the pressures of everyday life slip away. But he knew it was almost certainly asking too much, that there was a poor chance of the exuberant Dutchman allowing him to relax for long.

'So what have you planned for tonight?' he asked resignedly, pretending it was all the same to him. They were greedy for each other's company, these two, but, after twelve years, Vincent's gregarious spirit was bound to overcome his own preference for privacy. Well, Lowell could live with that. This, after all, was the essence of their relationship and why he paid these flying visits to Amsterdam. It was the younger man's vigour and general *joie de vivre* that continually replenished his own flagging vitality. He had no real objection to being dragged round the clubs and brown bars of this marvellous European city where anything went and no one ever condemned.

'Well, Henk and Willem and a few of the boys will be meeting up at the Koophandel later but we've time to grab a meal before then. Maybe even do a little clubbing if you're game.'

Lowell laughed. Vincent didn't change; one excellent reason why they still remained so close.

Leaving Lowell to sleep off his jetlag, Vincent slipped out of the apartment next morning and headed back to his small, smart gallery on the Keizersgracht to complete the job he had left unfinished the previous day. He was still highly amused by Cora Louise's latest fantasy and grinned as he strode along the cobbled street. Knowing the Ravenel ladies all these years had brought a lot of entertainment to Vincent and Lowell. They loved them both as dearly as their own kin but couldn't help poking gentle fun at some of the wilder flights of Cora Louise's fertile imagination. Her problem was that she was so steeped in the archaic snobbery of a small Southern town that name-dropping came to her quite naturally and she never failed to be exhilarated if she stumbled across some far-fetched lead to what might prove to be another family connection, no matter how obscure. The Charleston Vandervoorsts might be illustrious sons of the revolution but the truth was that, like his hero, Jan Vermeer, Vincent van der Voorst had been born and raised an artisan's son in Delft.

Notwithstanding, despite his humble stock, he had had the great good fortune to be singled out at an early age and encouraged to stretch and develop his one special talent: a laser-like eye for excellence in art, combined with the ruthless tracking skills of a bloodhound. Not a lot got past Vincent; his reputation throughout the art world was legendary and it had always been only a question of opportunity before he broke away from academia to set up his own private gallery. Though his former colleagues at the Rijksmuseum still trusted his judgement sufficiently to seek him out if ever they had a particularly tricky problem of identification.

At eight in the morning, Amsterdam was at its best – clean and washed as though a great sweeping-machine had just been through, with clear, pale sunlight striking shards of amethyst off the purple windows of the Van Loon Museum and ricocheting off the metallic waters of the canal. The idea of fancy ancestors in the great American South was patently absurd. Vincent thought affectionately of his stolid, pale-faced mother, straight out of one of his beloved Dutch interiors, and chortled aloud. At times that divine pair went right over the top but he loved them all the more for it. Lowell said it was the climate that was responsible. The timeless claustrophobia and mystery of the steamy South certainly had a lot to answer for.

Vincent unlocked the varnished door of his smart corner

gallery and de-activated the alarm. When you dealt on a daily basis with paintings this valuable, you couldn't be too careful. He adjusted the narrow slats of the wooden window blinds to admit a fine filtering of morning sunlight, then settled down with his magnifying glass to continue his study of the exquisite brushstrokes on the canvas on his desk.

The purity of the colours was quite extraordinary, with that special quality of pearly luminescence he looked for in a genuine Vermeer. Vincent's heart beat faster as he felt the familiar tightening of the visceral muscles that always preceded a spectacular discovery. He moved across the canvas, inch by inch, and marvelled at just how masterly the work of this unidentified artist actually was. Quite remarkable. He thought affectionately of the threadbare little *hausfrau* who had brought it in; he might well be on the brink of changing her whole life and that gave Vincent a wash of genuine pleasure.

They lunched late in a bar on the corner of the canal. Lowell was there before him, drinking his Heineken and brooding over an article in the *Herald Tribune* while a bunch of jovial Dutch workmen caroused in the corner as they celebrated the end of the working week. Vincent knocked down two swift ginivers in a row, then joined his friend in a more leisurely pint of the local lager.

'Tough morning?'

'Exhilarating!'

The glow was still in the Dutchman's cheeks as he told Lowell of his discovery.

'And you really believe it could be genuine?'

'I do.'

There were times when Lowell envied Vincent's lifestyle.

Not only was he free to live the life he wanted, without fear of restriction or public censure, but he was also following his true vocation, which led at times to glorious moments like this. Lowell Prentice Brooks had been born to a quite different calling, one defined by birth and position with very little deference to free will or choice of profession. He glanced at his watch. The afternoon was advancing; duty beckoned.

'You have a problem?' Alert as ever, Vincent's blue eyes were studying him.

'Please don't hold this against me but I bumped into a colleague from the Bar on the flight across and couldn't get out of joining him and his wife for cocktails. Tonight at the Pulitzer.'

Vincent pulled a face. 'Always so conscientious. You should have told them you couldn't make it, that you had a prior engagement.'

'Don't tell me.' Lowell leaned across and lightly touched the other man's hand. 'Only what do you say when you have already revealed you are travelling alone for a four-day break? You know how my fellow Americans can be, as sticky and persistent as chewing-gum. There was simply no way they were going to allow me off the hook. It is just a blessing it is drinks and not dinner. I can meet up with you later for some Indonesian food.'

'And I'm not included.' It was a statement rather than a query but the Dutchman was feigning concern. After all these years, he was accustomed to Lowell's caution and reserve. Besides, he found most of Lowell's fellow lawyers tedious in the extreme, and as for their wives . . .

'Well, old boy,' he said heartily, in response to Lowell's embarrassed shrug, 'I shall just have to fill in the time more profitably on the Rembrandtsplein. I'll catch you later unless, of course, I strike lucky.'

And, laughing delightedly, he called for the bill.

'And how is your dear mother?' Marshall Tolliver might be a dull old stick but his wife, Mimi, was considerably worse. Twenty years younger and as alert as a bird, she had already divorced two fortunes before catching the eye of the judge. She had long had a soft spot for the elusive Lowell, who was nearer her age, and never missed a chance of isolating him from the group in order to cross-examine him. 'Husband Number Four' was written boldly in her scheming eyes. Lowell inwardly flinched as her enamelled claw closed on his jacket sleeve and a sickening wave of *Shalimar* enveloped them both as she leaned even closer to catch his response.

'In excellent health, thank you.' Lowell nodded confirmation and attempted to edge away. Across the table in the dimly lit bar the sad old buffer, her husband, was already beginning to nod. Lowell edged his wafer-thin watch from under his cuff and risked a discreet glance at the time; twenty to nine already and Vincent would be long gone. Off to the dives of the decadent Rembrandtsplein in search of erotic adventure. And all because Lowell was too stuffy and too scared to risk offending a colleague he couldn't bear. Because, if he didn't comply with convention, they might just conceivably smell a rat and word might filter back to his mother. Pathetic. He coughed.

'My goodness, just look at the time. Don't let me keep you. You must be starving and the food in this city is so good.'

The raptorial eyes were bright with speculation. The old fart, her husband, was visibly wilting and she was keen to keep hold of her prey.

'Join us, Lowell, won't you? Our reservation is for nine and I'm sure they could squeeze in another one.'

'Thank you but no.' Lowell was already rising, glad of the chance to wriggle off the hook.

'I do have papers to look over tonight and I've already taken too much of your time.' If he moved like greased lightning, he might still not be too late. Or Vincent could even have been bluffing, though he wasn't sufficiently confident to rely on that.

'I thought this was a vacation.'

'Only partly. I really must go. You must both dine with me in Boston some time.'

'Do remember us to your mother.' Mimi was not pleased.

'I most certainly will.'

And he was out in the street at last, heart pounding, hands clammy, in urgent pursuit of the fallen angel without whose existence in his life he knew he would be lost.

On Sunday they slept late, convening at noon for scrambled eggs and Bloody Marys. Too many illegal substances the night before had dimmed even Vincent's unquenchable energy and lent a hint of redness to the brilliant eyes. At moments like this, he showed signs of middle-age. Lowell reflected sadly on the golden youth he had once been and sensed again the unnerving tramp of the years. He stood in the pristine kitchen wearing his robe, slicing limes with precision and delicately infusing the horseradish while Vincent brewed coffee. Vincent was a little heavier than when they had met but still agile and light on his feet with all that dancing and general clowning around, and the laughter was bright in his dear, dear face as he carried the pot to the table in the window and yelled for Lowell to get a move on.

'Patience, old boy,' said Lowell good-humouredly as he

tested his concoction for the right degree of spiciness. 'I'll have you know I still make the best Bloodies on the Eastern Seaboard and perfection always takes a little longer.'

Vincent spread snapshots across the cloth as they break-fasted and displayed some of his recent candid shots, each one captioned in his neat, precise hand, some with comic thought-bubbles issuing from his victims' mouths. Lowell roared. Vincent's wit was apt and incisive; in other circum-stances he could have been a cartoonist for he was also an extremely gifted draughtsman.

'My God, what was Pieter up to here? Decidedly illegal but looks dangerous too.'

'Don't ask. Far too risqué for a conservative fellow like you. As well as being positively corrupting.' Vincent's eyes shone with wicked pleasure. The vodka was re-adjusting his brain-cells effectively and a healthy colour was returning to his cheeks. He watched the judge flicking through the sheaf of snaps of men in all poses and reflected how much Lowell had unbent since they first got together. There was hope for the old codger yet; give him another twelve years and who knew how liberated he might become.

'And what are these?' Lowell reached for another yel-low envelope and a pile of shiny prints came slithering out.

'Antigua, last winter. Us and the gang on the balcony. Look, there's Fontaine with lotus blossom in her hair and the divine Jo looking as unsullied as a schoolgirl.'

Lowell thumbed through them. Everyone was smiling brightly and raising their glasses to the camera. Cora Louise, in her party frock, was as sleek and unruffled as always while her daughter was all over the place and looked positively pie-eyed. Jessica and Merrily waved from canvas chairs while Jo was perched diffidently on the corner of the railing, practically out of the picture.

'She is a nice girl, isn't she.' Lowell's face softened as he studied the picture, then moved on quickly through the set, searching for a better one. He found her standing leggily on the beach, demure in a white T-shirt over her costume, and another in close-up smiling shyly into the lens.

'Did we decide what she does for a living? I seem to recall you thought she might be a nanny.'

Vincent laughed. 'It was that air of incorruptible Mary Poppins innocence, as if untouched by human hand.'

'Though there was a boyfriend.'

'So she said.'

'Actually, what she looks like more than anything is a Flemish madonna, don't you think? With that pale, luminous skin and those strange mismatched eyes?'

'Circa fourteen hundred I would say. Before too much decadence crept into religious art.'

'Plus she's clearly a carer. Look how nice she always was to Cora Louise and how tolerant of that infernal Jewish Princess with her tedious self-centredness and endless complaints.' Lowell had little patience with women like Merrily; he considered them pushy and decidedly vulgar. He knew how his mother would react to such stridency; well-bred girls, according to Augusta Prentice Brooks, should be seen but scarcely ever heard.

'I'd guess she was an infant teacher,' said Vincent thoughtfully. 'Too smart to take care of someone else's children, pretty enough to still have some of her own.'

'But perhaps not ready yet.'

Lowell studied some further beach scenes, admiring Jo's radiant smile and coltish energy, the unassuming gracefulness as she cavorted on the sand with Vincent. Someone else must have taken that shot; Merrily, most probably, or the languid Fontaine.

'Poor Fontaine is certainly piling on the pounds,' he said. 'If she isn't careful she'll end up fat.'

Vincent tutted. 'And that would never do!'

'Not if she still wants to catch herself a husband.' Lowell was infinitely fond of Fontaine yet well aware of her weaknesses. And the silliness that sometimes spoiled her natural charm when she went too far, usually when she'd had a drink or two.

'I think she reckons she's done that already,' said Vincent slyly, starting to clear the plates. 'Look at the way she's eyeing you in this snap, positively drooling. I had trouble getting that one without her being aware. Had to take it sneakily, if only to prove my point.'

'And what point's that?' Lowell's grey eyes were genuinely puzzled as Vincent snorted with mirth.

'Don't try coming the innocent with me,' he said. 'It's clear for all to see that she dotes on you.'

At times, if he were honest, he found Fontaine's cloying adoration of the judge quite irritating. Tolerant he might be but her blindness where he was concerned was unbelievable. Where had she been all her middle-aged life if she failed to recognise what was right before her eyes? Though in no way possessive, Vincent got heartily tired of appearing not to exist in any significant way in his friend's life. And Antigua, more than any other place in the world except here, he saw as a sanctuary where they could both relax and be their true selves. If it weren't for that blasted Southern belle with her perpetual hots for Lowell.

'I'd watch that one, if I were you.' Vincent's voice had

darkened as he returned to the attack. He paused for effect. 'She could turn out to be dangerous.'

'Dangerous, who?'

'The fair Fontaine, who else? Still carrying a major torch, even though you refuse to take it seriously.' Lowell saw that Vincent was only half joking.

'It will all end in tears, mark my words. I'm not sure that one's entirely stable.'

Lowell flicked back through the snapshots. 'Oh, you think I need to watch my back,' he said, amused. 'Rabbits in the stewpot, that kind of thing.'

He had moved on and was now studying photographs of Jessica, neat and contained in the shadow of a palm tree, slightly apart from the rest of the group, her nose in the inevitable book.

'This is the one I'm not yet sure about,' he mused, recalling his first, strong impression and how he had been instantly attracted to her, with that clear, fearless gaze and the laughter lines about her mouth, yet not entirely decided about what he actually felt. There was strong feeling there, he knew it instinctively, and possibly also some hidden sorrow. 'I still haven't figured out Jessica.'

'What's the problem?' Vincent was behind him, peering over his shoulder. 'She's quite a sweetie, in her quiet, Brit way. Slightly buttoned up, maybe, but she's undoubtedly shy.'

'Aren't they all?' They laughed. It was a popular excuse but occasionally accurate. And if anyone could get to the bottom of things, it was Vincent.

6

Jessica clanked her rusty old bicycle down the final flight of stairs and out into the street. It was raining but by now she was used to that. Bath, with its elegant architecture and air of faded gentility, was all very well in summer but at this time of year, when the wind had begun to blow, bad weather was setting in and a strange sort of dankness had begun to issue from the walls of her cramped lodgings. She stood outside by the railings and tugged down her woolly hat firmly over her hair in a vain attempt to keep it dry. She searched in her basket for the mittens she had found in the Oxfam shop but appeared already to have lost. Jessica sighed. If she weren't careful, it would be chilblains again this winter and that was something she'd do almost anything to avoid.

Simon, for once, was there ahead of her, standing at her desk like an overgrown schoolboy in his ill-fitting suit, apparently searching for something.

'Yes?' she said with an element of froideur, tugging the sodden hat from her streaming hair. 'Can I help you?'

Simon Pratt, what a totally apposite name. She really couldn't abide this lanky young man with his air of erudition and permanent nasal drip but he was nominally her boss, so what was she to do? It was grossly unfair. Just because he had emerged from Cambridge with a better degree than hers and an aunt who was something influential on the Bath Festivals Trust, Jessica was forced to kowtow to his sanctimonious superiority even though, to her certain knowledge, he had virtually nothing between the ears. Or the legs either, from what she had observed.

'I was looking for that leaflet on the Monteverdi choir.'

Jessica yanked it out of her top drawer and thrust it into his hand. What was it with this bloke, always snooping around her own pet projects, unable to activate anything original of his own? Why couldn't he do the job he was paid for and get out there after new talent? The year was racing towards its end and they had a whole new festival to put together by May.

'And could you make me a cup of coffee?' His smile was watery; he had no charm.

Make it yourself, thought Jessica impatiently but she mutely hung her steaming coat on the rack and went to fill the kettle. It was easier just to shut up and get on with it while what she really wanted to do was bash him over the head, then trample him to death.

Once Simon and his coffee were safely back in their corner, Jessica settled at her own strewn desk and flicked through the morning's mail. The room was stuffy in an attempt to keep out draughts and the ancient, sputtering gas-fire sucked out what oxygen there was left. No wonder Simon looked so pasty; she at least had that bracing bike-ride to pump up her heart and keep her circulation racing. If he had any balls, she thought, he would use his affluent connections to get them somewhere more congenial to work. With a bit of style, perhaps, so that visiting musicians would feel more pampered and prospective investors take them more seriously. But, oh no. All he ever wanted to do was mince and preen around celebrities, so that he could then rush off to his spineless friends and brag about who he knew. He was even an amateur recorder player of sorts – pathetic. She slashed open envelopes with her wooden knife. *Men,* she thought savagely. *Who needs them?*

The list of visiting conductors brought her up short. There was that name again and it set her senses whirling. She laid down the knife and stared up at the barred basement window which fronted a yellow brick wall and let in insufficient light. However much she tried to cauterise her memories, something would always come along to remind her of Tom and then render her fairly useless for the next few hours.

She glanced across at Simon's bent head, then up at the clock which showed ten past ten. The rain was still streaming down the grimy window and puddling outside the basement door. But she had to get out.

'Stamps,' she said. 'I've just remembered we're out. I'll pop down to the post office before it gets too crowded. Anything else you need while I'm gone?'

She walked this time because she was too disheartened to take the bike. Huddled in her camel coat, with her scarf wrapped round her chin, she sank her hands deep in her damp pockets and flitted from doorway to doorway in an attempt to avoid the worst of the weather. The Copper Kettle was almost empty so she ducked inside and shed her wet garment, then settled by the radiator and ordered herself a cappuccino. Let that lazy sod man the office alone for a while. That should teach him the more mundane side of the job, all those silly women with their endless bleating enquiries. She warmed her hands round the steaming cup and gazed back into a haze of memory. They said these things got less painful with time but so far she had no evidence of that.

Tom was all right, she'd known it from the start, straight and honourable and as talented as hell. Younger, maybe, but that was all to the good. His confident grin and gritty northern knowingness had complemented her own more refined upbringing. He had taught her so much in the few short months they'd been together – to relax and listen to jazz, and laugh and make love with the lights on. And she had taught him too – about Schopenhauer and Sibelius and the proper way to hold his knife and fork – while he'd joked and teased her and gazed at her in admiration.

'Who would have thought,' he had said fondly, stroking her soft, pale hair, 'that in one small head . . .' And she'd thumped him and run away and he'd chased her across the wet grass. And caught her under the trees and held her fast, and kissed her like no one ever had. Before or since, more's the pity. When the waitress came to offer her more coffee, she saw that Jessica had been crying.

The digs Jessica rented didn't have a kitchen as such, just an ancient Baby Belling and a sink concealed behind a curtain in the corner. And a one in seven incline to the hill she had to climb each day, though freewheeling down in the mornings made the extra exertion almost worth it. And she did have a spectacular view, over the whole of the beautiful city of Bath, even though it meant her shoving that blasted bike up two flights of stairs and then walking two more to her own front door. And at least this time she had privacy of sorts.

In Cheltenham last year she'd been forced to share, with a girl with a nasty cough who had chain-smoked most of the time and had regular screaming rows with her boyfriend over the phone.

On the whole, she really enjoyed the job, even though it paid only a pittance compared to some and involved working excruciating hours. But Bath was definitely one of the plums in the calendar, with architecture and historic ambience that more than compensated for the damp and the cold. The thing about music festivals was the variety; you never knew what you'd be doing from one day to the next and there was, of course, the music to keep you going. Which reminded her. She switched her transistor to Radio Three in time to catch Natalie Wheen's slightly fruity voice, interviewing some Czech violinist in Prague. Now *that* was a job she would really like. And some day, when she'd finished her peregrinations, she meant to have it. Finding a way into the BBC wouldn't be easy but she already had her plans.

She poked around in the minuscule fridge to see what there was for supper. A carrot, half a wilted lettuce, two courgettes that had seen better days and some bacon past its sell-by date. No eggs, so it would have to be Sutherland Spaghetti again. Jessica wasn't much of a cook and her repertoire contained just the two basic dishes: Spanish Omelette when there were left-overs to use up; her own pasta with bacon and courgette sauce when the fridge was virtually bare. But she did take seriously the minor culinary touches and would cycle an extra half-mile to buy really good olive oil or sun-dried tomatoes for the summer version of her sauce. She'd tried growing basil on the windowsill but it hadn't worked; she was far too chaotic to remember to water it and anyhow it always died, or developed white fly before she got round to using it. The same went for parsley so she'd learned to do without. She turned her nose up at the dried variety just as she swore she could never drink instant coffee. In her strange, haphazard way, Jessica was an elitist where the finer things of life were concerned. But she almost never entertained.

Once the pasta was *al dente* and the sauce sloshed on (no parmesan, she'd forgotten to buy any) Jessica poured herself a hefty slug of wine and carried the whole lot across the room to the oilcloth-covered table in the window where she could read the paper while she ate. No television for Jessica; she was far too much of a cultural snob. She liked to brag that she was the last of the Luddites and bashed away merrily on the ancient office Underwood because she felt that computers were unreliable and somehow too worldly for the esoteric circles in which she worked. Simon, however, had other ideas. He had started bringing in his Power Book to work and would spend hours in silence, poring over its tiny screen. Jessica had her suspicions about this latest piece of exhibitionism and was thrilled to be proved right when she caught him playing Solitaire when he was supposed to be chasing up bookings. Sooner or later she would properly catch him out and then she would have his job faster than she could even say gotcha.

She twisted the dial to the World Service and listened in desultory fashion to a crackling news report from the Middle East. Evenings in Bath were inclined to be dull when she wasn't out on the job, trawling around the neighbouring countryside, auditioning talent. And Jessica found it hard to make new friends, moving as she did from town to town as she diligently beavered her way up the arts festival ladder. Bath was marvellous but her ultimate goal was, of course, London. What wouldn't she give for a crack at the Proms, the largest and most prestigious music festival in the world, certainly the most exciting. Plus the chance to settle in that most exciting of cities, surrounded at last by a positive banquet of cultural delights. She couldn't imagine being lonely there. It would be one wild whirligig of sensual pleasure where companionship would be an unnecessary extra.

Which brought her thoughts back inevitably to Tom. She finished her insipid meal and gulped down the last of the wine, then dumped both glass and plate in the sink to deal with tomorrow when she felt more in the mood. On the old pine chest that served as a bedside table, half-hidden behind a pile of books and a flashlight, was a small, framed snapshot of a laughing young man, with a red-spotted kerchief knotted around his neck, crouching over a Primus stove in front of a backdrop of mist-enveloped hills. Windermere. Because of the flame he was trying so hard to control, he was squinting up at the camera and his features were indistinct.

Jessica took up the photograph and carried it over to the lamp. All she had left of last year's idyll, of the encounter she had thought would change the course of her life, was this single snapshot, over-exposed, so that all she could really see was the dark, curly hair and one minute gold earring. Elusive as a dream she only partly remembered. Jessica sat on her rumpled bed and once more wept.

The harpsichordist was pretty but her arpeggios were uneven and would simply not do, not on the professional platform. Jessica scrawled a comment in her notebook and closed it with a snap. She glanced at her watch. If she left the Pump Room now and took a taxi she should just make it on time to the next appointment, an all-male choir from the Rhondda, in Bath for a one-night stand on their way home after a Canadian

tour. She sighed. This winter had got off to an early start
and her toes in her insubstantial boots were already frozen.
She stamped her feet. Life had become a gruelling round of
nothing but work and these days Jessica's moments of joy
were few. She thought with nostalgia of that marvellous island
holiday and the group of jolly new friends she had made on
the beach. What a blessing they had turned out to be, after
all that had gone before. Lifesavers in their way, blissfully
unaware of her trauma, and that was what had eventually
saved her sanity. Fun, that was what she was lacking now
and Bath in mid-winter was certainly not the place to find it.
Tonight, when she got home, she would write again to Cora
Louise. So far there'd been no response to the last letter but
Jessica knew how much those Charleston ladies travelled.

Christmas seemed to start earlier each year and Jessica, who
both hated and feared it, was filled with despondency when
she saw that the shops already had their card departments
up and running. It wasn't even Hallowe'en, yet the glitter
and tinsel were already creeping in and pretty soon there'd
be lighted trees in every store window and cute little Santas
with collecting boxes waiting in doorways to waylay her.
Christmas in the office, too, was bound to be hell. Home-made
paper-chains spanning the room under the neon light with a
bunch of straggly mistletoe over the door; she'd been in this
poorly paid business too long and knew just what to expect.
At least the Prat was not the type to go buzzing off to the
ski-slopes, leaving her to cope alone, but she had no doubts
he'd have something exotic up his sleeve. Grandparents with a
Scottish castle, maybe, or a wealthy step-mother who wintered
in Florence. Because of her circumstances, Jessica had long
avoided all thoughts of Christmas; left to her own devices,

she'd simply go to ground and ignore it altogether. Last year had proved a miraculous escape, one of those aberrations to which she rarely succumbed but which had turned out to be more than worth it in the end. Especially in view of what had gone before. She closed her eyes as a familiar chill swept through her.

Money well spent, there was no doubt about that, but could she possibly afford it again this year? She thought of the beloved Cora Louise, the mother she would have liked to have had, and her amiable daughter, Fontaine, who seemed so relaxed about sharing her. Of Vincent, the life-enhancer, the elegant Lowell and the warm and sensible Jo. Jessica badly needed friends and longed to pursue those connections. Even the abrasive Merrily she had found she could stomach, once she'd grown used to the rapier tongue and those wicked, downbeat one-liners. For the first time in years, Jessica had felt part of an extended family and, even though they had parted before Christmas, the holiday had brought the year to a satisfactory end.

Now, nearly ten months later, she felt in sharp need of a similar happiness fix. A small bequest from a grandmother, long dead, was still invested in National Savings; it was so long since she'd felt like being extravagant, she'd forgotten exactly how much it was. As soon as she reached home, she would check out the figures and see if she could stretch to another escape to the sun. Just thinking about it made her that much warmer inside. She bent her head stoically against the sleet and pumped up and down on the ancient pedals as she manoeuvred her battered old bicycle home.

Jo seemed surprised to get Jessica's call. Surprised yet delighted. There'd been an exchange of postcards earlier in the year but they never had managed to get together and lately she'd been too busy to think about anything but work. She apologised. She'd just been talking to Merrily, she said, pretty fed up herself in New York and keen to get away from it all again. She herself had not given it much thought recently but needed, most definitely, some sort of respite from the job. For one reason or another, this year had been particularly gruelling. She still didn't say exactly what she did, but her voice sounded weary and furred with a cold she couldn't shake off. Jessica sympathised. Occasionally, when you were feeling low, those bugs just latched on and refused to be shifted. The thought of that smooth, white sand and flat, translucent sea was incredibly tempting. Lying supine in a deck-chair under a tree, holding out her hand for the occasional Planter's Punch and catching up on her reading, seemed like paradise. And the sunshine, out of that clear cerulean sky. Just the thought of it warmed her toes and the cockles of her heart.

First thing tomorrow, without fail, she'd go down to the travel agency and make her booking.

7

'Cocktails at seven in room 16. Dress informal.'

Jo laughed when they handed her the note at reception and she recognised Vincent's flamboyant scrawl. It felt good to be back. The moment the plane touched down on Antigua and she smelled the familiar hothouse aroma and the pulsating darkness caressed her face like a warm flannel, she knew she was right to have come. She followed the smiling bellboy along a corridor edged with palms, to the welcoming doorway of her own airy room, windows behind floating curtains already open to the friendly Caribbean evening.

It was ten past six. She shook out her meagre holiday wardrobe to allow it to uncrease in the humidity, then splashed water on her face and ran a brush through her hair. Ten minutes out on the balcony, breathing in the clean, salt air and allowing her head to clear, and she was ready for the short, fragrant walk along a winding path between bread-fruit trees to the flight of stairs at the end of the complex that led to Vincent and Lowell's spacious suite. They always booked the same one, another of their traditions. She could hear laughter even before she turned the corner and a bright dart of happiness shot right through her.

Lowell opened the door with a flourish and bowed low to kiss her hand; Vincent was busy doing the honours at the makeshift bar, a pitcher of martinis already mixed and waiting.

'Unless you'd rather have juice,' he joked, dropping everything in order to envelop her in a bear-hug.

He looked svelte and dapper in immaculate white jeans and a yellow shirt while Lowell was more formal in blazer and Harvard tie. The Ravenel ladies were already well settled; their connection from Miami had landed at four so they'd managed to slip in a proper nap before the reunion. Fontaine, Jo observed, had put on a little weight but her mother was as tiny and exquisite as ever. Both seemed genuinely delighted to see her.

'Quite like old times,' said Cora Louise, embracing her. 'Now all we need is those other two gals and our little family will be complete.'

Fontaine, in startling fuschia which clashed dramatically with her riotous hair, was rather like an overblown rose as she fluttered her inky eyelashes at Lowell, but no less ravishing for it. Her skin was as clear and flawless as porcelain; only the high arched nose with its broad flattened tip stopped her being a total beauty. Huguenot blood, Jo imagined, with a name like that. Next to her Jo felt dowdy and uninspired.

'How ya doin', doll?' asked Fontaine fondly, crushing Jo to her billowy bosom and kissing her firmly with her full, scarlet lips. 'Isn't it just dandy to be here again? Can't wait to get out of

mah clothes and on to that beach.' The smile she shot at Lowell
was positively lascivious but he, apparently not noticing, had
moved across to the bar and was slicing salami.

'You know that guy from Vancouver,' remarked Vincent,
who had already been out on his rounds. 'Norman, who
we met last year with his wife? Well, he's here again, in the
same beach-front suite, only the wife's a good thirty-five years
younger this time.' He chortled as he handed Jo her martini.
'Either that or she's had one hell of a face-lift.'

'Now, now,' scolded Cora Louise. 'You bad boy. You just
keep your nose out of other folk's business, you hear?'

Vincent was incorrigible. Nobody's secrets were entirely safe
from him. He smiled at the others with his oh-so-innocent
blue eyes, guileless as a choirboy at a church picnic. But
secretly Jo felt that she had the last laugh. *He may think
he's pretty damn smart,* she thought. *But what does he really
know about me?* They still hadn't cracked the secret of her
profession. Silly really, but it made her feel a little smug.
She would tell them some time but not while they were
on holiday. Sebastian had been right about all those minor
ailments; there were people on the beach who could talk of
little else.

'The Barlows are back too,' said Lowell. 'Marjorie still
wittering on about interior design.'

'I'll bet she's brought her photographs,' sighed Vincent. 'Actually, I can't wait to see them. From the way she was talking
last year, the place will resemble a tart's boudoir by the time
she's done.'

There was a tap at the door and in walked Jessica. Everybody chimed a cheery welcome and she smiled with delight,
pleased and surprised by such a warm reception. She looked,
if anything, even more fragile but her hair was glossy and

bouncing with good health and the unhealthy smudges had gone from beneath her eyes. She had come in on a charter flight from Luton, thus missing Jo at Heathrow.

'What a shame we didn't think,' said Jo, making room for her on the bed. 'We should have arranged to travel together.' Jessica, she reflected, looked better than she had expected from their recent conversation. Clearly a survivor. Jo looked forward to getting to know her better.

Glasses filled, they all drank a toast, to the island, to renewed friendships and, in half an hour's time, the sunset. Lowell checked his watch.

'We must get down there in time for the green flash,' he said. 'All part of the great Antigua tradition. Especially on the first night.' It was something to do with the angle at which the sun hit the sea. Even Lowell was hazy about the physics but nobody really cared.

'Magic,' said Vincent solemnly as they all trooped out. 'That's all you need know, all that really matters.'

Merrily arrived at midnight, in a sunnier mood than last year. The gang had all loyally waited up and were grouped on the terrace under the stars, drinking gimlets to the rhythm of a jaunty steel band. Vincent had more than done his duty as an escort, waltzing each of the ladies energetically about the floor, but Fontaine had monopolised most of his attention because she was such a fantastic dancer. *It's odd that*, thought Jo comfortably as she watched, *all that extra baggage yet still so light and agile on her feet.* She had never seen Fontaine look more beautiful as she twirled around in Vincent's practised arms, head thrown back in ecstasy, twinkling feet in their ridiculous strappy sandals matching his, step for step.

'What a star she is,' said Lowell admiringly and was rewarded by Cora Louise with a proud mother's smile.

Then Merrily made her entrance and everybody clapped.

'Jesus,' she said, as she sank into a chair. 'That was some bitch of a flight, I can tell you.' But, from the light in her eyes and the radiant smile, it was clear she didn't mean it.

They laughed next morning when they met for breakfast and saw where their table had been placed. Right in the corner of the L-shaped room with a healthy space between it and the other, less raucous, guests.

'That tells us something,' said Vincent gaily, gallantly escorting Cora Louise to her place at the head of the table. 'They obviously had enough of us last year and last night was clearly the clincher.'

'Well, that's fine with me,' said Merrily. 'Who needs envious strangers gawping and eavesdropping?'

'They're just jealous,' said Fontaine, resplendent this morning in a candy-striped beach-robe, 'because we're having more fun than they are.'

Which did, indeed, appear to be the case. Apart from one family engrossed in their own conversation, the other tables were occupied by stiff, unsmiling couples, none of them in the first flush of youth and all eating in silence. Glancing round the half-filled room, Jo silently thanked her stars once again for her huge good fortune in having fallen in with this cheery group. Her eye caught Jessica's and she smiled back. Now *there* was someone to get to know better. Jo had a gut feeling that, given time, the two of them could become really good friends. She admired Jessica's knowledge and quick-witted intelligence and sensed there might be considerably more below the surface than she ever allowed to show.

Merrily, for once, was in dazzling form and kept them in stitches throughout the meal with hair-raising stories about life in New York. By the time she was through, Cora Louise's eyes were starting out of her head while Fontaine was positively enthralled.

'Mercy me,' she said theatrically, one plump white hand to her bosom. 'It surely can't be as bad as you say?' She was envious.

'Worse,' said Merrily darkly, fixing her with an evil grimace.

'Go and stay with Merrily, I dare you,' said Vincent. 'And sample it first-hand. Sounds as though you'd like to. Am I not right?'

'Heavens, no,' shuddered Cora Louise. 'The last time we were in New York we were petrified for our lives. All those darkies jostling us on the sidewalk. Never left our hotel room after sundown. Lived on room service the entire four nights.'

'Jesus!' exclaimed Merrily, startled into outrage. 'What planet have you been living on?'

She was genuinely shocked by the political incorrectness, though Cora Louise merely looked bewildered.

'You have got to be kidding!' Her tales of big city lust and debauchery might be way over the top, but this ignorant Southern belle was daring to criticise the city she loved and that simply wasn't on.

'But I'll bet you enjoyed the late-night blue movies,' said Vincent, the peace-maker. 'Come along, Cora Louise, 'fess up. You can tell us, we're all family here.' And the older woman's feeble protestations were lost in a gale of complicitous laughter.

Merrily was diamond bright this year and more determined

than ever. And the clothes she produced, outfit by stunning outfit, were good enough to grace the boards of a fashion show and made Jo's own humble collection look very charity shop indeed. Jessica sympathised.

'I'd like to know what she earns,' she said, not without a touch of envy. 'It must be top dollar to support a lifestyle like that.' Like Jo, she had brought the minimum of sensible beach-clothes, with a couple of faded Indian cotton skirts for evening. Yet Jessica, too, had a style all her own and managed always to look chic and rather striking. She favoured pale apricot and soft, warm browns to go with her autumn colouring and, as her pale skin began to take on a little colour, needed only a lick of lip-gloss to perfect her appearance. Of course, that hair was a help. Jo noticed how men glanced at it as she passed, following her skinny, almost adolescent, figure with appreciation, even lust. If only she would throw off some of that pseudo-intellectual tweeness, Jessica could really make an impact.

Merrily was inclined to dominate the conversation, with stories of big spending and the fast track in New York, but even as she chatted she never missed a trick. Eyes bright as a magpie's, she watched each movement on the beach or in the bar, ever alert for the challenging new arrival, someone into whom to sink those immaculate, silk-wrapped claws. Or was she being unfair to her? Jo wondered; studying Merrily in action, she really didn't think so. Even Fontaine, for once, was outfaced. Her own collection of clothes was pretty spectacular, but this year Merrily left her standing.

Lowell, however, was privately disapproving. He abhorred vulgar exhibitionism and considered Merrily well over the top. He watched Cora Louise silently sharing his disapprobation and beamed her a smile of support. In the South all show of conspicuous wealth was strongly frowned on, certainly in Ravenel circles. His mother would approve of Cora Louise; they were fashioned from the same fine clay, sadly out-dated these days. But Vincent told him sharply not to be so stuffy.

'Give the girl a break,' he said. 'She's funny, feisty and I'm starting to like her a lot.'

What he admired in Merrily was her shrewd, calculating business brain, a lot like his own, and her unashamed eye for the main chance, which he found refreshing.

We're both whores at heart, he thought, though didn't say it. Under almost any circumstances they'd have got along well together. As it was, he found himself seeking her out and laughing riotously at some of her stories. Jo, too, was rapidly warming to Merrily. Behind the spiky facade, she intuited genuine kindness and felt instinctively that this was someone she could trust, should the need ever arise, with more than just her secrets.

'I've sussed out the Canadians,' reported Vincent over lunch. Formal meals were confined to the evenings; at noon the hotel laid on a sumptuous buffet, served on the terrace under a canvas awning. Provided you covered your top half, bare feet and the briefest of shorts were permitted. The group was assembled round a wrought-iron table, close to the low, white wall that divided them from the beach. Brilliant birds, unfamiliar to Jo, hopped on and off the backs of chairs, hopeful for rich pickings from the exotic food.

'The beloved Myra, dear to us all, is still alive and well in suburban Vancouver. Tending her garden and doing good works in the neighbourhood. This substitute is his "personal assistant" from the office, here to sustain him body and soul and take dictation, should the need arise.' Everybody laughed.

'How on earth did you find out all that?' asked Merrily.

The Dutchman's eyes were innocent. 'I asked.'

'I'm surprised he didn't tell you to get lost.'

'I asked politely. Besides, Canadians aren't like that. They take life more . . . philosophically.' Vincent glanced at his watch. 'I need more film,' he said, 'and I'd quite like a jaunt into town. Anyone care to come along for the ride?'

Everyone glanced at each other then shook their heads. Merrily was off for a nap in her room once she'd finished her beer. Fontaine had booked a manicure and Jessica wasn't yet through telling her life story to Cora Louise, who was engrossed in a *petit point* cushion cover. She was all too happy to remain seated right here if Jessica would stay and keep her company. Vincent raised a querying eyebrow at Jo but she was feeling unusually restive and decided to go for a walk.

'Well, come into town with us and walk round the shops,' said Vincent. 'That should be all the exercise you need and I could use a lady of discernment to help me with a little light shopping.'

But Jo was firm. 'Some other time,' she promised, but not today. Today that fine, white sand was beckoning; she longed to go off on her own along the shore and sort out some of the turmoil that was beginning to surface now that she had relaxed a little.

Lowell was leaning against the Jeep outside the main front door when Jo came out, his feet in pristine espadrilles, a wide-brimmed straw hat stuck elegantly on his head.

'You look like Cecil Beaton,' said Jo.

'Please!' The judge pulled a face, pretending displeasure, but he knew he made a striking figure in his blue silk shirt and khaki shorts.

'Hop in,' he said, when Jo explained her destination. 'We'll drop you off a couple of miles along the coast and you can walk back.'

That seemed a sensible idea. Together with the boys, she had more or less explored this side of the island; there were so many deserted beaches that she decided to be adventurous.

'But do take care,' warned Lowell, once Vincent had joined them and they were on their way. 'All sorts of gruesome stories occur from year to year. Last year there was that unfortunate drowning and this year, I gather, there's already been a mugging. Some poor, unwitting American tourist was confronted by a man with a machete who chopped off her finger in order to get her rings. Or so they were saying in the bar last night.'

Jo shuddered. Was no place safe from violence these days? 'Better not let Cora Louise hear that,' she warned, 'or she'll not venture even as far as the beach.'

'Probably an exaggeration but still,' said Lowell, stopping the Jeep at a bend in the road to let her out. 'And if you're not back by sunset we'll organise a search party.'

'Don't worry about me,' Jo assured him jauntily. 'Remember where I come from. I'm pretty much streetwise.'

She stood on the empty highway and waved the Jeep out of sight, then took a sharp left and cut 'through a stand of sugar-cane to where she could hear the waves idly plashing on the shore. This was more like it; pure white sand stretching for miles each way, dotted with coconut palms and occasional man-made breakwaters but no sign of life in either direction. Exactly what she craved – alone with the elements with time in which to think, away from the gang for some quality time on her own. Way ahead she could just make out the outline of a rustic shack. She would make that her turning-point and maybe get a beer.

The past twelve months had been hectic for Jo and her head was still reeling from all she had absorbed. She still loved her work, was more dedicated than ever, but realised now how much she had needed this break. General medicine was stimulating in a less dramatic way than the daily trauma of hospital life but a general practitioner needed a far more wide-ranging knowledge, which meant continuing study, and Jo found herself working till all hours just in order to keep up. Each day brought its own new challenge. There was no way of knowing what problems might arise and any mistake could prove potentially fatal. The recurring image of that dying child flashed across her brain, but in softer focus. A year had gone by but she still couldn't erase it completely; nights when she was particularly strung up she knew she could say goodbye to sleep.

Growing apart from Sebastian hadn't helped. Without his comforting arms and rational outlook to calm and sustain her, facing a daily diet of sickness, panic and pain was sometimes almost more than she could take, but what else could she do? They were still good friends, still officially 'an item', but were actually drifting further and further apart as they got more caught up in their separate lives. Sebastian's music was taking precedence in his. Although he was still fascinated by the workings of the sick mind, his obsession with the flute was beginning to take over and Jo privately wondered that the Tavistock Clinic allowed him so much time off for his gigs. The truth was Sebastian's life had always been charmed; he was bright and well-liked and things usually worked out for him.

She reached the beach bar at around four but found, to her disappointment, that she was not alone. Apart from the barman, still and mute as a sand-creature merging with his surroundings, a man was seated at a corner table, shaded by a wooden beach umbrella and absorbed in the notebook on his knee.

'Hello there, young lady!' boomed the barman, springing to life like an automaton, his face splitting in a gigantic grin. 'And what may I get for you today?'

Jo jingled the coins in the pocket of her shorts and decided on a beer. Thirsty work this, walking on sand, and her legs were telling her she was more tired than she had thought. The stranger raised his head and smiled abstractedly. He was tall and lightly tanned, in well-pressed chinos and a spotless white shirt. She headed for the furthermost table in order not to disturb him but he raised his hand and beckoned her over. Not wishing to appear rude, she felt obliged to join him.

'Hello,' he said with a more focused smile, 'you're the first living creature I've seen in a while. Please sit down.'

Close to, she could see that his clothes were discreetly expensive and certainly no local barber had ever touched that hair – longish and soft but skilfully cut and artfully streaked by the sun. Scandinavian would be her first guess, or possibly even West Coast American though, from the little he'd said so far, his voice seemed accentless. Off one of the floating gin-palaces, no doubt, or the fancy hotels clustered around the English Harbour.

'Make that two,' he said to the waiter when her beer arrived, then closed his notebook and leaned comfortably back, pushing his dark glasses back into position on his fine, patrician nose. And with that one simple gesture, something in Jo's chest seized up, squeezing the breath right out of her. His skin was golden, his hands long and expressive. She couldn't see his eyes but his teeth were perfect, his smile warm and welcoming. This was the most stupendous man she had ever been close to, in the flesh and not on the cinema screen. Come to think of it, there was something vaguely familiar about him. Maybe he was a real celebrity; all kinds of people came to these islands. Dare she ask?

'Your eyes don't match,' he observed casually when she removed her own glasses to polish the lenses. Jo smiled shyly and replaced them on her nose. Normally she wore contact lenses but found them uncomfortable in this scorching sun.

His own eyes were effectively obscured by black mirror lenses which gave him an anonymity that went with the aura of celebrity. He had, she found herself thinking, the most kissable mouth she had seen. Then felt herself flushing with confusion and tried to hold on to her sanity. He seemed to be watching her intently so she groped for something to say that was halfway sensible. The sun, the beer and a sudden leaden lethargy all added up to a feeling of pleasant euphoria. Jo wanted this moment never to end, content just to sit here beside him for eternity.

'So tell me,' he said, after a lengthy pause. 'Who exactly are you and what are you doing here?'

'Joanna Lyndhurst,' said Jo obediently. 'I'm here on holiday. From England.'

'Alone?'

'Yes. Well, no. I met up with friends.'

'And is this your first visit?'

'No, we were all here last year.'

'Same time?'

'Exactly. The week before Christmas.'

'And staying?'

She told him. He seemed to want to know a lot of trivia, an odd way of making small talk. She would have liked to believe it was personal interest but he seemed too professional, too detached. And Jo had no false illusions about her own pulling-power; she knew instinctively that a man of this calibre would not be interested in the likes of her. His looks, the cut of his clothes, his air of lazy insouciance, put him as far out of her class as the wafer-thin Rolex on his wrist. Out came the notebook and he made a couple of brief notes. Maybe all he was was some sort of travel writer, out here to assess the local hotels. It seemed unlikely but you never could be sure. One of the truths Jo had learned since entering medicine was that people often come in deceptive packages.

He glanced at his watch. Soon he would walk out of her life and the idyll would be over and there wasn't a thing in the world she could do to prevent it. Instead he nodded to the barman and indicated another round. Then leaned back lazily and flashed her that megawatt smile.

'Tell me about your friends,' he said, with apparently genuine interest. So Jo plunged right in and described the group and watched his interest increase as she talked. He was flatteringly attentive to every word; it was just disconcerting that she couldn't see his eyes. He seemed riveted by what she had to say about Merrily and Jessica; Fontaine, too, until he heard about the mother. But it was Lowell who really caught his attention and he stopped her abruptly right there.

'A judge, you say? How fascinating. Would I perhaps know the name?'

Jo could not believe she could be so indiscreet but the power of his questioning, combined with an urgent desire not to let him go, made her throw caution to the winds and plough right on, ingenuous as a school-girl and, as she later realised, every bit as foolish. Once he had probed her for every piece of information, he glanced again at his watch and said he must be off. He didn't shake hands or even say goodbye, just patted her lightly on the shoulder and left. Jo sat there leadenly watching him stride away, tall and elegant and infinitely desirable – a god of a man, destined to haunt her dreams.

Vincent took one look and led her straight to the bar. Although he knew she usually preferred wine, he ordered her a double cognac and another for himself.

'So tell me,' he said, as they settled in a corner. A single glance at that stricken face and he knew something fairly momentous was up but, for once, he didn't pressure her. He was always curious but also kind. Jo knew she could trust him, more even than the rest. And, no matter how foolish she might feel, she badly needed to unload.

'He was, quite simply, the most beautiful man I've met,' she said solemnly. 'I can't explain it but it went beyond just physical.'

Vincent nodded, for once not wise-cracking. 'You mean his soul was beautiful too?'

'Why, yes, that's it.' Jo was quite startled. Vincent spent so much time playing the buffoon, it was a surprise to find him attentive and not poking fun. 'How could you possibly know that? It was almost as though I had met him before . . .'

'In some previous existence?'

Now she was suspicious, but he was still playing it straight. Bless him, he was taking her seriously. She squeezed his hand and he raised hers to his lips.

'Don't worry,' he said softly. 'I've been there and I know. I hate to sound corny but it's commonly known as love.'

'As fast as that? We only talked for about twenty minutes. I never even found out his name.'

'Nevertheless. Stranger things have happened.' Lowell entered the bar, unseen by Jo, but Vincent fractionally shook his head and Lowell took the hint and left them alone.

'Don't knock it,' said Vincent. 'It is all too rare. But the *coup de foudre* is definitely a phenomenon. If only you have the courage to face up to it.'

'We'll find him,' he reassured her the next morning, as he brought round the Jeep. 'This island's minute, there are few places he can hide. And, anyhow, why would he want to?' Cynical though he might be, at heart the Dutchman was a true romantic and could observe a rare beauty in this serious young woman of which she herself was entirely oblivious. Which was part of her intrinsic charm, her utter lack of self. Any man with any sense would surely find her a delight. She was, as he had already joked to Lowell, almost enough to turn a guy straight.

Shopping, he'd said when they'd asked where they were off to. Jo had been right in her choice of confidant; Vincent was an enthusiast who would never betray her. Fontaine had looked as though she might like to tag along but Vincent remained firm.

'There's something important that Jo wants to look for. Expect us when you see us.'

He was expert, he told her, at tracking people down and once they had more or less circuited the island – or at least the places where the tourists went – they started stopping off at the more likely bars and having a quick snifter while they looked around. *At this rate*, thought Jo, *we'll soon both be plastered*, but her confidence was growing with Vincent's persistence and she was possessed by a recklessness that grew with each successive pit-stop. What she would do if they actually found him she hadn't yet worked out. Running after a man was the last thing Jo would normally do but these were special circumstances. For the moment it was the chase that mattered; she knew in her heart that what they were doing was right.

It was always a pretty wild gamble but they might have found him, though they never did. A huge orange sun was plummeting to the horizon as they finally gave up and headed home, tired, despondent and more than a little pissed. Lowell was leading a line of sunset-worshippers, cocktails in hand, down to the beach for their nightly vigil but one glance at the bleak, sun-ravaged faces told him all he needed to know. Later, he knew, Vincent would fill him in but he could see that poor Jo was dangerously close to tears. Whoever would have thought it of the cool, enigmatic Miss Lyndhurst, but that was just one of the more fascinating things about these vacations. Scratch the surface of practically any person and you never did know what you might uncover.

8

The pure, hypnotic beauty of a Mozart flute concerto wafted through from Sebastian's study as Jo lay on his living-room carpet, surrounded by Sunday papers. Christmas was long past; a raw January wind agitated the trees in Gordon Square and rattled the casement windows. The music stopped.

'You're quite sure you won't come?' Sebastian stood in the doorway, buttoning his cuffs. 'I still have that extra ticket. It's criminal to waste it.'

'No thanks.' She pulled herself to her knees and set about tidying up. 'I'm way behind with my case-notes as it is and was relying on this afternoon to catch up.'

She smiled up at him from under her fringe, anxious not to cause hard feelings. She'd only stayed over, as it was, because of last night's bash.

'There must be someone else you can ask. Even as late as this.'

But Sebastian was not one to harbour a resentment. Easy come, easy go had long been his motto, though this time he'd secretly rather relied on her keeping the date. But to tell her why now would be positively wet so he wasn't about to do it.

'Sure there is,' he said with a grin. 'But I guess it's your loss. One of the rare performances of a truly great maestro. I can't imagine how you can bear to miss it, Philistine.'

Jo laughed. Sebastian and his enthusiasms; he didn't change. With his Peter Pan good looks and compelling smile, he was still the charmer she had fallen in love with all those years ago at university. She rose to her feet and gave him a quick hug.

'When does it actually start? Have we time for a rapid lunch, if I get a move on?'

'Three. And yes, before you ask, Eggs Benedict will do me fine.' He'd ring Amelia, though it wouldn't be the same. And the surprise he had kept up his sleeve until later would simply have to go by the board. It seemed a shame but he knew his Jo. If he told her the truth she would change her mind and come, and then her case-notes wouldn't get done and she'd fret. It was a tough, competitive world they both inhabited but they were equal over-achievers; without her dedication he would probably love her less. And, with luck, there'd be other occasions, particularly if he got the job.

Jo felt guilty as she poached the eggs and knew she wasn't being entirely fair. Music had always come first with Sebastian; it would be such a small sacrifice to go with him today, and catch up on her paperwork later. It was just that, lately, she couldn't seem to concentrate and the thought of three hours stuck in the Festival Hall was absolutely more than she could face in her present jumpy condition. It was certainly

something she could never explain; the truth would be far
more cruel.

As she rode home on a number 11 bus, Jo's thoughts were
far away, on a sun-kissed beach. Since that chance encounter,
more than six weeks ago, everything else in her fevered brain
had been superimposed by one longed-for image, the face of
her mysterious stranger, mocking her forever from behind
dark glasses, as inaccessible as a fading dream. It was totally
ridiculous; she saw that with perfect clarity. How an intelligent
grammar-school girl like her could be susceptible to such
hysterical flights of fancy she couldn't say; her headmistress,
who had always praised her so highly, would be shocked and
disappointed if she knew. For Jo, if anything, had only ever
erred on the side of common sense. Even her romance with
Sebastian had been conducted with propriety and carefully
controlled. They hadn't slept together at all that first year
and once they were fully committed, the exclusivity had been
mutual. Both sets of parents had thoroughly approved and Jo
felt as much at home with the jolly Lucas family as she did with
her own parents in Hampstead. Her mother steered well clear
of the subject, as was her way, but Molly Lucas was forever
dropping hints and talking hopefully of dates and hats and
the best time of year to take a sunshine holiday.

And now this had happened, quite literally out of a clear
blue sky. Shona, to whom Jo had already unloaded, was
inclined to scoff and make light of holiday romances. She'd
felt the same about ski instructors, she said; it was not an
unusual phenomenon. But imagine bringing one home to
the rain and dirt of London; his fairy prince allure would
fade as soon as his tan. Shona had always been partial to
Sebastian and would snap him up in a second, she always

said, if ever he became available. Jo knew that what she said made sense yet she couldn't throw off her amazingly mixed feelings, a kind of ongoing euphoria combined with a deep, dark sorrow that kept her constantly on the brink of silent tears. What was going on? It wasn't hormones as she was not pre-menstrual and it couldn't even be overwork since she'd just returned from holiday.

The more she thought of it, the more guilty she became. The closer she drew to home, the worse she felt about missing this one concert to which Sebastian had so specially looked forward. Their relationship generally might be on the decline, but he was still her dearest friend in the world and she really ought not to have let him down. He would take the insipid Amelia, she knew, and she'd love every second and enthuse right through. And then they'd go to supper together and analyse it, movement by movement, and Amelia would insist on paying her share because she was that sort of girl.

But it wouldn't be the same for him and that was where Jo had acted selfishly. Not only was it a top-ranking symphony orchestra, but it was conducted today by Sebastian's number one idol, the world-famous conductor, Richard Stanford Palmer, here in London on a flying visit in the middle of an international tour.

I really boobed, thought Jo with some shame as she let herself into her flat. She'd make it up to Sebastian somehow but she knew she didn't deserve his constant patient forgiveness. Time he moved on to someone more worthy; she thought of the eager Amelia and winced.

There was something about the weather in January that always got to Jo. Temperatures dropped and flu bugs thrived; the surgery was filled with coughing and sniffling and it was a miracle they didn't all go down with something nasty. Mrs Constantine, one of her long-term patients, finally succumbed to a chest infection and Jo had the down-trodden daughter weeping on her shoulder, blaming herself for what she felt was neglect. There wasn't a lot anyone could say to comfort her. The poor harassed woman, with four children of her own, lived in Chingford and simply couldn't afford the fares. Her mother had been a doughty old thing whose life had been full of colour and activity. Seventy-eight was a good age to go; still with all her faculties in order, untouched by the blight of failing health. Except, of course, she had died. Jo didn't know what more she could usefully say but made a resolve to attend the funeral.

It was the deaths that always got to her, even when a patient had been ailing for years and she knew in her heart it was really a blessed relief. It was by no means as traumatic as the casualty department, where anything could happen in a chill split second, but Jo sometimes wondered if she'd ever have the stomach for this job. Memories of that dying child often came back to haunt her at night.

'You did all you could do,' Sister had told her comfortingly but to this day Jo couldn't help wondering perhaps if she'd only acted faster . . .

'You worry too much,' Sebastian was always saying, but surely that was the essence of the job, the driving motivation that kept them all working so hard.

'What you need,' said Shona sympathetically, 'what we *both* need is something to take ourselves out of it. Living life on the edge is all very well, provided you don't let it get to you.'

Then off they'd trundle to a meal or a film, or to one of the Leicester Square late-night joints that Shona particularly favoured. For a registered nurse of her distinction, she was surprisingly fun-loving and able to let herself go. Jo envied her that indefatigable bounce, her seemingly endless ability to switch off when necessary, to put it all behind her and really let her hair down.

Jessica phoned. She'd had a terrible winter, she said, and the job was running her ragged. She adored being in Bath but the weather was dire. She still had the same cold she'd had all through Christmas and couldn't seem to shake off. Jo sympathised. She was in the same predicament and her heart lightened just to hear Jessica's cheery voice. Too much responsibility; too many late nights. Jessica had a plan. There were a couple of concert promoters she needed to see in London, so she thought she'd treat herself to a long weekend and take in a bit of culture too. If Jo were free at all in the next few weeks. Jo was delighted. Life was in danger of turning into one interminable slog and she knew she didn't take nearly enough advantage of this wonderful hub of the universe she lived in.

'Come and stay here,' she said, without a second thought. 'It's fairly cluttered but there's room enough for you, if you don't mind climbing five flights of stairs.'

Jessica thought of her own steep dwelling-place and laughed. If only Jo knew. At least she could leave the bicycle behind and rely on the capital's efficient transport system. They fixed a date for two weeks' time but then, the very next morning, a post-card arrived from South Carolina so Jo phoned Jessica back.

'Talk about synchronicity! Guess who I've heard from this very morning? The Ravenel ladies, on the road again; can you beat that! Off to South Africa on one of their jaunts and planning to return via London.'

They both agreed it was too good a chance to miss, so

Jessica said she'd postpone her appointments and aim to be with Jo when Cora Louise and Fontaine arrived, a couple of weeks before Easter.

'We'll have a dinner party here,' said Jo, delighted. 'Nothing fancy. I'm not that good a cook.'

'I'll bring dessert,' offered Jessica, running her mind's eye swiftly over her winter wardrobe, slightly daunted at the prospect of encountering Fontaine away from the informality of the beach.

So it was arranged. And two days later another postcard arrived, this time from Vincent and Lowell, skiing in Aspen. Jo's heart softened. Just when she felt that she was being neglected, all her new friends were converging together with the same serendipity that made the island holidays such magic. She could hardly wait to let Merrily know in one of their regular late-night phonecalls. Merrily was going through a bit of a rough time at work. She'd be green.

Jo showed the Ravenels the Aspen postcard and saw Fontaine dart a coy glance at her mother. They admitted they'd be passing through Boston, too, just in time to catch Lowell home from his trip.

'He's such a total angel, that delicious man,' Fontaine gushed. 'Can't do enough for the two of us. Says he'll take us to the symphony, with dinner at the Harvard Club thrown in. Can you beat that?'

'They're simply divine, both those boys,' agreed her mother. 'Gentlemen in the real sense of the word and such inseparable friends. Like David and Jonathan in the Bible. I swear we are all the better off for knowing them.'

For this special occasion, Jo had pushed the boat right out and slaved all afternoon making authentic paella, with real saffron from Harvey Nichols' foodstore and fresh shellfish from a stall in the North End Road.

'Looks as if you've been pond-dipping,' said Jessica, sticking her fingers in the pan and trying to snatch a prawn without burning herself. 'I used to enjoy that as a child.'

'Lay off, will you! Keep your piggy paws to yourself! I'm not at all sure there's enough to go round as it is, without you picking before we've even sat down.'

But when she carried the steaming platter through to the crowded living room, everyone applauded.

'It smells quite delicious,' said Cora Louise, closing her eyes in rapture like a Bisto kid. 'Makes me feel as though we are right back home.'

Fontaine pulled a face. 'Please, Mama! It cost us enough as it was to get away. Don't go wishing us back there until it's absolutely necessary!' She winked at the others. She loved riling her mother about her beloved Charleston. South Africa had been a triumph, they said, particularly Cape Town. And now they were all set to do a little light shopping in Bond Street and Knightsbridge.

'I feel such a fright,' said Fontaine, immaculate as ever. 'We've been on the road so long, I can't imagine how I must look!'

Like a bird of paradise and then some, thought Jo silently and saw from Jessica's quick glance that she agreed. But there was no denying it, Fontaine had style. It wasn't just money that turned her out so well. Jo glanced down at her own worn skirt and was uncomfortably aware that the cuffs of her shirt weren't clean. These days she found she worked so hard, there simply wasn't time to get through everything and laundry, by default, came quite low on her list. Along with cleaning the bath and hoovering under the bed. After all, a starched white coat can cover a multitude of sins.

Still, Fontaine did look magnificent and so did her mother, dressed to the nines in the highest couture fashion, and loaded down with authentic jewellery. With their fear of crowded places, Jo wondered how they dared. Jessica was wearing a nifty little something picked up in Oxfam, discreetly mended – a tie-dyed cotton wrap-around skirt, worn with a slinky, sage-green body that subtly enhanced her freckled skin. Amongst them all, Jo felt positively drab. She ladled out the last of the rice and left the platter in the sink to soak.

Now they were on to the subject of clothes, they weren't going to let her off easily.

'Come along, sugar,' breezed Fontaine over the coffee. 'Let us into the secrets of your closet and we'll pick you apart then help put you back together again. You are so darned pretty, it's wicked to waste it.'

Jo winced. Flats were what she favoured, with pleated skirts in serviceable grey, teamed with men's shirts, with the sleeves rolled up. So much of her life was spent in the surgery or paying house-calls to rundown homes that, even if she could afford posh clothes on her doctor's meagre pay, she would rarely have occasion to wear them. This isn't the United States, she wanted to point out; here doctors, along with teachers, came very low in the financial pecking order.

But there was no gainsaying Fontaine. Coffee cup in hand, she led the way into Jo's cramped bedroom and threw open the closet door with a flourish.

'This looks OK,' she said, pulling from the crowded hangers a thick-knit fisherman's jersey in heavy clotted cream. She threw it on to the bed and Jessica retrieved it and held it against herself before the mirror.

'Yes,' she said approvingly, admiring the way it offset her own pale colouring and glowing, russet hair. She could team it with jeans or her sixties' velvet, drainpipes; it would even look good with one of her Indian skirts.

'But you're only half my size,' said Jo, watching the way Jessica's mind was working. Jessica smiled and handed it back.

'Nevertheless, some time when the weather's cooler I'll have to borrow it and see how it looks. This season, according to the magazines, baggy is in.'

'Thanks,' said Jo grinning, though she knew what Jessica meant.

Later, once they were quiet again and starting to think about going, the doorbell rang. It was Sebastian, on his way home from a late shift at the hospital, irresistibly drawn by the light in Jo's window, curious to meet her new friends. He sauntered in and shook hands all round, tall and attractive, bright-eyed and boyish. Jo saw Fontaine eyeing him speculatively and was pleased. It still gave her pleasure that other women admired her man even if she was feeling distinctly lukewarm herself.

'So *you're* the Antiguans,' said Sebastian insouciantly. 'Somehow I imagined you all quite different.'

'Black, you mean,' said Fontaine coquettishly and Sebastian gave her a thoughtful stare, then settled down next to her on the sofa. Jo put on another pot of coffee but Sebastian wanted brandy.

'It's been a long, hard day,' he said, aiming his irrepressible charm at Cora Louise and immediately she responded in pure Pavlovian style, with respectful talk about doctors worldwide and the sacrifices they had to make. *He's such a ham*, thought Jo, amused, then remembered that her guests did not yet know her secret and wondered if Sebastian was about to blow it. Not that it mattered now. These women felt like members of her family; away from the beach they could gossip as much as they liked. Jo would even be happy to listen to talk of their ailments, should that ever arise.

But Sebastian had turned his attention to Jessica and, when he heard what she did for a living, his eyes lit up. Anything to do with the world of classical music always got him going and soon they were immersed in insiders' chit-chat – who they knew in common, which concerts were coming up, and what Jessica planned to include in this year's festival. Jessica was interested to hear that he played the flute and named a couple of musicians she thought he might know.

'You'll have to come down to Bath,' she said eagerly, warmed by his enthusiasm and the light in his toffee-brown eyes. 'We're doing a lot of Mozart this year and I can easily get you tickets.' Sebastian hesitated. There was something he hadn't yet got round to telling Jo and he didn't want to spoil his surprise in front of strangers. But Jessica was waiting for an answer, so he had to say something. Subject to pressure of work, he told her, he'd definitely leap at her offer.

'Sounds like fun, don't you think?' he said to Jo. 'We could both do with a bit of a summer break.'

Jo said nothing. Somehow she got the impression she was not included in this invitation but it really was of no consequence to her. But now Sebastian was talking about his idol and at the mention of Richard Stanford Palmer, Jessica grew alert. No, she said cautiously, she didn't exactly *know* him but of course she knew many people who did, some who were part of his charmed circle. Sebastian's eyes positively gleamed. What wouldn't he give . . . Though he should be meeting him himself fairly soon. If all went according to plan.

'*Now* who are they on about?' asked Fontaine, a touch plaintively. She hated not to be in the centre of things, a childish trait not improved by the fussing of her over-indulgent mother.

'Some boring musician,' said Jo with a twinkle, refilling her cup. 'The great be-all and end-all so far as Seb is concerned.'

'*Only* the greatest conductor in the world,' said Sebastian indignantly. 'Jo's such a Philistine she can't tell genius from mediocrity.'

'Childhood prodigy, playing publicly at eight,' recited Jo, who loved to tease.

'Bit of a tyrant, so they say. Once married to the Chinese violinist Mei-Lim Choy,' added Jessica unexpectedly. 'But that was years ago.'

'I didn't know that.' Sebastian, upstaged, was stopped dead in his tracks. He focused more closely on this sandy-haired stranger; maybe she really did know her stuff. Where women were concerned, Sebastian suffered from the typical dismissiveness of the Oxbridge-educated man. Except, of course, in the case of Jo and she could do no wrong.

'Can't remember what happened but there was some sort of tragedy and then they split up.' Jessica was enjoying this moment in the limelight. A becoming flush enlivened her normally pale cheeks and she sat up that much straighter.

Just as Sebastian was about to move over to perch on the arm of Jessica's chair, Fontaine made her own move and clutched him possessively by the sleeve. There was no way this divine young man was going anywhere, not when Fontaine Ravenel was in the room.

'Me, I'm far more interested in jazz,' she told him huskily and started to discuss the merits of various New Orleans groups, neatly eclipsing her rival. Jo and Cora Louise swapped a smile; it was funny watching them fight over Sebastian, particularly since wise old Cora Louise perceived him to be Jo's beau all the while and therefore well out of bounds.

'You be sure y'all come and see us now,' she told him approvingly as they prepared to leave. 'Then we'll show you how we do things in the South.'

'Hominy grits washed down with Jim Bean?' grinned Sebastian.

'Real Southern comfort, isn't it, Mama?' Fontaine's eyes were agleam with excitement; the wine they had consumed had gone right to her head. After kissing all round, she made them a promise that they'd pass on good wishes to Lowell when they saw him, though Jo had the distinct impression that the edge had gone off the Boston jaunt now that she had met Sebastian.

Sebastian put them both in a taxi then returned for a final drink with Jo and Jessica.

'They're really something, those ladies, aren't they?' he said, still delighted. 'Those folks from the Deep South are all so deliciously, decadently interbred. Charming on the surface and pure delight to spend time with, while deep-down they're probably all as mad as meat-axes.'

Later, as they finished the dishes, Jessica brought the subject back to Sebastian. He had left them reluctantly at a quarter to two, with the prospect of a drive across town when he was definitely over the limit. Jo begged him to stay but he had, he told them, an early start and needed all his wits about him in the morning.

'He can talk about mad as meat-axes,' she said fondly, as she rolled off her rubber gloves. 'He lives like a lunatic most of the time. It's only amazing he's survived this long.'

'He's nice, though, isn't he.' Jessica was probing and Jo, with a secret sigh of inevitability, felt she had to be honest.

'Frightfully nice, one of my dearest friends. We've been together so long, I can't imagine life without him but one of these days, I'm afraid, some other lucky lady's bound to snap him up.'

She watched the speculation in Jessica's eyes.

'So you don't feel especially proprietorial about him?'

'Absolutely not.' It wasn't entirely a lie and Jessica deserved some sort of a break. Sadly, in her heart, Jo faced the fact that it really was time to let him go.

'The festival sounds a terrific idea,' she said, switching off the living-room lamps and leading the way to the bedrooms. 'I know he'd love to take you up on it but I'm afraid my own work schedule just won't allow it.'

'Your life always seems so hectic,' said Jessica, a shade wistfully. She finished cleaning her teeth and climbed into Jo's spare bed. Jo stood hovering, just like her mother, waiting politely to wish her guest goodnight.

'But from all you've told us, you're pretty busy too. It must be fascinating, mixing with all those musical folk.'

'Yes, but you seem to have such an active social life too, friends who really care for you. Not like me, with nobody in the world to call my own.'

Jo thought grimly of the long, exhausting evenings and frequently broken nights. The hours spent pounding the pavements or poring over medical books till the small hours. If only Jessica knew the truth but right now was not the time. They had both had an exhausting evening, and she was due in the surgery by eight. It was time to turn off the lights. But she made a resolution to spill the beans bright and early the next morning. Who, after all, could she trust if it weren't her inner circle? And what had seemed an important omission, a bit of a lark, in fact, on holiday, paled now to insignificance when faced with a proven friend. How hurt she would be, were she ever to suspect that Jessica, or any of the others, was holding out in a similar way on her.

'They're your friends too,' she reminded Jessica gently as she closed the door. 'And now you can add Sebastian to your list.'

Generous or what? she asked herself as she rubbed in handcream and pulled back the duvet. But fair's fair, Sebastian deserved a future too and Jessica was so beguiling she doubted he'd be able to resist her. Once he'd finally got the message that their own romance was over.

9

When Cora Louise dialled the Dover number, Augusta Prentice Brooks took the call. Lowell spent the week at his chambers in Boston, she crisply informed the caller then, recognising the illustrious Ravenel name, mellowed immediately into gracious charm. She was lonelier than she cared to admit, living her declining years in the fading splendour of the family mansion, and yearned for more company than her son was able to provide.

'I'm not quite on the scrap heap yet,' she would tell the world defiantly, yet daily felt life beginning to pass her by. If only Lowell would marry and settle down but still, after all these years, he showed little sign of that. Despite his looks, wealth and family provenance, the wretched man persisted in evading commitment. Whatever was the matter with him? He had left it late still to be waiting for Miss Right so Augusta decided it was time she lent a hand, as she had on more than one occasion in the past. She invited both mother and daughter to dine the following evening, then called Lowell to inform him of what she had done.

'Be home early,' she commanded. 'And wear your good blue suit with one of the shirts I gave you for Christmas. And be sure to open a few bottles of the St Emilion in plenty of time to breathe. We'll be having grouse.'

Lowell was appalled.

'This time she really has gone too far,' he spluttered to Vincent over the transatlantic phone. Fontaine on the beach might be barely containable but at least he had to face her only once a year. Fontaine in his family home was something else entirely, particularly with that fondly indulgent mother in tow and his own mother ready to wreak whatever mischief she could. He knew Augusta only too well and could just imagine the plotting and colluding that was likely to go on; the cosy exchange of recipes and family secrets, the sending of Christmas cards and weaving of connections that would prove impossible to break. His life in the future would not be worth living. If only she'd learn not to meddle in his affairs.

Vincent just laughed. He thought he might have a buyer for the putative Vermeer and had more important matters on his mind than Lowell's pathetic little social worries. 'Get a life, man!' was his constant cry when what he really meant was: 'For God's sake be true to the one you've got.'

'Maybe she'll pounce on you,' he remarked abstractedly, totting up figures on a pad and wondering how far he dare push his mark-up. 'She was certainly hot to trot when she turned up in Amsterdam. Couldn't stop talking about you and asking questions, worse than any lovelorn teenager.'

Though he knew Fontaine presented no real threat, Vincent

nonetheless continued to resent his long-term lover's persistent denial of the truth of their relationship. These were, after all, the so-called permissive nineties though, from all accounts, Boston society was still stuck a century back.

'Got to go,' he said, checking his watch. 'Have fun!'

When Lowell arrived back at the faded old family home, he found his mother had been hard at work, organising her staff into putting on something of a show for these Southern ladies of whom she had heard so much. Out came the family silver and the second-best dinner service, with stemware thickly coated with dust from the back of one of the capacious pantries that still housed a substantial section of the dowry she had brought here as a bride. Baskets of lilies waited in the hall to be carefully positioned by Augusta herself, who preferred to keep the finishing touches from the hands of ignorant servants. A warm smell of baking wafted through from the cavernous kitchen and the gardener's boy was even polishing the downstairs windows, as if that would make any difference after dark.

Lowell was faintly irritated and a feeling of anxiety enveloped him. When Fontaine and her mother saw the extent of his property and the trappings of a solidly inherited wealth, who knew what foolish ideas they might get, as if the current situation weren't bad enough. It wasn't that they were gold-diggers, far from it. He knew they came from good old Southern stock and were likely to be better-heeled than the Brookses had become in recent years. But the gleam in Fontaine's eye alarmed him each time they met. He saw it again now when the maid ushered both ladies into the drawing room.

'Cora Louise!' he said with genuine pleasure, taking both her hands and kissing her powdery cheek. 'And Fontaine!'

Throwing propriety to the winds, Fontaine stepped forward and embraced him fiercely, kissing him on both cheeks while his mother looked on, intrigued. For this occasion Fontaine had really gone to town and wore a Hartnell gown she had had altered in London, in a heavy, bronze-ish silk that made the most of her flamboyant hair. Her shoes were rich chocolate suede with four-inch heels and she moved in a cloud of *Bal a Versailles* that made Lowell long to throw open a window. She was altogether too much.

'Come and sit by me, my dear,' said Augusta mildly, leading the way to a faded sofa by the vast log-fire and leaving her son to deal with the drinks. A dart of hope had sprung in the old lady's breast the moment she saw this handsome, stylish woman; a tad on the loud side, maybe, but that could easily be toned down. What mainly struck her was that Fontaine was neither too flighty nor too young to be suitable for her son. Her shrewd old eyes examined the mother and took in the discreet cut of her dress and the authentic lustre of the diminutive stones at her ears and throat. There was a lot to be said for these Southern belles. Centuries of in-breeding had not only refined their blood, but consolidated their family fortunes too. She'd check out the Ravenels as soon as she had the time but was increasingly comfortable with what she saw now. Something at last to get her teeth into and give her an added incentive to live on.

She looked from the flushed Fontaine to her handsome son, once again dancing attendance on the mother, and could already see them walking together beneath a flowered arch. It was time they had a wedding in this ancestral home; they'd owed it to Massachussetts society for far too long.

'Help!' said Lowell urgently from the fastness of his study, to which he had fled with a cigar and glass of port on the pretext of making an essential business call. The evening was turning out a total success and tongues and wine were flowing freely below. Lowell felt more trapped than almost ever; he turned to his best friend for reassurance.

But Vincent merely laughed. His meeting had proved more profitable than he had hoped and the representative of the Mellon Museum had named a figure that was more than satisfactory. Lowell's minor persecution by a foolish woman past the first flush of youth was nothing more than a laugh, so far as he was concerned. One, if the truth be told, that he was growing more than a little tired of.

'Get real,' he said, 'or at least get a grip. Worse things have happened to you before. Bluff your way out as you've always done.' He laughed and exhaled a stream of expensive South American smoke. 'Or else just relax and enjoy it.'

The truth was Fontaine was not the first. Nor, as Lowell was dully aware, likely to be the last unless he put an end to it now. By default, because of his background and position, he had spent a lifetime in the public glare, always a favourite for tennis parties and debutante dances, becoming, as the years rolled by, one of the most eligible bachelors in New England. The formidable Augusta had stood by and watched, at first fiercely protective of her only child, latterly growing more and more despairing as matchless chances presented themselves and were rejected. There had been the Fitzgerald daughter and the Auchincloss twins, not to mention the spirited Melissa Vanderbilt who had very nearly lured him to the altar. On that occasion the engagement had been announced in the *Globe* and the silver pattern registered at Tiffany before Lowell's cold feet had led him to duck out and quit the country for the safety of Buenos Aires until the shouting had eventually subsided.

Augusta rarely alluded to that grim period and shuddered when she did so. Lowell had only preserved his honour by pleading an inherited blood disorder and relying on the discretion of the Vanderbilts not to take matters further. Luckily, his former intended had been swept off her feet by a Latin American playboy with a larger fortune, so she no longer hung around to accuse him. On the two occasions they had glimpsed each other in the past few years, she had merely fluttered her fingers in greeting and hurried on by, clearly content to be shot of him. But, make no mistake, it had been a close shave. It still brought him out in a sweat just thinking of it.

Fontaine had slipped away to the Little Girls' Room and taken the occasion for a rapid snoop. The two mothers were still going like the clappers, talking nineteen to the dozen about the comparative merits of apple jelly and home-baked bread. Nothing, apart from a few veiled hints, had been said so far about their respective children but each was shrewdly summing up the other and, behind the fan, they had already reached agreement. All that remained now was for them to iron out the niceties of etiquette and Fontaine was quite content to leave all that to them. Even in her forties, she was used to Cora Louise taking charge. It gave her mother something concrete to worry about and allowed her own thoughts and desires to wander at will.

Nice house this. The powder room was the size of a whole bedroom, with an old-fashioned high cistern and solid mahogany seat. Once she had splashed cold water on her face and wrists to cool them, brushed her torrent of hair into some semblance of order and powdered the shine off her nose, she peeped out of the window at the

dark, scented garden before setting off to explore the rest of
the upper floors. Somewhere, in one of these rooms, Lowell
must be incarcerated. She longed to come across him as she
felt in the mood for an intimate tête à tête and surely no time
could be better than this.

The house was over a hundred years old and the ancient
oak floors squeaked and shivered in protest as Fontaine
assailed them with her formidable heels. On the landings
were hand-hooked rugs, lovingly laboured over by some
earlier Prentice or Brooks but still as colourful as when they
were first completed. And at the curve of the staircase on
each floor was a deep and comforting window-seat where
a person might pause to draw breath and admire the view,
or pull across the heavy drapes for total privacy. Fontaine
was insane about this house already. It made the shaking
old wreck on Tradd Street look like the pile of rotting
clapboard it was. She was heartily sick of the heat and
tropical climate; she pushed open the casement window a
fraction wider and inhaled the rain-soaked freshness of the
balmy New England night.

Downstairs the ladies had moved from the dining room
and were settled before the fire with coffee and *petit fours*.
Lowell had been gone a full twenty minutes and now Fontaine
seemed to have vanished too. Beneath her demure expression,
exhilaration was rising fast in Cora Louise and she only hoped
her slightly austere hostess could not detect the excitement
she was feeling.

'What a truly gracious room this is,' she twittered, glancing
round. 'Large enough to throw a ball in if you had the need.' In
Savannah they said you were not really rich if your townhouse
lacked a ballroom. This room had space enough for the whole
of the Tradd Street ground floor, and then some. She hoped

Augusta would not come to Charleston, not until everything was signed and sealed.

'The ballroom's at the end of the passage,' said Augusta apologetically, poking the logs to elicit more heat. 'I'm afraid we've rather neglected it in recent years. It's more of a conservatory now.'

But she took Cora Louise's meaning. It was long overdue that this doughty old home had a new and younger mistress to restore it to life. When she thought of the balls and garden parties they had enjoyed here when she was a girl; it was on this very sofa, now as faded and threadbare as herself, that Lowell's father had first kissed her, more than sixty years ago.

'It all needs a bit of a facelift, I'm afraid.' In contrast to Cora Louise's smart wool serge, Augusta was wearing her habitual faded chintz, a uniform she scarcely heeded any more. Her once abundant hair was now quite grey and pinned up untidily on top of her head, with floating tendrils that had escaped and gave her the look of a woman far younger. Her skin was lined from too much gardening but the bones beneath it were perfect and patrician. Augusta Prentice in her youth had been quite a noted beauty. Her posture was rigid, her carriage erect. A formidable opponent, should that ever arise, but also a loyal and redoubtable ally. Cora Louise thought of Louella Petigru and her like and shuddered involuntarily. What she had always needed in her life was someone strong and fearless like this to back her up.

Augusta was thinking how sweet the dainty little woman was, foolish in some ways, like a child, but nonetheless appealing. She was small and exquisite like a little sparrow and that lilting Southern accent was positively beguiling. Since the death of her husband, more than twenty years before, Augusta had allowed herself to become something of a recluse. With Lowell always so preoccupied and often away, she had come to enjoy her own company, which was just as well. But the light, inconsequential chatter of this exotic stranger reminded her forcefully of what she had missed so long. Yes, something had to be done, and without a moment's delay, before that numskull of a son of hers allowed another opportunity to pass him by. An idea began to form in her fecund brain.

One of Lowell's formal fund-raising events was coming up in about three weeks' time. A white-tie affair at the Lincoln Centre in New York, followed by dinner at one of his fancy clubs. Occasionally Augusta liked to accompany him to these dos as it gave her the opportunity to dress up a little and mix in circles she had neglected for too long. But this was one opportunity she was not going to risk spoiling. Lowell could take Fontaine as his partner and both mother and daughter could spend the weekend here. Or even, if they preferred, the week. It would give them space to get to know each other better without applying too much pressure. Yes, that was an excellent plan. As soon as they'd left she would broach it to her son.

Lowell glanced into his mother's bedroom as he returned to the drawing room to face the music. He saw the door ajar and the lamps all lit and popped his head inside, hoping to catch Augusta before she ran away with any fancy notions. He knew the way her mind worked and what damage she could achieve. What he saw made him take a great intake of breath and his lips tightened in non-amusement.

Unaware of his entry, Fontaine sat there dreaming, comfortable on the sagging dressing-table stool, admiring herself in the three-way glass. Augusta's brushes were tarnished silver and the cherry-wood surface was clustered with framed photographs. A handsome man in tennis whites who must, she supposed, be Lowell's dead father, a portrait of Lowell as a student, serious in Harvard cap and gown, and several smaller informal snapshots of him in all sorts of sporty poses – wielding a fishing-rod, playing with his dog, navigating a small sailing-boat with the breeze whipping through his hair. Emotion welled up inside her as she looked. More than anything in the world she knew this was what she wanted. A move to Massachussetts away from the rumours and tittle-tattle; a clean start in life as the wife of a prominent man.

Later that night, Lowell even laughed a little once he'd chauffeured the ladies back to their hotel and his mother had heated the milk for her chocolate and taken herself up to bed. It was the middle of the night for Vincent but he was a light sleeper and never seemed to mind being wakened. When he was home. Lowell poured himself another cognac and settled down for a long grouch.

'And now my mother has got it into her head that Fontaine is definitely the girl for me, that I should be pursuing her actively and taking her to the Stanford Palmer concert to show her off to society.'

'Too much.' Vincent was barely conscious but good-natured enough not to let it show. These dialogues in the small hours had been part of his life for a long time now; he cherished the links that kept them so close, even when the ocean divided them. 'And shall you obey her?'

'Shall I hell! Much though I adore both those lovely ladies in moderation, to do so would be virtual suicide. Take my word.' He glanced at his watch as he spoke but, at this hour, even New York would be soundly sleeping.

First thing next morning he planned to ring Merrily Morgenstern and see how she was fixed for three weeks on Thursday. Over the years he had become adept at holding off the pack but Merrily, he realised with relief, was another thing entirely. His initial reserve, caused by her upfront brashness, had gradually faded as he'd got to know her better and these days he found her a refreshing change from the airhead debutantes with whom he normally mingled. She had a first-class brain and a job to match; if she spoke her mind too forcibly, he accepted she had the right. She was fun, she was stylish, she knew how to behave. Most important of all, she already knew the score. It would be a relief, for once, to spend time with a genuine pal who would expect nothing more from him than a pleasant evening.

10

As it happened, Merrily was feeling pretty bruised. Since there was no one close to her she felt she could really trust, she had lately got into the habit of calling Jo long distance and almost, though not absolutely, unloading on to her. Jo always seemed so calm and unhurried and apparently pleased to hear from her. More than that, she actually listened and, furthermore, remembered – almost unheard of qualities amongst Merrily's own New York set. Despite her fine performance on last year's island holiday, all the time, beneath the sparky facade, she had secretly been dying with terror that she might lose her job. The bank was irrational, to say the least, and still making relentless cuts, downsizing like mad. One of these days, it was only logical to suppose, her own number was likely to come up. And then she really would be up shit creek and no mistake.

Doing the job she did, in personnel, she was highly visible

where the action was and couldn't kid herself she still had many friends left in the corporation when she had been, for so long, perceived to be the one wielding the axe. It wasn't fair but when was life ever? Merrily had always run in the fast track and knew, from bitter experience, that that was where you were likeliest to come unstuck. At the end of the day, when the offices were clearing and her colleagues going home to their separate lives, she would put in a call to her new best buddy in London and Jo, usually on the point of collapse and just climbing into bed, would know instinctively who it was and wearily pick up the phone. Sebastian, on the rare occasions he stayed over, suggested she tell Merrily not to be so selfish and remind her of the five-hour time difference, but that wasn't Jo's way. The compassion that had led her in the first place into medicine made her soft-hearted towards well people, too. In the eighteen months they had been acquainted, she had grown very fond of the abrasive New Yorker. And sensed the panic growing beneath the breezy veneer.

'Hi there!' Merrily would greet her in that husky drawl. 'How ya doin', doll?' And then, without waiting for any sort of a response, would launch straight into her own dire tale, spiced with the usual jokes and hilarious anecdotes so that Jo was never entirely sure how much was serious or whether Merrily, the joker, was simply having her on. Though these days she had a pretty good idea. The American would rattle on, sometimes for as long as half an hour, while Jo lay drowsily listening, careful not to drop off altogether, waiting to get a word in so that she could gently remind her of the time.

'I mustn't run up your phonebill,' was one of Jo's stock ploys but Merrily always brushed that aside with a growled response that the bank could bloody well afford it. Jo was not at ease on an international call but then she was a doctor,

119

used to working among the poor and deprived, and could not shake off the awareness of how much these things cost. Trivial things, frivolous in their way, though she could tell it was probably worth it to Merrily who was bleeding inside and in need of a sympathetic ear. One she knew she could trust.

'You ought to be charging her overtime,' Sebastian would grumble but, considering how little he was around these days, it really wasn't any of his business.

'How's your love life?' Jo would occasionally venture, to which the snappish response was always: 'Don't ask.'

In Antigua it had always seemed that Merrily's life was a laugh a minute. Jo remembered those endless stories, embellished, no doubt, for the benefit of the gullible Ravenels but which must, surely, still have some basis in truth. Parties, rave-ups, weekends in the Hamptons, even the occasional blind date. She had seen the envy in Fontaine's credulous eyes and watched her mother's air of slight censure as Merrily wickedly, knowing full well what she was doing, laid it all on with a trowel. Merrily was sophisticated and gorgeous with a glossy lifestyle and salary to match. She lived in the centre of the most exciting city in the world and appeared to lack for virtually nothing, except, maybe, for that special Significant Other but they were all in the same boat in that department. Even that, Jo would assure her patiently, was bound to come with time; Merrily was still barely in her prime. Otherwise, from all appearances, Merrily lacked for nothing. If only Jo knew.

'Hi, babe,' Byron had said on that fateful Sunday the previous year, not even attempting to cover up his infamy. 'Now why doesn't it surprise me to see you here this fine Sunday morning?' His implication was obvious. Doll she might be but it was no secret within Chase that Merrily was mainly wedded to her work. And not entirely from her own choice, either.

He had lolled back comfortably in Merrily's swivel chair, his fingers still ranging idly across her keyboard, and smiled that slightly lascivious smile through narrowed eyes and wet, fattish lips. His gaze was trained straight at her upper torso; instinctively she had drawn her coat closer and shivered slightly from more than just air conditioning. From the moment of first meeting, Byron had been eyeing her up. Despite his bulk and his baldness, maybe because of them, Byron had famously always had a keen eye for the ladies. In principle, Merrily didn't especially mind; she had always been a looker and it was par for the course, but it had been getting increasingly worse. Since the firings had started and downsizing become the new Chase slogan, a wild recklessness had seemed to possess her boss and he had thrown political correctness to the winds as if he no longer cared what anyone thought. Goddammit, in this town the corporate buck stopped with him. Let any person who stood in his way either shut up or ship out.

Merrily didn't especially dislike Byron, never had, but found his perpetual leering wearisome, especially so since she rather liked his wife. Shirley Kaminsky was overweight and defeated, even though she was reputed to have money of her own, and had never been anything but friendly and hospitable towards Merrily; in Merrily's view she deserved better than the klutz she had married. But this was not the time for minor issues of that nature. Byron was invading her territory. Suddenly this was war.

'Just exactly what are you doing?' Merrily had demanded through clenched teeth.

'Cool it, babe,' Byron had said, still smirking. 'Just checking up on one or two vital statistics.'

'Like what?' She couldn't believe him, he was so blatant. This was exactly the behaviour that Ed and Stanley had complained of and look what had happened to them, minutes after. In a bank as eminent as the Chase Manhattan you expected certain standards of behaviour. This just wasn't on. But Byron, unfazed, was still smiling his wolfish smile and staring at her chest as if he could see right through her T-shirt.

'You certainly do have great boobs,' she had heard him saying. 'How's about we knock off now and go get a little . . . lunch?' He was outrageous.

'Get the hell out of my office,' she had snarled, before she lost it completely. 'And leave me, please, to do the job my own way. The job I was hired to do.'

She had got away with it then but only just, because the phone had rung and it'd been his wife, summoning him home for lunch, and suddenly he had found he had to go, though clearly only reluctantly.

'See me in my office tomorrow at eight,' he had barked, saving face. Then shoved her roughly against the desk in his rapid retreat, bruising her breast and causing her to recoil in distaste and something suspiciously like fear.

Grotesque, thought Merrily as she snatched a fast fettuccine at *Il Toscana*. The man she was looking at had a beer belly like an eight and a half months' pregnant woman, roped in over his jeans by a leather belt almost at its final gasp, with a scrubby, greying beard, no doubt concealing a receding chin. He was gazing in rapture into the eyes of his female companion – Korean, or possibly Japanese – who was as thin as a chopstick, with hair down to her ass, as thick and glossy and impossibly straight as a waterfall. And at least twelve years his junior. However did they manage it, these generally unappealing and menopausal men, in a world where the likes of Merrily, with their straight As, fixed noses and Homecoming Queen diplomas, were out there battling against varicose veins and cellulite? Not to mention the total absence of eligible men, combined with a definite social stigma against those who visibly hadn't made it?

It just wasn't fair. Although fractionally less repulsive than the man in the restaurant, the thought of Byron's chubby hands anywhere on her body brought Merrily out in mental hives. And yet, in her long and chequered career, there had been times . . . The stories she loved regaling in Antigua, mainly to invoke the look of pure alarm in Fontaine's trusting mahogany eyes, were true in the main, truer than Merrily cared to admit. In all the years she had resided in Manhattan there *had* been beach parties, and dates and glitzy occasions and all the things she claimed, except . . . At times the gloss she laid on inches thick, in order to entertain and (*let's be honest*) also impress her new Antiguan friends, covered a truth that verged towards the sordid. The long and the short of it was that Merrily was lonely. It was not always easy, working the hours she did, to keep on meeting witty and attractive men, not in a closed society where women outnumbered them three to one. And the other, less occupied bimbos had more leisure hours to spend at the gym and beauty parlour. Particularly since anyone at Chase was automatically out of bounds. So far.

Byron Kaminsky might be unprepossessing but he did represent power. Ultimate power, the way things were going right now, when none of them knew for sure what the future

123

might hold. And if the awareness of his eyes forever crawling over her skin made her feel unclean, she had to admit it also gave her a perverse wetness between the legs when she thought of where such an obsession might lead . . . if only she could bring herself to do the unimaginable. Byron's balding scalp was often filmy with sweat and a slick of visible desire dampened his chin whenever she caught him looking at her. He was loathsome; in saner moments, she recoiled in disgust at the way he behaved behind the back of his trusting wife. Two PAs had left in quick succession and the rumours about him in the securities department were beyond belief. And yet, and yet. If she were honest, she had done worse for no reason, for instance after a ropy night in a singles bar with only too many Manhattans to blame next morning. *Get real*, Merrily told herself on occasions like this, when she was feeling particularly low. *You're pushing thirty-seven so stop behaving like a pathetic virgin from the Midwest, saving herself for her one true love.* Ha.

Jo recounted to Merrily the evening with the Charleston ladies and Jessica. Merrily, inherently suspicious, jumped the jokes and went straight to the crux.

'I wouldn't trust that broad,' she said, when Jo related the amazing musical connection with Sebastian.

'Oh, come on.' At times Merrily's predictable cynicism got on Jo's nerves and she wanted to thump her. New Yorkers were all the same, or so it seemed. World weary before their time. Out to get everyone else before they got them. 'It's only Jessica, our friend – remember? With Sebastian? My closest pal in the world?'

'Not as far as I could throw her.'

'Lighten up!'

Despite herself, Jo was laughing. However hard her own day might have been, she actually relished these late-night hen sessions with Merrily. Merrily was so sophisticated, so constantly alive with crackling wit. Whatever her mood, she always left Jo chuckling and that was a gift not to be taken lightly. It concerned Jo, however, that she seemed not to have taken to Jessica. Could it be jealousy? she wondered. Sebastian would certainly say so.

'Jessica's a very good friend. All they have in common is the music and that they can keep.' Now she came to think of it, all Jo could remember was the light in Sebastian's eye, the unaccustomed glow in Jessica's cheeks. Preferable, if she were honest, to the mealy-mouthed Amelia. But she wasn't quite ready for it yet; she banished the thought.

'But the Ravenels, mother and daughter, were out in full force. You should have seen them.' Jo remembered the luminous quality of Fontaine's skin as she talked of Lowell. Was everyone, all of a sudden, in a mood to fall in love? She put that thought aside for later. 'They're crazy, the pair of them. But, boy, did we have a riotous evening. I only wish you'd been there.'

She sensed from Merrily's silence that she'd said too much. One of her friend's surprising limitations was her basic inability to share – the result, perhaps, of being an only child. Jo blundered on.

'How's things at work?'

'Lousy.'

'You always say that.'

'Would I lie?'

Probably, thought Jo, *in order to regain centre stage*. But she let it go. A bright thought struck her.

'Jessica was talking about this year's Bath Festival.'

Was she ever.

'Maybe you should make it an excuse to come over and we'll all go together. Jessica's put so much into it, I know she'd be thrilled if you came too.'

Like hell.

The maintenance was heavy too, thought Merrily before she switched off the light. It might resemble a suite in a midtown hotel but when she thought of what she'd invested in this place. The rent, the service charges, the maid, the general upkeep. The new double windows to cut out the draughts and traffic noise; the automatic ice-maker in the kitchen; the security system with its sensors and alarm. Not to mention what it cost just to keep herself standing still. *Oy vey*, as her long-dead *Mutti* might have said. Michael Morgenstern, given the chance, would simply tell her not to be so choosy and who, at this age, did she think she was? What was wrong with settling for a nice Ohio Jewish boy? A dentist, maybe, or some sort of businessman? A furrier, something steady in insurance; even, at a pinch, a tailor like himself? She shuddered. Whatever the future held regarding her prospects at Chase, she would die rather than return to Dayton a failure.

And then, by some miracle, next morning the telephone rang and it was Lowell Brooks, sounding just a shade embarrassed as he veered around in gentlemanly confusion, taking way too long to come to the point. Yes, he was well and he hoped she was too and yes, Vincent was thriving and sent his love. *Cut the small talk.* He cleared his throat. The thing was he had tickets for a white-tie fund-raising bash, in Manhattan in two weeks' time, and he rather hoped . . . well, he wondered if she could spare the time to accompany him. As his partner.

'It's a concert at the Lincoln Centre,' he ventured diffidently. 'For my sins, one of the causes my family has always supported.' He did not add that he normally took his mother and that there was a fair chance she'd be there this year anyhow, catching up on old friendships, shooting the breeze, generally making mischief. The trouble with Augusta was she was hard to control.

'Followed by dinner at the Knickerbocker Club.'

He knew Merrily led a hectic social life but hoped he might be lucky. 'Do you think you could bear it?' he said. 'It might be fun and give us a chance to catch up.'

Merrily took a great gulp of air. *The Knickerbocker Club, eh? Did they allow in Jews?* She cast around wildly in her mind for something appropriate to wear; the black Donna Karan was probably the most suitable but was already two seasons old. The trouble was right now her accounts at Saks and Bendels were up to their limit and any second now she had a tax bill looming. Plus the health club subscription which she really couldn't afford yet equally couldn't bear to lose.

'I'd love to come,' she said, at her most gracious. As accessories went, Lowell was one of the best. And at least, with him, she knew she would be safe.

She met him at the Avery Fisher Hall with minutes to spare. He'd offered her champagne at the Harvard Club, where he was staying, but she'd had trouble, in any case, getting away in time. She arrived breathless and concerned, with her sable jacket thrown over the trusty dress, but her pulse immediately steadied and a genuine smile enlivened her face the moment she saw him standing there, calm and rock-like with his distinguished silvering hair, immaculate in tuxedo and white tie.

'Hi there.' Merrily's voice was even lower and more sexually charged than usual as she advanced towards him and allowed him to take her hand in both of his.

'You look quite ravishing.'

The admiration in his eyes was genuine. Together she knew they made a striking pair. In an instant she felt the cares of the week beginning to recede; for one night of magic she was determined to forget it all, to allow herself to enter the fantasy this charming, urbane man was opening up for her. She felt like a princess as she preceded him into the concert hall and when the audience broke into applause, for one heady second she almost believed it was for her. Then she saw the tall, elegant man running lightly down the stairway and remained on her feet, clapping wildly, joining in the mass hysteria as Richard Stanford Palmer took the podium.

God, but he was good. Even Merrily, with her limited musical knowledge, felt the thrill as he raised his baton and plunged the orchestra into the stirring opening chords of Beethoven's magnificent Fifth Symphony.

'It's a bit of an old chestnut,' muttered Lowell at the end of the first movement, 'but I have to confess it never fails to stir me.'

Merrily sat transfixed, electrified by the whole event – the muted lights of the auditorium, the well-heeled crowd, the pure sexual charge of the charismatic man standing so powerfully in the centre of the stage with the orchestra and the audience held so lightly in the palm of his hand. Never much of a one for culture, Merrily had dribbled away her youth in the bars and dance halls of downtown Dayton. She knew quite a lot about rock 'n' roll and sixties' pop music but had to confess she was hard pressed to name the composer of even a classical piece as familiar as this. As the symphony thundered to its cataclysmic close, she was on her feet with the rest of them, clapping till her palms were sore, her breathing short with the sheer excitement as he took bow after bow to the delighted audience.

'Wow,' she said later, as they lolled with glasses of chilled Chardonnay, overlooking the surging crowd in the foyer below. 'I hadn't realised music could give you such a charge.'

Lowell smiled in sympathy. 'I know what you mean. Sheer visceral magic. It takes a maestro to infuse that kind of electricity.' She was looking so beautiful tonight, he was glad he had invited her. Small and stylish in her chic black dress, there was not a hair out of place nor a chip on her perfect fingernails. He knew from what she had told him that she worked like a demon, but to the eyes of the charity crowd that night Merrily Morgenstern might have spent all day labouring over her toilette.

She smiled up at him, her eyes like diamonds.

'Thanks so much for asking me,' she said. 'I can't remember when I enjoyed myself more.'

Lying in bed that night, in a daze of happiness, that marvellous music still pounding in her head, Merrily reflected that she could do a great deal worse. Lowell was handsome, educated, charming and good company, all the things you looked for in a fairy prince. He had money and breeding and, most of all, culture. She liked him a lot and, more important, it would appear he must also like her. Something she hadn't been sure of before, on the holidays they had shared, when she had sensed his disapproval. Lowell was the sort of old-fashioned guy she knew instinctively found her over the top. Too bright, too brash, altogether too mouthy; not at all the type of broad he would introduce to his mother. Well, she'd shown him tonight and she knew he'd been impressed. It was a start.

Imagine what her folks would say if she swanned home to Ohio with a man of that calibre in tow? That should render her father speechless and just think of the kudos at the country club! Well, stranger things had happened; sex wasn't the be-all and end-all of life – and she hadn't imagined she'd ever be thinking *that*. Lowell Brooks was a gentleman and could be the answer to all her dreams, at the moment in her life when she desperately needed him.

Eat your heart out, Fontaine, she murmured as she finally drifted off into a dream-filled sleep.

11

At first Vincent failed to recognise the voice. It was months since they'd last had contact and right now Jessica Sutherland could not be further from his thoughts. But he quickly pulled his wits together and didn't think he had given away his vagueness. He greeted her with his customary ebullience, though his heart did sink a little when he heard why she was calling. It was usually the way. The most casual of acquaintances had a habit of turning up when circumstances led them to picturesque Amsterdam and it was, Vincent acknowledged, partly his own fault. He did go on so about his adopted city; Lowell was forever scolding him about being too prodigal with his favours. She had, she told him, reason to be in Rotterdam next week so thought she would make a long weekend of it and perhaps come on to see him, if there was a chance he'd be around.

'Wonderful!' enthused Vincent, racking his brains for an

excuse to avoid her. He liked Jessica well enough but cherished the exclusivity of his weekends, preferring to spend them alone or with his close, inner circle. 'Ring me the second you get in and I'll be happy to lay on the full scenic tour.'

Jessica travelled by coach, in order to save money, and when he collected her from the hotel, he was appalled by how cramped and down-at-heel it was. Surely she could have done better than this. He wondered if she was really hard up or merely close-fisted. They sat in the spacious art deco splendour of the Café Americain and, before he could stop himself, he heard himself issuing the invitation.

'Why not move in with me for a couple of nights? I've loads of room and that place is little better than a dog-kennel.'

'Do you really mean it?'

Jessica's eyes brimmed with gratitude and suddenly Vincent felt glad he'd made the offer. She was good at heart and he had just been being selfish. Besides, now he thought of it, those subsidised arts jobs were always badly paid. He remembered his own early years at the Rijksmuseum and thanked his stars his life had turned out so well. But, from what Jessica was telling him now, she didn't have much left over for life's little luxuries so the least he could do was show her a good time while she was here. He wondered idly how she'd managed to scrape up the money for Antigua but that was really none of his business. As Lowell was forever reminding him, he must learn not to stick in his nose where it wasn't wanted.

'Drink up,' he said, dropping his credit card on the bill and hoping that Dirk had had the good sense to remove all trace of himself when he finally awoke from that drug-induced slumber. Ah well. Vincent made a speciality of living dangerously; it added to the spice of the delights of Amsterdam. And Jessica was not a child; she must surely by now have picked up on some of the secrets of his lifestyle.

Jessica's eyes popped when she saw the opulence of Vincent's apartment. Pale gold walls framed a perfect view of the canal and the furniture looked too good to sit on. Vincent led the way into the guest suite and dumped her shabby knapsack at the foot of one of the beds.

'I guess it is a little over the top,' he laughed. 'I was going through my Marie Antoinette phase when I had it done.'

Jessica was struck speechless. After the cramped conditions of the Hotel Paris, this was like the Ritz and Savoy rolled into one. Vincent went round the room ahead of her, opening closets, putting out clean towels, then left her to freshen up in the *en suite* bathroom. Jessica couldn't help peeking inside the mirrored cabinet and found it packed with Penhaligon's products still in their cellophane wrappers. This man had thought of everything and he hadn't even known she was coming to stay. She hung up her two crumpled dresses and brushed her hair, then went back in to join him. Vincent was standing by the window, gazing down at the canal and he turned and handed her a flute of champagne.

'So how was the Rotterdam Symphony Orchestra?' he asked. 'We'll just knock this back, then you can tell me all about it over dinner.'

Actually, Vincent reflected after he'd escorted her to her room and wished her goodnight, Jessica was better company than he'd remembered. There was something rather touching about her gratitude when all he'd done was provide a room for a couple of nights and spoil her a little with a slap-up dinner. She looked as if she needed it too; she was definitely thinner than the last time they'd met and her freckled skin was too

133

pale to be healthy. He wondered if she ate properly, then chided himself for fussing. Absolutely none of his business. All she was was a distant acquaintance and that was the way he intended it should stay.

'You didn't!' said Lowell, with a snort of amusement when Vincent, from the privacy of his own bedroom, made his regular late-night call. 'You don't even particularly like her. Must be getting soft in your old age.'

'Actually, she's rather good company. Very informed about classical music. Well read, too.'

Jessica had chatted away over dinner and Vincent found himself warming to her considerably. Once she was into her favourite subject, music, she really opened up and the slightly pinched look around her nose and mouth softened and went away. *She's really quite pretty*, reflected the Dutchman. *If only she'd learn to be a little less intense*. Something had obviously happened to Jessica, he deduced, and not too long ago. He studied her shrewdly in the flickering candlelight and kept her wineglass topped up. Before she left this town, he'd get to the root of her secret. Vincent was a past master at delicate sleuthing; his fascination with the minutiae of other people's lives was inexhaustible.

It rained next morning, as it so often does in Amsterdam, but Jessica was quite undaunted. She'd brought her mac and some comfortable shoes for walking and couldn't wait to get out there and explore.

'My hair will drip dry,' she told Vincent cheerfully, earning herself brownie points if she did but know it. One thing Vincent couldn't abide was women who grizzled. He expected good spirits and an energy to match his own and in Jessica he wasn't disappointed. They deliberately missed out the Anne

Frank house – not even for Jessica would Vincent stoop to that and, in any case, the line went right round the block – but managed to cram in almost everything else. He was particularly pleased to discover that, in addition to music, she also had a healthy interest in art and remained unflagging in the face of both the Rijksmuseum and the Van Goghs.

'You're certain you're not tired?' he kept asking her then, when she continued to say she wasn't, gave in himself and dragged her into a bar for a breather and a glass of Dutch gin.

'A middle-aged man like me,' he teased, 'no longer has the energy of the young.' And Jessica, with flushed cheeks and sparkling eyes, just laughed; if there was more than a handful of years between them, it certainly didn't show. She was having the time of her life and wanted this weekend never to end. Vincent was a kind and thoughtful guide as he led her along cobbled streets and over tiny bridges, telling her the history of his beloved city, glad to have such an appreciative audience.

'It sounds as if you're falling in love with her,' said Lowell drily.

'No, but I find I like her a lot more than I had thought.'

One refreshing aspect of Jessica was that she didn't want to go shopping and for that her host was inordinately grateful. He rewarded her by taking her to his gallery and unlocking his priceless paintings for a private view. Jessica was impressed.

'My goodness, where did you find them all?' she asked and Vincent told her of his endless expeditions to out-of-the-way places, tracking down masterpieces on the basis of the slightest rumour.

'That sort of shopping I do enjoy,' he said. 'The thrill of the hunt with its subsequent kill.

'It's a pity you're not staying on a little longer,' he told her. 'Or we could drive out into the bulb fields for a change.'

It was not at all the sort of thing he usually did but he found her guileless enthusiasm faintly touching. *Sucker*, he could imagine Lowell saying but, for once, he knew his friend would be wrong. There was something vulnerable about this sandy-haired girl he found infinitely appealing, along with that bloodless skin with its hint of tragedy beneath.

For her own part, Jessica was thrilled with this impromptu weekend. Being with Vincent, just the two of them, was an unexpected delight and she saw for the first time a more sensitive side to him, underlying the joky exterior. Just to cross the rain-slashed street, with him holding on to her elbow for protection, made her feel truly feminine and cherished in a way she wasn't used to. It was a long time since she'd had a regular male escort, certainly one as considerate as this. And walking into restaurants and bars, she was aware of eyes – male as well as female – being focused on them as a couple. A feeling she liked.

Vincent was elegant and striking with his cropped blond hair and those piercing amethyst eyes and she liked the way he dressed and carried himself. He was also a lot of fun as a companion and made his dissertation on his city lively as well as informative. She couldn't remember when she'd enjoyed herself this much; probably not since the last group holiday in the islands.

A shadow flickered across her face, which Vincent instantly caught. They were sitting in a canal-side restaurant close to his home, eating a late Sunday lunch while they rested their feet, and he leaned towards her and squeezed her hand in instant empathy.

'Tell me.'

'What?'

'Whatever it is that's troubling you. I've been catching snatches of it all weekend.'

Jessica coloured and looked a trifle flustered. Did this man with his piercing eyes miss nothing? In an attempt to change the course of the conversation, she grabbed his hand and studied his impressive ring.

'Tell me about your ring,' she said, but he wasn't about to be deflected.

'It was a gift,' he said simply. 'I've had it for years.'

'The stone matches your eyes.'

'So they say.'

'Is it hugely valuable? It certainly looks it.'

'There's a history attached to it. I'll tell it you some time. But first I want to know what's troubling you.'

She gazed down at her plate in confusion but he wasn't going to let her off the hook so easily; this, he realised, was his golden opportunity.

'You're sad about something and that makes me sad too.'

'It's nothing.'

Vincent leaned still closer and tilted up her chin with one manicured hand. His searching eyes gazed into her confused ones and caught just a glimpse of the bleakness she was attempting to hide.

'What? You can tell me. I'm your friend.'

There was just a hint of tears there now and he drew out his white silk handkerchief with a theatrical flourish and made quite a show of dabbing them dry.

'Go on, sweetheart, tell me what's the matter. Is there anything at all I can do to make things better?'

Now she really did feel like bawling. She pulled away from Vincent's hand and busied herself in her handbag, searching for a tissue. Beneath the sudden wave of emotion, a blast of happiness was making her feel quite dizzy. What was it about him that she found so compelling? It was years since anyone had paid her this sort of attention. She pulled herself together with an effort and ventured a watery smile.

'I'm afraid I was just feeling foolishly sentimental,' she said. 'I haven't had so much fun in years. You've been more than kind.'

Vincent sat back in his chair and studied her keenly. Now that the threatened storm had passed, the colour was returning to her cheeks and she looked quite handsome. There was something about this young woman that touched him profoundly; a sameness of spirit, perhaps, another cat that walked by itself.

'For a moment there,' he told Lowell later, 'she really got to me. I thought that maybe you were right and I *was* falling in love with her. There's definitely a great deal more there than meets the eye, depth and personality I hadn't suspected.'

Jessica sketched out briefly a little of her rather desolate childhood. Parents who had died when she was still a young child and a loveless upbringing by an uncle and aunt, doing their duty but patently not enjoying it.

'I shouldn't complain,' she said with a rueful smile, sipping her beer and running nervy fingers through her hair. 'What they did for me was way beyond the call of duty. Imagine inheriting someone else's brat when you were well into your middle years and had avoided having kids of your own.'

She had been well educated, she had them to thank for that; also her in-born love of the arts, from an affluent home that was always filled with music and books.

'Many have had it worse,' she told him bravely. 'It's just that I was so lonely, I suppose. Never quite belonging, always aware of being on trial, so to speak. Afraid to make a noise or have an opinion. Or bring home a friend to their spotless house.'

Vincent longed to ask what had happened to her parents but an instinct told him to keep his mouth shut or he'd stop her flow. She was really relaxing now and letting it all come out. He longed more than anything to give her a hug and tell her it didn't matter. She was grown up now and her own fine person – independent and safe, most of all loved.

'You're just an old softie,' said Lowell, growing impatient. His recent encounter with Fontaine had left him wary. He couldn't bear the thought of Vincent falling to a similar fate.

'No, but wait.' Vincent was unusually serious tonight. 'I swear there's something else she hasn't told me. The parent thing is only part of it, the reason she feels so out of it and alone.'

'And you, I suppose, are the one to winkle it out?' Lowell had known him too long. Vincent grinned.

'I'm certainly going to have a jolly good try. We've just one more glorious night together and I plan to pull out all the stops. Watch this space.'

She really hadn't meant to tell him but somehow she found she had no choice. Talking to Vincent was the easiest thing in the world and over their sumptuous Indonesian rice table, the words had just started coming and she didn't need too much persuading in the end to cough up the whole sad story. Vincent just sat and listened, feeding her occasionally with delicacies from his chopsticks and making sure she always had plenty to drink. Lowell would have laughed at him and called him too obvious, but it worked. Like a charm before he was through. Which of the two of them, he often wondered, would make the better interrogator?

Tom. Where to start? Jessica sat and gazed at her hands, with their red knuckles and stubby, bitten fingernails, and tried to conjure up words to describe how it had been. Tom the *Wunderkind*, who had sprung miraculously from a Newcastle housing estate and captivated the world of music, and her heart, with his quite formidable talent. Tom, six years her junior, with his gypsy curls and dazzling smile, his nasal intonation and shabby clothes, who had waltzed straight into her life when she wasn't paying attention and transfixed her as surely as a butterfly on a pin.

'I'd never really been interested in a younger man before,' she said apologetically from behind her mane of tousled hair, made worse by the frantic scrabbling of those same roughened fingers. Vincent sat silently, observing her agitation, but made no effort to help her along now she'd started. He watched in silent fascination as the pain hit the surface and knew he had finally scored. But he also felt a twinge of shame. Who knew what he had summoned up, he told Lowell later, as he watched the slow disintegration of a formerly rational person.

'He was beautiful,' she said simply, gazing into the past, 'in every sense of the word. Yes, he was a rebel and no, he wouldn't let them tame him, though they tried. He was pure, untutored talent and God knows where he sprang from. Not his immediate parents, that's for sure, for they were quite ordinary folk and as much in awe of him as the rest of the world.' She stopped, remembering. 'And somehow,' she said humbly, 'he fetched up loving me.'

Vincent was unbelievably moved. But still he didn't speak for fear of breaking the moment. With her light green eyes

awash with emotion, Jessica took on a new kind of beauty
and he was able to forget the tousled hair and the ungainly
hands as her soul shone through. Lowell would have nudged
him into rationality but he wasn't here; that, as always, was
Lowell's loss. He missed the moments of pure poetry.

'And then?'

'And then they tried to interfere. Them upstairs, the people
with power.' He watched her eyes narrow and something very
like hatred shine through. 'They tried to come between us and
in the end they succeeded.' Just like that rigid old uncle and
aunt, thought Vincent, and it did occur to him that maybe
they were the 'they' to whom she referred. But no.

'They said he had a talent not to waste and that love was
not an option in this phase of his life. They tried to send him
abroad, away from me, but we fought them and, for a while
at least, we won.'

Her eyes were growing feverish now and her skin was
blotched with colour. Instinctively Vincent filled up her water
glass but she ignored him. Her frenzied silence lasted so long
he could bear it no longer.

'What happened?'

'What happened?' Those eyes found his and stared as
though she could not believe the question.

'He died.'

Her voice was so low he barely caught the words but she
gazed at her tortured hands and he knew the confession was
over. Shocked as though a bolt of electricity had entered his
chest, Vincent just stared at her, speechless. *How?* he wanted
to scream, and *Why? Give me the details!* But her silence was
so absolute he knew he didn't dare.

'And then,' he reported to Lowell that night, 'she just cried.
Bitterly and hopelessly till I thought she would never stop. I

longed to do something to help her but she seemed to have gone away from me, off into some miserable scenario of her own which I knew she would never let me enter.'

'Well, knowing you,' said the judge sagely from the sanctuary of his study three thousand miles away, 'that's by no means the end of it. You never could leave well alone and I doubt she can resist you. Give her time.'

'Not too much, though,' said Vincent more brightly. 'She leaves tomorrow and we've only a few hours left.'

He stood outside her room later that night, listening to her breathing. Then, when he heard her stirring, tapped on the door and asked if there was anything she needed.

'Come in,' said Jessica huskily, and he found her sitting up in bed, widely awake. Vincent opened the curtains a little and allowed the lights from the canal to lighten the darkness. Then he perched at her feet at the end of the bed and asked the one question he hadn't been able to utter.

'What happened?'

She shook her head. The tears were now long gone but she had no more words.

'I can't talk about it now,' she said. 'But I'll tell you one day. I promise.'

Then he leaned across and took her in his arms, rocking her gently against his chest, protecting her. She smelled evocatively of cold cream soap and fresh air and rain and something deep within him stirred so that he held her again at arm's length and studied her face. Then crushed her once more to his chest and kissed her fiercely on the mouth, too full of emotion for speech.

And she kissed him back. With a passion that almost shocked him. Without comment, they clung together, like survivors of a shipwreck, and he knew as he gently disentangled himself that this was one part of the story he would not be telling Lowell.

'Goodnight, my darling,' he said softly, as he dimmed her lights.

'Thank you,' she said, from the security of her bed. 'For being my friend. For listening. For everything.'

Next day, after he'd waved her on to the bus and spent a few hours at the gallery, Vincent opened the guest-room closet and found traces of Jessica left behind. A wrinkled dress on a hanger, a sweater in one of the drawers. Her hairbrush in the bathroom and a pair of worn slippers under the bed. *Oh dear*. This he definitely wasn't telling Lowell. He knew he'd never hear the end of it.

12

That useless klunk, Silas, had only gone and put his great foot right through the rotting timber of the veranda so that now, in addition to everything else, they would have to find the money for some urgent repairs. The way things were looking, this old house would soon be falling down around their ears and what, in heaven's name, would they do then? Living on Tradd Street – indeed, anywhere south of Broad – was costly enough as it was, what with all the painstakingly restored historic homes to maintain and having to apply to the Preservation Society before you so much as laid a lick of paint on your own property. Hurricane Hugo surely had a deal to answer for; the eighty per cent devastation of 1989 had set the town back at least a hundred years and turned it into a living memorial to itself.

'Lordy, lordy,' said Cora Louise in despair, rocking herself back and forth in her agitation.

'Don't fret, Mama,' said Fontaine placidly from the sofa in the parlour where she was idly painting her toenails scarlet. 'Silas knows enough to fix it when he's good and ready. Meantime, we shall just have to take care to tippy-toe around it and leave the porch light on after dark. Maybe we should invite the beloved Louella over and see if we can't persuade her to trip and break her neck.'

Fontaine chortled, the thought amused her mightily, but her mother was on one of her worrying jags and not to be diverted. Christmas was fast approaching; they had yet to raise the cash for their annual excursion to the islands, an absolute must if they were not to go stir crazy, shut away in this incestuous small town. With much lamenting, Cora Louise took herself off upstairs for a long, calming soak and while she was gone the mailman dropped by with another letter from Jessica. Fontaine merely glanced at it, then left it on the table for her mother to discover once she was through with the vapours. Living day in and day out with her mother was tricky, to put it at its mildest. Maybe some news from their new friend in Bath was what was needed to improve her day.

'Is that it?' asked Cora Louise disappointedly when she reappeared, swathed in her oriental robe while she decided what sort of a face to assume for the day. She fluttered the thin, blue envelope between nervous fingers and glanced suspiciously at the empty table as though impelling something better to materialise. Something important; a stiff, white, embossed card, perhaps, adorned by Louella Petigru's distinctive handwriting. But, alas, the plain oak surface remained depressingly bare.

'Toughen up, Ma,' said Fontaine laconically. 'I guess that vile old woman has finally gone and done it this time and poor Cinders and her mother won't, after all, be going to the ball.' As if she cared.

'Hush, child,' said Cora Louise automatically. In this town *nobody* spoke that way about a Petigru, even one guilty of delivering such a grievous snub to two entirely innocent victims. Weren't the families, after all, distantly connected? And didn't that still count for something? A frown creased her unblemished skin and there were signs of panic in the bright, chipmunk eyes.

'For the life of me, I cannot imagine what can have possessed Louella to be actin' so contrary after all these years.'

For this was the season when an invitation to Louella's traditional musical soirée was quite the most coveted in town; it was unthinkable that the Ravenels should have been dropped from such a fancy list. Nothing, surely, from the past could be bad enough to warrant that.

'And there's no chance he simply overlooked it?' persisted Cora Louise, still hopeful.

'No, Ma. We had quite a chat.' Fontaine was ruthless in her determination to stifle her mother's dreams. This foolish preoccupation with ancient history was outdated and unhealthy as well as playing merry hell with Cora Louise's nerves.

'What do you hear from Jessica?'

Cora Louise looked down abstractedly at the crumpled letter in her hand and only then took in who it was from. But now was not the time to be opening it, no matter how fond she might be of Jessica. Life was cruel and getting crueller. They could barely exist, as it was, on the little that remained from Fontaine's trust fund and her seasonal earnings as a tour guide. What remained of the Ravenel splendour was rapidly vanishing down the plug hole. Something drastic was going to have to be done; there was no denying that obvious truth a second more.

Cora Louise took a couple of turns about the room, then stopped stock still and drew herself up to her full five foot two.

'I'm afraid there's nothing else for it,' she announced dramatically. 'I shall simply have to find mahself a job.'

'Gracious, Mama!' Even Fontaine was caught off balance. All trace of her former amusement vanished as she stared at her parent in startled horror. The idea of a Ravenel forced to earn her own living was unheard of in the low country, even in these so-called enlightened times. How utterly degrading. It was bad enough for herself, deprived of a formal education and having to lead those dreary tourists round the town's haunted sites, but at least she could laugh that off as a hobby, albeit a cranky one. For her mother to be seen touting for work would be a scandal indeed. Imagine what the likes of Louella Petigru and her deadly demolition crew would make of *that*.

'And what exactly do you suppose y'all could do?' The words were harsh but she had to be made to face facts. Like most Southern belles of her generation, Cora Louise had been raised to be purely decorative; to cook and curtsey and do exquisite needlework; to keep a trim household budget and control her servants; to gaze at her husband in devout admiration at all times and button her lip, at least in public. But there was a steely glint in her eye which heralded trouble. Cora Louise was determined; now that her mind was finally made up, there was no avoiding the inevitable. She knew exactly where her calling lay. Was she not, after all, a Daughter of the Revolution, with a knowledge of her birthplace second to none?

'I shall become a guide,' she said firmly, 'in one of our

historic homes.' A bright thought lightened her sombre mood. If she did it at all, she'd be sure to do it properly and family strings were there to be pulled, or so her papa had always said. She would start at the top and offer her services to the Calhoun Mansion, where she had first set eyes on the man destined to ruin her life.

How beguiling Gabriel Ravenel had been on that summer's night long ago, lithe as a whippet with his foxy, Mephistophelian beauty, and not a sign yet showing of the latent devilry and paranoia that would carry him away from her in such a shockingly short time. In the oldest dance of all, their eyes had met across that enchanted candlelit ballroom and he had swept her into his arms and off into a waltz even before they had been formally introduced, whispering blandishments into her perfumed hair and thereby stealing her heart forever. And she only seventeen and a half and not yet officially out.

Cora Louise glanced down at her daughter, watching the paint on her toenails dry against a great heap of cushions, and wondered whether she had the remotest inkling of the hornet's nest she had created, right from the start, by the very fact of being born. If only there'd been more time to get properly acquainted, to discover more of each other's personal histories before plunging into the ultimate grown-up commitment of parenthood, they might still have been strong enough to stand up to the forces of evil that had relentlessly set out to destroy the magic of that night. But it was not to be. Thirteen months after that first doomed waltz, Gabriel Ravenel had flung out of the house on Tradd Street, returning only to collect his possessions. Leaving his under-age, feckless bride of less than a year alone, with a baby, to face the wagging tongues. Mother and child had scarcely been parted since.

Even her own kinsfolk, the Bees and the Hugers, had turned their backs on poor Cora Louise, preferring to listen to the malice of the town than believe her defence of innocence betrayed. But she had fought back valiantly and done whatever she could. She had made it her life's crusade to nurture and protect this unfortunate child and, all things considered, had succeeded pretty well if only it weren't for the viperish gossiping of certain idle souls with too little to occupy their rancid minds. There were times Cora Louise truly hated Charleston, no matter how hard she tried to conceal it, but how, for pity's sake, except for occasional excursions, was she ever going to escape? For the South was in her blood and the prognosis bound to be fatal. She heaved a great theatrical sigh.

Well, there were important things that needed to be done. She'd show them yet, she most certainly would.

Life, wrote Jessica, was tiring yet exhilarating and she'd pulled off something of a major coup by managing to sign up the Rotterdam Symphony Orchestra for next year's festival. She was feeling the cold, though, in her draughty lodgings and had a nasty crop of chilblains, a childish ailment she thought by now she might have outgrown.

'Poor lamb,' said Cora Louise, instantly sympathetic. Whatever their own troubles, here at least they were warm. She had heard of those harsh British winters, without adequate heating, and had no doubt at all that the child didn't take proper care of herself. Maybe she should send her a care package for Christmas – warm underclothing and some jars of Angelina's spicy gumbo.

Jessica was very much hoping to get away and join them again this year, though her tiresome work colleague was not making things easier by announcing, out of the blue, that he was off on an East African safari at approximately that time. Typical behaviour of the selfish male, she wrote. Making those decisions without discussing them first.

'She's far too soft,' remarked Fontaine idly as she fanned her toes. She'd heard enough on the beach about Jessica's brilliant career to admire as well as envy. Of the odious prat, Simon, Jessica's constant bugbear, put there to trip her up rather than assist her. 'Make the little beggar work, I say. Why keep a dog and bark yourself?' And this from a woman who had never known full-time occupation in her life.

'Wait!' said her mother, continuing to scan the page. 'Why, bless my soul! Says here she's been in Amsterdam, visiting with our Vincent.'

'I'm amazed she could afford it,' said Fontaine acidly. She privately thought Jessica a little on the cheap side, never in a rush to put her hand in her own pocket. 'But doubtless the City of Bath was paying.' As, indeed, turned out to be the case.

'*Strictly business,*' read her mother aloud, '*with a couple of days' holiday thrown in at the end since I was in the country already. And what an enchanting city Amsterdam is . . . the cobbled streets, those romantic canals . . . pure magic. And an opportunity to get to know each other better . . . such a lovely man and an excellent host.*'

'Well now!' said Cora Louise with a wicked gleam, flashing on down the page. 'She certainly does go on about him, to be sure. Could it be, do you suppose, that they're sweet on each other?'

Ever the dreamer, the idea appealed hugely to Cora Louise;

she felt quite cheered up. There was nothing she liked better than a hint of romance and she'd had a soft spot for the disadvantaged Jessica right from the start. There was something endearingly vulnerable about her, as if she didn't laugh enough, that had quite touched Cora Louise's sentimental heart. Nice girl, thoughtful with it; with always the time to sit and chat to the older folks when she might have been off on the beach having fun with the others.

'Perfect!' said Cora Louise, clapping her hands with childish satisfaction. Now she came to think of it, what could be more suitable than a liaison with the delectable Dutchman, another of her favourites. They weren't that far apart in age and apparently both unattached. It was a shame they didn't live nearer but that could be easily remedied; these days the European boundaries were falling and soon they'd be opening that tunnel. And there was still this year's winter holiday. Ten days together in an island paradise should do it, especially with Cora Louise there to do a little fixing.

Her daughter, however, was having none of it.

'Bosh!' she exploded, in genuine annoyance, leaping to her feet and ruining her morning's handiwork. 'Get real, Ma!' And she slammed out of the room.

It wasn't that Fontaine had anything specifically against the sandy-haired Englishwoman. Along with the rest, she could take her or leave her and actually, at times, found Jessica could be great fun. It was simply that, in her current frustrated state, constantly on edge with nerves as taut as fiddle-strings, Fontaine couldn't bear even the slightest suggestion that anyone else might threaten the exclusive threesome she had formed with Lowell and his elegant friend. They were just so good together, a near perfect combination.

At times of high emotion she saw herself part of a lasting *ménage à trois*.

Jessica was certainly closing in on her ma, with these regular letters and constant cosy chats. Did she have no life of her own without having to sponge off other people's? Fontaine thundered upstairs in a rage and threw herself, weeping, on to her bed. Hearing her, Cora Louise raised her eyes to the heavens and uttered another great sigh. Life as a single parent in a small, hidebound town had certainly not been easy, not with all the mindless tittle-tattle. The Lord alone knew how they'd managed to come this far.

Luckily, equilibrium was restored next morning when Lowell phoned to catch up on their latest doings and see if the ladies were planning their annual jaunt.

'Wouldn't be the same without you,' he warned and Fontaine, thrilled just to hear his voice, wriggled her fat rump in ecstasy and purred into the receiver in her most sultry tones. Seeing her there, slumped on the stairs like a coy teenager, the phone wire coiled round one soft white hand, Cora Louise bit her lip and bided her time. Poor Fontaine; life so far had not been good to her. She deserved better luck. And why not, indeed? Lowell Brooks was a fine New English gentleman. What mother would not be proud at the prospect of maybe one day welcoming him into the family? Thoughts of Jessica were swept aside in a new irrational rush of hope. Gabriel Ravenel could not have known the damage he had wrought by leaving alone these two ditsy belles, balanced precariously on a lifetime's razor's edge of anticipation.

'Yes,' said Cora Louise, claiming the phone. 'Y'all will definitely be seeing us this winter. Just try and keep us away!'

'You know something?' she said later, as they dressed for

dinner. 'What say if we bring Jessica back down here for Christmas, right after the vacation, and show her some real Southern comfort for a change?' She still had those chilblains on her mind. A bit of cosseting was what the girl needed and who better than Cora Louise to provide it?

'Poor child,' she pondered, spraying on scent, 'no family of her own, not a single livin' one. And forced to abide in rented lodgings like a servant. It just ain't right, it surely ain't.'

'Really, Ma,' laughed Fontaine, restored to full bloom. 'You and your lost causes.' But she made no objection and actually approved the plan. Cash might be a little on the short side right now but there was love enough in plenty to go around, especially for an orphan and at Christmas.

Vincent wrote a couple of days later, sending captioned snapshots and apologies for his silence. He had had an unexpected windfall, he said, and would tell them all about it in Antigua. He enquired after Cora Louise's health, included a handful of zany newspaper cuttings and generally sounded in his usual high spirits. Fontaine's heart melted. She venerated Lowell, she genuinely did, and her knees went wobbly at the very thought of him. But she also loved Vincent like a brother and brightened at the prospect of seeing him so soon.

They'd be there on the eleventh in the normal way, he wrote, and had booked their usual suite. Cocktails were at seven on the terrace with the gang; Jo would be there and also Merrily, though she, as usual, would be arriving late.

Can't wait to see you all, he added, *and catch up on the news. This miserable weather seems to drag on. Be sure to pack your dancing shoes and an infinite supply of energy.*

Of Jessica he wrote not one word.

13

'Wake up, lazybones! Time to shake a leg.'

Jo was jolted out of half-sleep by Vincent's sandy toe in her ribs and she peered over her dark glasses to find his friendly face beaming down at her. It was mid-afternoon and the sun was at its highest. She felt uncomfortable and sticky with oil and sweat; time for a shower and a change of pace.

'We're off into town. Care to join us?' Lowell was already changed and ready, in pressed white shorts and a floral shirt, a far cry from the conservative judge who had greeted them the previous night.

'Two seconds and I'll meet you out front.' She pulled her towelling wrap over her head and bolted barefoot towards the hotel. The rest of the group were still sunk in lethargy on the beach: Merrily out of it with a heavily creamed nose and what looked like used tea-bags protecting her eyes; Jessica and Cora Louise safe in the shade, intent on needlework and intimate conversation. Of Fontaine there was no sign.

'Gone for her nap,' said Lowell when asked. 'Too much exertion last night on the dance floor.' He grinned. His tan was already maturing nicely and contrasted effectively with his silvering hair. He looked elegant and distinguished; most definitely a man of some substance.

They piled into the Jeep and off along the bumpy road that led to the centre of St John's. Vincent had film and another lens cap to look for and Lowell had promised duty free perfume to his mother, while Jo was just there for the ride. All along the way they passed friendly native Antiguans who waved and smiled and flashed their marvellous teeth. This island was noted for its pleasant informality; notwithstanding the horror stories from previous years, it was one place where Jo felt really safe. She sat in the back seat and closed her eyes as the salty breeze fanned through her hair and dried it. One easy way to get instant highlights, a beauty treatment that would cost a fortune in London. It had been another long hard year. Sitting here with the sun on her face, she felt a load of tension and despair beginning to shift and determined to enjoy every second of this holiday. She had certainly worked hard enough for it.

Purchases achieved, they hopped back in the Jeep and Vincent drove them up a steeply winding road to the highest point of the island, which overlooked a harbour.

'The English Harbour,' he explained. 'So-called because that's where Nelson parked his fleet.'

The water was a brilliant azure blue, the colour of Vincent's eyes, and the grass was bleached and battered by the wind as they bowled down merrily along the zigzag road to take a closer look at the boats. Incredible. They strolled along the sun-baked harbour wall and lingered among the wayside stalls, displaying brilliant tie-dyed cotton dresses and T-shirts, coral and seashells and woven bead jewellery. Jo bought a white linen hat to protect her head.

'You look like Christopher Robin,' said Vincent approvingly.

The harbour was crammed like a film-set with tall, full-masted schooners, picturesque reminders of an earlier age. Jo was amazed; she had had no idea. This was a flourishing port after all, not just a backwater holiday resort.

'It's the climax of the Tall Ships Race,' Lowell told her. 'The winners are just coming in but there'll be more to follow.'

'How do you know?'

'It's an annual event. They leave from London and sail out here by way of Bar Harbour in Maine. Pretty impressive, don't you think? All that sail power in this motorised age?'

Indeed. Totally entranced, Jo wandered on, inhaling the sharp, salt smell of the nets, spread across the indigenous fishing-boats, left out to dry until the next night's haul. Lowell and Vincent, camera-happy as always with a new, expensive lens to test, lingered way back among the clamouring stall-holders, admiring and fingering and engaging them in happy chat while all the while that insidious shutter worked up and down like an automaton with a life of its own. Recording them for posterity.

And all of a sudden, there he was, right in front of her – her stranger. Seated on a bollard, in rolled-up jeans and an open shirt, tanned and healthy, utterly at his ease. Jo stopped dead in her tracks, unbelieving, but he recognised her at exactly that moment and waved a lazy hand in greeting.

'Hello there,' he said with that heart-stopping smile that had, for a whole year, haunted her dreams. 'How nice to see you. The girl with the extraordinary eyes, if I'm not very much mistaken.' And he walked towards her and lifted her glasses, to check her eyes and prove himself right. Jo's heart was hammering so hard she could scarcely speak; she spun around frantically to look for the guys but they were way behind, still socialising. He grinned at her, as though it were the most natural thing in the world to be meeting here. Despite the tan and the rough salt on his skin, she could not help noticing the suppleness of his fingers and the dull shine on his nails that spoke of a regular manicure. This was no ordinary seaman, but who in the world was he? Here one moment, gone the next; elusive as the legendary Flying Dutchman.

'Come sit.' He led Jo to the sea-wall, patting the warm stone beside him. He produced a solid gold lighter and a packet of thin cigars and offered her one before he lit up.

'No thanks.'

'No vices?' He seemed amused. Little Miss Goody Two-shoes, Sebastian called her, and now Jo felt foolish at appearing such a prig. He blew a thin stream of aromatic smoke high into the air, then turned his full attention on to her. She felt herself blushing, as awkward as a child. Against charm this potent she found she had no armoury. She kicked her heels against the rough stonework and studied her fingernails in embarrassment. He was still wearing the mirror-lenses so she couldn't tell what he was thinking, but his fine, tanned features were creased into a smile and the teeth were as white and perfect as she remembered. Irrationally, she wished the boys would catch her up. They'd know what to say to break the ice and Vincent, with his bloodhound's instincts, would be in there pronto, finding out all he could.

'They're quite a sight, aren't they?' He was studying the boats and Jo just nodded mutely, feeling gauche and a fool.

'There she is, my beauty.' He pointed into the middle distance and indicated a fine, low-lying cutter, comfortable on the water like a swan at rest. Across her bow was painted the one word – *Leonore* – and a look of dreamy contentment was on his face as he caressed her with his eyes, the way a racehorse owner regards his winner.

'My one true love,' he said softly, 'the lady of my dreams. Do you understand that or perhaps you think me mad?'

'She's beautiful.'

'She's more than that. My escape, my sanctuary, sometimes even my sanity.' He glanced at the thin gold watch on his wrist. 'We're just in from London and have made record time.'

He was distracted at that moment by distant shouting from the dock where two jeans-clad sailors, with *Leonore* emblazoned across their chests, were waiting to row him back to the boat.

'That's it, must go. We'll get together for a drink some time and then you can tell me all about yourself.' He rose to his feet and stubbed out his cigar, then stretched like a cat and waved to his crew. For one glorious second he remained smiling down at her, stopping her heart and sending her pulse into overtime.

'I'm at the Mill Reef,' he said casually. 'I'll see you around.' Then began to run, in long, athletic strides, down to the jetty and on to the boat without a further glance in her direction.

'What gives?' said Vincent suddenly, into her hair. 'You look as though you've lost a pound and found a penny.'

'Something like that,' muttered Jo without turning her head. Even in this bright light, she could still make him out, tall and erect and completely at his ease as he lounged in the bow of the small dinghy and allowed them to row him out to the *Leonore*. He was laughing – she could hear the mellow tones across the water – and the sunlight glinted off his hair.

'Oh dear,' said Lowell, coming up behind. 'I can see somebody who could really do with a drink. And fast.'

'The Mill Reef,' Lowell told them over dinner, 'is one of the most exclusive clubs in the world. Virtually impossible to crack unless you have influence. But there I may just be able to help . . .'

'Oh please,' begged Merrily with shining eyes, almost panting at the prospect of finally invading some worthwhile territory. This was turning out better than she could possibly have hoped; she even had the outfit for it – a divine, understated little creation that was barely there, snatched at the Versace sale and not yet worn. Lowell laughed. He loved to make people happy and this request was so simple. He made his excuses to the ladies and went to call a distant Mellon cousin who owed him a couple of favours.

'Do you think he'll be there?' Jo asked Vincent in a low voice, scarcely daring to hope.

'You bet. Why else do you think he told you where he was staying? Get in there and wow him, kid. I can't see how he can resist you.' And he meant it. With her week's tan and the light of excitement in her eyes, Jo was as pretty as he had ever seen her. No more the pallid, fourteenth-century Flemish beauty but a living fire-cracker of a woman, hard not to fall for, even for him. He kissed her gently on either cheek and sent her off to get changed.

Jessica was watching him; Cora Louise too, from the shadow of an indoor palm where she had decided to settle, rather than go gadding with the rest.

'I'm too old, my dear,' she told Jessica gently. 'Y'all get

out there now and cut a caper and leave me here with my patchwork and my memories. That's about as much as I can hope for at my age.' But the glint in her eye and the barely suppressed laughter told an entirely different story. Cora Louise was just being a brick, keen not to put a damper on the adventure. And from the admiring glances she was getting from the bar, Jessica had a shrewd idea she'd not be lonely long. Well, good for her, she was a game old bird. All she cared about herself right now was quality time with Vincent on the dance floor, if only she could disentangle him from Fontaine who seemed never to be able to let go. That weekend in Amsterdam was still glowing in Jessica's memory. She was certain she hadn't imagined it, that something ground-breaking had happened that final night. Well, now was the time to prove it to them all; she swept back her chair and followed Jo.

The ride to the Mill Reef Club was dark and bumpy, and all the way there Merrily was practically wetting herself with excitement, particularly when they swung through the gates and Lowell uttered the magic Mellon name to the guard. Private houses were built within the grounds and they passed between two rows of mailboxes bearing some of the most illustrious names in the United States before they reached the lighted entrance to the club and trooped inside. *Just fancy,* thought Merrily, *me here tonight,* while beside her Jo was virtually fainting with terror. What had she started – and could she carry it off? He was so suave, so handsome, so way out of her league. She ground her fingernails into her palms and prayed that he wouldn't be there.

He was, of course, and she spotted him instantly, tall and distinguished, standing at the bar in a blazer and white pants, his gold wire-rimmed spectacles adding a touch of gravitas to the otherwise sensational face.

Lowell led them all to a table and Vincent immediately claimed Fontaine in a dance. Jessica, elegant in apricot silk, had swept up her hair and was actually wearing make-up; she watched as the merry couple swung on to the floor but nobody noticed the tightening of her jaw.

Jo just wanted to be lost in the crowd but she couldn't take her eyes of him as he drank and laughed with his friends. That nose was aesthetically perfect and she loved the way his hair curved in elegant wings above his ears.

'Come on,' said Lowell, patting her arm. 'I can't compete with Fred over there but let's get out there before it gets too crowded.' And he pulled her from her chair before she could resist and carried her protesting into the music with a skill she had not suspected.

Round and round they waltzed and each time they swung she could see her idol laughing and drinking toasts with his friends. And then he'd grown still and the laughter was gone and she dared not turn her head when at last the music ended, for fear he might be looking. Which he was. Lowell had slipped off into the crowd again with a more than willing Fontaine, leaving Jo to brave it out alone. She fumbled with her bag and when the band struck up again, found he had moved and – oh Lord – was heading her way. Right to where they were sitting, with the candlelight flickering on his lenses so that she couldn't distinguish the expression in his eyes. Maybe it was Merrily who had caught his attention; she was certainly looking beautiful tonight in her midnight blue strapless silk. But no.

'May I have the pleasure?' – or words to that effect – and Jo was stumbling awkwardly to her feet and he was leading her back to the floor, that strong, sensitive hand enfolding hers as comfortably as though they were long-time partners.

He spoke very little, the music was too loud, but held her firmly against his chest and moved with a fluidity that surprised her. Up there, by the bar, celebrating with his friends, he had looked so outdoors and masculine, but now, as the beat grew heavier and the rhythm more lively, he merged with the melody so expertly she felt like Ginger Rogers re-born, her feet barely skimming the floor. Dancing with this stranger left even Vincent cold; with her cheek pressed close to the starched white shirt, she felt his heart beating in unison with her own. Jo closed her eyes in ecstasy, willing it never to end.

But eventually the band called for a break and he led her politely back to her table where Jessica had turned as white as a sheet and Vincent was bending over her, talking urgently.

'What's up?' asked Jo, momentarily distracted, and when she turned to thank him he'd gone, without even waiting to ask her again. But even though she kept it to herself, Jo was a doctor and that came first. She pushed through the group to where Jessica was slumped and took one limp hand in her own. 'What's wrong?'

'I have to go home,' said Jessica dramatically and swayed on her feet as she attempted to rise. Her skin was even more transparent than ever, with a purple pulse beating visibly at her temple, and she looked on the point of passing out. Jo was seriously concerned.

'Migraine,' hissed Vincent, taking her aside. 'Apparently she's had them all her life.' He shrugged regretfully. 'What else am I to do?'

What indeed? They were all of them in the one vehicle and the journey was just too long and erratic for Vincent to make two trips. Or so it had already been decided while Jo was dancing. She wanted to argue but what was there to say? They'd set out late and now it was almost midnight. She glanced around for her dancing partner but he appeared to have vanished into the crowd and when she looked for Merrily, she'd gone too.

But now she appeared from the centre of the throng, flush-cheeked and radiant, one heavy lock of raven-black hair loose about her neck where it had escaped its pins, hand in hand with the man she had been dancing with most of the time they'd been there. She looked like the cat who had finally got the cream.

'Meet Dimitri.' He was dark and exotic in a well-cut tuxedo and embroidered velvet waistcoat with diamond studs. He bowed low over Jo's hand when presented, like a foreign dancing master, though his voice was pure California.

'Enchanted,' he said softly, meeting her eye. His own eyes were almond-shaped and catlike; he was, she guessed, in his early forties and gave off an almost tangible musk of money and class. Right up Merrily's street, in fact. Jo almost laughed when she saw the looks he was getting. All Merrily's dreams rolled up into one elegant package; despite her own deep disappointment, she was pleased for her friend and shared her obvious delight. But how would she take this sudden departure? Merrily was accustomed to getting her own way.

'No problem,' she said airily, Dimitri would take care of her. The night was still young and they had barely started yet. Lowell appeared a little apprehensive. The guy looked just too smooth for his taste and he'd met that type before, many times, usually on the wrong side of the bench. But Vincent led him aside and did some fast talking.

'Come on, old boy, don't be a party wrecker. She's not a

child, she's a fully fledged adult, and it's time we injected a little excitement into her life.' Lowell still looked doubtful but Jo couldn't help but agree. From the very first meeting, Merrily had made no bones about the fact that she was out here in search of adventure. And finally, it appeared, she had found it. Good luck to her; there was little likelihood of her coming to any harm, certainly not in this most exclusive of venues with this aristocratic-looking stranger at her side.

So they left her to it and climbed into the Jeep and Vincent drove them home in subdued silence. Jo sat beside him, her eyes prickling in the dark, while Jessica slumped at the back with Lowell and Fontaine. It was all so unfair but what else could they have done? This might be Merrily's lucky night but the gods clearly had it in for Jo.

'I'm sorry, babe,' said Vincent as he parked. 'But don't you go fretting about it. You'll see, we'll find him in the morning. We know now where he's staying and there aren't many places he can hide.'

Jessica was recovered by breakfast but there was no sign of Merrily. Eyebrows were subtly arched at each other but no one was saying a thing in front of Cora Louise who ate her cereal serenely and enquired politely about their night out.

'Great,' said Vincent, winking at Jo. 'Merrily literally had herself a ball and is doubtless still sleeping it off.'

'I hope she did get home,' said Jo worriedly, as they slipped away. 'Should we make enquiries at the desk, do you think, just in case?'

'Leave it,' said Vincent, ever the man of the world. 'I doubt that babe could ever come to harm. She probably keeps a dagger in her garter-belt. I know the type. Along with the compulsory packet of three. Besides, she's been asking for it so badly for so long, it would have been unchivalrous of us to get in her way.'

They climbed into the Jeep, just the two of them, and drove in silence back to the English Harbour. This morning the sky was unusually overcast and a strongish wind rattled the leaves of the palms. Trees were roped off with 'Beware of bread-fruit' signs and there was even the occasional spot of light rain in the air.

'Nothing to worry about,' said Vincent easily. 'These mornings are fairly usual in the islands. By lunch, you'll see, the wind will have blown the clouds away and this afternoon we'll be back on the beach.'

The tall ships were still there, most of them, but fewer people were lingering on the quay, probably because of the change in the weather. Jo climbed out of the Jeep in a hurry and went to stand at the water's edge. She'd paid scant attention to her appearance this morning, just jeans and T-shirt with a sweater around her neck, so anxious was she just to find him. She didn't know what she would say if she did; all that was uppermost in her mind was that she couldn't bear to let him vanish again.

With one hand above her eyes to shield them from the glare, she stared across the harbour where little grey ripples had replaced the azure pond. A stiff breeze had now developed so that all she could hear was the twanging of the steel halyards mixed with the mournful, wheeling cry of seabirds.

But, try as she might, she could not distinguish the *Leonore*. Her mooring was empty. She had slipped away in the night.

14

'As far as I can remember, I've always had them,' said Jessica from the swing. 'Part of my murky heritage, I suppose.'

She was out there on the veranda with Cora Louise this fine Christmas morning, while Fontaine, with a less than perfect grace, banged around in the antique kitchen, throwing together turkey hash in a variety of mismatched pots and pans. Alarmed by Jessica's bout of illness on the island, Cora Louise was treating her with exaggerated care, keeping her replenished with a series of mint juleps and covering her frail knees with an exquisite, hand-stitched quilt even though the temperature was as moderate as any average summer's day in England.

'We don't want to risk you getting a chill,' she said.

In just a few days, all trace of Jessica's fleeting tan had faded so that her fine, transparent skin was restored to its familiar paleness, with mauve smudges, like heavy thumbprints, under each eye. She held the highball glass carefully in both hands and swung herself gently back and forth as Cora Louise plied her with affectionate questions. One thing she had noted about Jessica: she seemed always to be cold. Thin blood probably; they were well accustomed to that sort of thing in the South.

'Hell,' muttered Fontaine from the sanctum of the kitchen, where normally no foot other than Angelina's ever trod. But times, they were a-changin', and this Christmas their long-term retainer had shattered tradition by boldly asking permission to visit with her family, an unparalleled piece of impertinence that had left even the liberal Cora Louise agape. The nerve of it all and also the shame, should word ever get back to Louella Petigru. As well, as it turned out, that the two households were not at present on speaking terms.

Fontaine was by no means at ease in this small, dark room but at least it kept her out of earshot of her mother's banal conversation with the ersatz invalid who was beginning seriously to stick in her gullet.

'They usually last no longer than a day or two. I can't imagine what brought this one on. They're never quite sure what actually triggers it.' Underlying which, of course, lay the unspoken message that poor Jessica had no relatives of her own to ask. And Fontaine's mother, ever the sucker, was right in there lapping it all up. She sat erect on a narrow Shaker chair, frowning over her delicate stitches as she empathised with her guest.

'Guess it must have been real hard for y'all growing up alone. Was there no one at all to take proper care of you? Nobody close?'

Such a thought was truly shocking to the tender-hearted Southerner. She also sensed beneath the surface of her guest's equilibrium a constant muted sadness but somehow Jessica's natural coolness, that well-known British reserve, unnerved even this most direct of interlocutors.

'Just my uncle and aunt.' Jessica paused reflectively but continued to swing. 'They took me in at an early age and I suppose I was lucky. They did more than their duty.'

Cora Louise, mindful of the wise old owl, stitched on in silence, content to bide her time.

'Ma,' shouted Fontaine crossly from the kitchen. 'Where, in heaven's name, do we keep the jalapeno sauce?'

The fact was Jessica was not chilled but terrified, though the shaking shock of that recent near confrontation had manifested itself in her veins as ice. Just when she had thought it was safe to breathe again, she had turned a corner, as in one of her worst nightmares, and found herself face to face with the enemy, though luckily she wasn't certain she'd been spotted. Thank God for Vincent with his natural chivalry; in his unwaveringly dear way he had come to her rescue and whisked her out of danger before an ugly incident could occur. She tried to attend to what Cora Louise was saying but inevitably her mind kept travelling back to Tom and that last, wonderful summer they had spent together before disaster struck.

She had discovered him first (so what happened was doubly unfair) at a music workshop at the Durham Festival, where she was acting as a tutor and he her most gifted pupil. He was in his last year at school, kept on against his wishes by the intervention of an enterprising teacher who, recognising his musical ability, had persuaded the authorities to grant him a late scholarship.

'It's all a lot of rubbish,' he'd confided. 'What's the point in all that boring book-cramming when all I ever want to do is play me music?'

Her features softened as she thought back to that time, those merry dark eyes and the gypsy curls, and the small gold earring he'd insisted on wearing even though it was frowned on by the school.

'Pansies wear jewellery,' his dad had always growled, reason enough to make Tom instantly do it.

'Me da doesn't rate me,' he'd confessed to Jessica. 'Thinks that music is only for cissies. Would have me down the pit in a flash, given the chance.'

The festival ended but they'd stayed in touch. Newcastle was close enough so they'd managed to get together most weekends. It was only a matter of weeks before he'd lured her into bed and she'd been astonished, and quite bowled over, by his sexual maturity and the depth of his passion.

A tear slid from the corner of her eye; Cora Louise, observing it, said nothing but continued to stitch in silence.

And what had happened next had really been all her fault; if only she hadn't been quite so ambitious, had kept him under her personal aegis and not tried to share him with the world.

She had heard, through her job, of a master-class in London, to be given by the celebrated conductor, Richard Stanford Palmer, aimed at young players of special talent. Just the thing, she reckoned, for her Tom; he would benefit from some top-flight tuition and it would bring him to the notice of one of the truly greats. For Jessica's ambition, even then, extended beyond her own career to that of her inamorata. Better still, it would give them some valuable time together, away from the probing of nosy neighbours or the approbation of her colleagues and his family. They travelled down to London on the coach and stayed at a down-at-heel hotel in King's Cross. It had been sordid and uncomfortable but also heady and blissful. That long weekend had cemented their love; from that point on they vowed to stick together.

But it was not to be. All their planning went by the board the moment the maestro heard Tom play. His talent was rarer than even Jessica had recognised and Palmer was renowned for his encouragement of up-and-coming youngsters. Before she had really understood what was happening, Tom was in his clutches and under contract to Worldwide Concerts, Inc. Unknown to either of them, their deep and precious love was, as it turned out, already doomed.

Cora Louise was startled when Jessica put her head in her hands and silently started to weep.

'There, there, my dear, it can't be as bad as that,' she said, laying down her cushion cover as she rummaged for her own lace hankie. But Jessica was inconsolable. That ruthless man, that reptile, had taken advantage of Tom's innocence to further his own ends and eventually drive them apart.

The bells of St Michael's were peeling forth merrily in the square and God-fearing folk of every denomination stepped out gaily in their Sunday best to worship the Saviour and give thanks for His birth. Normally the Ravenel ladies would be right along with them, only this year they were saddled with a house guest and that house guest was feeling poorly. Not too poorly, however, to hog the veranda swing and knock down a series of powerful juleps, allowing other folks to do all the work. Dark thoughts were festering like a horde of maggots in Fontaine's brain but, blessedly, just at that moment, the telephone rang and it was Lowell calling from Boston before his own late lunch, to wish them all the compliments of the season.

'Augusta sounded in sprightly form,' said Cora Louise approvingly later, shaking out her linen napkin and nodding to Jessica to help herself to wine. Beaming now with restored good humour, Fontaine carried in the huge earthenware platter and ladled steaming turkey on to the guest's plate first. The mere fact that the austere Mrs Brooks had seen fit to speak to them at all on Christmas morning had surely to mean something, so Fontaine reasoned.

'She most certainly did,' she said with satisfaction. Lowell had sounded mellow and at ease, a gentle babble of voices in the background where they were entertaining close family and friends. She had wanted to talk to him for longer but first Cora Louise and later Jessica had hogged the phone so that in the end she had missed her opportunity to wish him a special Merry Christmas of her own. Still, hearing his voice and knowing he was thinking of her gave her the incentive to enjoy this meal. Some day soon, she vowed to herself, they would no longer be parted on these occasions but would be together, entertaining as a team.

Later, while they were all doing the dishes, the phone rang again and this time it was Vincent. No sign of lethargy or depression in Jessica now; she was jostling to get to him, to corner him for herself, her eyes suddenly brighter, a new flush to her cheeks. Amused and intrigued by this startling transformation, Cora Louise tried to catch her daughter's eye but Fontaine just stood there with tightened lips, grimly determined not to cede any ground and allow this interloper to come between her and a friend.

In the end, however, Jessica prevailed and Fontaine went back to the kitchen in disgust. Jessica sat like a child on the stairs, cradling the phone and talking in a low, rapid voice.

'Go listen and find out what she's saying, child,' prompted Cora Louise, still curious, but Fontaine, pouting, had had enough. She stomped upstairs to freshen up, glad, like her mother, that at least Vincent had made the call and the extortionate charge would not be appearing on their own bill.

At home in Holland Vincent was baffled and ended the call with an element of relief. He was entertaining friends for lunch and still had the table setting to perfect, the gravy to make and the Harrods pudding to steam. Always a traditionalist, he was so steeped in British culture that he liked to amuse them with a Victorian meal on Christmas Day. His annual ritual of calling up old friends had gone somewhat awry when it came to Jessica so that now he found he was running late. All he had been doing was updating her with news of the gang but she had behaved as though her life depended on the call, as if the two of them were closer than they were and had some sort of unfinished business. Most odd.

He had already rung London and spoken to Jo who had no real news of Merrily. The last they'd seen of her had been at the Mill Reef Club but Jo had spoken to her on the phone and all she had deduced was that the boyfriend, conveniently, lived in New York and kept a permanent suite at the Pierre. And that, for once, Merrily seemed ecstatic.

'I really think this might be it for her,' she said. 'I certainly hope so; she's wanted it for so long.' Privately she had doubts about the briefly met dazzling stranger, but wasn't going to air them, not even to Vincent. All she wanted for Merrily was the best of happy endings and if this should turn out to be it at last, then well and good. On closer acquaintance, she would learn to like him; of that Jo was determined.

'What was he called again?' asked Vincent. He knew it was something unlikely, something daft.

'Dimitri Romanov. I believe there's a title there somewhere, too.'

'Hmm.' Vincent was no particular scholar but knew enough about recent Russian history to have his doubts. But for once he allowed that it was really none of his business; he liked Merrily, found her amusing and wished her only the best. If this was what she wanted, she should go for it. At the very least, it was grist for some excellent gossip and that, for Vincent, was always a certain lure.

He'd been slightly more circumspect when it came to matters relating to Jo. Although he knew Jessica was a privileged friend, he remained loyal to Jo's trust and kept her secret. It was up to her if she decided to confide in others. Although widely reputed to have a mouth like a torn pocket, when it mattered Vincent's silence could be absolute. He had done his best to reassure Jo that all would be sorted out once he found time for some private sleuthing.

'All boats above a certain size have to be registered,' he told her, having checked it out with one of his maritime friends. 'And that is where we'll get him. Given time, I am bound to track him down; a boat that impressive can't vanish completely. And then, at least, we should know who he is.'

He was touched to the core by Jo's single-mindedness, as only a fellow romantic could be. He'd barely glimpsed the delectable stranger, but that was enough. Ever a connoisseur of beauty, particularly male, Vincent was one of nature's predators and knew how much he was going to enjoy the chase, even vicariously.

'Don't worry, babe,' were his parting words. 'You *shall* live happily ever after, I promise. That's what we fairies are all about.'

Jessica seemed entirely revived, and hummed as she polished the table. Cora Louise was delighted. She loved to see her guest happy and perked up instantly at the hint of intrigue. Like Vincent with his sleuthing, she had an inborn antenna for the slightest ripple of romance and would do anything she could both to foster and encourage it. And something had certainly changed suddenly to put Jessica into such an unusually sunny mood. Could it be, she started to wonder, that she might even yet achieve a double whammy and get both of these girls off her hands in one go, Fontaine with Lowell, Jessica with Vincent?

'Those boys,' she said, her chipmunk eyes merry with anticipation, 'are both so utterly special, y'all could do a great deal worse than snap them up. I mean it, the pair of you.'

'Shush, Ma,' said Fontaine only half-playfully but her mother was off on one of her romantic jags and would not be stopped.

'A double celebration would be neat, don't you think?'

'Hush your mouth!'

'On the island so's we could all take part.'

'With an arch of crossed water-skis, I suppose, and garlands of hibiscus round our necks.' Fontaine might laugh but she was also enraged. It was unforgivable that her mother should mortify her like this, and in front of the house guest too. But Jessica merely smiled and seemed to go along with the fantasy so that Fontaine, through her rage, was quite startled. Whatever it was they'd been talking about so snugly on the stairs, Jessica and Vincent, it had certainly put her in a better mood. Maybe Mama wasn't quite so silly, after all, and she was carrying a torch for the elegant Dutchman. Well, thought Fontaine, she'd heard crazier things than *that*.

15

Morale in the office sank to an ultimate low in January as Mother Chase marched relentlessly on with her layoffs. Any team spirit that might once have existed fled as worker turned against worker and ugly rumours began to abound. The crowd no longer gathered round the water-cooler; each was too busy protecting their own patch to risk a knife in the back. The feel-good factor had evaporated entirely; this was the beginning of anarchy. To avoid the gathering hostility, Merrily took to arriving even earlier and skulking in her office for most of the day, rather than risk facing her disgruntled colleagues. It wasn't her fault – well, *she* knew that – but try explaining company policy to a bunch of brain-dead drones, in mortal fear of losing their livelihood. It was all extremely depressing and the single bright light in an otherwise overcast sky was her overwhelming passion for the new man in her life who continued to make her deliriously happy.

Merrily still couldn't quite believe her luck. She woke with first light, if she slept at all, and leapt out of bed with a new vitality. Her skin glowed, her hair was glossy with health. Emotion had caused her to shed nine pounds so that she was as svelte as she'd been as Dayton's Homecoming Queen. She had even cut down on her smoking since Dimitri's sheer presence in her life was sufficient narcotic. He was, quite simply, the best thing ever and, amazingly, seemed to feel the same about her. No wonder she looked so good.

From the very first moment they'd met at the Mill Reef Club, this pair had had eyes only for each other. Two people of quite extraordinary beauty, they could not have made a more perfect match. His chiselled Cossack cheekbones and slanting eyes complemented her more Caucasian features; they were both small in stature and slightly built, with a natural grace that could have come from the same bloodline.

'You'll certainly make stupendous babies,' joked Jo, on one of their midnight chats, when Dimitri was fleetingly out of town and Merrily, unusually, alone in her apartment, washing her hair and catching up on some sleep. Merrily preened; right from the start, she had had that thought too. At forty-three, Dimitri had never been married and was surely at that crucial stage when he might just allow himself to be caught. All fantasies about Lowell's patrician background shrank to the shallow make-believe they had been. Wait till Michael Morgenstern got a look at *this* veritable prince. He wouldn't believe it; his daughter couldn't.

Dimitri was cautious about the use of titles. These days, he told her, it was not necessarily good for business as he didn't want to appear too much of a dilettante. Though he continued to be vague about what he actually did. But privately Merrily dared to style herself Princess-Elect and posed before her mirror, imagining the Romanov diamonds in her hair.

'I hadn't realised the Tsars had Cossack blood,' remarked Jo innocently, provoking a snort of amusement from Sebastian, at her flat on one of his now rare visits, browsing through her Sunday papers. Victoria would turn in her grave at the very notion, he told her, but Jo continued to keep her counsel. Now she was in love, Merrily was suddenly vulnerable. It was nobody's business what he passed himself off as, provided he didn't end up breaking her heart.

Even that, said Vincent wisely, need not necessarily be the end of the world. At thirty-six, Merrily was no chicken. It was surely a scenario she had played often enough not to fall to pieces when it ended.

'No, this one's special,' said Jo staunchly.

Vincent had called to update her on his investigation. 'I plan to be in Rotterdam in a week or two's time,' was all he would reveal, sounding dangerously like the cat who'd got the cream. 'And after that, who knows what I'll be able to tell you.' Beyond that he refused to be drawn. He enjoyed an intrigue, did Vincent, and had positive hopes of satisfying her in the end.

The time Merrily managed to spend with Dimitri was mainly after dark, since each worked such crippling hours. They could really only ever contrive to meet once the phones had stopped ringing, which was often as late as ten. Dimitri had a leaning towards café society and favoured a series of trendy and ill-lit bars. Merrily grew accustomed to hanging around, for even then he was likely to arrive up to an hour late.

'Sorry, sweetheart,' he would breeze when he did finally put in an appearance. 'Got stuck in a meeting,' or, 'on a call to the coast.' Or: 'Those Hong Kong financiers are just too much. Don't know where to draw the line. Would have had me there all night if I hadn't been meeting you.'

Once arrived, however, he gave her his full attention and waved aside any attempt she made to turn the spotlight on to him by assuring her that it was all too dull for words and that he'd far rather be talking about her. He certainly showed a flattering amount of interest in her work and his knowledge of Chase and its inner functioning was surprisingly thorough.

What he actually did out there remained very shadowy but obviously, in some unstated way, he was very much a mover and shaker. The truth was Merrily was so besotted that she gave it only the minimum of thought. These days, all she lived and breathed for were those late-night meetings; she found herself restive even while they ate, screwed up in anticipation of what was to follow as soon as they reached her apartment. For he rarely ever took her to the Pierre. Too public, he explained, and also too degrading. He couldn't risk her appearing like a tart by being seen in the early hours wearing clothes from the previous night.

'Things will change once I've managed to sort them,' he promised, sending a thrill of visceral excitement right through her. He was so damned sexy, she couldn't get enough.

'Quite the most devastating lover I've had,' she sighed to Jo. 'A veritable Tarzan in the sack.'

Thin and supple, he worked out daily in the gym; his muscles were elastic, his stomach as flat as a board. In bed he was agile and inventive, in public the most devoted of escorts. In short, to Merrily's mind, perfection. The sole cloud in an otherwise flawless sky was his voracious appetite for cocaine.

'You've got to be joking!' he said the first time she refused it.

'You won't get better stuff than this. Try a snort and see what it does for your sex life.' And he wasn't kidding. At the best of times, Dimitri Romanov was hard to resist. With a regular supply of his insidious nose candy, Merrily stood in danger of fast becoming a crack-head.

Jo was appalled when she heard what was going on.

'You ought not to be even talking about it over the phone,' she protested, hating the prim schoolmarm she heard in her own voice but quite unable to approve. 'Think what could happen to your career if you were busted or word ever got out. And have you any idea how addictive that stuff can be?'

But Merrily was already past caring. Anything Dimitri wanted was all right with her.

'Your problem is you worry too much,' said Sebastian dismissively. 'Most of those Yanks have disgusting habits and, from what you've told me, Merrily has always been pretty decadent. Booze or drugs, there's not a lot to choose between them. Either one will get you in the end.' He shook his head grimly. 'Wouldn't surprise me if she was HIV positive too.'

But Jo loved Merrily and refused to give up on her. She thought for a moment of confiding in Vincent, a fairly prolific drug-user himself, but felt she shouldn't break Merrily's confidence. Sebastian was one thing, since he didn't even know her, but Vincent and Lowell quite another. Lowell, after all, was a judge and it wasn't fair to burden Vincent, since he divulged most things to his partner. So she worried in silence, but worry she did. It seemed that Merrily was unhealthily hooked, on the man as much as the substance.

A social animal like Dimitri took quite a lot of living up to and put considerable strain on Merrily's resources, even with the lucrative Chase salary still coming in. For how much longer that would continue she really had no idea. Despite the universal despondency in the office, she tried to shut her mind to the precariousness of her own position. She could face up to only one crisis at a time and holding on to the man of her dreams took most of her spare energy. She stayed clear, whenever possible, of Byron Kaminsky and his lascivious stare, by lying low in her office and avoiding the local eateries and bars. Whatever was fermenting in his deranged mind was bound to emerge in time. For all she cared, Chase were welcome to keep their piddling little job. Merrily Morgenstern had matters more urgent on her mind.

Although she possessed more clothes than anyone she knew, she would not be satisfied with recycling outfits; like royalty, she felt obliged to turn up in something new each time they met. Apart from Saks and Bendels, where she had accounts, she took to trawling further afield, uptown to Lowmans to seek out designer bargains which once would have been anathema to her retail sensitivity.

She recklessly sold a block of Chase shares and then some more. To herself she reasoned that this could count as serious investment and was better than leaving them to moulder in some bank. And, while she still had this well-paid job, there'd be more and better stock options at the end of each year, and so on up the corporate ladder. Everything she'd got went into this roll of the dice but she thought of it as seed money and therefore worth the risk. If you wanted something sufficiently badly, you were almost certain to get it. She had never lusted after anything more fervently than she did Dimitri Romanov.

Another of the Chase employees' perks was free checking facilities with few questions asked. Plus access to some of the best financial advice it was possible to get. Traditionally the bank had always taken good care of its workers and Merrily rested snug in the assurance that her money was safely invested and quietly growing. Dimitri, however, a man of wide-ranging financial experience, was forever cross-examining her. He alarmed her by expressing doubts that the bank was doing its utmost best on her behalf.

'The Chase Manhattan Bank,' she protested, as they lay satiated in her bed, 'has to be rock solid, as solid as Fort Knox.' Dimitri merely smiled and leaned across her to light another joint. He kept his dope in a fake shaving-foam canister, which he left boldly displayed on the bathroom shelf.

'You're such an innocent, my sweet,' he said fondly, kissing her hair. 'Look what they're doing to the work force throughout the world. Downsizing at a rate of knots. What makes you imagine that you're so special? Where streamlining a major corporation is concerned, you're little more than a pawn. Like the rest of them.' And she knew it made sense. She pressed her face against his taut, hairless chest, which always smelled pleasantly of vanilla, and tried to put such sordid matters out of her head. But Dimitri was determined not to let it go.

'We'll run through it one more time,' he said, placing the joint carefully between her lips. 'Tell me exactly what you have invested and where.'

'It's not my money you're after, is it?' She was only half joking, he seemed so intense. He gave his familiar, catlike smile, his eyes narrowed to slits.

'I am far too attached to you, my darling, not to be concerned about your investments. I just want to make doubly sure that no one is ripping you off. Remember I'm an expert in the cut-throat world of banking. Not a lot gets past me.'

Heady words from a powerful man. Her head was reeling

from the aromatic smoke and the steel in his voice made her horny all over again. She rolled towards him seductively but he moved away and lay looking up at the ceiling, puffing and absorbed in private thoughts. Merrily felt cosseted and very, very special. Not one of the previous louses in her life had paid this sort of attention to her welfare. He must really care for her.

Mustn't he? she asked Jo that night. Jo was altogether less certain but keen not to let it to show. She'd been talking again to Vincent, who had discussed it in detail with Lowell. Lowell, the keen-eyed lawman, pulled no punches. There were, quite simply, no stray members of the last Tsar's family alive apart from a well charted few. And, far from carrying the Cossack genes so apparent in Merrily's dashing beau, recent generations had been strongly German with direct connections to the British royals.

'Of course the man's a fake,' said Vincent. 'But tell me what else is new. Stands out a mile – he is far too flash. And why has he told her so little about himself? If he really were the hotshot he purports to be, then what's wrong with a little bragging? If he had a clue about what makes Merrily tick, he'd know she's more than just a blatant star-fucker; a ballsy high-achiever herself, turned on by power.'

The jungle drums had clearly been working overtime and the Antiguan network earning its laurels for caring. Jo smiled. Soon, no doubt, she'd be hearing from Cora Louise and Fontaine, adding their pennyworth to this kangaroo court.

'And what's with all this travelling he supposedly does? Why all the secrecy from the lady he is bedding?' They'd obviously given it a lot of thought. Jo faced up reluctantly to the obvious truth that was staring her in the face.

'You think he has a secret life? Is that what you're saying?'

'Precisely. A man that gorgeous is unlikely to come untrammelled and how come he seems to live permanently in a hotel?'

'You think there's a wife and family somewhere?' Jo was appalled.

'Or worse.' Vincent sounded amused. Fond though he might be of Merrily, he remained a voracious gossip at heart and this was about as good as he'd come across. Jo, however, was far more concerned with Merrily's welfare; if this came unstuck she might easily crack up.

'Well, continue to keep shtoom and we'll see what we can dig up,' said Vincent. 'Meanwhile, wish me luck in Rotterdam. Quite the little private eye, me.'

One bright February morning, when the leaves were back on the trees and the crocuses in the park were beginning to show, Merrily went into the office with a singing heart. Dimitri had not been away for a couple of weeks and she'd seen him already four times in as many days. There was something urgent he was keen to discuss; tonight he was treating her to dinner at *Lutèce*. Her mind was racing. If it was what she thought it was, and she was sure she must be right, it was essential she looked her optimum best, which meant an entire new outfit. If she cut out lunch, she could make it to Saks and might even fit in a manicure too. She had put in so many extra hours lately that no one could object if for once she came back late.

But, alas, it was not to be. As the elevator doors opened on the twenty-second floor, she sensed immediately something was wrong. There were half-filled tea-chests blocking the corridor and evidence of frantic rearrangement. And when she reached her own office suite, she found the door fixed open and a couple of security men waiting to greet her.

'I'm sorry, ma'am,' said Gus, the black guard she had always thought of as something of a friend, 'but you can't go in there. Orders from upstairs.'

And that, quite simply, was that. Her private door had been locked and sealed and written authorisation required to enter, and even then, with a guard in attendance. She had to be out of the building by noon. Merrily Morgenstern was out on her ear, just when she least expected it, without so much as a chance to appeal. Fired. Kaput. Discontinued.

Oddly enough, when the crunch actually came, Merrily didn't go running to Dimitri for comfort but instead took the coward's way out. She was insufficiently sure of him to risk divulging this ultimate bombshell until she'd had time to withdraw and regroup and properly plan her strategy. So she simply told him she was coming down with a bug and would have to cancel their date. No new outfit, not for tonight; no *Lutèce*. There was a nasty chance the good life had gone for good, she just didn't know. And she wasn't risking her future with Dimitri, not without a proper fight.

He sounded detached and a little impatient and said he'd get back to her when he was less busy. He hoped she'd soon be better and then they'd have that talk. Though he wasn't now sure when that was likely to be since he had, that night, to return to the coast and might be gone for a while. Cold terror gripped at Merrily's heart and it was all she could do not to blow it on the spot. But she'd die rather than let those buggers win and that included him.

'Sod off, Kaminsky,' she muttered through her teeth. 'I'll see you in hell yet before I'm through!'

185

She wasn't keen to share her news, not even with Jo. She gazed bleakly around the apartment she'd never much liked and told herself it would have to go. Midtown rents were suddenly out of her reach; soon she would have to start looking around for something more humble she could realistically afford. But not until after a period of ritual mourning. A creature of tradition, Merrily took to her bed and for four days existed solely on vodka and ice-cream. Dimitri's unexplained absence was a boon, for one thing was vital: he must never find out what had happened to her, for she knew that in weakness lay her ultimate downfall. And if she lost Dimitri, then she'd have lost it all.

After four days, with blotchy skin and hair in need of a wash, she rose and showered and finally raised the blinds. Outside it was spring and the sun was high. Time at last to put on her armour and venture once more into the world. There was a lot of fighting still ahead but of one thing she was quite certain. She wanted Dimitri more desperately than ever and would do all in her power now to pin him down.

16

In March a postcard arrived from Vincent. Not one of his customary over-the-top ones, with windmills and tulips and cute little Dutch girls in clogs, or muscled he-men flaunting more than they ought, but for once unusually restrained. Just a Durer engraving of aesthetic hands clasped in prayer, with Vincent's excited scrawl across the back.

> *Eureka, darling!! I really think I've cracked it and finally identified your elusive Prince Charming!!! Wait till you hear the half of it!! Far too classified for a postcard, I'm afraid. You'll just have to curb your impatience till Easter. Well worth the wait, I guarantee!!!*

Then, as an emollient, he had added a postscript: *The picture is a clue.*

Now what was he on about? Jo picked the postcard off the

doormat and, despite her frustration, couldn't help laughing out loud. Trust old Vincent, always prepared to make a meal of things and keep a person on tenterhooks for the sake of a punch-line. But he did succeed in brightening up her life even on a morning as dismal as this. She sat on a chair in the hall while she laced her boots. Outside London was dark with drizzle and she had a formidable list of house-calls to get through. Easter would be late this year but then the guys would be arriving, staying at the Ritz for a week of culture and fun. She could hardly wait, especially now she knew that Vincent had news. She studied the postcard again. Whatever did he mean by that mysterious PS? How utterly frustrating. She dropped it into her bag for further study, snatched her car keys and was away.

Her first instinct was to call Merrily and bounce it off her. For such a dyed-in-the-wool cynic, the American had remarkably good instincts where anything to do with human relations was concerned. She had been more than generous with her time already, letting Jo bore on about her mysterious stranger without attempting to shoot her down, as others might have done.

Jo knew she was making a bit of a fool of herself with this crazy adolescent crush but was quite unable to help herself. It was, as they said, like getting measles late in life. Since that mesmerising moment when she'd first clapped eyes on him, she'd been quite unable to get him out of her mind. And actually dancing with him had only made things worse; having proved him conclusively solid flesh and blood, her obsession had magnified about a thousand per cent.

Yet Jo sensed Merrily had problems of her own and lately had been conscious of a slight withdrawal. She wondered what could be wrong. Nothing she had said or done, of that she did feel confident. Merrily might be touchy but could always be relied on to spit any grievance straight out. That was one of the things Jo liked best about her; she always fired from the hip. Ever on her guard, occasionally belligerent, but not one to brood or maintain a lasting grudge. It was most likely something to do with her job. That, or the dubious Dimitri giving her grief. She'd find a way to call her later and elicit the truth without burdening her with her own childish perplexity. Meanwhile, dying to discuss Vincent's postcard, Jo opted instead to talk to Jessica.

Jessica sounded oddly on edge but pleased, nonetheless, to receive Jo's call. Life right now was a bitch, she confirmed, with the festival opening in just two months and so much still to achieve before then. She had a huge amount of travelling to fit in and wondered if she might grab a bed occasionally as she zipped through London, auditioning musicians. Jo was only too delighted.

'I'll let you have a key,' she said spontaneously. 'Then you can come and go as often as you please and leave some basics in the flat so you don't always have to bring a bag.'

She found Jessica excellent company, on the rare occasions that they managed to meet, and could use a bit of intelligent conversation, what with the overwhelming workload of a National Health practice and Sebastian so frequently away. She'd find out in a minute if Jessica had news of him; first there was the postcard to analyse.

'What do you imagine Vincent means? You understand the workings of his devious little mind.'

At first she'd been cautious about discussing her stranger but they'd all been there on that fateful night and it was, after all, Jessica's migraine that had mucked things up. Though she was far too forgiving to mention that now. Jessica sounded slightly guarded and more interested in Vincent than his postcard.

'When exactly did you say they're arriving?'

'April the thirteenth. You knew that. You should have it in your diary from last year.'

Jo had bought tickets for the National Theatre and was planning a dinner in her cramped little flat. There had been a chance that the Ravenels might be over too but the last Jo had heard they were headed instead for Bruges.

'We missed it last time,' Cora Louise had written, 'and cannot resist those mediaeval cities in the spring.' How ever did they manage it? From what Jessica had implied, they were less well-heeled than appeared and all that travelling must certainly set them back. But Bruges was only a hop and a skip from London, particularly now that the Eurotunnel had opened. What fun if they could make it after all and nip over for a night or two in London. She'd certainly do what she could to persuade them. Apart from Merrily, they might all be together at Easter.

But the enigmatic postcard. They still hadn't cracked it.

'What do you suppose those saintly hands signify? It's all very perplexing.'

'I really haven't a clue.' Jessica sounded less than interested as well as faintly fraught. 'I talk to Vincent quite a lot and he's certainly mentioned nothing to me.'

Did she indeed; how odd she hadn't said. But Jo was pleased she could trust Vincent's discretion, even if it brought her no nearer to knowing the truth. Curses! She felt like ringing him right now and forcing the truth out of him but knew she ought to wait. If she jumped the gun, she'd only spoil his surprise and that would certainly never do. Vincent was such a darling man who derived infinite pleasure from doing favours for friends. She would just have to hang on patiently, like he said, and wait to see what magic he had up his sleeve.

She chatted to Jessica for a further few minutes, then rang off. Only later did it occur to her that she never had got round to asking about Sebastian.

Sebastian's big news, almost a year ago now, was that he had been, in the teeth of incredible competition, selected to audition for a touring orchestra under the baton of his idol, Richard Stanford Palmer. Jo laughed incredulously when he finally told her.

'How could you possibly fit that in with your studies? Are you crazy?' Doing psychiatry as well as general medicine was surely already enough of a burden. But Sebastian was determined, never more so.

'I don't suppose I'll get it but it's an honour to be asked,' he said, privately miffed at Jo's proper lack of reaction to this dream of a lifetime so nearly within his grasp. Amelia would understand its true importance, Jessica too. But Jo, alas, lacked soul, or so he thought. She hadn't a musical bone in her body but he loved her nonetheless. Which was a pity in a way since Amelia – and Jessica – were far more on his wavelength.

To his secret surprise, though, he romped through the auditions and when he eventually met the great man himself, the engagement was in the bag. The maestro, it emerged refreshingly, was all in favour of young musicians living as normal a life as possible, provided it didn't get in the way of the music. He felt it added more substance to their playing, to see a bit of real living and not be confined to the concert platform.

'I was rather in danger of making that mistake myself,' he said frankly, as they sat and chatted in the empty auditorium. 'You know what they say about all work and no play.'

He was younger and less formal than Sebastian had expected and engagingly relaxed. But then, as Jessica had pointed out, he'd been in this game since childhood; professional music was his life.

'Well, I'll see you around,' said Palmer eventually, checking his watch and realising he was running late. 'We start in late February with the European tour and then, if all goes according to plan, we are doing the southern United States next summer. Do you think you could manage to fit that in as well?' His smile was infectious.

'You bet!' said Sebastian, with shining eyes. 'Just try and stop me!'

The Tavistock would have to allow him a sabbatical; that or he'd quit. He had all his life to become a psychiatrist; this was an opportunity that might never come again.

'I got it!' he shouted as he bounced into Jo's flat and she rose from her desk, laughing at his excitement, to give him a heartfelt hug. She might not be particularly musical herself but she knew how much it meant to him and was glad. She felt she'd given him a bit of a raw deal lately. By achieving this dream, he could put all that behind him and, with luck, their friendship needn't suffer.

'I only hope success won't change you,' she said as he swung her off her feet.

'It hasn't changed him, or so it would appear. You'd be surprised what a regular guy he is.'

There would be some paperwork to follow. Richard Stanford Palmer had a tough Hollywood management handling his affairs but that ought not present any problems. They were simply there to sort out the small print; it was what the maestro wanted that counted.

'Well done, sweetie. I'm so proud of you.' Jo put aside her

case-notes with a smile and took Sebastian round the corner to *Kartouche* for a celebration. With his bright, hazel eyes and Peter Pan smile, it was hard to believe he was thirty-two and no longer the idealistic youth she had fallen for on the banks of the Cam. She knew she would miss him when he finally went away but it wouldn't be forever and their lives were already diverging. The important thing was he was achieving a lifetime's ambition. In her heart she wished she might some day do the same.

Occasionally, as an antidote to the job, Jo would take herself off to a West End matinée or else to the Tate Gallery for an hour's peaceful browsing among the Turners. Living as she did in one of the world's great capitals, she often felt guilty that she didn't manage to do more, to avail herself more fruitfully of all it had to offer. It was the same with most of her friends. Even the few with regular nine-to-five jobs found themselves burdened with overtime, homework or, like Sebastian, extra-curricular studying. It was a throwback to the work ethic of her father's generation. Today's bright achievers put competitiveness in the workplace far ahead of plain quality leisure time.

She thought of Merrily, with the spectre of downsizing constantly clouding her horizon. Merrily hadn't said much about her worries but now and again felt the need to unburden and Jo's ear was always available and receptive. Jessica, too, spent every waking hour labouring for far too little money in pursuit of her eventual aim. In the case of Jessica, however, the actual work brought its own rewards. Again, like Sebastian, music was her life; her ambition was to find a way into the BBC and one day get her teeth into helping organise the Proms.

Living in Chelsea was bliss to Jo. Having grown up in distant

Hampstead, with its huge houses and spacious gardens, she now felt North London was too far out and relished the short walk from the practice back along the busy King's Road. Her parents had laughed when they first saw her cramped quarters and could not understand how she could abandon panelled luxury for this. But Elm Park Mansions represented more than just grown-up status. Her flat stood for freedom and emancipation, the end result of all she had worked for.

Jessica loved the flat. After the dismal digs she was used to, gaining a key to Jo's cheerful two-bedroomed eyrie was better than anything she might have hoped for, particularly in this expensive city. She rapidly filled the spare drawer and hanging space Jo had thoughtfully provided and these days left her toilet things on the washbasin and her slippers under the bed. She would arrive from Paddington mid-morning, make herself a cup of coffee in Jo's cramped but tidy kitchen, then run down the five flights of stairs and out into the enclosed courtyard to which massive elms gave the air of an enclave out of provincial France. And all within spitting distance of practically everywhere she needed to go. Sheer delight.

Jo, too, liked having an occasional house guest. Without Sebastian, she sometimes found life lonely and loved the secure feeling of turning the corner at the end of a long, hard day and seeing a light on in her flat. It meant there was someone there to talk to, someone with whom to share a meal and a laugh and take her mind off the grim realities of the job. Jo and Jessica were fast becoming best friends; Merrily might have her reservations but then she always had been a bit of a dog-in-the-manger, reluctant to relinquish centre stage.

'If only she'd go wild and join us at Easter,' mused Jo. They still weren't certain of the Ravenel ladies but Jo had her hopes that the lure of Lowell would prove irresistible bait. While simply being together with those two marvellous men would be pleasure enough for Jessica. The special understanding she felt she had with Vincent kept her, these days, on a permanent high, so that even the pain of losing Tom was finally fading into perspective. Gradually Jessica's heart was beginning to thaw.

Jo didn't know about that, of course. Jessica played her emotional cards close to her chest and only Vincent knew what she'd been through before she met them. Cora Louise had a bit of an inkling but the subject of Tom had never really been broached. Jo occasionally wondered what Jessica did for social life but, since her evenings were mainly filled with concerts and listening to recordings, she understood how work might take priority even over love. Since Sebastian, it was much the same with her. *What a pathetic pair we are, to be sure*, she sometimes reflected as she microwaved her solitary supper while she watched *EastEnders*. *Working ourselves into an early grave, letting real life pass us by*.

Jessica occasionally brought a contribution – flowers or pâté or some classy olive oil – but not very often. Jo didn't care; she knew that Jessica worked on a limited budget and didn't begrudge her what meagre hospitality there was. Friendship was, after all, about sharing. Jessica more than sang for her supper with her cheerful company and lively conversation.

But Easter would soon be here and with it Lowell and Vincent. Jo made a special effort to clean the flat and laid in wine as if for a siege.

'Drink the Marks and Spencer stuff,' she instructed Jessica. 'Keep the snobby labels for the boys. They notice these things.'

The beginning of April came and went and Jo intensified her

preparations for the get-together. Jessica was in and out and there had been no word from the Ravenels but Jo continued to plan menus and spring-clean the flat in fits and starts, ready for the great day. Vincent, she knew, was a gourmet cook and Lowell accustomed to gracious living. She tidied up her living room, schlepping piles of old medical journals to be recycled, and even took her dingy curtains down and round the corner to the cleaners.

Then she tackled the spare room and stripped off the candlewick bedcover for the wash. She put Jessica's toilet things tidily into the cupboard and saw, with surprise, how much was already there – sweaters, underwear, a couple of shirts and a raincoat. Even one of her own favourite scarves and the grey velvet beret Jessica so much admired. Jo laughed. Talk about taking liberties. She really didn't mind but, in Jessica's place, would have thought to ask first.

There was a new exhibition at the Hayward Gallery and live jazz at Pizza on the Park. She couldn't wait for Vincent and Lowell to arrive since there were so many good things she could share with them and she loved showing off her city. On top of which, of course, she was dying to hear what Vincent had discovered about her stranger. She managed to curb her impatience but it wasn't easy. She tried her hardest to persuade Merrily to join them but something was obviously still not quite right there, so in the end she let the subject drop. Merrily would tell her in her own good time. No point in prying and ending up upsetting her.

Jo's excitement was not to last. Just two days before the projected visit, she had a sombre, late-night call from Lowell.

She could scarcely believe what he was saying, nor hear him properly, for he was almost incoherent. There would be no Easter celebration after all. Vincent was dead, found battered and strangled, alone in his Amsterdam flat.

17

'How exactly did it happen?' asked Jo when Lowell finally made it to London. He was on his way from the funeral and the upsetting task of talking to the police and sorting through Vincent's possessions. She was shocked by how the death had aged him. His skin was thin and papery and his hair pure white. He had put on ten years in a matter of weeks. Inside him, a vital light seemed to have been extinguished.

Lowell spread his hands in helpless despair. 'Who knows? In some ways, with the life he led, it's a wonder it hadn't happened earlier. He was a dear, dear fellow but inclined to go off the rails.'

Jo nodded. She'd had a fairly shrewd idea of the life Vincent lived; no need to go into detail. She knew a certain amount about the gay life and some of the things she had seen in casualty had shocked her profoundly. She didn't understand it but then, who did?

'So you think it may have been a casual pickup?' She hated to hurt him.

'One assumes.'

He was found in his living room, face down on the floor, with head injuries and a tie knotted round his neck.

'One of his favourites. His yellow silk Hermès.' It was an inconsequential detail but important to Lowell. He'd been over and over it in his mind, almost to the point of lunacy.

'Had anything been taken? Was the apartment ransacked?'

Lowell shook his head. 'That's the oddest part. He had a vast stash of cash on him because he was going to buy a painting. Yet nothing was touched. No sign of a break-in or even a struggle. Whatever happened, happened quickly. The police said he probably won't have suffered.'

Lowell's eyes filled and he looked away in embarrassment. Jo's true profession was no longer a secret. He badly needed to talk to someone and had instinctively chosen her, hence this visit. He was a lost soul but a brave one. Her heart ached for him, he was so vulnerable yet so dignified.

'The only thing that was missing was his ring. Ripped from his finger apparently.'

In an odd way, that was the cruellest thing, the epitome of all he had lost. Apart from bequests to his immediate family, Vincent had left Lowell the bulk of his estate but it was the ring that symbolised their fourteen-year relationship and now that too was gone.

'That beautiful ring!' Jo remembered its intricate design and the bright blue stone, the colour of Vincent's eyes. A gift, he had said but had never expounded. At the realisation that she'd not see him again, she too began to weep and they stood together in Lowell's hotel room, clinging to each other in desperation through the storm of their shared grief.

Jo had thought about going to the funeral but wasn't quite sure of the etiquette. She came from a family of non-believers and had no strong feelings about religion except that people's customs should be respected. And Vincent was Dutch with a family she'd never met. As a doctor, she had an ever-widening acquaintance with the whole paraphernalia of bereavement, yet still felt uncomfortable about the conventions of mourning and hated to intrude on private grief. She had rung Jessica to see what she thought but found her so shattered by the terrible news that she wasn't making much sense. So instead, after some thought, Jo had dialled International Enquiries and put in a call to South Carolina. There was just a chance that Cora Louise and Fontaine hadn't yet heard about Vincent. Lowell had been so distraught the night he told her, she'd not thought of asking, until it was too late, if there was anything at all she could do on his behalf. This was something she *could* do off her own bat, though she dreaded to be the bearer of such appalling news.

The phone rang and rang, then someone picked it up and a sleepy Southern voice announced the Ravenel residence. Jo could almost feel the sultry stillness of a Charleston afternoon in early summer, lawn-sprinklers spraying the rock-hard earth against a background of chirruping cicadas. Cora Louise would be taking one of her naps and Fontaine – well, who could guess what Fontaine got up to at home. For a moment she panicked and felt like hanging up but then the retainer told her that the missees, they were not home at this time, and to try again in a couple of weeks when they should be returnin' from their travels. Jo was quite shaken. Did that mean they really hadn't heard from Lowell or had he, perhaps, caught them before they'd left? She'd no way of knowing but, whatever the truth, couldn't imagine how badly they would take it. They'd been so close to Lowell and Vincent for so long. Losing either one of them would be like losing one of their closest kin.

Next she tried Sebastian but, even as she dialled, knew that would be hopeless too. This music tour was taking up all his time. He only returned to London for occasional flashes and she was lucky if she heard from him from one month's end to the next. Well, she couldn't really complain. She had turned away from him of her own accord. If he chose to strike out on his own and make a new life for himself, she had no one to blame but herself.

But oh, she felt so lonely; lonely and sad.

In the end, Lowell told her, only immediate family and a gaggle of vacuous luminaries from the international art scene had turned up to pay their respects. But that was all right. Vincent, too, had had no formal religion and was doubtless up there, laughing on his cloud, thinking what a lark it all was, while down below they strutted and pontificated and praised his contribution to twentieth-century culture. Not to mention Mammon.

Walking back along the towpath from Richmond to Kew, Jo finally found the courage to broach the subject of Vincent's postcard. For three nights they had talked themselves hoarse, sitting up late and sharing a bottle of whisky, and now were getting a needed breath of fresh air. Lowell was wearing a well-cut leather jacket and his white hair fluttered in the breeze. Jo clung to his arm for comfort; he was taller than she was by a good six inches but her stride matched his.

'The postcard.' At first he looked vague, then some sort of recollection dawned but he simply shook his head. Vincent had babbled something about it over the phone but he hadn't really taken in the details. Hadn't really been interested was the truth. There was usually some sort of intrigue going on in the younger man's life. Lowell had so many pressures of his own, he hadn't kept up with the trivia.

'His trip to Rotterdam. You don't know anything about that?' She really hated to chivvy him at such a time but it was important. Vitally important, but she wasn't about to say so.

'Afraid not. Although we were so close, there was a lot about Vincent I didn't know. He had his own friends, led a separate life. Whatever he was up to, he'd have let me know eventually.' But not till all was resolved. And certainly not over the transatlantic wires.

So that was that. Jo bit back her disappointment and clung a little closer to Lowell's arm. All things considered, it was probably for the best. In the face of what had happened to Vincent, she was ashamed even to have raised the subject. She would let it drop now and try to return to being a rational being. One good thing, Jessica was joining them for supper. She had all sorts of exciting things to tell them, Jo knew, about her recent travels and the festival; about her new job. That ought to help divert poor Lowell. With a little luck, they should get through the evening intact.

On his way back home to Boston, Lowell called on Merrily too. His own life might have ended but he knew he had to struggle on, and touching base with trusted friends was one way of keeping Vincent's spirit alive. Or so he reasoned. Merrily was startled to receive his call and apparently tongue-tied with embarrassment. He swiftly tried to put her at her ease but her angst went deeper than he realised and she perked up only when he suggested they meet midtown. For lunch at

La Reserve on West 49th Street; he couldn't face the Harvard Club in his present state of melancholy and guilt.

Merrily arrived only fifteen minutes late, dressed demurely in stark navy with a crisp white shirt. She was wearing her Jackie Onassis shades and he saw at a glance that she dreaded meeting his gaze. Poor Merrily. It was hard to handle raw grief at the best of times and the last time they'd met she'd been in a state of euphoria. Lowell stepped forward and, gripping her firmly by both elbows, gave her a kiss on either cheek to help put her at her ease.

'Thank you for coming at such short notice,' he said, and she shook her head, mute with emotion, entirely unable to speak.

They ordered. Then, to help her out, Lowell asked how things were going and if she were still in love.

'Yes,' he laughed, when he saw her astonished look. 'You needn't think you have any secrets from me. Vincent was a constant mine of information.'

There, it was out. Merrily started and looked on the point of panic. His name had been mentioned but Lowell still sat there at ease and hadn't fallen to pieces.

'I'm sorry,' she gulped and started to improvise but Lowell leaned across and touched her hand, giving permission to waive convention and answer his question without demur. She was grateful. The colour crept slowly back into her cheeks and the eyes behind the shades were sparkling. She took them off and slipped them into her purse. If he wanted diversion, he'd certainly chosen right. On this particular subject, Merrily could talk forever.

She didn't tell him that she'd lost her job, that Mother Chase had fucked her royally so that soon she would have to give up the apartment. That she was in hock up to the gills as well as scared out of her wits. That she hadn't a clue how she was going to survive or even if she'd get another job. Oh no. Lowell, as it happened, would have been exactly the person to unburden to but Merrily had too much pride to let him know. He was so distinguished himself and so well-heeled. Why would he want to concern himself with another faceless victim of downsizing, particularly now, when he had just been so brutally bereaved? So she prattled on instead about Dimitri and, as she talked, her eyes grew even brighter until she lost her appetite completely and could only toy with her food.

'He sounds some kind of a guy.' The warmth of Lowell's smile was genuine; for the first time in weeks he was sharing another's hope and it felt good.

'He is.' No doubt about it. They had been together till the early hours but had still not had that vital conversation. There was definitely something brewing but she didn't know what. Being with Lowell was a welcome diversion, even in such tragic circumstances.

'And you say his name is Romanov?' He wouldn't throw cold water, wouldn't undermine her happiness. Vincent had constantly nagged him about being a wet blanket so now, belatedly, was the time to learn to stay shtoom. In Vincent's memory, if for no other reason, Lowell would hold his tongue and merely listen.

'He's a descendant of the Tsar,' said Merrily proudly. 'A genuine prince of the blood.' Didn't they teach them history in Ohio? Had she no education at all? 'But he hates to talk about it because he's a true democrat. He likes to be treated naturally, like just an ordinary guy. He's smart as they come and drop-dead gorgeous. Wait till you meet him properly.'

From the glimpse he'd had of Merrily's prince in the dim

light of the Mill Reef Club, he'd looked about as appealing as a Rottweiler, but still Lowell held his tongue.

'What's his line of business?' That, at least, should be safe.

Merrily shook her head, outwardly serene. 'I've no idea. Something to do with buying and selling, I think.' She giggled like a schoolgirl. 'We don't get very much time for talking. If you catch my meaning.' She was so elated, he dared not deflate her. But he racked his brain for something cautionary to say, without letting show his real, deep-seated dismay.

'Has he met your folks?'

'Not yet.' They had talked about Christmas but that was still some way off. Dayton, or a trip to the Virgin Islands; she knew which one she'd prefer, as she explained to Lowell.

'So you won't be joining us?'

She looked surprised. 'Will you?' Surely not.

'Why not.' Lowell sat comfortably facing her, sipping his claret as calm as the judge he was. He'd taken a firm grip on his emotions and wouldn't crack up again. Not in public and certainly not with Merrily. Jo had given him enormous comfort but she was altogether a far more caring girl. 'Vincent would want me to, I have no doubt. And I'm certain he'll be there in spirit himself.'

He paid the bill and helped her find a cab. He didn't realise she would rather walk, that she no longer had the wherewithal for this kind of petty extravagance. But with a man like Lowell Brooks you had to maintain a facade; at least, that's how Merrily felt and she breathed a sigh when he was out of sight.

'Round the block!' she told the driver, and hopped out again when she knew she wouldn't be seen. It was getting harder and harder to play this game with Dimitri but she didn't want him to know about the job until she was sure there was another in the bag. He had loads of money for both of them but she didn't want to appear a gold-digger. When he got round to marrying her, it had to be on equal terms. She'd worked hard enough for it up till now. When the time was ripe, she planned to return to Dayton a total success, professionally as well as in the marriage stakes. Then, perhaps, she would finally see in her father's eyes the approval she had striven for for so long.

Lowell waved her off then turned back down Fifth, to 44th Street and the Harvard Club. Time to go home now and face a desolate world, devoid of meaning and devoted only to duty. To resume his cloak of staid respectability, to sit on the bench and help dispense the law. Let the poor girl believe in this fairy tale if she must. The light might have gone off permanently in his own life but, if she truly believed she had found her Mr Wonderful, bully for her.

There were flowers in his Boston chambers, great sheaves of them, with an overpowering scent that polluted the air. His first action was to force open the protesting casement windows, then he turned to his desk and the pile of pencilled notes. He groaned. Fontaine – he might have guessed it – and a beautifully penned note on lavender paper from Cora Louise, inviting him to stay.

Our hearts bleed for you, she wrote. *The least we can do is share with you some of our love.*

Lowell sank his head in his hands and sighed. They meant so well, he knew they did, but still; the very last thing he wanted now was cloying sympathy. He needed to be left in peace, to work and face the burden of his empty future alone. Luckily, his friends in Boston had no knowledge of this tragedy. Even his mother had only the vaguest sense of

Vincent and who he was. Just a pleasant holiday companion, met on his travels. Someone who sent Christmas cards and piles of jokey snapshots. He hadn't even told her about the tragedy, just that he had pressing business to attend to in Europe and would be gone at least a couple of weeks. He couldn't deal with the Ravenel ladies right now. He scrawled a note on his official stationery to say that he'd be in touch. Then instructed his clerk to hold all personal calls until further notice.

Down on Tradd Street in the steamy South, Cora Louise was lying supine, exactly as Jo had imagined, on her canopied bed in a darkened room, with an ice-cold washcloth over her eyes. After a lifetime of foreboding and fearing imaginary calamities, one had finally hit them four-square like a meteor, worse than almost anything her fevered imagination might have dreamed up. Vincent van der Voorst, that lovely boy, dead before his prime and for no reason she could possibly understand. Lordy, lordy, whatever was this bad old world coming to?

Along the passage, in the cathedral-ceilinged chamber that had always been her personal territory, Fontaine was dancing. Surrounded by her rows and rows of Victorian dolls, with their porcelain complexions and simpering smiles, she gazed at herself full-length in the glass and admired what she saw. She wore only a cerise satin teddy, trimmed with Brussels lace, and her profligate hair hung about her creamy shoulders in a riot of Titian curls. She was humming along to a pile of cracked old 78s, played on her mother's ancient Dansette, left over from the days when Cora Louise herself was a girl. Cole Porter and Gershwin, they really hit the spot. Not for nothing did the Ravenel ladies live just around the corner from the mythical Cat-fish Row.

'*They laughed at me wanting you, said it was reaching for the sky,*' sang Fontaine along with the lyrics. Cora Louise winced at the reverberations from her daughter's thumping feet but Fontaine was oblivious as she pranced and shuddered in an ecstasy of happiness.

Ho-ho-ho, who's got the last laugh now?

18

The Pump Room was filled to capacity, but Jessica led the way down the centre aisle to the second row, where she had reserved seats right in the centre.

'A perk of the job,' she whispered in the semi-darkness, groping for Sebastian's hand.

She was proud to be seen in public with him. Just back from his European tour, he had gained in stature as well as in elegance and wore a grey pinstripe suit with the distinctive cut of a Bond Street tailor about it. Poncey, Jo would have called it, but he didn't care; he was weary of her fond mockery and knew he looked good. It was Sunday night and an evening of early music, selected specially by Jessica because she knew he'd enjoy it.

'Come for the weekend,' she had said when she made the call. The flautist in tonight's ensemble was somebody he knew and they were invited for champagne afterwards with the rest of the players.

'It's a shame you can't stay on for tomorrow,' she said as she handed him his programme. 'We have the Leipzig Quartet playing Mozart and Stravinsky and the Prague Symphony at night.'

'Sorry,' said Sebastian, returning the pressure of her hand. 'Gotta get back to the sweatshop some time. I've been away long enough as it is.'

Jessica was looking particularly fetching tonight. In marmalade shantung, a shade darker than her hair, she was wearing amber ear-drops that subtly enhanced the effect. And her light green cat's-eyes were ablaze with passion as she listened attentively to each word he said and caressed the back of his hand with thin, pale fingers. She was a strange one, Jessica, and he wasn't at all sure how he'd come this far, almost without his noticing. Since the night he'd met her at Jo's flat, a year ago, they had somehow managed to keep in touch and now he found himself dating her irregularly and sleeping over in her cramped little room, on the lumpy bed intended for just one person.

She was light years away from Jo but perhaps that was part of the point of it, an integral sea-change he had needed to make before he could completely escape Jo's spell. He still wasn't sure. All he did know was it was good to be with someone who shared his musical mania and who gazed at him in frank delight as though he were the wittiest fellow alive. A change from Jo, with her calm, appraising eyes and that serene, untroubled countenance which entirely belied the turmoil churning beneath. Madonna-like he had heard Lowell call it. Certainly she had the goodness and the strength which often made him feel inadequate, never the best basis for a sexual relationship.

Whereas Jessica quite obviously adored him. She sat as

close to him as she could, still holding on to his hand, so that he could hear her light, rapid breathing as the quintet mounted the platform and took their places there on dainty gold chairs. Jessica looked fragile and her bones, beneath the transparent skin, were as light and delicate as a bird's. Not at all like his sturdy Jo but appealing nonetheless. Jo was a great one for tennis and country walks but Jessica looked as though she might blow away in the breeze and brought out the macho instincts in a bloke. The sort of girl you'd fight a duel for or end up carrying over a threshold. Sebastian preened. He had had the most enlivening ten weeks ever, basking in the light of the maestro's approval, and these days felt he could achieve almost anything. The Tavistock, too, had been good to him and he totally appreciated their forbearance. But if there should ever come a parting of the ways and push came to shove, he now knew without a doubt which way he would jump. Richard Stanford Palmer had given him the confidence; Sebastian did not intend to let him down.

He talked of his idol in the interval and a wary look crept into Jessica's eyes which Sebastian didn't recognise. Jealousy, maybe – she was an intense little person – or maybe just another aspect of her general competitiveness.

'You ought to have him down here for the festival some time. He travels an awful lot but is far more approachable than one might think.'

'He's supposed to have a management that repels all comers.'

'Yeah, the original bunch of junkyard dogs. But the thing is, he's not like that at all himself. That's the whole point.'

'How would I ever get to him?'

Sebastian smiled, his toffee-brown eyes gleaming with pleasure.

'Via me, old thing, nothing simpler. He really is a good fellow and keen on popularising the arts. There's a rumour he may be conducting at the Proms next year. It would be a laugh to get in on that, don't you think? Playing the old flute for all the odds and sods one knows?'

Sebastian was sick of his medical colleagues taking the mickey. Even though he had been, in his time, a star on the rugby field, they still seemed to think there was something slightly effete about the world of classical music. He often wondered if they would be so sneering if he played instead in a rock band.

Now Jessica was preening too. 'I knew that.'

'What?'

'About Richard Stanford Palmer and the Proms.' She had a secret too but wasn't ready to divulge it yet. Sebastian's curiosity was a huge aphrodisiac; let him tickle it out of her later, if he would.

They ran into Simon Pratt at the bar and Jessica had no choice but to introduce him. Simon looked his usual droopy self, with a knitted waistcoat visible beneath his jacket.

'My colleague from the office,' was what she said, holding her breath that Simon wouldn't betray the small fib she had always told and reveal that he was actually top banana and she merely his lowly number two. She need not have worried. Simon was far too occupied with the horsy, smothering woman at his side who looked at least five years older yet seemed as possessive of him as Jessica was of Sebastian. Well, she thought with relief, there is certainly no accounting for taste. The Prat must be a bigger catch than she'd realised; why else would the Honourable Anthea be clinging so lovingly to his arm?

He did take notice, however, when he heard that Sebastian played the flute and had been on tour with Richard Stanford Palmer. And the Honourable Anthea had her tongue practically hanging out.

'That man is utterly *divine*,' she breathed. 'I saw him conduct the *Emperor* at the Hollywood Bowl and the audience was just *swooning*, he was so dishy.'

Jessica stared at her with distaste. The Honourable Anthea had a velvet hairband and lipstick on her teeth. But Sebastian appeared in no way put off, far from it; his eyes sparkled with endorsement as she gushed on about his hero.

'He does have that effect. More groupies round his dressing-room door than you could shake a stick at. I never realised serious music had such a potential FQ until I travelled with the maestro. Quite an eye-opener, I can tell you.'

'FQ?' queried the Honourable Anthea.

'Fuckability quotient,' explained Sebastian, causing Simon to draw in a sharp, shocked breath. 'It's a Hollywood term.'

The second half was about to start so they parted company and returned to their seats before Simon had the chance to embark on his own private passion, the recorder.

'What a pill that man is,' hissed Jessica fiercely, glad to be shot of them. But Sebastian wasn't listening.

'You really must meet him some time, old thing,' he said. 'Blow your socks off, he would, I promise. He's doing the Horn Concertos at the Barbican in two weeks' time. I'll get tickets if you like.'

But Jessica, for once, was mysteriously not keen. Sebastian sensed immediate withdrawal once more and was puzzled. There was something he hadn't been able to get hold of, something from her past that caused her occasionally to change the subject or just clam up. He had tried probing gently but succeeded only in causing her to hyperventilate. He would have to tread carefully; maybe Jo would know.

Jo had been surprisingly relaxed about Sebastian's friendship with Jessica. To begin with, he had kept off the subject but, when he discovered Jessica had no such inhibitions, allowed himself to mention her, though only fleetingly, in passing. It wasn't quite the thing, he felt, to let one of his lady loves know about another but if they were going to discuss him behind his back, what the hell. Locker-room chat was something he abhorred; it made him uncomfortable to think about the notes these two might be swapping.

But when he asked Jo about Jessica's past she couldn't help.

'I know she's an orphan but that's about it,' she said. 'Vincent was the one who got to know her best, along with Cora Louise, but any secrets he might have gleaned will have gone with him to the grave.'

'What can she possibly have against Richard Stanford Palmer? I sense there's something but I really can't imagine what.'

'Don't know. Maybe she's bored with you constantly banging on about him. Jealous, perhaps?' Jo was laughing but there was sufficient truth in what she said to make him uncomfortable. 'Try asking her, since you seem to be so close.'

It *did* stick in Jo's throat a little, if truth be told; she was, after all, only human and she and Sebastian went back a long way. But Jessica had been completely upfront about it and cleared it first before she had phoned him the first time.

'I'd invite you too but I know it's not your thing,' she'd said. 'You must come down another time on your own, once the festival is out of the way.'

Jo was privately annoyed but didn't show it. She had always made a bit of a thing about not caring for music, primarily to keep a check on Sebastian, who was inclined to go ape with his enthusiasms. But actually, in the privacy of her home, she listened to Radio 3 much of the time. It was too late now, however; she had made her point and was bound to stick by it. She had given her blessing; what else could she do? Now it was up to them how things worked out.

Merrily, however, was a lot less forgiving.

'What a cow!' she said, when Jo updated her. 'Never trust anyone who's so consistently nice.'

'Oh, come on. It's only Sebastian. Practically family – and, besides, I gave my permission.'

Merrily snorted. 'Like lending her a library book, how extraordinarily generous! You have to remember, hon, that life's one great jungle. Never turn your back on a friend or, take my word for it, they'll be knifing you in the back.'

'Surely not. Female friends, too?'

'Are you kidding? What other kind is there?'

'Tell me more about yourself,' said Sebastian cosily. They were lying together on his threadbare sofa in Gordon Square, listening to Mozart and idly fooling around. He had found her standing outside in the street when he finally emerged from the clinic. He felt her thin shoulders tense.

'Like what?'

'Oh, just things. Where you grew up. Your favourite colour. The first bloke to kiss you. Stuff like that. I feel I know so little about you.'

But Jessica wasn't playing. She'd looked pale and strained when he'd stumbled across her, with no satisfactory explanation for being there except that she'd happened to be in town and passing. Now she got off the sofa abruptly, altering the mood, and went to stand by the window, looking out across the trees in the square.

'What's wrong, sweetheart? Is there something you're not telling me?' said Sebastian, crossing the room to join her.

She flinched as if he had struck her, then turned to face him and laid her cheek against his chest.

'Hold me,' she said simply and he obliged without further words.

'There *was* someone,' she said eventually and he could feel her beginning to shake again. 'A musician, like you, with an amazing future.'

'And?'

'I'd sooner not talk about it. It's just that everything I care about gets snatched away. And sometimes it scares me.'

Sebastian tilted up her chin and kissed her gently.

'Goose,' he said with genuine affection. 'I've never known anyone so insecure and all without reason.' He kissed her again. 'You can rely on me; I'm going nowhere. At least, not for a long time. Far too busy.'

'Promise?'

'I swear.'

One Friday morning in July, Jessica arrived early at the office, to find Simon for once there ahead of her. He sat at his desk, hunched over the mail, and she could tell from the set of his shoulders that he was in a snit. Well, that was nothing unusual; this man had the equanimity of a hornet.

'Morning,' she said breezily, dropping her battered handbag on her chair and proceeding to fill the kettle. Outside the sun was high in the sky and the city of Bath was bathed in light. The festival was over for the year and she and Simon would

soon be going their separate ways, once they had tidied stray
ends and generally cleared up behind them. She had plans to
get away with Sebastian. He had exams looming, which meant
a lot of studying, but still she reckoned she could convince
him they needed the space. Greece would be nice, or back to
the Caribbean, just the two of them this time. She hadn't much
money but they'd manage somehow. They didn't need a lot in
the way of comfort, just seclusion and the chance to be alone
together for a while. Away from ringing telephones and Jo.

'What gives?' She dumped a coffee on Simon's desk and
paused when he failed to react. He looked up at her from
under knitted brows, pure murder in his eyes.

'Now what have you been up to?' He stuck the letter, with
its BBC heading, in front of her, scowling as she picked it
up. Nicholas Kenyon, she read, glancing at the signature,
then whooped incredulously as she read on. It had worked,
after all, and she was in there with her toe in the door. Her
application had won through and now they were asking
Simon for a reference.

'I don't believe it! How utterly fantastic!' She looked down
at him with a radiant smile and almost plonked a kiss on his
balding pate. 'The Proms next season. Can you beat that?' It
had been a long shot but worth it; her wildest dream come
true. Utterly amazing, but how on earth had it happened?
Millions must apply so how come they'd picked her?

'Someone's obviously been pulling strings,' grumped Simon.
He'd lately had his doubts about Jessica and suspected she
might have friends in high places. But Jessica was frankly
puzzled. She genuinely hadn't a clue.

'Jobs like that don't fall out of trees.' Everyone knew the
BBC was a closed shop and getting to work on the Proms a
sinecure. Simon had got his own job through the intercession

217

of a relative but that, for the moment, was conveniently forgotten. Much as he disliked Jessica and was dying to see the back of her, it stuck in his craw that she'd been offered this elevation and all, as it would seem, out of a clear blue sky.

'That boyfriend of yours, the musician,' he said, unable to leave it alone. 'Perhaps he's been sticking his nose in and pulling a few strings. It just isn't fair; I'm far more qualified than you.'

Jessica said nothing. She had written the letter months ago, not thinking for a moment she would have a response but keen to further her career by whatever means she could. She knew it couldn't be Sebastian, that was daft. He was up to his ears in his medical studies and his musical connections were tenuous at the least. Besides, she'd never told him she was planning to move on. The letter had been a secret, a coin flipped into the fountain of fortune. Whatever, she most certainly was not going to look a gift horse in the mouth. It was the job she'd always dreamed of, come sooner than she'd hoped. It would take her away from the odious Prat and up to London where she'd always longed to be.

Just think of it. To live in the metropolis and work for the BBC, with all that entailed and its accompanying perks. London was expensive but she could always move in with Jo – or perhaps even with Sebastian who was bound to share her delight. *Wait till I tell him*, thought Jessica gleefully, impatient to see the back of Bath and get on with her life.

19

That winter in Antigua they were a sad little band indeed. Lowell, apparently functioning on automatic pilot, had taken the same spacious suite as before and dutifully welcomed them all for cocktails the first night. Their hearts weren't really in it, though. Without the fizzing effervescence of Vincent's ebullient charm, the holiday spirit was almost entirely extinct. They sat politely in a row along the veranda, peering through bougainvillaea at the darkening sea and sipping spritzers for some extraordinary reason, proof perhaps that not one of them was in the party mood. Nor did they bother to troop down to the beach at sunset, to watch for the mystical green flash. That had all been part of Vincent's magic, vanished now along with his exuberant spirit.

'Remember that Englishman who drowned? The first time I was here?' said Jo suddenly.

'Vaguely.'

'We never did hear any more about him. I wonder who he was, what actually happened. How he came to drown in completely still water.' She knew a fair bit more about these things since then. How green she'd been, how innocent, pathetically pretending not to be a doctor. If it happened now she'd be more alert; at least show some responsibility and be in there, asking questions on behalf of a fellow countryman.

'I don't think I knew about that,' said Jessica, without curiosity. 'Must have happened before I arrived. How odd no one's mentioned it till now.'

But none of them really cared. Without the spur of Vincent's probing curiosity, they couldn't be bothered to pursue the subject and simply lapsed back into torpid silence.

Merrily, too, was missing this year, snatched away at the eleventh hour to an idyll for two in the Virgin Islands with her fairy prince. Lucky Merrily but, oh, how Jo missed her already. It wasn't the same without that caustic wit. Lowell's face was as pallid as parchment and Fontaine, heavier than last year and hopelessly over-dressed in pink chiffon with bugle beads, watched him warily from where she sat and scarcely raised her voice at all. Had they made a terrible mistake in coming? In hoping to replicate the same old magic, year after year, even when things had irrevocably changed?

Eventually Cora Louise took the initiative, grabbed Lowell's sleeve and marched the lot of them downstairs to the dining room which was still only filling up. Not their usual style, by any means. Even the waiters seemed surprised.

'Hello, there!' called Marjorie and Donald Barlow, crossing the room, svelte and sun-tanned and in their second week. 'We were dreadfully sorry to hear about poor Vincent. What a shocking thing.'

Lowell, granite-faced, merely nodded; it was Cora Louise who took their hands and, tears in her eyes, spoke the appropriate words. Marjorie, trim in cornflower-sprigged Laura Ashley, touched Jo lightly on the shoulder in passing and murmured that they must meet up by the pool. Then she followed her husband with a brisker step as the band struck up with a lively calypso and the mood around them began to mellow.

'Guess what!' Merrily had crowed, ten days earlier. 'He's actually come through this time and we're off to St Thomas. Can you believe it? I never thought he'd do it, not when it came to the point, without the usual last-minute change of plan.' She was jubilant.

It was still not too late but Jo didn't dare say that. No point in alarming Merrily when she was on such a high; she sincerely wished her every happiness in the world.

'How many new outfits have you bought so far?' she teased, wondering, as ever, where on earth Merrily stowed them all. 'It's a shame you're such a shrimp, else I could have your cast-offs. I could certainly use them, I can tell you.' This year, with Jessica firmly in possession, there'd be no cadging from Sebastian's wardrobe. It would just have to be good old M & S again; her budget, once she had cleared her bills, didn't stretch to much in the way of frivolity. At least without Merrily there'd be less sartorial competition, but that wouldn't make up for how much she would miss her.

Merrily fudged the answer. The question of clothes was becoming a major headache. She felt the need to be outfitted like a bride, yet scarcely had the wherewithal, as things stood, to cover even a bikini with a decent label. All her cards were right up to their limit; she had shed some more of her Chase shares but still that wasn't enough. And unless she got another job soon, who knew where that might land her. In Central Park in a cardboard box, her worldly possessions stashed around her in plastic bags. If only he'd get to the point and make things official. All her hopes were pinned on this vacation. Which was why she was prepared, if necessary, to take out a bank loan to cover the costs.

'Good luck,' said Jo, alert to the unspoken. 'I'll keep my fingers tightly crossed for you and will think of you all the time you're there. Go for it, girl! You deserve it!'

Merrily nodded, at the far end of the line, but in her heart was more anxious than she showed. The pressures of keeping up a pretence in front of Dimitri had finally cracked her iron resolve. Jubilation about the trip and the prospect of where it might lead, combined with perhaps one too many snorts of cocaine, had last night led her to blow her cover and confess to her darling the truth about her job. That there wasn't one any longer, that she was currently unemployed. She had snuggled up against him in her own impersonal bed, fearing to tell him the worst of it, that shortly she would also be having to move. And Dimitri had said not a word. Had lain there in the semi-darkness, his narrow eyes virtually closed, and done magical things to her body with his fingers that had blown away her worries along with her mind. What would be would be, she comforted herself as she gave way to raw lasciviousness. Today she was not quite so sure.

The sea was unusually choppy so the group camped round the pool on yellow recliners. Jo industriously did her thirty laps but the rest of them were entirely indolent and lounged around with their books and newspapers, with towels draped over their legs because of the breeze. It was quieter without

Merrily and Vincent, and they were less inclined to chat. Jessica sat under an umbrella with Cora Louise, watching her embroider and talking intensely in a very low voice, while Fontaine laughed and gambolled around poor Lowell, who looked as though he were waiting to see the dentist. Did she really believe, thought Jo as she swam, that she could shake him out of his present depression with these ludicrously girlie antics? Now she was leaping about on the grass, flashing her rather good legs as she chased a giant beach ball tossed to her by a group of grinning Germans. Far better to show a little tact and simply let him be, but that, unfortunately, was not within Fontaine's canon.

'Has anyone got a camera?' she shrieked but this year nobody had. They were too accustomed to Vincent's paparazzo antics; every Christmas they had all been treated to a fat batch of hilarious holiday snaps, most of them with outrageous captions. Certainly Fontaine, in that jazzy neon Lycra number, would have proved natural fodder to the Dutchman's wicked lens.

The Barlows joined them and Marjorie waded into the pool to talk. Was Lowell all right, she wanted to know, and did the police know if it was murder?

'I assume so,' said Jo. 'He was battered to death. But beyond that, I don't believe they have any leads.'

Marjorie shook her head in dismay. 'He was such a sweet fellow, we loved him so much. How ever can Lowell carry on without him?'

They turned to where Lowell sat engrossed in the *Herald Tribune*. Fontaine was now rubbing oil into his shoulders but he did not, by so much as a glance, acknowledge her presence. *I wish she'd leave him alone*, thought Jo, but what was the point? In her clumsy way, the flamboyant Southern belle was right;

Vincent might be dead but life went on. Sooner or later he would surely have to snap out of it.

Beneath their umbrella, Jessica was telling Cora Louise all about Sebastian. *Odd*, thought the older woman as she quietly stitched, *last year it was poor dear Vincent she had her eye on*. Still, it was healthy that Jessica's feelings could mend so quickly. One of the assets of youth, no doubt. Though right till this day, when she had trouble sleeping Cora Louise still dreamed of her lost Gabriel, and the moonlight gleamed just as brightly on his coal-black curls. *Guess I'm just an old-fashioned romantic*, reflected Cora Louise.

Jessica's outpourings were making her a little confused. She remembered Sebastian, that enchanting young man, but had been under the impression that he was Jo's beau, not Jessica's. Yet all she had heard since they'd arrived this trip was Jessica banging on about him. She glanced across at Jo, to see if she minded, but was countered by the customary serene expression, which, if she did but know it, concealed a tumultuous soul. *Well now, I'll be darned. Whatever next?* She would talk to Fontaine when they went upstairs to dress, and see if she could make head or tail of it all.

Walking along the beach one morning, Lowell asked Jo if this new man in Jessica's life could possibly be the same Sebastian he had always thought was Jo's. Jo laughed and confirmed it was. All they had heard, these last few days, were constant coy references to him – Sebastian this and Sebastian that – until others besides Jo were beginning to grind their teeth.

'How come?' asked Lowell mildly, as they splashed along at the edge of the surf, enjoying the heat of the sun on their backs. 'From what I'd gathered, you were something of an item. How ever did Jessica get in on the act?'

He might well ask. But Jo just laughed and told him the bare facts: how Jessica and Sebastian had met through her, that they shared an enthusiasm for classical music which had rapidly drawn them together. So that these days they were fairly inseparable, especially since Jessica was now moving to London and was popping up and down all the time, sorting out her living arrangements.

'And it doesn't bother you?' Lowell was inordinately fond of Jo. He hated to think anyone might do her wrong.

'Not really,' said Jo honestly, scrambling over a seaweed-covered breakwater and gratefully grabbing for Lowell's steadying hand. 'We had been together for over twelve years and the relationship had more or less run its course.'

Lowell said nothing. The fickleness of youth. He had known Vincent fourteen and a half years but the pain was as intense as if they were still at the honeymoon stage. Sensing his distress, Jo held on to his hand and for a while they walked in silence, peacefully communing with the elements.

'Still,' said Lowell after some thought, 'it does seem a tad unfeeling. Forever on about him when you'd think she might show an iota of tact.'

Jo smiled, he was so sweet, but her mind had moved on to more urgent matters. They were approaching the bar where she'd first seen her stranger, and she felt the familiar rush of adrenaline and her heartbeat quickening as foolish hope rose in her throat. It was surely simple logic: if he'd been there once, then why not again? Or had he really been the Flying Dutchman, a hallucination brought on by the sun and too much rum, on top of the evaporation of her love for Sebastian?

It was practically noon so beers seemed in order. The same smiling barman served them and they settled, in isolated splendour, right at the water's edge with an umbrella to protect them from the worst of the sun's rays. Lowell kicked off his canvas espadrilles and soaked his feet in the foamy brine. Jo sensed him starting to unwind and was glad of it. Mourning was a long, relentless climb, which had to be achieved before the healing process could begin. She sighed with the pure pleasure of the moment on this white, deserted beach and closed her eyes. Maybe, if she wished extremely hard and promised to be good for the rest of her life, magic would happen again and her stranger would rematerialise.

'Did you ever find out any more about that guy?' enquired Lowell, as if reading her thoughts.

'Not a thing.'

'Shame. I sensed you were rather taken.'

'I was.' *So help me.*

'And we still don't know what Vincent discovered,' mused Lowell. He had been through Vincent's private papers and found his affairs more or less in order. Vincent had always been meticulous; clearing up after him had proved relatively easy.

'No, more's the pity. Something to do with his trip to Rotterdam. But what, I have absolutely no idea. Unless it was something to do with the boat.'

'Boat?'

'Don't you remember, the *Leonore*? Vincent's thinking was that she had to be registered somewhere. Rotterdam's a major international port. Maybe that's what took him there.'

'We'll never know now.' Lowell was sorrowful but able to contain it. This nice young woman, with her earnest eyes and unfeigned sympathy, was a welcome tonic to his battered spirits. He rose from his chair and went to rinse his feet. Back at the hotel they would be serving lunch and for once he felt his appetite returning.

'Come on,' he said. 'There has to be an answer somewhere. We'll think better with food inside us. Trust me.'

The others were sitting together on the terrace, round a table with a starched white cloth. Cora Louise waved as Jo and Lowell approached but Jo could see that Fontaine was looking quite peeved. Well, tough luck, baby; she could have come too if she'd not been so busy flirting with the Germans. Nevertheless, Jo pulled a chair up next to her and chatted brightly about the glorious scenery and the healthy trek they had just had.

'Come with us tomorrow,' she said, and meant it. 'There's this picturesque little bar several beaches along, totally deserted except for the barman.'

'Sounds too much like hard work for me,' said Fontaine but her eyes softened and she even began to smile. 'Shall I get you something from the buffet?' she asked Lowell and, before he could answer, was up and about it while he smiled resignedly and winked at Jo. There was simply no stopping her but it was all quite harmless. Jo grinned back and went to forage for herself.

Jessica was still chattering on about Sebastian, her eyes bright with happiness, a glow in her sallow cheeks. She had, she told them, wanted him to join them, but this year he'd been too busy with his exams and hospital duties. This was the first Jo had heard of it but she didn't say a word. The Greek break Jessica had planned had also fallen through and all she had managed to see of him these last few months was a few fleeting weekends in London when she had stayed with

Jo. And even then, if she were honest, he'd seemed perpetually preoccupied.

'The way he throws himself into his music,' she said proudly. 'Always practising, more dedicated than a professional.'

'He *is* a professional now,' objected Jo but Jessica, in full flow, didn't hear her.

'They're touring the Southern States next summer,' she said, 'so he'll be heading your way.' The Charleston Symphony was on his schedule and there were other bookings in Savannah and New Orleans. Jessica hoped to wangle an invitation; right on cue, Cora Louise came up trumps.

'What fun,' she said. 'Y'all must come visit with us on Tradd Street.' The epitome of the gracious Southern hostess, she could always be relied on to deliver the goods. Fontaine groaned silently. There went Mama again, promising the moon. Had she forgotten the gaping hole in the veranda, the fact that the house was practically threadbare? Not to mention the ignominy of doing paid work? How did she intend to explain all that away?

'I thought we might all convene in New York first,' continued Jessica brightly. 'They open in June at the Lincoln Centre.'

That too was news to Jo. Normally she followed every step of Sebastian's itinerary but lately they'd been largely out of touch. Now she knew why.

'A half-yearly reunion? What do you guys think of that? I know Sebastian wants me along,' bragged Jessica. 'I'm sure he'd be thrilled to see the rest of you too.'

Lowell was in favour, so that meant Fontaine too. She perked up at the prospect of a trip to New York, more so than ever since the horror of Vincent's death. She felt the need of some serious retail therapy and where better to do it than on Fifth Avenue? They were building a Saks back home on King Street but that was small beer compared to the original. And as for the shops in fashionable Charleston Place, forget it.

'The second we get back,' she told her mother eagerly, 'I'll call the Plaza and make our reservations.'

Jo wasn't certain she could get away, or even that she wanted to, but the others were insistent. An excuse for a get-together in Manhattan was altogether too good to miss; and this time they'd make sure that Merrily joined them. Jo softened. Right now, with Jessica behaving like the cat that got the cream, she felt more than ever in need of a Merrily fix. Besides, in truth, Sebastian deserved the support of his oldest friend. She had let him down once in the past; she was determined not to do it again.

'I'll see what I can manage,' she promised. She could always bunk down with Merrily, in that palatial pad that sounded as big as the Ritz. And East 62nd Street was slap bang in the heart of town, perfect for a fleeting visit to a city she had always wanted to see. Provided, of course, that Merrily was still there. Right now, in St Thomas, who knew what might be happening? Maybe they'd end up combining the New York jaunt with a wedding party in Ohio. Now *that* really would be one for the albums.

'Come on,' said Lowell softly in her ear. 'I took the precaution of renting the Jeep for the afternoon. Let's get the hell out of here.'

First, by mute assent, they drove back to the English Harbour and up the steep hill to the highest point which gave such spectacular views. The sea was flat and as blue as Jo had ever seen it and the harbour crowded with a profusion of luxurious boats.

'Look!' said Jo in excitement, pointing. Across the expanse of shimmering water tall sails were just visible, heading towards land. A fleet of them, vast and stately, making good time despite the balmy weather.

'The tall ships,' said Lowell. 'What perfect timing! Come on, let's get down there and watch them come in.'

Please, prayed Jo, her heart in her mouth, as giddy and light-headed as a teenager. They stood on the quay and watched the first boats arrive amid the sudden bustle and movement on the dock. Ropes were unfurled, anchors dropped and triumphant shouts came echoing across the water.

'Can you read their names?' asked Jo, frantically searching, even with her lenses unable to see that far.

'*Amazon, Sea Crest* and *Myrtle*,' said Lowell. 'No sign of the *Leonore,* I'm afraid. Not yet.'

And that was how it remained. They stayed for most of the afternoon, just watching, then climbed back into the Jeep and drove to the Mill Reef Club for tea.

'Are you certain they'll let us in?' asked Jo anxiously, perched on the edge of her seat with tension. Lowell smiled. With his name, pedigree and impeccable connections, there were few doors in the world he couldn't open.

'I guess so.' He slowed to speak to the smiling guard, dropped a name even Jo had heard of, and watched in satisfaction as the guard lowered the chain and nodded him through into the grounds of the exclusive club. Today the public rooms were bathed in sunlight and only a few guests sat in distant corners, talking quietly over afternoon tea or early cocktails. Lowell paused by the notice board in the lobby, to read a list of recent arrivals. A futile exercise, he realised immediately, since they had no idea of the mystery man's identity.

'The race is finishing right now,' he said, once they'd ordered and moved to seats by the window. 'Who knows what might be hoving into sight even as we sit here?'

Come on, Leonore, *please show yourself*, urged Jo silently. But, alas, she never did. As dusk began to gather they made their way thoughtfully back to the hotel.

'Well, no one can say we didn't try,' said Lowell, consolingly. 'But I'm sorry we didn't find him. I know how much it must mean.'

Fool, thought Jo that night as she undressed. Luckily Lowell was such a gent she knew he'd not make fun of her. Though she certainly deserved it, acting like a child; losing her heart so badly to a man she hardly knew. Not like Merrily, she reflected, as she slid beneath the single sheet and flicked off the lamp. She, at least, would be having a holiday to remember. Jo envied her her happiness. The second she got home, she would call New York and catch up on all the details.

At that very moment, back in New York, Merrily sat motionless at the window, bourbon in hand, moodily watching snow drift across Madison Avenue. All around her were half-filled packing cases containing her clothes, books and china. Tomorrow morning early, removal men were coming to transport her, lock, stock and barrel, out of this classy building and across town to a far less prestigious address. Just hours before they were due to leave, Dimitri had left a message on her machine to say there was a crisis on the coast and that the trip would have to be postponed.

'Sorry, doll,' he had breezed, 'but I guess that's the way the cookie crumbles. Have a good holiday and I'll call you when

I'm back.' She'd had no time to tell him just how things were in her life, to explain she was having to move and why. She had mulled it over for several days while she tried to persuade the exclusive stores to refund the cost of the clothes she was returning. Then, with a couple of strong drinks inside her, she screwed up the courage to call the Pierre.

'Sorry, ma'm,' said an impersonal switchboard operator. 'We have no one of that name staying here.'

20

'You know what you should do with this room?'

'Rip it apart and start all over again?'

Jessica laughed. She was standing in the middle of Jo's second bedroom, in jeans and a faded sorrel shirt of Sebastian's that went miraculously with her marmalade hair. It was Sunday afternoon and they'd just cleared away lunch. Sebastian was off to some quiet place with his flute, leaving the girls to get to grips with the living-space.

'Nothing that drastic. Simply a matter of readjustment with, perhaps, a lick or two of paint.'

All Jo's papers had been moved, as it was, and were now stacked tidily in the tiny hall, ready to be stashed in the cupboard under the sink. Once Jo had been through them one more time to check what might be discarded altogether. It was a lot of work but worth it, she now realised. This sort of drastic spring-clean was occasionally essential; she was fortunate to have the methodical Jessica to oversee it. The narrow ottoman had been pulled out from the wall and its dusty red upholstery covered with an orange paisley throw.

'You could start by replacing that uncomfortable bed. A properly sprung sofa bed should not be beyond your means. Not if you go to the Sofa Bed Centre or, better still, to the Lots Road auction rooms.' Jessica had certainly done her market research.

Jo demurred. 'I'm not sure that I'd fancy a second-hand bed.' Then realised, as she spoke, that once again she'd allowed Jessica to win. Oh well. High time she faced up to being an adult and having a proper, grown-up spare bedroom instead of a study-cum-boxroom-cum-den. She grinned.

'Then what?'

Jessica pondered. 'If you moved the desk away from the window you'd have room for an armchair, perhaps even two. And a portable telly that could stand over there – on the corner of the desk once you've shoved it next to the door.' She smiled. 'That's it. And a huge mirror on the opposite wall to add depth to the room and give it more light. And a few extra shelves might come in handy too. Now all we need think about is colours. If we hurry we can get to Homebase before they close.'

'Hang on, it's Sunday. And I really haven't the energy.' Jo's single day off and Jessica had hijacked it. And now she was suggesting an exorbitant investment of cash Jo didn't have. But Jessica was moving on, eyes ablaze with the fervour of refurbishment. Whatever was she going to suggest next? An extended wardrobe, probably, to cater for her own influx of clothes. As well as a second bathroom no doubt, though, luckily, there wasn't room for one. It was lovely having Jessica here at weekends, particularly since it meant seeing more of Sebastian too, but this makeover of the flat was precipitant, to say the least, especially since Jo had always liked it as it was.

They compromised by making a pot of coffee and carrying it back to the living room to watch *Farewell to Arms* and catch up on the papers. After that, they'd take a stroll down the King's Road. Sundays in Chelsea were always enjoyable, a lot more lively than Cheltenham or Bath. Habitat might be open and also the new Heal's. And Designer's Guild, though that was way beyond Jo's means. What she really loved was the elegant Shaker shop, though that, at present, was definitely out of the question. One day, maybe, when she had more money and someone significant to share the costs. Which brought her back inevitably to her dream and the ache in her heart that never quite went away.

'What are your plans for tonight?' she asked and Jessica, deep in the Books section, simply smiled and said that depended on Sebastian.

'Crikey!' he said, as he spun through the door at seven and crashed on the sofa which Jo had just vacated. 'That was one tough session, I can tell you, chaps!'

'Where've you been?'

'To the maestro's house for an impromptu rehearsal, only his manager was there and he's one hard dude. I'm not kidding. Papers to sign and questions to answer. All of a sudden it's become heavily contractual. They say his team go around the record shops and break the fingers of the managers who don't hit target. I thought that was all a cod until I met him. Jesus, what a scary guy. Let's hope he stays in the background, where he belongs. Who needs a Rottweiler when making music?'

He was serious. Jo laughed.

'I've not heard you mention him before. What's his name?'

'Conrad Silver and the less said about him, the better. Came in last night on the red-eye to make trouble. A nastier piece of work I don't think I've ever encountered.'

'How's that?' Jo was instantly curious. It was not like Sebastian to wax so dramatic.

'Oh you know the type. Handsome, suave, impossibly condescending. Wearing a seven-thousand-dollar suit and strutting his stuff as though he were the one with the talent. Whereas, like all agents, all he really is is a parasite.' It was clear Sebastian hadn't taken to him.

'Poor sweetie.' Instantly Jessica was over there, perched on his knee, smoothing his hair and fiddling with his tie. 'Come and have a lie-down, I am sure you could use one.'

Sebastian grinned but didn't object. He cocked one eyebrow at the highly amused Jo, then followed Jessica from the room like a lamb.

'I'll cook supper. What do you feel like?' asked Jo but all she heard was the silent closing of the spare-room door. Her house guest was in control; guess she'd just have to wait till they emerged. But she'd feel a lot better if they weren't quite so exclusive. She missed having Sebastian to herself.

She compromised by calling Merrily but all she got was another tale of misery and woe. She was in the new place and more or less settled, if settled was what you could call it in a dump like that. There was still no word from Dimitri. Not that he could track her down now even if he wanted to; she had quite inadvertently effectively covered her tracks, as he had apparently done with his.

'Surely there's someone the two of you know in common,' said Jo.

'No.' He had always insisted on keeping her to himself. At the time Merrily had thought it romantic; now she saw it in a far more sinister light.

'And they still have no knowledge of him at the Pierre?' Despite Vincent's initial reservations, that did seem awfully odd.

'Nope.' She'd called several times, using different personas; had even asked a friend to try for her. Zilch. Dimitri Romanov, whoever he really was, appeared to have evaporated into thin air. 'You know something? I've a nasty feeling he was only using me for my Chase connections.'

Illicit money-laundering – what Vincent and Lowell had feared but never actually said. Jo felt bad. But, quite apart from Dimitri, she worried about Merrily's future. Now that the truth was beginning to emerge, she was aghast at what her friend had been through. Being publicly humiliated and kicked out of such a high-flying job was worse than anything she could imagine, and all without any warning. At least in the medical profession you had to do something pretty dire to get the chop. From what she knew of Merrily's performance, it had been one success after another until now. It sounded distinctly like sexual harassment; Merrily had told her about the loathsome Kaminsky and his slimy little ways. But the mood she was in these days, there was little point in pursuing it. When it came to the crunch, it was his word against hers and Jo knew how dicey that could be. Besides, it was probably too late.

'Hang on in there, kid,' was all she could think of to say. 'Jobs are like taxis, there's always another one behind.'

'Not these days,' snorted Merrily glumly. 'Right now downsizing is the most emotive word in America. Everyone is terrified and clinging on like grim death. The same applies to boyfriends,' she added sourly. 'Once you're past thirty.'

She did sound bleak. Jo had an impulse to leap on a plane and go to comfort her; instead she tried to make her laugh by telling her, *sotto voce*, about the recent invasion of Jessica. But Merrily was not amused. She had never really warmed to 'the Marmalade Cat', as she'd dubbed her, and this latest piece of what looked like pure selfishness only endorsed what she'd thought all along. First she'd coerced Jo's boyfriend; now she was invading her home. Before Jo knew it, she'd be wearing her clothes and doubtless borrowing her car. Jo laughed but couldn't argue, not at the moment. Next door Jessica and Sebastian were as silent as the dead. She only hoped they weren't lying there listening to her talk.

'Bye now,' she whispered, suddenly paranoid. 'Take care and be sure to ring me when there's news. I have to go and cook supper for my guests. Never a dull moment for a busy landlady!'

When she got home the following night, exhausted after a particularly gruelling day and dying only to kick off her shoes, pour herself some wine and relax on the sofa, Jo was startled to open her bedroom door and find her furniture all moved around. The bed had been shifted from the window into the corner, to make room for her desk. Which meant she could only just open her wardrobe door, and the chair on which she liked to sit and read was crammed in between the two big pieces of furniture so that she couldn't possibly use it. *What the . . . ?*

'An improvement, don't you think?' said Jessica cheerily from behind her. She was draped in one of Jo's big, fluffy bath towels, flushed from a leisurely hour in the tub. Lute music was playing softly from the darkened room behind her and Jo could smell the scent of sandalwood candles issuing forth on a cloud of steam. She bit back her irritation.

'We thought it would give you more privacy,' said Jessica. 'So you can study without us disturbing you.'

'Thanks,' said Jo, throwing her coat on the bed. 'Very thoughtful of you, I'm sure.'

But Jessica was back in the bathroom, crooning softly to the pervasive music as she pottered around and did fancy things to her hair.

Jo opened the fridge but the last bottle of wine was half-empty. It was too late now to go out and buy more; besides, she couldn't face all those stairs again.

'Are you in for supper?' she shouted, trying hard to suppress the anger in her voice, but Jessica called back that she was meeting Sebastian.

'Thought I'd get out from under your feet for a change,' she said cheerfully, when she reappeared, wearing his dressing-gown. It was far too large for her but she'd rolled up the sleeves and, with the cord knotted twice round her trim little waist, she did look distinctly appealing. *Hmm*, thought Jo grumpily, since it was the one she'd bought him herself last Christmas. Did this woman have no scruples at all? She always bragged that she travelled light; on closer acquaintance the reason became obvious.

Jo was in the kitchen, stirring eggs, when Jessica came in, fully dressed, to wish her goodnight. 'I'll probably be back late,' she said. 'Seb's taking me to a concert, then on to a party. Don't wait up.'

As if she would. Jo ate her frugal supper in a frightening rage and decided to give herself an early night. The way she was feeling, there was no point in trying to study. She was far too upset to be able to concentrate. Inspired by Jessica, she unearthed some expensive bath oil, then carried her transistor and a book into the bathroom to soak away some of her angst. If Jessica was going to be late, there was no chance of being disturbed. For such small mercies, let her at least be grateful. She turned on the tap but the water was stone cold. Her bloody house guest had emptied the tank.

Jo was studying, glad for once of the silence, when there came a timid tap on her door. It was Jessica, whom she'd thought was still out.

'Mind if I come in?' Jessica was carrying a Conran carrier and looked apprehensive, even scared. Suppressing a sigh, Jo closed her book and flashed a bright smile at her friend.

'Of course, silly. When did you have to knock? And what time is it?' The light was fading fast but she hadn't noticed. Almost eight, wherever had the hours gone? 'Why don't we both have a drink?'

'I'll do it.' Jessica was out and back again with a bottle within seconds. Nice wine, already chilled, with two elegant glasses Jo hadn't seen before.

'What's the toast?' She was intrigued.

'You, you chump, for being such a brick. For putting up with me all these weeks and letting me push you around.' Jessica ran her fingers through her gold-streaked hair and looked as though she had weightier matters on her mind. The shadows beneath her eyes were more pronounced; if anything, she seemed a little nervous. 'Don't think I don't know my own little foibles. I must be driving you mad.'

Jo was touched. 'Don't even mention it,' she said accepting a glass of wine and raising it to her friend. 'You know what they say, *mea casa, sua casa*. The pleasure's all mine, I assure you. As house guests go, you're the best.' She felt dreadful for telling such a porky but what else could she do? All these weeks she'd been resenting Jessica only to find that the consciousness had been there all along.

'It's just that being close to you makes me feel closer to Seb.' Jessica was faltering now and positively embarrassed. She reached into the Conran carrier and produced a tissue-wrapped package.

'Open it,' she said and watched while Jo fumbled through the wrappings and produced two elegant pewter candle-sticks, the very last word in contemporary chic. They were wonderful.

'They're for your bedroom,' said Jessica, watching her. 'Or for anywhere else you care to put them, of course. It's still your flat. Don't think I don't know it.'

'You're a dear and you shouldn't have,' said Jo, rising to kiss her. The candlesticks were expensive; she knew Jessica couldn't afford them. The gesture made her warm inside and fiercely keen to make up for her earlier intolerance. This was her friend, after all, and the woman Sebastian was dating. The odds were she'd be around for a long time, permanently if Jessica had her way.

'I can't get over how generous you've been,' said Jessica, reading her thoughts. 'I feel dreadful grabbing your boyfriend like that. All I can say is it wasn't intended. It's just that we seemed so right for each other and he assured me you didn't mind.' She was almost pleading.

'Nor do I,' said Jo staunchly, suddenly meaning every word. Jessica was a poor, sad creature at times, deprived all her childhood of a normal loving relationship. If she was over-inclined to close in on the happiness of others, it was nobody's fault but the parents who had so thoughtlessly died.

'Don't give it another thought,' she said, meaning it. 'Sebastian and I will always be buddies; I'm only glad he's found someone else splendid to love.'

And in her heart she vowed to make it up to Jessica in little ways. Family, after all, was an accident of birth; as the saying went, thank God you could choose your friends.

Jo was still hard at work on Saturday afternoon when Jessica and Sebastian came in from the match. It was raining hard and Jessica was wearing Sebastian's blue and white Chelsea supporters' scarf round her nose with her hair a wet tangle that rather became her. All she wanted to talk about was the football.

'How was it?' Normally Jo was genuinely interested; there was a time when it was her he would honour with a ticket. But all of a sudden Jessica had become sports mad. Knew the names of the players and the positions in which they played; had even apparently studied form or, at least, read a couple of in-depth newspaper analyses. She burbled on about Ruud Gullit until Jo had a sudden impulse to slug her. Saintly resolutions were all very well, but there were times when Jessica was altogether too much. Sebastian, warming his hands on the radiator, was watching her and laughing. Jo grinned back.

The thing was, the flat was too cramped for the three of them. But Jo, not wishing to appear inhospitable, hardly liked to mention that. Why they couldn't spend more time in Sebastian's bachelor quarters in Gordon Square, she really didn't know. Except that Sebastian shared with two others and was also probably far too fly to allow Jessica over the threshold on anything more than a casual basis. Though, she had to admit it, he did seem fairly besotted.

Jessica went into the kitchen to make the tea and came back crunching a biscuit. She looked sexy and waif-like in Sebastian's cricket sweater with her delicate fingers barely showing under the sleeves. Apparently incapable of leaving him alone, she went to rest her head against his chest, strewing crumbs on the carpet as she ate. Sebastian ruffled her damp hair indulgently.

'My little carrot-top,' he said fondly, causing Jessica to giggle and then choke. She coughed and wheezed as the biscuit went down the wrong way, until Sebastian swung her round and caught her roughly from behind, wrapping his arms around her upper abdomen and joining his hands below her rib-cage. With a sudden jerk, he pressed his balled fist into her stomach, causing her to double up sharply and cough up the remainder of the biscuit, her hair clouding forward over her face. She had turned positively blue and was panting with fright as she tottered to a chair to recover. Jo leapt to her side to check she was all right then shot into the kitchen to fetch her a glass of water.

'Drink this and then stay quiet for a moment.' It was frighteningly easy to choke; the oesophagus was inefficiently narrow.

'Right,' said Sebastian proudly, once he'd reassured himself that the crisis was past. 'What's that action called, doctor? You have one minute to answer.'

'Heimlich Manoeuvre. Give me some credit, please.' They'd done it in first year, though she'd never had to use it. It was interesting to see a live demonstration, though. Jessica was fortunate Sebastian had been so alert. Left to herself, she wasn't at all sure she'd have remembered what to do.

'It just goes to show that you need all your wits about you. One minute more and Jessica could have been a goner.'

243

'Oh, stop!' Jessica didn't like it when they started to get medical. Or was it, Jo wondered, that she hated to lose the limelight? She watched Jessica thoughtfully as she towelled her hair dry and some dim memory flickered fleetingly and was gone.

Concentrated practice was what Richard Stanford Palmer preached and, all of a sudden, Tom had little time for almost anything else. He had to move to London, to attend the Royal College of Music, and Jessica found herself a job in Cheltenham, which was as close as she could get to being with him. Life became a mundane routine of commuter trains and sordid lodgings, and Tom lost a lot of his sparkle as he drove himself harder in order to reach the maestro's exacting standards. Romance flew out of the window though love remained. It wasn't at all what they'd planned, though Tom was ecstatic at the progress of his career.

'You need some time off,' said Jessica that winter. 'You can't work all the time, you know what they say.'

But Worldwide Concerts was planning a glittering tour and if Tom made the grade, there was a good chance he'd be included.

'Can't risk letting this one slip by,' he had said regretfully. 'Richard says now is the time to slog my guts out. If I don't make it soon, I'll not even get on the ladder. Perhaps after Christmas, if I don't get selected . . .'

And that was it, at least for a while. Jessica was obliged to bite back her frustration and continue with the lonely waiting game.

'Mightn't it be cosier if the two of you were permanently

under one roof? I mean, it's great having Jessica here . . .' She hated to bring up the subject so crassly but this was one of her rare moments alone with Sebastian, and Jo was loath to waste it. It was Jessica's turn to make supper and she had popped off down to the Fulham Road to buy some fresh pasta from Luigi's. To go, no doubt, with her stalwart courgette and bacon sauce. Jessica's repertoire risked becoming predictable.

'But?' Sebastian looked startled, even shocked.

'But the reason I choose to live alone is that I actually like my own company.' There, it was out; she felt all the better for it. And she felt no shame at all at contradicting the white lie she'd told, on an impulse, to Jessica.

For several months Jessica had been flitting in and out and, little by little, eroding Jo's space. Her toothbrush and flannel were permanently in the bathroom, while her robe (or Sebastian's) hung on the inside of the door. The furniture had all been swapped around and a couple of faded tapestry cushions had found their way in unannounced and now graced the sofa. Which was all very well but they weren't to Jo's taste. Jessica's books were piled high on the coffee table and her CDs littered the carpet. Now she was talking about changing the decor. Sudden alarm took a grip on Jo; if she didn't act quickly, who knew where it might lead? Already she was forced to listen to the World Service in the morning instead of her favourite Radio 4 and when she rushed home one night for a rerun of *Hill Street Blues*, Jessica was there already, engrossed in a documentary on Zubin Mehta.

This was her moment to strike out in her own defence but she could see at a glance that Sebastian wouldn't be much help. He was clutching the colour supplement with whitening knuckles and the expression on his face made Jo lose her stern resolve and break, instead, into peals of helpless laughter. That was men for you every time, pathetic and useless. Why could they never finish what they started? But Jo was used to clearing up Sebastian's messes and, deep inside, had to admit to a small twinge of relief.

'So what do you intend to do?' she said, settling down for a heart-to-heart with one ear cocked for the door.

'God knows.' Sebastian closed the magazine in relief and dropped it untidily on the pile at his feet. 'Jessica's a sweetheart, and I really do mean that, but lately things seem to be getting out of hand.'

'To put it mildly.' Jo was still laughing and, after a moment, Sebastian joined her. It was a relief to get it out into the open. He should have known that good old Jo would turn out to be the brick she always had been. Why on earth had he ever strayed? With a little more effort he could surely have held on to her. But this problem was urgent; soon Jessica would be back.

'I honestly don't know what I'm going to do. There's not room for her in Gordon Square, what with Guy and Ravi and their various hangers-on. And in June, remember, I'm off to the States.'

He looked at her appealingly with the familiar boyish charm but this time Jo hardened her heart and refused to be drawn in.

'She's not staying here. It's your mess, you started it. Now it's up to you to sort it out. Before it's too late.'

There wasn't the slightest doubt in Sebastian's mind, Richard Stanford Palmer came first. But looking at Jessica, with her pale, transparent skin and the light of pure devotion shining in her eyes, his courage deserted him one more time and he hadn't the heart to disillusion her.

'Shouldn't you be looking for a place of your own, old thing?' he had tried. 'It's not really fair on Jo, having both of us under her feet all the time.' But the look that crossed Jessica's face at the mention of Jo warned him to tread warily. Jo might be taking this new arrangement in good heart; Jessica certainly wasn't.

'Jo should find herself a man of her own,' she had said acerbically. 'She's getting quite old maidish with her solitary routines. And she works far too hard.'

The last was undoubtedly true and Sebastian had broached it many times. But Jo's dedication was unswervable. In a few years she had become a devoted GP.

'They really need me,' she had tried to explain. Then couldn't resist adding: 'Which is more than anyone can say for you. I can't believe the hospital's letting you go off on this gig.' Sebastian was coming up to his psychiatry finals; surely not the time to be taking a sabbatical.

'This just happens to be more important,' he had told her. 'The chance of a lifetime, too good to miss. Do you realise, this will put me right into the big time, musically speaking. Richard Stanford Palmer is simply the best.'

'So you keep telling me. Well, all I can say is you must be a damn fine musician.'

'You know something,' said Sebastian confidently, eyes ablaze with manic enthusiasm, 'I'm a bloody good psychiatrist too.'

He didn't feel so confident now, with Jessica thumping around Jo's flat, blindly sorting herself out while he waited to take her out. Perhaps he had been a little harsh, suggesting she find herself a place of her own, but he'd only spoken the truth. It was his fault she was spending so much time with Jo and, before he jetted off, he had to sort things out. Besides, if she had her own flat, it would be better for them all and less embarrassing where his friendship with Jo was concerned. That was something he was determined not to damage, if it wasn't already too late. But he doubted Jessica would see it that way.

'Come on,' he called, glancing at his watch. 'If you don't get a move on, we'll miss the main picture.'

Then he looked up, startled, as Jessica appeared before him, wearing a pair of his old pyjamas, the sleeves rolled up over her bony wrists. Her face was drawn and drained of all colour, chicken-pale with a miserable, drippy nose.

'You don't understand,' she said in an anguished voice. 'I love you, I love you, and can't bear to be on my own again!'

Then she hurled herself against his chest, hammering him hard with frantic fists, and burst abruptly into great juddering sobs.

Despite the maestro's edicts and the ferocity of his management, they'd managed eventually to sneak a few days' break. Tom had been quite nervous but Jessica had remained adamant; if this slightly oddball relationship were to survive, they needed time to themselves, and space.

'You'll see,' she'd said, lying beside him that first night. 'With a little sunshine and relaxation, you'll soon have things back into proper perspective.'

Alas, it was not be. However they did it, they had managed to track them down and Tom was ordered back to base on the threat of breach of contract. She'd begged, she'd pleaded, but all to no avail. As with Sebastian, when it came to the crunch, music came first with Tom. Richard Stanford Palmer, as always, took precedence; they were forced once again to put their romance on hold. And less than twenty-four hours later, Tom was dead.

21

The new apartment wasn't half as bad as Jo had expected, though it might prove a bit of a tight fit for the two of them. Still, she was only planning to stay a few nights and nothing could equal having to share with Jessica. It was really just one large studio with a neatly planned kitchen and serviceable bathroom, the sort you find in middle-of-the-range hotels. By far its best feature, in Merrily's opinion, was the short corridor of walk-in closets which connected the main living area to the bathroom. Plus a doorman, really an essential in a city this tough.

'You ought to have seen the last place,' lamented Merrily as Jo hung her raincoat in her own bit of closet and shoved her bulky holdall out of sight. Like Jessica, she travelled light but was also self-sufficient. All she needed from her hostess was the use of a hair dryer and, perhaps, an iron. She turned and gave her a grateful hug.

'Don't you worry, this is perfect. You should see the space I've got at home. And before you know it, you'll be back on your feet again. Wait and see.'

She couldn't contain her excitement at actually being here in New York, a city she had always longed to see. They strolled a couple of blocks up to Second Avenue for a late brunch in an unpretentious bistro. The area was far less daunting than she had imagined, full of ordinary residents going about their business, walking their dogs and carrying home brown paper bags of groceries, and rows of enticing little ethnic shops which shouted out to be explored. More like Fulham than she had expected. Whatever Merrily's feelings about leaving Madison Avenue, here Jo felt immediately at home.

'One thing they say is an absolute must,' she said, digging into an outsized burger and chips, washed down by a glass of the rough house red, 'is the Circle Line boat trip around the island.'

Merrily groaned. In all the years she had lived in this city, she had not yet succumbed to its obvious tourist attractions. Now, with Jo in town on her very first visit, she supposed she might have to break the habit of a lifetime. Oh well, right now she had little else to do and it might help to take her mind off other things.

'If you insist,' she growled, mock-severely, 'though I warn you, at this time of year it'll be thick with tourists. Loads of fat-assed visitors from the Midwest, herding kids crunching popcorn and dribbling ice-cream.'

Jo laughed. 'Maybe we should ask Jessica to join us. It's her first visit too.'

Merrily looked startled. She'd forgotten all about her. 'Where the hell is she?' she asked.

'With Sebastian at the Hotel Ansonia, bunking down with

a couple of fellow musicians. They arrived a couple of days ago. I'm surprised she hasn't called.'

Merrily wasn't but she kept that to herself.

'So they're still together,' she said, amazed. 'I'd rather imagined they'd have split by now.' However hard she tried, Merrily still couldn't condone Jessica's behaviour, muscling in on Jo's man despite Jo's protests that she really didn't mind, that the couple thing was over. There was a code of honour which Jessica had ignored, that you didn't pick up the leftovers from the table of a friend. To Merrily's mind, she was well out of order. Not a person to trust long time.

'They seem quite happy,' said Jo quite calmly. 'They are travelling together so apparently all is well.' Though what well was, she was not prepared to say. She remembered Sebastian's stricken face last time they'd met, then shrugged it aside. Not her business, nor Merrily's either. Not any more.

Michael's Pub was more Merrily's scene so the following night, while they waited for the music to begin, the three girls sat huddled round a tiny table, shouting to be heard above the increasing din. Jessica looked tense and a trifle thinner, though her eyes were friendly and her smile as bright as ever. Sebastian, she reported, was still closeted with the maestro at the rehearsal rooms, frantically running through the opening programme a couple more times.

'He really works them hard,' she said. 'But this tour should be the making of Seb.'

As a flautist, maybe, but not as a doctor. Privately Jo still disapproved since she couldn't help thinking his medical career should come first.

'So how come you're not there too, holding his hand?' asked Merrily. From what she had heard, Jessica rarely left his side. With her own intense interest in all things musical, she should be right in her element at the Lincoln Centre. But Merrily's question was secretly barbed; she was so much enjoying her time with Jo, she resented this intrusion into their cosy twosome. She had never really quite hit it off with Jessica; found her too fey, too precious to be real. Jessica smiled a tad smugly and waved her hands in that affected way she had.

'I can't be with him all the time, poor love. He's far too involved in making wonderful music and Richard prefers them not to be distracted.'

Richard, thought Merrily acidly. 'So you know this paragon, do you?' she asked. She had heard Jo's jokes and was curious about him. 'Tell us, is he all he's cracked up to be? Is it true he walks on water?'

Jo gave a short, sharp snort of delight, which she covered up by blowing bubbles through her straw. She loved to hear someone else poking fun at Sebastian's idol. It was an ingrained habit, born of years of intimacy, but Jessica was overdoing it and starting to get up her nose. *Wanker* was the word that leapt immediately to her mind, though Jo would never be that coarse. Not out loud. She didn't mean to belittle Sebastian's huge achievements but friendship like theirs was founded on something solid. And that included cutting through the crap, though just try explaining that to Jessica.

Jessica was momentarily silenced. She loved to talk about Sebastian, however, so it wasn't long before she was back on the defence.

'I have met him, actually,' she told them archly, 'though it was so long ago, I doubt he'd remember.' Not like Jessica to be quite so self-effacing; normally she liked to brag and drop illustrious names. 'It's really his management that is causing all the trouble. They behave like mafiosi, absolutely terrifying, a gang of mindless bouncers, supposedly protecting the players.' She laughed nervously. 'Even from their nearest and dearest.' She wasn't faking either; Merrily was suddenly alert.

The colour had faded from Jessica's wan cheeks and she chewed a hang-nail abstractedly. Just the mention of that unsavoury bunch of thugs brought back memories she would sooner suppress. Tom and her life with him were now part of the past; let the poor fellow remain there and rest in peace. Once she had believed she could never recover from that crippling experience but lately things had begun to change and the bitterness was draining away. Sebastian had brought new meaning into her life; for the first time in years, she had someone worthwhile to live for and an exciting new future to plan. This time nothing was going to mar the relationship; Jessica was there to protect him from every outside force.

Her thoughts were interrupted as Woody Allen strolled on to the stage with his clarinet and the room broke into rapturous applause.

The next few days were a whirl of sightseeing and shopping and Jo risked wearing her shoes out, walking for miles, dragging along with her a protesting Merrily.

'Jesus,' Merrily gasped, panting with exertion. 'Haven't walked like this in years, not since I left Ohio.' Secretly, though, she was having the time of her life. The June air was fresh and balmy and the weather so warm they wore only their lightest clothes. After years of long hours, confined in a hermetically sealed office, she wasn't used to the feel of sunshine on her skin. She felt like a newly released prisoner or a plant in the sun after too long in the shade.

'Do you good,' said Jo briskly. 'Plenty of exercise and Vitamin E. Should save you a packet at the health club, too, if only you'd learn to cut down on taxis.'

She was nearer the mark than she could possibly realise but Merrily was resilient enough not to let it show. And, indeed, her calves felt firmer and her butt a little tighter; keep this up and she'd be back to a size eight in no time. For the first time in ages, she found she was having fun; straightforward, girlie fun with a compatible kindred spirit. They tried on clothes and tested make-up, visited the Museum of Modern Art, took the ferry to Staten Island, shared a ride in a hansom cab. Even whizzed to the top of the Empire State Building and stood there marvelling at the stupendous view . . .

'Remember *Sleepless in Seattle*,' said Jo with eyes on stalks. 'Maybe he's out there somewhere, your Prince Charming, dreaming of you and waiting for you to find him.'

'If he is he can shove it,' said Merrily harshly. The last few months had by no means been a joke; only the restorative presence of Jo gave her the spirit to laugh at all. She'd been surprisingly restrained about Dimitri up till now and managed hardly to mention his name. The hurt went so deep, she preferred to bottle it up, she feared she might really lose control if she once allowed Jo to glimpse the extent of her misery. Until one evening, when she'd had too much to drink, and ended up screaming her heart out.

'I really believed he loved me,' she bawled. 'When all the time the bastard was just using me. Because of my Chase connections.'

'Oh, come on, lovie, you can't know that. There's probably another explanation entirely, a hidden agenda you're just not aware of.' Married would be Jo's personal shrewd guess, though she was far too caring ever to say so. All she knew was that Lowell and Vincent hadn't approved, and they were both experts at character analysis. It had all been too much of a fairytale to ring true; what a depressing comment on contemporary life.

'He picked me up and used me, then tossed me aside like a used condom.' Merrily was crying in earnest now, her face red and ugly like an outraged child's. 'And you know the worst part? I really thought I had it sewn up, was so damn smart. Little Miss Manhattan High-flyer who had seen it all and could take anything in her stride. Then along comes this jerk and craps all over me. Sod the bastard, may he rot in hell!'

That was more like it; getting mad was healthier. Jo gave her a hug, then put on some water for coffee. Far better for Merrily than the wine she was consuming. She was bound to see things more rationally in the morning.

Merrily was on edge with nerves. She'd had a call from a prestigious firm of head-hunters, keen to see her as soon as possible. It could mean a job, a whole new beginning. The appointment was for four so she arranged to meet Jo later and then play the rest of the evening by ear.

'How do I look?' It was weeks since she'd had a real reason to dress up; the light navy linen with its mint-green camisole was fresh and smart and ultra-chic, and the recently lost pounds made it fit that much better.

'A million dollars,' said Jo approvingly. 'Wear your Paloma Picasso earrings and they won't know what's hit them.' She was relieved to see Merrily animated again. The great grey eyes were alive with hope. With luck, this time something good would come of it.

'Meet me at the *Café des Artistes*,' said Merrily, checking her purse. 'There's loads of stuff we can do in that area, take in a movie or just have a quiet meal.' She grinned. 'It all depends on the mood I'm in.' She had no idea how long she would be but six seemed a likely compromise. Jo hated entering bars on her own, a throwback to her student days, but the restaurant was famous and suitably well placed. And at least she'd be under cover and sitting down.

'Good luck!' called Jo gaily as Merrily left. 'Remember you're a star and then you can't go wrong.' A job was what Merrily needed more than anything; then she could start thinking about restructuring her life.

Jo spent a leisurely two hours in the Frick Museum then, uplifted by its peace and elegant other-worldliness, sauntered on down Fifth Avenue in the sunshine and across the road to the Plaza for tea. This was certainly the life, a total contrast to her normal daily scramble. Soon the rest of the gang would be turning up too, to join in the celebrations for Sebastian's big night. After she had indulged in some wicked Black Forest gâteau, she continued her stroll up Columbus Avenue to the Avery Fisher Hall to check out the posters. Then, on a further block to their meeting place; she willed Merrily, for once, to be on time.

As it happened, she need not have worried. The bar was dimly lit and virtually deserted. She carefully chose a corner booth where she could see but not be seen and settled down with a spritzer to catch her breath and watch the world go by, all the while keeping out a watchful eye for Merrily. She was sad for her friend's unhappiness but sensed that, in the long run, she'd be better off without that particular disruptive presence in her life. She remembered her boasting about cocaine and the sexual antics they got up to when they were stoned. Though by no means a prude, Jo was still fairly conventional; the drug scene had always been anathema to her and was likely to remain that way.

On the far side of the room a group of men was assembling and their laughter and good spirits floated across to where she sat. They all wore tuxedos, presumably forgathering for some special event and, for one startled moment, she fancied she saw among them the dark, satanic features of Prince Romanov himself, eyes screwed up with merriment, laughing fit to bust. Then the group shifted and he was eclipsed. Jo shuffled around to get a better view, then dismissed him sternly as pure imagination.

She had, after all, only ever seen him once, on that memorable night at the Mill Reef Club, and then for a matter of seconds. She remembered the lean, dark, smiling face above the crisp white dress-shirt with its diamond studs, and the look of besotted rapture on Merrily's face as he took her hand and drew her into the dance. He'd been overshadowed then, in fact as well as memory, by a taller, fairer presence in glinting gold-rimmed spectacles, who had just as effectively snatched Jo's heart then trampled it underfoot in similar cavalier fashion.

And then, quite suddenly, there he was before her, unmistakably her stranger, in the centre of the group. He was leaning against a table with his face partially obscured but there was no way Jo could forget that noble forehead or fine patrician nose. His hair was longer than the last time she'd seen him and his small, rimless spectacles glinted in the lamplight. Jo's heart started hammering and she felt positively faint; if only Merrily would make her appearance and tell her what to do.

Already they were starting to move. Scared of losing him again, Jo acted right out of character. Without a second thought, she shot from her hidden booth and propelled herself across the room towards him.

'Hi!' she said, feeling gawky and foolish. 'Remember me?'

They all turned to stare at her and she wished the floor would swallow her up. How could she have been so crass; what on earth would he think of her now? He turned towards her slowly, frowning for a second, then held out his hand to her with a beaming, welcoming smile.

'Well, I'll be blowed! If it isn't the elusive Miss Lyndhurst, the girl with the mismatched eyes.' He stretched towards her and reeled her in, then held her loosely encircled by his arm as he introduced her round. 'I discovered this mermaid on a tropical island. How come you're not there now?'

Feeling embarrassed and immeasurably silly, Jo stood lumpishly beside him, racking her brains for a snazzy riposte, terribly afraid she was about to cry. She couldn't see Dimitri any more but that made no difference; they were all of them laughing now, apparently at her. Her courage deserted her.

'I'm sorry,' she mumbled, disentangling herself. 'I have to go. I'm meeting someone.'

Then she ducked beneath his arm and ran blindly out into the street, where she promptly hurtled headlong into someone laden with packages, who dropped them, cursing roundly, and grabbed instead at her arm.

'Jesus Christ!' said Merrily urgently. 'What the hell's going on?'

'We've got to get out of here!' said Jo frantically, as they scrambled around on the sidewalk. Then she felt a firm hand descend on her shoulder and watched the wonder on Merrily's face before she turned slowly to confront him.

'I'm sorry,' he said as he helped her to her feet. 'That was rude of me and unwarranted. It was just that you took me by surprise.' He wore a white silk scarf slung casually about his neck, over an expensive top-coat beneath which she glimpsed white tie and tails. His eyes behind the small, clear lenses were filled with concern and, now that she saw him in proper light, he was even more gorgeous than in her dreams. Tall and poised, elegant and at ease; no wonder Merrily stared.

'Look,' he said, glancing rapidly at his watch, 'there's loads I need to say to you but I really do have to go.' He patted his pockets as though looking for something and swore softly under his breath as he failed to find it.

'Hang on a second.' He shot back into the *Café des Artistes* and returned, scribbling something on a card.

'You can reach me there. Give me a call tomorrow. Though perhaps not too early,' he added with a smile. And was off again, back into the café while Merrily gawped and looked as if she were trying to remember something and Jo stood, stricken, just gazing at the card.

Conrad Silver, said the discreetly engraved inscription. *Worldwide Concerts, Inc.* Now where in the world had she recently heard that name?

'Jesus,' said Merrily as she flagged down a cab, 'I wish I could remember just where I've seen him before.'

22

'Are you crazy!' shrieked Merrily when she heard what Jo was planning. 'There's no way you can go off and meet him just like that, not in a city as dangerous as New York. For a start, you don't even know who he is.' For such a sophisticate, she really could be tiresomely bourgeoise. Jo, right out of character, merely smiled and stuck to her guns.

'One of Sebastian's "junkyard dogs", if I'm not very much mistaken,' she said calmly. A quick call to Jessica had established that. Jessica, having heard so much from Sebastian about this potentially lethal man, shared Merrily's terrible misgivings and in spades. But Jo was having none of it.

'Also,' she added in a quieter voice, 'quite simply, my destiny, the one great love of my life.'

'Bullshit!' said Merrily rudely. 'It's nothing more than an immature crush, brought on by frustration due to overwork and because you fucked things up with Sebastian and allowed that cow to snatch him. At least give *him* a call and find out if this guy's kosher.'

Jo shook her head. *Not on your life.* It was rich, Merrily talking like this after the way she'd behaved over Dimitri. Talk about kettles and pots. Besides, Jo knew only too well how Sebastian would react and didn't want to risk upsetting him so near to his big night. It was her life and she'd live it as she damn well pleased. No more Miss Goody Two Shoes, thank you; at thirty-something it was time to get a life.

First thing that morning she had fished out the charmed card, then remembered his warning about not making it too early. It was entirely against Jo's principles ever to call a man she didn't know but these were no ordinary circumstances; she was simply following her heart and fulfilling a three-year dream. She might never get another chance; she wasn't going to risk losing him again. She paced Merrily's modest apartment, drinking cup after cup of strong black coffee, until she judged it time to make the call. Merrily watched with amused tolerance. Yesterday's interview had brought forth two possible openings and she was feeling good. If it weren't for her apprehension about the antics of her idiot friend.

At ten forty-five, Jo's patience finally ran out and she dialled Conrad Silver's number at the Sherry-Netherlands.

'Who wants him?' asked a brisk female voice, then put her on hold for several minutes. Maybe he'd block the call. Maybe he'd not even know who she was. If it was only her strange, odd eyes he remembered, then what chance had she with a man that stupendous? At last the tinny music stopped and he came on the line; Jo's stomach instantly began to churn. She had actually spoken to him only three times, yet knew she would recognise that mellow voice anywhere.

'Hel-lo!' he said and sounded pleased. 'So you actually called!'

He needed to talk to her urgently, he said, though it wouldn't be easy to get away since he had an impossible schedule. Right now, he was rushed off his feet and could only manage a meeting late at night. How was she fixed for this evening; would that do? Jo's spirits plummeted with sudden disappointment but she'd come this far and was not going to falter now.

'That's fine with me,' she said bravely, hoping it wasn't just a fling he had in mind.

'I'll pick you up after ten,' he told her, 'and we'll go for a drink. There's a lot we need to talk about. Where are you staying?'

'East Seventy-Ninth, in a friend's apartment,' she told him and heard a distinct hesitation in his voice.

'OK,' he said, after a minimal pause. 'I tell you what. Be on the steps of the Plaza at ten-thirty and I'll find you there.'

'At least be careful,' warned Merrily, still worried. 'Remember the crime statistics and try to take no risks.'

But Jo wasn't listening. She had dreamed about this man incessantly, even broken a steady relationship for him. She had lived a good, safe life this far and see where it had landed her. Alone, unloved and in her thirties, while Sebastian was shacked up with her friend. This time she was going to follow her instincts regardless, even if it turned out to be just for one wild night. Even thinking about it made her shiver.

'I've done careful,' she told Merrily with a grin. 'Now it's time to live a little.'

But what to wear? Jo had travelled with just one medium-sized holdall into which she had crammed the requisite

T-shirts and cotton skirts, sneakers and underwear enough for a week. For a date this important she had made no provision. If Merrily weren't a petite five three, she might have borrowed something from her capacious closet but Jo stood a good five inches taller. She groaned with despair as she remembered his expensive clothes. She hadn't the time, nor the cash, to go shopping now.

'What's this?' asked Merrily helpfully, riffling through Jo's small collection of hangers and pulling out something long and pale in the finest of embroidered cottons. She shook it out. It was a demure, scoop-necked dress Jo had bought for a summer wedding, in palest primrose with elbow-length sleeves and buttons right down the front to mid-calf. She had worn it with gold slippers and a wide straw hat; it was pretty and demure but was it sufficiently chic?

'What do you think?' asked Jo doubtfully, holding it against her in front of the long mirror.

'Could do with a bit of a press,' judged Merrily. 'Otherwise I'd say it's perfect.'

'You don't think it's a bit little-girlish? I'd hate to appear too much of an ingénue.' With her shaggy, mountain pony haircut and those amazing, mismatched eyes, Merrily thought Jo would look enchanting, dangerously so. Did she really not realise what an impact she had on men? Part of Jo's irresistible charm was her total absence of self. Merrily scrabbled about in her jewellery box.

'Here, take these.' The plain gold hoops were exactly right to set off the simplicity of the dress and far more expensive than anything Jo had ever owned.

'Thanks, you're a pal,' said Jo, delighted, giving her friend a hug. 'I'll take good care of them, I promise.'

'It's you I worry about, not them,' said Merrily sharply. 'If anything happens to you, he'd better watch out.' And for once she wasn't kidding.

Precisely at ten-thirty on the dot, Jo stood waiting on the steps of the Plaza, nervous as hell as she watched the comings and goings of smartly clad revellers from restaurants and theatres. Suddenly her courage was waning and she wondered if her friends might be right after all. She didn't know this man from Adam; three brief encounters hardly constituted even a nodding acquaintance. She knew nothing about him apart from his name and the dire warnings hinted at by Jessica. Sebastian would go spare if he ever found out. To a man this deadly, in his opinion, she would be little more than tiger feed.

But Sebastian Lucas was yesterday's news and when did a woman in love ever listen to reason? Besides, this hotel was about as respectable as you could get; witness the fact that in two days' time, Cora Louise and Fontaine would be checking in. Any second now he was likely to appear and what harm could possibly come to her here, snug in the middle-class cosiness of the Oak Room bar among all those solid citizens? It would be a drink, a brief chat and, if she was lucky, more; she trembled with delicious anticipation as she conjured up that tall, imposing presence. The style, the aristocratic good looks, the megawatt smile. She was acting like a kid and knew it but it was far too late now to be thinking of turning back.

A cab had drawn up in front of the hotel and the burly driver was shouting something unintelligible. After a while Jo figured it was her he was addressing and went down the steps to meet him. She couldn't make out a word he said, he was some kind of Serb or something. But he seemed quite adamant she should get into his cab so, after a moment's hesitation, that's what she did. Golly, she thought, as he screeched off through the traffic and hurtled down Fifth at a reckless speed, this time she really had gone and done it, thrown caution to the winds. But since there was nothing she could do about it now, she settled back comfortably and tried to relax, keen to discover what fate had in store and where in the world he was taking her. They shot past the Empire State Building, then made a sharp left which took them down to FDR Drive and the river. Jo had never been this far east and could see no more landmarks she recognised.

They stopped eventually outside a cluster of tall, brown towers, built apparently over the water and approached by a narrow bridge. The driver gabbled and pointed. Moored directly below them was a glass-enclosed barge, full of light and sound, with a horde of party-goers thronging its decks. *The Water Club*, said the sign. It looked exotic and wildly expensive. The driver opened Jo's door and beckoned to her to get out. She fumbled in her bag for money but he waved it aside.

'Go,' he said, pointing towards the river then sped off, leaving her quite alone in the middle of the night, in an unknown area of a foreign city, and uncertain of her destination. Or how she was ever going to get home again. For a while she just stood and admired the jumble of boats and bobbing lights, then set off boldly down to the water's edge to find out what might be waiting for her there.

As it happened, she located him easily. Moored alongside the glittering barge was an elegant tea-clipper with its sails tightly furled, lying long and low and silent on the water, showing only a glimmer of light. Excitement clutched at Jo's heart as she recognised the three tall masts and slim, graceful lines of the boat, with the single word *Leonore* just discernible on the projecting bow. Then, as her eyes grew accustomed to the gloom, she saw him standing on deck in the fading light, tall and relaxed as he leaned upon the rail, calmly smoking a cigarette.

'Welcome aboard!' said Conrad Silver, bending to offer her a steadying hand. 'Sorry about the theatricals but there are reasons. Let's go below and get ourselves a drink.'

Below deck, the *Leonore* was luxurious and furnished with discreet and expensive taste. Jo was surprised at how spacious the main cabin was; apart from the slight curvature of the panelled walls and a barely detectable rolling underfoot, it was scarcely like being on a boat at all. There were two comfortable-looking sofas, covered in soft brown suede, and a swivel armchair in antique leather standing next to a roll-top desk. This space served obviously as office as well as haven. The walls were hung with framed gold discs and a row of bronze and silver statuettes was discreetly spot-lit in a corner cabinet.

Conrad crossed to the well-stocked bar and asked Jo what she wanted to drink.

'Bourbon,' she said daringly. Normally she stuck to wine or a spritzer but if she was going to live life dangerously, she might as well go the whole hog. Her heart was still beating painfully; she hoped he couldn't hear it.

'Do sit,' he said politely as he poured them each a hefty shot. He handed her a crystal glass, then leaned back casually against the bar, darkly silhouetted against the dim glow from behind.

'Your health!' He had tossed aside his formal jacket and rolled up the cuffs of his starched white shirt, unbuttoned now to reveal his strong, tanned neck. He was the most beautiful man Jo thought she had ever seen; her heart was beating fit to burst and she found her hand wobbling with sudden nerves. She carefully placed her untouched glass on the table in front of her, fearful of spilling it.

'Don't be nervous,' he said gently. 'I shan't eat you.'

She looked up at him but all she could see, against the back lighting, was the flash of the familiar smile and the glint from his rimless lenses.

When Jo first encountered Sebastian, she had been drawn to him gradually by his warmth and unflagging energy and the exuberant charm that usually worked in the end. They were both in their first term at Cambridge and attending the same lectures. They had studied together and shared each other's books, ridden their bicycles and grown to know each other slowly. The empathy had been immediate but she'd looked on him first as a trusted friend before succumbing, quite a while later, to a sexual involvement.

This was different. From the second she had first clapped eyes on this man, Jo had been motivated by pure lust. From that first giddy moment, three years ago, she had been electrified by his sheer physical presence. The touch of sunlight on his skin, the hint of gold in his hair, the knockout effect of his dazzling smile, the poetry of that perfect nose. She had never known a longing like this; all she wanted to do was touch him. Beneath her deceptively virginal dress, Jo's skin was alive with desire. Terrified of giving herself away, she glanced round wildly for any distraction to break the terrible tension of the moment.

On the desk, beside an onyx inkstand, stood a silver-framed photograph of a lovely slant-eyed child, her head cocked cheekily up at the camera with the sweetest, naughtiest of smiles. Searching for something to say, Jo leaned across and picked it up.

'What a truly beautiful child!'

'My daughter.' He turned and groped for a cigarette while something radical, deep inside Jo, twisted sharply and snapped. He offered her the pack but she shook her head. Inside, the tears were beginning to well and she was scared he might see them. All of a sudden she felt cheap and cheated as well as an utter fool. Had she come all this way and risked so much for this? A tawdry late-night encounter with a man she scarcely knew? Married no less; she felt ashamed. Now she understood the need for the cloak-and-dagger secrecy. What in the world did he think she was, nothing more than a tacky one-night stand? Despite her former recklessness, Jo had her standards; she knew she ought to rise and leave but her knees had weakened and she couldn't stand.

He had crossed to the porthole window and stood gazing out at the water.

'She died,' he said eventually, in a quite different voice. 'And it was all my fault. I neglected her, didn't love her enough, allowed my career to come first.'

'How dreadful!' She could see from his stance that he was really suffering and all her natural compassion came flooding to the fore. Enough of her and her own petty vanity. This man was in pain and she longed to be able to comfort him.

'What happened?'

He stood there, not moving nor even hearing her, the lights from the river glinting dully on his hair. Jo waited, silent. Suddenly she was no longer in a hurry; all she could feel was the terrible sorrow emanating from this beautiful, troubled man. In the years she had been a doctor, she'd encountered grief in all its aspects, but never quite like this. His agony was almost tangible; she could feel it from where she sat. The creases on his handsome face, usually so amiably smiling, were now the marks of suffering and the hair, close to, was streaked with grey. This was a man who was not what he appeared, who had been through a lot and was in the habit of dissembling. It was all she could do not to take him in her arms.

'Just eight years old,' he said eventually, in a soft, strange voice as if to himself. He turned abruptly to look at her and, against the dim light, she could see his bitterness. 'Running away from me. Her own father.'

Then he stubbed out his cigarette savagely in an ashtray and tugged at a cord so the curtains closed, totally extinguishing the light and plunging the cabin into darkness.

'Right,' he said briskly as he moved towards her. 'Enough of sentiment, let's get down to business. Pull up a chair, we've a long night ahead.'

'Tell me,' said Conrad Silver moments later, seated astride the swivel-chair and turning it to face Jo. 'There are things I need to know and you seem to be the one to give the answer.'

He had switched on a single powerful lamp on the desk and its beam levelled, hard and probing as a searchlight, straight into her face. The mood in the cabin had altered abruptly and she was filled with a sudden, terrible fear. Now she could feel the movement of the boat, the creaking of the old timbers beneath her and, from through the half-open porthole, the miasmic smell of the river. For all she knew, he was going to ship anchor and then what? She had come here hopefully, for the fulfilment of a dream; now suddenly she felt like a prisoner in a Gestapo cell, guilty of some unexplained crime, facing a remorseless interrogator. Whatever it was he had on his mind, it certainly wasn't seduction. How vain she'd been, how utterly childish, to have believed that possible even for a second.

His voice had lost its mellow charm as he paused to light yet another cigarette. Then the question he threw at her knocked her for a loop and made her blink with astonishment.

'What were you doing in Antigua that first time?' He checked his notebook. 'In 1992?' The smile had vanished and the soft gleam from his lenses had hardened into sparks.

'And who exactly are these people you hang out with? Names and addresses, please, it's urgent. I need to know.'

23

When Jo failed to come home that night, Merrily was seriously alarmed. Her reluctance to let her guest go out unescorted had been quite genuine yet, at the same time, she knew such caution to be absurd. Jo was a responsible, intelligent adult, streetwise through living her entire life in central London. And a doctor, too, accustomed to seeing life on the seamier side. What business was it of Merrily's to try and stop her pursuing her dream? Hell, she'd been wild enough herself all these years and still had come to no serious harm, if you discounted the incipient coke habit which she was now attempting to kick.

She left it till one a.m. before ringing the Sherry-Netherlands. They told her Conrad Silver's office was closed till next morning and advised her to try again then. If she could wait that long. Merrily paced the floor of her cramped apartment, slugging back whiskey like a Bowery bum and wondering frantically what to do next. Half of her hoped Jo was having the time of her life, yet she was also filled with a nagging dread. It was so out of character for Jo to behave this way; because she loved her, Merrily could not help fearing the worst.

Eventually, feeling a bit of a fool, she risked waking Lowell and called him in Boston. He was a judge; he'd know what to do and he always had a calming effect on Merrily's nerves. He picked up at first ring. No, he reassured her, he was still very much awake and rarely turned in until the early hours. Since Vincent's death he had found it hard to sleep and often sat up reading half the night, though he didn't tell Merrily that. Just hearing that calm, kind voice made Merrily feel a whole lot better. She told him briefly what had occurred and asked if she ought to play safe and alert the cops.

Definitely not, said Lowell, Jo was not yet officially a missing person. She was able-bodied, adult and of sound mind; down at the precinct they would merely laugh in her face.

'Let's hope, for Jo's sake, that she's simply having a whale of a good time somewhere wonderful,' he added, echoing Merrily's own sentiments. 'I really don't think you need worry. She's a sensible young woman.'

Lowell had always had a lot of time for Jo. He admired her unfussed style and straightforward manner. She must be a wonderful doctor, he thought, and her patients must surely adore her. Of all the Antigua group, Jo had always come first with him, and Vincent had shared his view. Let Merrily's fears be unjustified; in any case, he would soon be in New York himself.

'I'm booked on tomorrow's eleven o'clock flight,' he told her. 'Let's aim to have lunch. I'll call you when I get in.' This time, for a change, he was forsaking the all-male sanctum of the Harvard Club and staying instead at the Carlyle, largely out of deference to the Ravenel ladies who would be arriving that same day. The Carlyle was closer to the Plaza and far more their style; he knew them well enough to know they'd prefer the discreet opulence of that hotel to something a tad more masculine. And he always aimed to please.

Merrily went reluctantly to bed but lay awake much of the night worrying, ears alert for the sound of Jo's key. From time to time she drifted off but whenever she jerked awake she was all too aware of the empty divan across the room. Silly really, considering her own lifestyle, but there it was. Jo might be streetwise but she certainly wasn't promiscuous. As far as Merrily knew, there had been just the one serious relationship, with Sebastian, and that had lasted as long as most modern marriages. What could she be thinking of, staying out all night with a man with a dicey reputation she barely knew? The least she could have done was touch base with her hostess. Surely it would occur to her that Merrily might worry. But, on reflection, maybe not. Merrily recalled all too clearly how she had set out to shock Cora Louise and Fontaine in Antigua with her wildly embellished stories about the crazy life she led in Manhattan. Perhaps Jo would consider it wimpish to feel she had to ask permission to stay out late.

At seven she was up, tired and headachy, but there was still no sign of Jo. She waited till nine, then called the Sherry again and this time got through to a crisp, unfriendly PA who told her brusquely that Mr Silver was out of town and not expected back for a while. So finally, really panicked, Merrily sought out Jessica's number and called her at the Ansonia.

The phone was answered by Sebastian. Jessica had popped out, he said. Was there anything he could do? Anxious not to alarm him, Merrily found herself in a bit of a quandary.

Tomorrow was Sebastian's big night, his opening concert of the tour, and she knew how careful Jo always was not to upset him before he went on stage. She was also aware that he still had feelings for Jo. That was manifestly clear whenever he looked at her, even with Jessica clinging to his arm.

'Come on,' said Sebastian impatiently, as Merrily continued to waver. 'You sound as if there's something up. Let's hear it.'

Merrily wasn't sure what she thought about Sebastian. She could see he was fairly dishy, in a superficial English sort of way, but not sufficiently dark or dangerous to set her own hormones humming. She wasn't sure that she liked the public-schoolboy type, especially since this one was indiscriminate enough not to prefer Jo to Jessica. But Sebastian was waiting; she couldn't not tell him now.

Jo had gone out on a date, she explained, and not yet returned. She sensed, rather than heard, his sharp intake of breath but she'd started now and had to continue.

'Who with?' he demanded, as if it were any of his business. She told him.

'Conrad Silver!' gasped Sebastian, appalled. 'That pig of dimension! How come you let an innocent like Jo get entangled with an animal like that? And in this hell-hole, too.'

Merrily was startled and instantly put on her guard. She deeply resented such unwarranted criticism of the city she loved and the implication that somehow it was all her fault. She thought of the elegant stranger she had only glimpsed, with his stylish clothes and to-die-for smile, and considered Sebastian was overreacting. *Come on, get real. She's a big girl now.* And who wouldn't prefer that paragon, flawed or not, to this posturing ass-hole of an Englishman?

'How on earth did she meet him in the first place?' Sebastian was growing disillusioned with the strained atmosphere at rehearsals; even Jessica had been ordered to stay away though, oddly enough, for once she appeared not to mind. You never did know about people. Sebastian's initial impression of the slightly fey woman who now shared his bed and lodgings had been that she was, above all things, a passionate music groupie, obsessed with the world in which she worked. Yet, given the unique opportunity of rubbing shoulders with one of the world's foremost conductors, suddenly she was holding back.

'The man's an absolute heel. I wasn't even aware he was in town.' He should have known better. Conrad Silver was an expert cage-rattler and sooner or later contrived to turn up, to keep an eye on things, he said, but really to undermine the confidence of the orchestra. What lousy timing.

'You know him?' Merrily was suddenly hopeful. Sebastian would be the one to fix things; she cursed herself for not having called him first.

'Of course I know him.' He was getting agitated. 'He's only the promoter of this tour. A dope-head from the coast with a finger in too many pies. Rich as Croesus and as evil as Satan. Or so it is said.' Actually, the man was disconcertingly charming with a suavity of manner designed to disarm. Sebastian trembled when he thought of the effect he might have on Jo, an innocent if ever there was one, particularly in affairs of the heart.

Sebastian's growing alarm, however, was acting inversely on the hardened New Yorker. She preferred her men wild and wicked and Conrad Silver was gaining points with each new piece of information. At first glance he'd looked like a bit of a dandy, with that foppish haircut and those prissy John Lennon specs, but Sebastian was talking as if you needed garlic and an inverted crucifix to ward him off. Good for Jo. It certainly sounded as if the legendary Mr Silver possessed more balls than might at first appear. If Sebastian were going to make this sort of a fuss, he should not have let her come here in the first place.

'So how come you're involved then, Sunny Jim?'

'I've told you. He's the most influential impresario in the world, as well as the most ruthless. A chance like this happens once in a blue moon. I'd be a fool not to have taken it, regardless of his morals.' He heard himself sounding pompous and realised, too late, that Merrily was baiting him. But Jo still mattered a lot to him; he needed to hammer home his message.

'Find her, please,' he said more calmly. 'And call me when there's news. Leave a message with Jessica if you can't get through to me.'

'*Jawohl!*'

Typically selfish male, thought Merrily as she rang off. But the conversation had cheered her immensely; somehow Sebastian's yelping self-concern had helped put things back into perspective. Jo could look out for herself, especially now when she was where she most wanted to be. Merrily hoped she was having herself a ball, bonking her brains out with the man she worshipped. They came along all too rarely, these *coups de foudre*; since Dimitri's dramatic defection, she had lost her faith in love. But Jo was special – honourable and good. If anyone deserved a break in the romance stakes, it was her. She only hoped this stranger would have the sense and discernment to see her real qualities and not demean her by looking for cheap thrills. He might be a louse but what man wasn't and he certainly had the looks and charisma to compensate.

She stepped into the shower, still smiling. One thing had just become crystal clear; Sebastian still carried a mighty torch for Jo. She wondered if Jessica knew and rather hoped she did.

Lowell called her from La Guardia and Merrily strolled across to Madison to meet him. There was still no word from Jo but it was a fine, bright morning and just the thought of seeing Lowell again bucked her up immensely. Also, she had an interview later with Merrill Lynch, so had gussied herself up and felt pleased with the result. Neat, pale suit in softest dove grey over a white silk top, and discreet jewellery. Her glossy dark hair was piled high in a severe knot that suited her small, oval face and her skin gleamed healthily with her new summer tan. Merrily was regaining her fighting spirit. Just the fact of the interview had given her renewed hope and lunch with Lowell should set it off nicely.

He was waiting for her in the lobby of the Carlyle, distinguished in a lightweight suit but still looking shockingly older since Vincent's death.

'My dear,' he said, kissing her lightly on the cheek, 'you look quite ravishing, a tonic to an old man's heart.'

'Don't give me that!' He had a similar effect on her; she felt proud to be seen with him in public.

He led her to a corner table and a waiter brought champagne.

'To your interview!' said Lowell, raising his glass.

'Don't let me drink too much,' she protested. 'Can't have them thinking I'm a lush.'

'A glass or two of this stuff won't harm you,' said Lowell. 'I won't send you off half-cut, I promise.'

He knew things hadn't been easy for Merrily, though she

did always manage to put on a brave front. She looked
wonderful today and he was glad to see the bloom returning
to her cheeks, assisted by the vintage Bollinger. They ran once
more through the details of Jo's disappearance but Lowell
seemed fairly unconcerned.

'I'm sure she's well able to take care of herself,' he said
placatingly. 'It's probably nothing more sinister than a case
of *cherchez l'homme.* You'll see. By the time you get back,
she'll be home safe and sound, shagged out and longing to
tell you all about it. Trust me.' But privately he was less sure.
Bad things could happen in a city like this and lovely Jo was
a foreigner and an innocent.

There was something Lowell needed to discuss with Merrily,
hence this lunch, but he decided to wait till they'd eaten before
broaching it. She, as always, found his company stimulating
and soon got him talking about some of his recent court cases,
a surefire way of taking him out of himself. As he talked, she
studied the handsome face and remembered her ingenuous
fleeting dream of one day becoming this man's wife. She must
have been out of her mind at the time, as deranged as that
crazy dipstick Fontaine. The advent of Dimitri had soon put
an end to all that but look what a disaster he had turned out
to be. Maybe the concept of a 'white' marriage wasn't so silly
after all. At least it might have protected her from constantly
getting so burnt.

Stopped in his tracks by the expression on Merrily's face,
Lowell looked concerned.

'Hey, what's up? Was it something I said?'

'Of course not. You just reminded me of that bastard,
Dimitri. Are there no good men left in this bad old world?
Under eighty, I mean, and single as well as . . .' She stopped.

'Straight?'

Merrily was embarrassed. 'Something like that.'

Lowell laughed and patted her hand. 'I know how you feel, believe me, more than most. But the bad times do eventually pass and there's always another dream. It might sound sexist but a girl as pretty as you . . . Before you know it, you'll be swept off into some other lucky man's arms.'

'And you?'

'For me it's different. Also, I'm too old.' He changed the subject abruptly. It was not something he cared to discuss.

When the meal was cleared and the coffee poured, Lowell produced his bombshell. From his jacket pocket he took a shiny yellow packet which he handed to Merrily.

'Vincent's last film. I only just found it, unfinished in his camera, and had it developed out of curiosity. Take a look.' She flicked through the pictures.

'Vincent always was snap happy,' she said, with a grin. 'What's the problem?'

She thought back, with affection, to the regular delivery of neatly captioned snapshots that followed each holiday, lovingly prepared mementoes of a particularly happy time, captured forever by Vincent's perceptive eye. He rarely bothered with the obvious or banal, focusing instead on the outrageous and absurd, his vision as sharp and incisive as a cartoonist's. What a truly amazing talent he had had, and what a tragic waste. Merrily felt her eyes beginning to mist as she flicked through the pictures, feeling a bit like a Peeping Tom.

Lowell watched her impassibly. 'Just keep looking.'

They were clearly shots of Amsterdam, a city Merrily didn't know first hand. Small humpback bridges, canal scenes, cobbled streets. Quaint and pretty, straight from the pages of a guidebook, unusually straightforward and picturesque for Vincent. Not at all his usual style.

'Why,' said Merrily eventually, 'these are all tourist pictures. What on earth was he up to?'

'I wondered that too. He normally only carried a camera when travelling, or occasionally professionally, for a record of people or things he valued. Then I figured it out. I guess he was showing a visitor around, he often did that. This film was probably destined for that person though he never finished it, which is why I have only just found it. But go on looking. The most interesting shots come last.'

Merrily obliged. There were a couple of windmills and whole fields of brilliant poppies, then a sudden change of scenery and a much brighter sky. High scudding clouds and sunlight on water; a harbour scene crowded with boats of all sizes. Lowell craned across to see where she had got to, then watched expectantly for her reaction. Merrily continued shuffling through. Rows of boats moored closely together, some bearing the legend *Rotterdam* across the stern.

With dawning comprehension, she looked up at Lowell. He nodded.

'Go on.'

And then a couple of mid-distance shots of an elegant, low-lying masted sailboat, with two men leaning on the rear rail, deep in conversation. Merrily squinted but could not make out their faces but the next snap was taken with the zoom lens and she could plainly read the legend *Leonore* on the pristine white paint. So he really had found her, after all. No wonder Jo had reported that he had sounded so excited.

'See,' said Lowell, pointing. 'What do you make of the last two?'

Merrily crossed to the restaurant window and held them up

to the light. One man was unmistakably Jo's elusive stranger, tall and nonchalant in blazer and slacks, longish fair hair ruffled by the breeze. She had seen him only a couple of times, and then only fleetingly and in dim light, but he was easy to recognise with that comfortable elegance and the look of faint amusement on his face as he shared a joke with his companion. Then she froze.

'Jesus Christ Almighty!' said Merrily, stunned, beckoning urgently to Lowell to join her.

'What is it?' Now he was alarmed. Merrily's face had lost its colour and her hand was positively shaking as she pointed.

'It's him, that bastard, I'd know him anywhere. Dimitri Romanov, as I live and breathe! How come he got in on the act? What the hell's going on?'

And indeed, now that he looked again, Lowell recognised him too, the smaller, slighter man with the distinctive high cheekbones, flashing film-star smile and give-away Cossack eyes. He had glimpsed him only for seconds before, on the dance floor in Antigua, but well recalled his own blunt cynicism when he'd joked with Vincent about wrong-side-of-the-blanket hanky-panky in the Tsar's royal line.

So this was what Vincent had been doing in Rotterdam that fatal final weekend. He had tracked them down and taken these pictures and shortly after he'd died. Was this the secret of his jubilant postcard to Jo and, if so, what exactly did it mean? Lowell tapped his teeth and stared uncomprehendingly at the snaps. Now, he had a nasty feeling, they were unlikely ever to know.

24

The changing patterns of light on the ceiling just above her gave Jo the illusion that the boat was actually moving. It was an odd sensation. Then she shifted her eyes to the right-hand porthole and recognised the outline of the floating *Water Club*, ghostlike in the grey of early dawn. She turned her head to look at the man stretched out beside her and a warm clamp of happiness clutched at her waking heart. It had been some night and she had nodded off, exhausted, only when the sky was already beginning to lighten.

'My love.' He moved and murmured and drew her to him again and she went quite willingly, to snuggle against his chest and relive some of the exquisite memories she knew would be with her for the rest of her life. The interrogation had been unpleasant but she put that out of her mind. It was over now and she was safe, close to the man she had loved from the start, whose side she never intended to leave again. Conrad.

Conrad Silver. She smoothed her hand over his taut, tanned skin and felt a ripple as he moved towards her and drew her back into a lasting embrace.

Without his glasses he looked much younger, vulnerable and helpless as a sleeping child. His thick, sun-streaked hair lay tousled over his brow and she fondly traced the line of his perfect nose. Against the rising light, a memory stirred and was gone. Sunlight on the water, the echoing notes of a piano beautifully played. But he was moving now and his lips were back on hers; Jo closed her consciousness to everything but the immediate and sank back into the luxury of love.

The night before, she had told him everything, all she could think of about her friends: Vincent and Lowell, the Ravenel pair, Merrily, Jessica and Sebastian. Even as she answered his brusque, hard questions it felt like treachery and she was ashamed. But also scared. He gave no reason for this brutal behaviour, just pumped out the questions and waited till she answered, a little like an automaton, as if by rote. His eyes, behind the clear glass, were cold and impersonal, his expression a mask. Any resemblance to her romantic Flying Dutchman was gone. This steely eyed stranger possessed no visible humanity and she feared for her life.

When she came to recount it, there really wasn't a lot she could tell him. She had met them quite by chance, on an impulsive trip to the islands, and their group friendship had grown and developed from that point. All except Sebastian; he'd been with her a long, long time and she could swear any day to his credentials – stalwart and straight, an excellent doctor, a talented musician.

'Go on.' At intervals throughout those hours he had paused to light another cigarette or scrawl a brief note in a small black book. But there wasn't very much more she could add. Before Antigua, none of them had met, though Cora Louise and Fontaine had been acquainted with Vincent and Lowell for several years longer than the rest. Their lives were totally separate; the glue that held the group together was this annual shared holiday in the West Indies, the week before Christmas. She had fluttered helplessly and racked her memory, feeling all the while like an arrant traitor. This was her inner circle of friends they were discussing; she wished she had the will-power to tell him to go to hell.

Eventually, wearily, he snapped the book shut, took off his glasses and massaged his eyes. Then he rose and stretched and held out both his hands, his grimness replaced by sudden gentleness as he drew her slowly into his arms.

'Forgive me,' he murmured in a quite different voice. 'I didn't mean to bully you. At times I just forget myself.' Then he raised her gently in his surprisingly muscular arms and carried her, unresisting, into the inner cabin.

Now he roused her again and she realised she had been sleeping. The light in the cabin was white and brilliant and she heard the urgent scudding of water birds, low over the surface of the river.

'What time is it?' asked Jo sleepily, raising one hand to shield her eyes from the glare.

'Late,' he said, and she saw that he was dressed, his hair still damp and tousled from the shower. 'I'm sorry to leave you like this,' he said, 'but I'm afraid I have to be going.' He was wearing plain grey pants and a white silk shirt and now he grabbed a navy cashmere sweater and knotted it loosely around his neck. His eyes, when he looked down at her, were filled with affection; he pushed back the heavy fringe from her sleepy eyes and bent to kiss her lightly on the forehead.

Outside a car horn sounded and he ran up to the foredeck and raised an imperious hand. Then came back down and asked for the number where she was staying, and left her, despite her protests, fifty dollars for her cab-fare home.

'Conrad,' she protested, catching at his arm. He stopped and hesitated, as if about to tell her something. But the horn sounded again, more urgently, and he glanced quickly at his watch and slid his wallet back into his pocket.

'I'll call you, I promise,' he said as he swapped his glasses for anonymous dark ones, 'and then I know I've a lot of explaining to do. I really hate to treat you in this way but right now my time is literally not my own.'

Then he blew her a final kiss and was up and off down the gangplank; Jo reached the left-hand porthole in time to see the rear of the receding Cadillac. She flopped back on to the crumpled sheets and into a daze of muddled thoughts, weak with emotion and the night of strenuous love-making. Just wait till she told Merrily.

Merrily, oh my goodness! Sanity returned with a resounding thwack and she looked at the heavy maritime clock on the wall and saw it was almost eleven. What must Merrily think about this extended absence? She'd be out of her mind with worry and rightly so. She glanced around for a telephone, then remembered she was on a boat. There must be one there surely, among all that technical equipment, but she realised she didn't have time to look. Cora Louise and Fontaine were arriving this morning and Jo had a date with them for lunch.

Merrily was out when Jo came scrambling home but an array

of yellow Post-it notes was stuck on the bathroom mirror. 'Gone to meet Lowell,' said one and 'Call Sebastian,' another. 'Dirty little stop-out,' was what she probably meant and Jo acknowledged she had every right to be cross. But her own spirits were so high this morning that all she could do was grin and hum as she raced around the apartment, showering and exchanging the crumpled yellow dress for a more practical shirt and chinos. Not jeans this morning. They were meeting at the Plaza and Merrily had already told her that there jeans were not allowed. She checked herself in the mirror, combed her thick fringe into a semblance of order and tried to modify her ear-to-ear grin.

Then she noticed the time. Ten past twelve. She could make it across town to the Plaza in ten minutes if she put on her skates. There was just time to ring Sebastian and wish him all the best for that night. Jo felt a little guilty as she dialled; normally she would have been there with him for part, at least, of his special day but somehow events had come crowding in and, in any case, she no longer came first in his pecking order. Which was something she sometimes found hard to remember.

Jessica answered. She sounded a little on the defensive and was reluctant to disturb Sebastian who was running through his solo flute piece one final time. But, when Jo insisted, she went to fetch him and suddenly he was on the phone and in a towering rage.

'Where the hell have you been?' he virtually shouted. 'Didn't you realise we'd all be out of our minds with worry?'

Jo was startled back into reality and the soppy smile evaporated.

'I'm sorry?' Now what was he on about? What in the world

287

was she supposed to have done? 'I'm afraid I haven't a clue what you mean.'

'Last night. Your date. That man.' He sounded close to hysteria now and Jo held the receiver further from her ear. Wasn't it possible to have any privacy in this life? But tonight was the culmination of all Sebastian's dreams so she wasn't about to slug it out with him. At least, not now.

'I rang,' she said sweetly, 'to wish you all the best. And to let you know I shall be out there tonight, rooting for you. Along with Merrily and Lowell and the Ravenels.' Jessica as well, if she wasn't too grand to slum it with the ordinary folk.

Sebastian, stopped dead in his tracks, merely grunted. She could imagine him standing there, enraged and indignant, his schoolboy quiff of butterscotch hair sticking upright on his crown as it always did. Tenderness engulfed her. This was her boy, her long-time best buddy, about to hit the professional limelight and become the star she'd always known he was. She was sorry not to be the one at his side tonight but she'd forfeited that privilege deliberately. But she'd be the next best thing.

'Break a leg,' she said, 'or the musical equivalent. Get out there on to that platform tonight and knock 'em dead.'

'Oh Jo,' said Sebastian huskily, suddenly subdued. 'You really are the limit at times, did you know that?' And she knew then that she'd won.

Fontaine screamed when Jo bounced into the Palm Court and ran to embrace her like a long-lost child.

'Hon, you look stupendous! What have you been up to?' And she clasped her to her bosom and kissed her heartily on either cheek. Behind her Cora Louise was waving from a table and Jo gently disentangled herself and went to greet the older woman.

'It's marvellous to see you both, large as life and in America, too.' They were on their first martinis so Jo obligingly ordered one too, though she did privately wince a little when the sharp, sour liquid first hit her tongue. She also wished she had dressed a bit smarter; Fontaine was her familiar flamboyant self while Cora Louise was decked out like the Queen Mother in full sail. Both beamed. They had arrived, they told her, on a Delta flight and were cosily installed upstairs, with a panoramic view of the park.

'Well, we thought we deserved a little spoiling,' twinkled Cora Louise. 'It's not too often we get to New York.'

'And we're itching to get out there and hit those shops,' echoed Fontaine.

'Now tell me, dear,' said Cora Louise confidentially, once their chicken salads had been served. 'What secret happiness is making you so radiant? Do I detect a spot of romance in the air?'

'Mama!' shrilled Fontaine, hugely diverted, crumbling a roll and leaning closer in order not to miss a single word.

'I guess so,' said Jo bashfully, 'though it's far too early to tell.'

'So it's someone here in this city?' persisted Fontaine. 'Though not the beloved Sebastian, I assume?'

They were too much, these ladies, but Jo adored them for it. Such warmth, such caring; they really did feel like family.

'I don't want to talk about it yet,' she said. 'Please understand. I'd hate to tempt fate.'

Cora Louise nodded and simpered. She was so well versed in the machinations of love that she needed no prompting where discretion was required. Fontaine too. She couldn't wait to catch up with her own beloved darling. They had called the Carlyle but found him still at lunch.

'But we'll all be together tonight,' beamed her mother. 'And then we really will push the boat out and celebrate in style.'

Sebastian was alone in a rehearsal room, doing some practice fingerwork on a piece of the Mozart with which he wasn't happy. His eyes were on the notes before him but his mind was fixed firmly on Jo. His agitation at her temporary disappearance had told him something he'd been reluctant to face. She still had a stranglehold on his emotions; compared to what he felt for her, Jessica faded to insignificance. Which was heady stuff but also a bit of a bind. He'd have to wait till the tour was over before he could sort things out and only hoped he hadn't left it too late. Jo had been the one to sever their relationship but he didn't believe there was anyone else on the scene. Not yet. Apart, of course, from the junkyard dog and that had to be an aberration. He closed his mind to it. Sebastian, when he really wanted to, was rarely unsuccessful when it came to conquest.

It was Jessica who was the problem. What had started off as a mild flirtation had deepened too rapidly and caught him off his guard. The fragility and neediness that had initially appealed to him were now beginning to threaten to stifle. Once Jessica entered your life, you certainly knew it; she lived, breathed, dreamed the object of her affection and it was all becoming too much for him. Firm words were called for. He hated to hurt her but couldn't risk having her follow him South. He needed all his concentration for the forthcoming tour.

The door swung inwards and Sebastian glanced up, irritated. Who the hell was bothering him here, particularly on a day like this? A red light outside announced quite clearly that someone was in session. They should know better than to interrupt. Then he saw.

'Hi,' he said, entirely without enthusiasm, stopping at the end of the adagio and shaking the saliva from his mouthpiece. This was insufferable, yet another thoughtless intrusion, at a time when he should be psyching himself up for the highlight of his career which lay just ahead. Anyone with the faintest sensitivity would realise this and stay away, but lately Sebastian had become beleaguered by a host of petty irritations both personal and professional. The last thing he needed right now was an argument but finesse had never been part of this particular intruder's repertoire. Sebastian sat back resignedly, tapping his fingers, and waited to hear what bad thing he'd done now.

Jo still hadn't been on the boat trip round Manhattan so, since the sun was high and the temperature balmy, they all decided to forsake the culture of the Cloisters and take to the water instead.

'Those tapestries have been there a good, long while,' grinned Fontaine. 'They surely will still be there on the next rainy day.'

'Wrap up well,' warned Cora Louise, returning from her room with her squirrel jacket. 'It may be stifling in the centre of the city but once you hit that river breeze it can get pretty chillsome.'

Jo didn't care; she was still in a dream world all her own. She had brought a jacket but didn't intend to wear it. She slung it over her arm and followed the ladies into a cab. All she could think of was Conrad and their incredible night; her lips were still bruised from his kisses, her limbs sore from their ardent

athletics. He had been so sensuous but also gentle; she longed
for the feel of his arms around her, the touch of his mouth on
her skin. Cora Louise, aware of her preoccupation, winked at
Fontaine and gave her a little nudge. Jo was oblivious. Some
time she would let them into her secret but not quite yet.
Telling it to anyone would make it seem less real; for now,
at least, she needed to hug it to herself.

Cora Louise and Fontaine, keen not to disturb their elaborate coiffeures, preferred to sit in the shelter of the main
lounge, but Jo leaned on the rail facing towards the city
and watched with delight as the boat pulled out from the
Forty-Second Street Pier and headed down towards the tip of
the island. The commentary was informative and entertaining;
she learned of Frank Sinatra's birthplace, the history of that
gigantic Maxwell House coffee cup and a whole lot of other
fascinating trivia as they chugged towards the Statue of Liberty
and caught the best view of the dramatic Manhattan skyline
as the boat swung round and back into the East River. The
brisk breeze whistled past her ears and made her glad she had
brought the jacket, and she closed her eyes in the sunlight and
thought with ecstasy of the previous night.

He had said he would call. Maybe, by the time she got back,
there would already be a message waiting. Possibly she'd even
see him tonight for he would, most certainly, be at the Avery
Fisher Hall. As Richard Stanford Palmer's manager, there was
surely no way he would miss the opening night, though maybe
he'd be too occupied backstage to have time to come round
to the front of house. That remained to be seen; just thinking
about it gave her a delicious frisson and she realised, perhaps
for the first time ever, what being in love really felt like.

Back in the lea of the deckhouse, Fontaine was sipping
coffee and prattling on about Lowell while her mother listened

indulgently, the collar of her jacket turned up against the breeze, a filmy chiffon scarf protecting her hair. Jo strolled back to join them. It was good to be with them again and hard to believe it had been so long.

'How do you think Lowell is bearing up?' asked Cora Louise. Jo had seen him more recently than they had, though they did keep in regular touch by telephone.

'Hard to say.' She pulled up a chair and joined them, her eyes still held by the unfolding river panorama. 'He's aged a little but that may be only temporary. His hair is whiter and he's lost a little weight. On the whole, I'd say he's doing well though he'll never replace poor Vincent in his heart.'

Fontaine remained silent; she wasn't so sure. She had thought about Lowell intensively these last few months and if willing things to happen were enough, she'd certainly have Vincent's death on her conscience. It wasn't that she hadn't loved him too. But this particular tragedy, devastating though it might be, was far too good an opportunity to let slip, if only she could be sure of playing her cards right. She had invested some of her savings on a spanking new wardrobe from Saks and was keen to add to it at Bendels once this boat trip was over and they were back on dry land.

There it was, the beginning of the Lower East Side, and suddenly Jo spotted the now familiar glass-topped barge with the elegant, three-masted sailboat close by it, sails still furled and no sign of life on board. With luck, she would soon be back inside that cabin. He had told her he was bound for Bar Harbour once he'd sorted out a bit of business here. She wondered if there was a chance he'd take her with him; what could be more dream-like than life under sail alongside the man she loved?

*   *   *

The trip ended at four and they all three scrambled ashore, then taxied back to the Plaza for tea and a bit of a tidy. Draughty things, boats, but they'd all enjoyed it. Jo had a touch of windburn on her nose and Fontaine's mass of curls resembled a haystack after a storm.

'I really oughtn't to stay,' said Jo, over tea. They were reconvening at six at the Carlyle and she knew she had to get home first and make her peace with Merrily. Besides, there was just a chance he'd already phoned. And Merrily had had that Merrill Lynch interview; Jo felt suddenly guilty at her lack of house-guest manners. Best be off.

'Hi!' she shouted as she let herself in. She could see that Merrily was already home; her shiny patent shoes lay kicked off in the middle of the room and her jacket was draped on a chair. Merrily appeared from the direction of the bathroom, just pushing back the aerial of her cellnet phone. She looked so awful, Jo caught her breath.

'What's up?'

In total silence Merrily embraced her, then led her back into the main room. Aware of something momentous in the air, Jo went meekly. She was beginning to be alarmed.

'What?'

Merrily's face was chalk-white, her eyes like burning coals.

'Jo, there's no easy way to put this,' she said slowly, 'so I guess I'll just have to come right out and tell you. That call was from the Lincoln Centre. I'm afraid there's been an accident.'

A cold hand clutched at Jo's stomach and she sank into a chair. Sebastian? In a moment of chilling certainty, she knew what was coming almost before Merrily spoke. Dead. He had fallen mysteriously from the first-floor balcony and broken his neck. The concert, of course, was cancelled.

25

The next twenty-four hours were a whirl of confusion and pain. Jessica was hysterical and had to be sedated, while the rest of the gang clustered together in Lowell's hotel room, frightened and confused, shattered by this second terrible tragedy. At first it was assumed that Sebastian must somehow have slipped and stumbled over the balcony wall, though the officials at the Avery Fisher Hall remained adamant that such an accident was simply not feasible. So much had been going on that afternoon, with performers coming and going and the general hum of activity that precedes any opening night, that no one had a clear idea of when and how it had happened.

He had left his flute in the rehearsal room, so must have intended to return there some time. And since he had not changed into his penguin suit, he was presumably still rehearsing and not yet getting ready for the concert. The tour had been cancelled until further notice and Richard Stanford

Palmer was closeted with the police. The death had really got to the maestro, the cops reported to Lowell. Impressed by Lowell's calm dignity and his standing as a federal judge, they were telling him more than was usual in an attempt to elicit the truth.

'A real nice guy, caring and decent,' said the sergeant, 'with a positively patriarchal attitude towards his players.' Lowell was impressed by the man's delicacy of feeling; not like some of the uniforms he'd encountered over the years.

'The worst thing is he's been through it all before. Some bright, young prodigy, whom he looked on as a son, was lost under dubious circumstances a few years back. This time it's obviously hit him that much harder. For reasons of his own, he seems to feel responsible.'

Some time soon, the sergeant continued, the conductor very much wanted to meet Sebastian's friends. There were questions he needed to ask, leads to follow. Between them, maybe, they'd be able to shed some light.

'I don't know if I could face that,' shuddered Fontaine. She was heavily made-up but the circles under her eyes stood out, panda-like. Her mother gripped her hand.

'Y'all can definitely count on us,' she said firmly. 'I rely on you, Lowell, to take charge.'

In the afternoon, the police came back again and gave instructions that no one was to leave town. They would each have to be interviewed separately; they were Sebastian's sole close contacts in the city, apart, of course, from the other members of the orchestra. And the management, too, went without saying. Jo thought fleetingly and painfully of Conrad but the idyll was shattered, romantic thoughts all fled. That had been little more than an escapist dream, this brutal reality. She'd feel like a traitor even giving him a thought and needed all her concentration now just to keep from falling apart.

Lowell went first, as elected group leader, and emerged, after a couple of hours, thoughtful and grave-faced, with yet another piece of shattering news. Sebastian's fall had obviously been precipitated and there was one additional factor that had shaken Lowell rigid. Tight in his palm, he had been clutching a ring, an ornate antique set with a bluish stone. Lowell recognised it instantly, of course, and all his colour drained away. Vincent's ring, missing since the night of his own murder. Which was why they were now treating this death as murder, too. But what possibly could be the connection? In no way did any of it add up.

'Where exactly did the ring come from?' Jo asked Lowell later. She remembered it well and had always been struck by how much the clear blue stone matched Vincent's brilliant eyes. For some strange reason, it also brought to mind the Durer engraving; they never had established the mystery there.

'It had quite a history,' Lowell told her. 'It was given to him by a . . . protector . . . when he was seventeen, an affluent Viennese art dealer who took him under his wing at an early age and really had a lot to do with helping shape his career.' He fell silent for a while, raw grief still etched on his face. 'Of course, that was long before I met him.

'Its provenance was fascinating. It was fifteenth-century Italian from, according to Vincent, the school of Cellini, and had been previously in the possession of the Hapsburgs. It was presented to Vincent's friend's father, a lieutenant in the Austrian Army, in nineteen fourteen for an act of heroism on the Eastern Front. Not hugely valuable without its documentation but to Vincent's friend – and then Vincent

– an object of huge fascination and sentiment. He never took it off.'

'What happened to the older man? The protector.'

'He died tragically on his sixty-fifth birthday. Shot himself in his office because he feared old age.'

Lowell shook his head grimly. Just raking up the old story was bringing it all back. Not even Vincent had often discussed that tragedy; for the first few years they had been together it was something he had shied from altogether.

'I always thought it a bit of a bad-luck charm. Now, it would appear, I am proved right.'

'But where in the world did Sebastian get hold of it? It makes no sense. He never even met Vincent, did he?'

Lowell shrugged. 'Not that I'm aware of. It's something I've been mulling over since the accident, the police too. There seems no connection, yet the evidence is there.'

'And where, I wonder, has the ring been since it vanished off Vincent's finger?'

It was all exceedingly odd. Jo experienced a tiny frisson of fear as the full menace of the situation finally sunk in. Her mind switched instantly back to that night on the *Leonore* and the intensive grilling she had received from Conrad Silver. Just what exactly was it he'd wanted to know; they'd been so swept up in their mutual passion, she never had found out. 'I'll call you,' he'd said, and, 'I've a lot of explaining to do,' but Sebastian's death had got in the way of all that. She could track him down, she supposed, but what was the point? The maestro was already talking to the cops; anything Conrad had to contribute would presumably already be known.

Poor Sebastian, whatever had she done to him? His life had been so upwardly mobile and uncomplicated until she had managed to muddy the waters around him. If she hadn't gone on that first fated holiday, or at least had the patience to wait till he could join her, who knew what a difference that might have made? But where was the point now in bemoaning what-ifs and might-have-beens? The damage was done; Sebastian was dead.

Despite her almost insupportable grief, Jo's medical training gave her the necessary strength to carry on. Jessica was out of it completely; Cora Louise was coping, though Fontaine was constantly in floods of tears and turning to Lowell for comfort. Merrily remained stoic and for that Jo was grateful. Merrily, more than anyone, understood just how hard Sebastian's death had hit her. Even though Jo had ended the physical relationship, she had known him almost half her life and among her feelings of love and loss was mixed the insidious one of guilt. Merrily stood patiently by, ready, when required, with an attentive ear, a box of tissues or a bracing drink. Or a hug.

'I just feel so inadequate,' wept Jo. 'Not there for him when he really needed me.'

'You couldn't have known.' Merrily massaged Jo's back and shoulders and looked on helplessly while she cried.

'I just can't imagine who could have wished him so much harm. Seb was always so popular, the ultimate life enhancer.'

Merrily remembered her own last conversation with him and the acerbic note on which it had ended. No need for Jo to know about that; suffice it to reassure her how much he had still cared.

'How can you possibly know that?'

'Just do. You could see it in his eyes.'

'But what about Jessica?'

'What indeed? She was little more than a passing fancy, a sop to his vanity after you chucked him.'

'Please don't let her hear you say that.'

'Would I ever?'

Merrily grinned. Jessica was far too self-involved to question her own central role in Sebastian's life. The most annoying thing now was that she could really put on her widow's weeds and work the situation all she wanted.

'I don't know if I can go on without him,' sobbed Jessica. They had let her out of the hospital, after a night's sedation, and now she was in the Plaza, crying her heart out into Cora Louise's lap. The thin, brown hand, with its sparkling array of diamonds, caressed her hair and Cora Louise looked worriedly across at Fontaine and indicated silently that she should order tea. Anything to stem the torrent of tears; Jessica had scarcely drawn breath since her arrival.

'It was all going so wonderfully well,' she went on, raising her head to blow her swollen nose. 'We were mad about each other and he'd asked me to go on the tour. We were even planning on spending a couple of nights with you.' Again, the flood. 'I had told him so much about wonderful Tradd Street and Cabbage Row and the picturesque life of the South. It was going to be a sort of early honeymoon.'

'There, there, my dear,' said Cora Louise soothingly. 'Try not to take on so or you'll make yourself ill.'

'Why does it always have to be me it happens to?' wailed Jessica. 'Everyone I truly care for instantly snatched away.'

Fontaine was growing a little impatient. She did care about Sebastian's death, what a truly shocking thing, but her mother was more than competent to cope with hysteria. She wondered if she dared leave her to it and pop across to the

Carlyle. She was as shocked as the next person by the terrible occurrence but it was cutting into precious Lowell time and that would never do. Once the cops were through with their investigation, and it didn't look as if there was a lot more they could learn, they'd all be free to go and then where would she be? If he left town this time without a word of commitment, who was to say how soon she might manage to swing another meeting? Timing just now was crucial; Fontaine was unwilling to chance it.

'I guess I'll just slip out for a breath of air,' she murmured to her mother as she left. Cora Louise merely nodded. She wasn't fooled but she understood. And empathised with her daughter's frustration.

'Shush, sweetheart,' she crooned into Jessica's damp hair. 'Why not try and sleep a while? It can only do you good.'

Jo and Merrily were with Lowell when Fontaine arrived, going through the details step by step, reliving the previous day's events for about the twentieth time.

'Exactly where were you when it happened?' asked Lowell patiently. It was a sensible exercise to get things straight since the cops were sure to cover the same ground. It would save a lot of time in the long run if they started by getting their stories in sync.

'Out on the river with the Ravenels,' said Jo. Surely they'd never imagine *she* could be involved? 'Which means, I suppose, an alibi for all three of us.'

Lowell smiled thinly. 'I doubt it will get that far,' he said, 'but it is the sort of routine question they have to ask.'

'And I was incarcerated with Merrill Lynch,' said Merrily. 'For two solid hours, getting the third degree. With a bunch of suits who I know will support me. If they ever do decide to stick me behind bars.' She was looking quite cheerful; the interview had gone well. Maybe her luck was at last on the turn.

'And I was back here, having a nap,' volunteered Lowell.

'Did anyone see you?'

'Only the maid when she came in to turn down the bed.'

Jo smiled. 'We're not doing too badly as a group,' she said. 'Agatha Christie would be proud of us.'

'And Jessica?' asked Lowell.

Jo shook her head. 'Who knows? We've barely seen her since we got here. She's been closeted with Sebastian most of the time, hanging out at the Ansonia with him and his musician friends.'

She knew well Sebastian's gregarious lifestyle, at his happiest in the middle of a raucous group. There was the soccer crowd back home, and the medics and, of course, the merry band of itinerant musicians. It had always been the same with him, one of the things she knew had bugged Jessica, who was constantly trying to get him on his own, usually without success. Poor Jessica. However must she be feeling now? He had been an integral part of Jo's own life but Jessica was demonstrably in love with him. Jo had always been something of a loner; made no secret of it.

'Surely we can't be the only suspects,' said Fontaine. She shuddered theatrically, aiming to catch Lowell's attention. 'There must be others with closer access. And some sort of motive, for heaven's sake!'

Secretly, she rather liked the drama of being a possible murder suspect. How scandalised the ladies of Charleston would be. She could imagine the buzz round the mahjong tables and visibly brightened. She pouted her lips and arched her foot coquettishly. A fantasy flashed into her head of herself in the dock, dressed in impeccable black with an eye-veil, and Lowell out there on the floor, defending her.

'What about this management fellow?' asked Lowell, consulting his notes. 'The "junkyard dog" of Sebastian's description? He sounds a likely candidate, I would say, ruthless and drug-obsessed. What was his name again?'

Why did she feel all eyes were suddenly on her? The room fell silent and Jo's cheeks began to flame.

'Conrad Silver,' she said, after a pause. Then, too quickly and far too fast, 'though I'm certain it can't be anything to do with him.'

'No?' said Lowell surprised, one eloquent eyebrow raised.

'No,' said Jo, squirming. 'I just don't imagine he's that sort of a guy.'

'That doesn't fit with what Sebastian was saying,' said the judge, fixing her with a suspicious stare. 'According to him, the man is loathsome and utterly cold-blooded. The worst kind of creeping filth. Can it be you know something the rest of us don't?'

'Leave her alone,' said Merrily fiercely. 'Enough already. Can't you see what the poor girl's going through?'

Lowell apologised though he remained intrigued. There was obviously more here than met the eye.

The worst part of that horrible time was when the cops came to take Jo to the scene of the accident.

'Sorry, ma'am,' said the sergeant impassively when Merrily objected, 'these things have to be got through. Routine procedure, I'm afraid.'

'But what on earth can Jo contribute? She wasn't even there?'

'Shush,' said Jo calmly, fetching her bag. 'Anything I can do to help is fine with me, officer.'

But she didn't really feel that as she sat at the back of the patrol car and raced through the Manhattan streets towards the Lincoln Centre. And when they had led her up several flights of marble stairs and she stood at the spot where Sebastian must have stood and looked down from that dizzying height to the vestibule below where they'd found his broken body, a cold wave of vertigo swept right through her and she felt the familiar faintness swirling up and the pounding in her ears that always preceded an attack.

'Okay, ma'am?' asked the sergeant anxiously, gripping her arm to prevent her from falling.

'I'll be all right in a minute,' said Jo faintly, closing her eyes and wiping her sweaty forehead. It always took her this way, this tendency to black out when faced with too much of a drop, though it hadn't happened for so long now that she'd thought she might have grown out of it. The last time it had occurred was when they were skiing. Sebastian had laughed at her but she hadn't been able to face it since. She took several gulps of the cool, air-conditioned air and waved the policeman away when she found she could stand unaided. Bravely, she looked down.

'This is where he fell,' said the man, more gently. 'Right over the parapet and broke his neck on the floor.' It certainly didn't look likely; the wall was at least waist high.

'Must have been quite an athlete,' cracked the patrol man in attendance, then closed his mouth when he saw his superior's expression.

'Any ideas at all?' pressed the sergeant. 'We gather you were closer to him than most.' Jo shook her head. Sebastian was known for his larking around but this was beyond the bounds of probability. Especially on such an important day when his concentration would have been on the concert. Something, or someone, must have intervened but the implications were too ghastly too contemplate.

'Surely you're not suggesting he was pushed?' She could barely speak the words.

'Looks like it. Someone must have given him a mighty shove and forced him off balance before he could save himself.'

'But who?' It was unthinkable; spots appeared before Jo's eyes and she felt the faintness returning.

'You tell us. Someone with a grudge, maybe. Or else some random lunatic on the loose. Guess this city is full of those. Perhaps the poor guy just struck unlucky.'

After a little more questioning, they finally took pity on her and returned a shaken Jo to Merrily's apartment. All she wanted was to curl up and weep, with a pair of strong arms to comfort her.

'Don't you think you ought to call him?' said Merrily later, in the privacy of the apartment, once she had heard the whole story. Jo mutely shook her head. No, she wasn't up to it and he must be aware of the dreadful goings on. He was, after all, Richard Stanford Palmer's manager. Jo and Merrily had both been interviewed and cleared by the police and were relieved to hear that Jessica, too, appeared to have a watertight alibi. She had been down in the basement for a large part of that afternoon, doing the laundry with a couple of Julliard students. So now what was there left for them to do?

Jo had also had the upsetting task of telephoning the Lucas family in Chepstow to break the news of Sebastian's death. The police had offered to do it for her, but she felt this way was more humane. His parents had said they would fly straight out but Jo had insisted that wasn't necessary. She knew their finances were limited, that his father had retired on a headmaster's pension and also had the beginnings of a dicky heart.

'Leave it to us,' she had told them. 'The police investigation is purely formal. Once they release the body, we'll be on our way.'

In the event, however, Sebastian's body was not allowed to be removed from the police morgue, pending the probability of a post mortem. Even Lowell's intervention failed to sway them; although the cops had unearthed no firm evidence that the death was anything more than an unfortunate accident, they refused to let him go until every relevant fact had been sifted. Which could, according to Lowell, take months. Jo was torn between staying and escorting Jessica home. Staying meant hanging around and waiting but always with the chance she might still hear from Conrad. But Jessica was in such a frail and unstable state, she feared she would only deteriorate more if she remained too long at the scene of the tragedy. So home it would have to be while Lowell promised to keep a close eye on things here.

'Don't worry,' he told Jo, 'it will all sort itself out. And this one badly needs to get home before she cracks up completely.'

So tickets had been purchased for the night flight to Heathrow. Jessica was still with Cora Louise and shortly Jo would be going to collect her. Her things were packed, her goodbyes said. She did not relish the thought of going home but at least it was a relief to have something positive to do. She blocked her mind to all she was leaving behind.

Lowell was there when they reached the Plaza. With still

more news. Richard Stanford Palmer himself had been to see him and had stayed the best part of a couple of hours, talking, commiserating and generally swapping information. The cops had been accurate in their assessment; he seemed to be a humane and decent man. Distinguished and full of integrity, he appeared light years away from the popular image of such a stratospheric celebrity. Lowell had been impressed.

'He spoke of Sebastian with genuine affection,' he told Jo, 'and was full of praise for his musical abilities. Apparently only occasionally does someone come along with natural talent like that. He was obviously as cut up as the rest of us. A true mensch.'

He told Jo the maestro was keen to talk to her too and was waiting downstairs in the Oak Room in the hope of seeing her before she left. Jessica too, if she could find the strength. But Jessica was having none of it. With a low moan, she buried her face once more in Cora Louise's accommodating shoulder while, Jo, helpless, shook her head. She was torn by mixed feelings and didn't know what to do for the best. She longed to meet this kind, caring man but knew such an ordeal would be too much for Jessica. And she was the one to have to take her home; if Jessica were stirred up any more, she'd not be in a fit state to travel and they were due at the airport in a little over an hour.

'Tell him no,' she said regretfully, pushing away the possibility that his manager might be there too. At any other time, she would have been intrigued to meet this paragon who had exacted from Sebastian so much loyalty and admiration. Perhaps in London when things were a little calmer. But all her medical training hurtled to the fore and reminded her of her Hippocratic Oath. The patient must always come first, in this case Jessica, and all other considerations would have to be put aside.

But Lowell persisted. He had spent enough time with the man to recognise his sincerity and had learned things he still hadn't quite worked out. But now was not an appropriate time to divulge any of it to Jo. At least, not in this company with the weeping Jessica present.

'He was very insistent,' he said in a low voice. 'Won't you just slip down now while we organise the luggage? I think you'll find it worth it, particularly since it's you who has to face the family.'

Jo, however, remained adamant. It was too much of a temptation; she simply hadn't the strength. Jessica could rely on her. She'd not subject her to any more harrowing interviews nor run the risk of finding out something that might only distress her more.

So Lowell played his main and final card. He fished in his pocket and brought out a snapshot. Carefully weighing his words and pausing for optimum effect, he placed it on the table before her and slowly uncovered it.

'Who's that?'

'Conrad Silver,' said Jo immediately, feeling her heart beginning to race out of control. Then looked more closely and sharply drew in her breath. 'With . . . Dimitri Romanov? Can that be so?'

She stared at Merrily who nodded in confirmation. Then up again at Lowell.

'Rotterdam,' she said slowly. 'Was this what Vincent was after?'

'Apparently.'

'But how and why and what in the world . . . ? And where

do the hands on the postcard fit in? And what was Sebastian doing with Vincent's ring?'

'We still don't know everything. But, believe me, we're working on it.' He patted her shoulder and spoke in a gentler voice. 'Do what you have to, my dear, and God bless you. And rely on us' – he included Merrily – 'to get to the bottom of things while you're gone. And keep you fully informed.'

Jo nodded. Her mind wasn't working logically at all; just dealing with Jessica was taking all her energy. Lowell would sort things out, she trusted him. And Merrily, bless her heart, who was such a staunch friend. But now she had to be thinking of getting to the airport. The taxi arrived, the luggage was stowed and Jo helped Jessica, weeping profusely, inside while Cora Louise and Fontaine waved them off.

Merrily and Lowell, left alone, simply sat and stared incredulously at each other.

26

Without Sebastian, Jessica seemed lost. Where once she had been a truly free spirit, living alone in various undistinguished digs, riding her clanky old bicycle and leading a slightly eccentric, peripatetic life that verged on the selfish but was always good-humoured, suddenly she appeared to have lost all her spunk. Jo watched in dismay as she subsided into despairing lethargy. All at once that formerly fierce ambition appeared to have evaporated. She spent her free time sunk in gloom, often weeping, constantly lamenting the sadism of a fate that could deal her a second time such a cruel body blow. She was still firmly entrenched in Elm Park Mansions and now Jo hadn't the heart to ask her to go. That she had left to Sebastian to fix but, unusually, he had failed to deliver.

Luckily for Jo, there was the new job to keep Jessica occupied. Ironically, this summer of Jessica's despair was also the one that saw the fulfilment of her long-time ambition, to work in London on the BBC Proms. The concert season started in late July so that by the beginning of June, when they returned so despondently from New York, a vast work load had already accumulated. Jessica, functioning properly, should by now be steeped in it and firing on all cylinders. This, unfortunately, was not the case.

'Come along, love,' Jo urged her in the mornings, opening the curtains to let in the light as she brought her house guest tea in bed. 'It's after seven. You really ought to be up and about.' Jessica, pallid from a sleepless night, would groan and burrow back into the pillows so that all Jo could do, before racing off to the surgery, was run her a bath and leave her to it. Secretly, she was growing a little impatient with all this self-indulgent sorrow. Sebastian's death had left a huge hole in Jo's life too but she was practical and determined and knew that the best possible antidote to despair was to throw yourself whole-heartedly into work. Which, more or less, she was succeeding in doing. Seeing day by day the tragedies and setbacks of ordinary life helped get things back into reasonable perspective. Jo would never ever forget Sebastian, nor cease loving him, but the show had to go on which is what she knew he would have expected.

And, as a small niggling voice that she despised kept reminding her, Jessica had known him only a matter of months.

'How's it going?' asked Merrily, during one of her late-night calls. She was feeling pretty glum herself and needed Jo's cheery optimism to stop her from flagging again. The Merrill Lynch job had not come through. They had had, it transpired, over three hundred applicants and the appointment had gone to a twenty-four-year-old whiz-kid; male. She might as well not bother, she thought. At thirty-eight she was already over the hill.

'All right, I suppose,' said Jo doubtfully. 'I just wish she'd get a grip and sort herself out. Find herself some friends and sort out somewhere to live. She has all the opportunities she could possibly want, with that stimulating job and a whole new set of workmates.' Right now, Jo's own life was fairly static. Shona was leaving the practice, to live with her new boyfriend in Edinburgh, and the other three doctors were all married and settled. If her job weren't so draining, she'd do something really positive, like joining an art class or even some sort of club, as the columnists recommended.

Instead, she was stuck with Jessica. Each night, when she turned the corner into Park Walk, she would look up and see a light in her own flat, a beacon to warn her that Jessica was already home. She would wearily trudge up the five flights of stairs, to find Jessica settled in front of the telly or listening to a symphony or something obscure on the World Service.

'Hi,' Jo would say, 'have you eaten?' And Jessica would reply lethargically, 'Not yet.'

On the surface, Jessica was not really interested in food but, Jo observed with occasional irritation, her appetite was guaranteed to revive once she herself had scoured the fridge and store cupboard and got something aromatic bubbling on the stove. Her medical training, plus sensible parents, had instilled in Jo the importance of regular meals. No matter how late it was when she got home, she always put together something decent to eat, even if it often lacked imagination. Furthermore, Jessica was a late-night snacker and food that Jo had been relying on to see her through at least another meal had often disappeared by morning. She hovered on the edge of asking Jessica to shop, to try her hand at cooking and be a little less self-involved, but always ended up chickening out. Poor Jessica had suffered a major bereavement. Depth of feeling, she well knew, had nothing to do with how long you had known someone. She thought fleetingly and longingly of Conrad Silver, then sternly dismissed him from her mind. That way lay only madness. He had had his chance and he'd well and truly muffed it. Let there be no more foolish fond thoughts about him. He still hadn't called; Merrily confirmed that. It would appear that, after all, the man had been just another louse.

Except that it was hard to forget him with Jessica constantly around and talking about the Proms. Richard Stanford Palmer was arriving mid-September to take the podium on the celebrated last night. It was something of a coup for the BBC, and Jessica, slowly edging back to her normal gushy self-confidence, wasn't past taking a large slice of the credit herself.

'It took a bit of doing,' she boasted, 'but I finally persuaded him.' Jo's ears pricked up, though she managed to stay silent. Could it be that Jessica was sufficiently solipsistic to have forgotten? For she distinctly remembered Sebastian crowing about this particular event long before Jessica even had the job. If the American tour had been a success, there was a distinct possibility he'd be invited to play at the final Prom. And it had tickled his vanity to think he might perform in the Albert Hall, in front of his friends. *That* ought to show the lads at the football club, not to mention the mindless medics with whom he passed his days. But, being a nice person, she didn't say a word. Let Jessica have her moment of triumph, why not? What possible difference could it make now?

She caught her talking to Cora Louise, *again*, and shuddered slightly as she envisaged the escalating phonebill. Though inclined to be on the stingy side herself, Jessica displayed a curious unconcern when spending other people's money. The result, maybe, of being an orphan, of lacking parental guidance at a crucial age.

'They're almost certainly coming to London in September,' said Jessica, cock-a-hoop, bursting into the kitchen where Jo was serving up. 'Lowell booked ages ago, so I guess they thought they'd tag along. They are doing Edinburgh and the Scottish islands first, so things couldn't be simpler. It's great they'll all be here for the Proms. It is, after all, my major breakthrough.'

'That's nice.' Jo was silently disapproving of Jessica's sudden mood swing. Too much harping on death was unhealthy but now she risked sounding just the teeniest bit callous. Though Jo was planning to use this unscheduled get-together as a welcome carrot to entice Merrily over too. The poor girl had really had a rotten year; any sort of break was bound to do her good and Jo looked forward to sharing with her her own beloved city.

'We can have a little party for them here,' said Jessica happily. 'And if I can borrow your car, I'll take them round Bath and the West Country while you're working.' Typical of Jessica, always pushing herself forward. Even in her exasperation, Jo had to be amused, though. Jessica seemed to have forgotten entirely that this was Jo's home, not hers. And that Cora Louise and Merrily and Lowell were equally her friends. But at least her thoughts no longer centred on poor, dead Sebastian so Jo valiantly managed to curb her tongue. Time would surely help heal the wound and maybe the gang would assist in convincing Jessica it was more than overdue that she found a place of her own.

Then, of course, she felt guilty. She came home one night to find Jessica had completely scrubbed out the bathroom and rearranged all the foodstuffs in tidy rows in the crowded kitchen cupboard. And washed the tea-towels and dusters and hung them over the bath to dry.

'You've been so good to me,' said Jessica, hugging her. 'Letting me live here and share your life. Let's ask Shona and that boyfriend down for the weekend. There's a Truffaut season at the NFT that I know she'd love and we can maybe also take in the Harrods summer sale.' Jo grimaced to herself and thought longingly of her solitude. Jessica had met Shona only fleetingly but chattered away to her on the phone these days as if they were joined at the hip. Shona found it funny, Jo less so.

'If she'd only find a life of her own,' she complained, 'maybe I could get on with mine.'

The message on the answering machine was quite explicit. A man's voice confirming the theatre tickets booked by Dr Lyndhurst, the costs to be charged to her Visa card. Jo ran the tape back and listened to it again but there was no mistake. She was pondering the enormity of the situation and wondering whether to contact Visa this late and stop the card, when Jessica sailed in, looking fetching in Jo's blue sweater. Jo took this in but was more preoccupied with the phonecall. She was used now to Jessica borrowing her things.

'Something wrong?' For once Jessica had stopped to do a little food shopping and was unloading avocados and coffee beans, plus a slice of particularly ripe-looking camembert. Wine too. This was clearly a red-letter day. Jo told her.

'Oh yes, I booked them last week,' said Jessica casually, 'for Cora Louise and Fontaine when they arrive. Tickets for

315

Guys and Dolls are like gold-dust and I reckoned they'd prefer that to something a little more cerebral.' Her implication was that the show was beneath her but its new production at the National just made it acceptable. But that wasn't the point. Jo was outraged.

'And you used my name?'

'Yes, I hope you don't mind. Doctors, like professors, carry a certain cachet. I thought I'd stand a better chance of getting good seats that way. I do hope you'll join us.'

Jessica's smile, now that she had cheered up, was infectious. Against her instincts, Jo found herself giving in.

'And my credit card.'

This time Jessica did look a shade uncomfortable. She placed the avocados carefully in the yellow fruit bowl and unwrapped the cheese on to a ceramic plate, to breathe.

'Mine's currently over its limit,' she admitted, as if that made it acceptable.

'But how did you get the number?'

'It was on your dry-cleaning receipt.' Attached to the blue sweater. Which Jo had left in her closet still plastic-wrapped, until she had occasion to wear it herself.

Jessica glanced at her curiously.

'You're not cross?' she ventured, as she looked for and found the corkscrew. Jo held back on her real reaction; Jessica, after all, was her flatmate and a true and trusted friend. She accepted a glass of the fruity beaujolais.

'Of course not, idiot. Just ask next time.' And don't go pretending you're me in future.

Late in July the New York authorities finally declared the case on Sebastian closed and released the body for burial.

'They came up with no further evidence,' reported Lowell,

'and have now decided it was just a freak accident. Though that doesn't explain where he got Vincent's ring.'

'You mean they're leaving it at that?'

''Fraid so. In a city like New York the police are so overworked, they don't have time for guessing games about some poor, itinerant musician from out of town.'

'So what do *you* think happened?'

'I really haven't a clue. But I do think now he deserves to be left to rest in peace.' Vincent too.

Jo came home early the following evening, full of anxiety about the funeral. It wasn't going to be easy, having to see the Lucas family again, and she hated the idea of saying a final farewell to Sebastian. Jessica, luckily, would be late home tonight; her hours extended the closer they got to opening night. Jo trudged up the endless stairs, as usual pondering what to eat. She wasn't at all hungry but there had to be something, provided, of course, her flatmate hadn't already scoffed it.

She opened the front door and stopped dead in her tracks. Jessica, it would appear, had been at her tricks again. The narrow hall was piled high with opened boxes and it took her a second to realise it was her own shoe collection from under her bed. She shot into her bedroom and there chaos really reigned. The bed was awash with most of her clothes thrown casually around, and her empty jewellery box lay open on top of them. The drawers to her desk were all half-open and papers were strewn all over the floor. It certainly wasn't Jessica; it must have been intruders. Without a thought for her own safety, Jo shot into Jessica's room where she found a similar mess.

She called the police. And then began to shake uncontrollably so poured herself a whisky and lit a cigarette. After all she had been through in the past few weeks, this was the last thing she needed right now. She held back her tears until the policeman arrived, but her voice shook with emotion as she showed him around.

'A routine burglary, I'm afraid,' said the pleasant bobby, scribbling on his pad. He demonstrated how they must have got in, probably by using a credit card on the regular Yale lock. He tutted over Jo's lack of proper security but when he mentioned an alarm, she told him she had nothing worth stealing.

'Aren't you going to take fingerprints?' she asked, as he glanced at each of the ravaged rooms, then replaced his helmet, ready to leave.

'No point.' He was polite and sympathetic but entirely without optimism. There were so many burglaries these days, particularly in the more affluent parts of town, that they just didn't have the manpower to follow most of them up. He urged her at least to get herself a mortice lock, then left his name and a contact number and set off down the stairs for the next hopeless call.

Jo stood in the midst of all the mess and finally allowed the helpless tears to fall. It simply wasn't fair. As she tiptoed carefully about her strewn bedroom, her foot touched something hard and she saw it was her grandmother's diamond brooch. She immediately dropped to her hands and knees and felt carefully around and, indeed, all her small pieces of jewellery were still there, shaken from the box and left carelessly on the floor.

'I suppose they simply weren't worth enough,' she told Jessica later, once she had calmed down, 'though you'd think they might have made a bob or two in the Portobello Road.'

She had managed to tidy up most of it and between them

they found that nothing at all was missing, not, at least, from a cursory glance. Jessica was thoughtful, though, her face even paler than usual.

'Maybe it wasn't jewellery they were after,' she said. But beyond that she really wouldn't comment. It was just rather nasty to think they could be so vulnerable; Jo had always looked upon this place as her sanctuary. First thing in the morning, she would telephone the locksmith and do as the nice policeman had suggested. But she knew she would never feel quite the same again.

The funeral was fixed for Brompton Cemetery, on a stifling, hot Saturday when the earth was parched and dry. At first the family had wanted to take Sebastian home to Chepstow but Fulham was where his happiest years had been spent so they decided to leave him there, close to the hospital where he'd trained and the football ground he had supported. A small service in celebration of his life was held first in the hospital chapel, then the burial party moved on down the Fulham Road to the beautiful old cemetery where strings had been pulled to make room for him under the spreading plane trees, close to the stadium wall.

'You were the one he always loved,' said Molly Lucas emotionally, enfolding Jo in her arms and shedding a few fresh tears. Jo patted the sturdy shoulder. Jessica was following close behind and she didn't want her to catch what was being said. Lately Jessica had been bearing up so well, she dared not risk upsetting her again and possibly causing a relapse.

'I felt the same about him,' said Jo simply, watching with a flat, dull ache as they lowered the polished pine coffin into the earth and shovelled fresh soil upon it.

The burial service was brief and to the point and afterwards the mourners strolled, in twos and threes, back up the central pathway of the cemetery, skirting the crumbling catacombs, among rows of imposing Victorian tombs. Jessica was starting to flag again so Jo took her arm for mutual support. It was a wretched time and such a tragic, terrible waste. As soon as they got home, she would pour them each a brandy then make a reservation for that evening at *Kartouche* to try to inject some lightness back into their bleak little lives.

Close to the cemetery gates, just inside the red-brick entrance, a long, sleek, silver, stretch limousine was parked, its driver's door wide open, with a slim, dark man in aviator specs stooping to talk to someone unseen inside. At the slow approach of the burial party, he straightened up and stood there impassively watching them, his eyes inscrutable behind the lenses, as black and opaque as the windows of the car. There was something oddly familiar about him, as he fingered his neat silk tie, and Jo felt discomfited as he raked her with his gaze. She turned her head to check out the family behind her, but he totally ignored them as they passed.

Jessica saw him too and her snivelling stopped abruptly.

'Who's that, I wonder?' she whispered urgently, giving Jo a sharp nudge.

'Don't know,' Jo muttered, hoping he couldn't hear. 'Someone to do with Sebastian, I'm sure, though he hasn't the grace to acknowledge the parents.'

'Maybe he's some sort of private detective,' suggested Jessica hopefully. They had passed the limo and were through the iron gates, out on to the Brompton Road, teeming with Saturday afternoon traffic. 'Good thing too, it's time someone came up with something. Let's hope they catch the bastard who did this to my boy.' And Jo, still holding closely to her arm, felt with surprise that she was really shaking.

Jo was thinking fast. The accident had happened in New York and the case officially closed. There was no obvious reason for the British police to be involved so, if Jessica was right, who conceivably could be paying for an investigation? And why?

'Come on,' she said firmly, hailing a passing cab. 'Let's stop playing guessing games and get you home.'

27

It was an irritating coincidence but there was really nothing she could do about it now. The very last week of the Proms season, in mid-September, this blasted medical conference had come up in York which Jo knew she couldn't afford to miss. Damn.

'Don't you worry,' said Jessica, skilfully straining the piping hot pasta, 'I'll be here to entertain the gang. Fear not.'

They had all agreed to meet up in London, even Lowell who would be staying at the Connaught. He had, he felt, spent time enough in seclusion, silently grieving. It would be something of a relief to ease himself back gradually into normal living by socialising with old and trusted friends who knew about his secret life and didn't judge him.

'I know you will,' said Jo with a smile. 'You're a dear to be doing so much as it is, when you're this busy.' It was just that she had wanted to spend as much time as possible with them all, especially Merrily who was also coming over, lured reluctantly from New York. Jo had rather hoped for some private time with her friend, but that was clearly not to be. Not with Jessica in there officiating.

'She'll be quite comfortable on the sofa,' said Jessica confidently. 'She can hang her clothes in my closet, no sweat, and we'll all rattle along together as cosily as peas in a pod. You'll see.' But it wouldn't be quite the same.

The Ravenels were booked into Durrants Hotel in Marylebone, where they usually stayed. Jo had attempted to entice them across the park to South Kensington but they felt at home in that area, liked being within walking distance of Bond Street and Selfridges. After that, they were heading up to Scotland where they were treating themselves to a week at a famous hotel on the Isle of Skye for a bit of quiet relaxation, before returning to London for fun with the gang.

'It is run by a real lord and his lady,' wrote Cora Louise, 'and the food is reported to be quite excellent.' Jo had smiled. She loved the barely suppressed snobbery of these dyed-in-the-wool Southern belles; they'd be right in their element at Kinloch Lodge, awash with Labradors and the green-wellie brigade. Though how would Fontaine ever get around on a rocky island on those heels?

'We're here, doll!' screamed Fontaine the morning they arrived. 'Safe and sound and just rarin' to go. Mama insists on a nap before we hit Oxford Street but we'll be sure to be with you by six-thirty at the latest. Can't wait!'

For once Jo had begged off evening surgery and was planning another of her elaborate feasts to celebrate the arrival of the Ravenels in London. It was starting to become a bit of a tradition; she planned to push the boat out and make them a Thai curry, if only she could persuade Jessica to get off her backside for a change and help with the preparations.

'Why do you have to be so ambitious?' queried Jessica, snooping through Jo's copious plastic carriers. 'Fish sauce, lemon grass, what's this – galangal? What is wrong with macaroni cheese or good old shepherd's pie?' But she was laughing. Jo very rarely had the time to cook but when she put her mind to it, she was really rather good.

'I thought it would make a change,' she said, 'after all that gumbo and ladies' fingers and other exotica they exist on down there.'

Actually, Charleston was a sophisticated town but Jessica preferred not to spoil Jo's fantasy. And since she loved all kinds of oriental food herself, she wasn't about to stand in her way, provided she didn't have to do too much herself.

'If you'll just julienne those vegetables, to go with the egg noodles, and then set the table, that'll do,' said Jo patiently. Actually, she preferred to cook on her own. It gave her time to think and unwind from what was usually a gruelling day. And, just lately, there was more on her mind than usual; she had read in the papers of the recent arrival in London of Richard Stanford Palmer and his entourage, primarily to conduct the last night of the Proms. She remembered how keen he'd been to talk to her before she left. Weeks had gone by since then and Sebastian was safely buried, yet still she prevaricated about actually meeting the man.

He was also giving three concerts at the Barbican and Jo wondered whether she dared go. She wasn't by any means a music buff, though she secretly enjoyed listening more than she ever let on. Her Philistine pose had been mainly to exasperate Sebastian; it was part of the tragedy that he had died not ever knowing. If she went to a concert, maybe she could get backstage. And if she summoned up that amount of nerve, it was not impossible that his manager would be back there too . . . She knew she shouldn't even think of it but found the temptation too strong. She *couldn't* just turn her back on that amount of passion without allowing it at least a second chance.

But who should she choose to share this adventure with her? She risked making a gigantic fool of herself, so it had to be someone she knew she could trust who wouldn't poke fun. Shona was *hors de combat* through distance, so the obvious choice would have to be Jessica; Jessica who lived her life steeped in music, who went to concerts as often as she could and knew all the managements and many of the players. Who could probably even contrive, if necessary, to get them upgraded seats.

She was unprepared for the force of Jessica's refusal.

'No,' was all she would say, almost snappily. 'I hate the Barbican and am not attracted by any of his programmes.' That's all. No word of apology or explanation, just a flat rejection that was actually rather rude. Jo was stunned. Now what had she possibly done to deserve this rebuff?

In the end she chickened out and decided to wait till the last night of the Proms. The chances of bumping into Conrad by accident were too minimal to count on and Jo had to remind herself impatiently that she was no longer a louche schoolgirl, hanging around the bike sheds in the hope of glimpsing her favourite prefect, but a thirty-something career girl with a gruelling job and promising future. Provided she didn't crack up.

Merrily, when she arrived, reminded her that he had always had the phone number but simply hadn't called.

'I've been in enough in the past few weeks, God knows,' she grumbled. 'And there's always the machine. No, face it, babe, he's just another no-good rat who took what he wanted and then beat it.' She hated to see the light die in Jo's fine eyes but Merrily was never one to soften a blow. And, in her opinion, Joanna Lyndhurst was worth far more than any low-life, drug-dealing impresario, the scum of the earth by all accounts.

She was pretty pissed off to find Jessica still in residence but there wasn't a lot she could say since Jo was providing board and lodging and, these days, Merrily was virtually skint. It had been a bit of a gamble even to get this far. Really she should have hung on in New York and tried a bit harder to find herself a job but the months she had spent looking had started to get to her. She badly needed this breather and reckoned she deserved it. And she wanted to spend some time with Jo.

'Lordy, lordy, those stairs will sho'ly be the death of me,' said Cora Louise faintly as she wavered on Jo's threshold. Jo went forward, hands outstretched, to embrace her and relieve her of her coat. Behind her, Fontaine hopped around, bright-eyed and excited.

'We've just been followed by a man,' she said.

'Seriously?' Jo was startled. Despite the break-in, this was reputedly a safe area, especially at this time in the evening when it was still full daylight. Cora Louise raised both eyebrows and smiled, amused as ever by her impossible daughter.

'You wish,' she said, pinning back several loose strands into her immaculate hairdo. 'No, dear, don't worry. He was simply lurking about downstairs. Probably looking for a number he had forgotten.' For security reasons, in this prestigious block names were not displayed on doorbells.

'What was he like?' Merrily was always curious.

'Dark, good-looking. Rather a dish, in fact.' Ever-optimistic, Fontaine milked every incident for its ultimate dramatic effect. 'He was wandering in the courtyard looking positively ravishing. If you pop down now you'll maybe catch a glimpse of him.'

'No thanks,' said Merrily grimly. She'd had a basinful of men just lately and dark and good-looking was no longer on the agenda. Short and kind with love handles was more what she hankered for now, with a safe, dull job and insured security. Perhaps her father had been right after all and a dentist from Ohio was really her mark.

'Come on in,' said Jessica from the living room, where she was touching up the flowers. Jo had done the cooking, all of it, but Jessica was great when it came to the finishing touches. She had made poor Merrily collect up her belongings and stow them safely in the spare-room closet. Right now Merrily had mutiny on her mind; if it weren't for her finances, she'd move to a hotel. Three women living together in cramped conditions was certainly not her idea of paradise. Though she was genuinely delighted to see Cora Louise and Fontaine.

'Sorry it's not rum,' she said, pouring the wine. 'We thought about Planter's Punches but came down on the side of sobriety.'

'And anyhow, away from the tropics, those cocktails are inclined to lose some of their magic,' added Jessica.

They grouped together on the sofa while Jo fussed in the kitchen and Jessica handed nibbles around and acted as if she owned the place. Without asking permission, Merrily lit up.

She could just about take it for another few days; any more time and there'd be an explosion.

'When does Lowell get here?'

'Tomorrow week,' said Fontaine with eyes that shone. New York, she felt, had been a bit of a breakthrough. She relied on this London trip to consolidate matters. 'We'll just be back from Scotland that same afternoon.'

Tonight she was looking luscious in canary yellow linen with high black patent stilettos and a matching designer bag. Merrily, amused, had to admire her style. She certainly had a lot of dash for one of her size and flamboyance; not quite Manhattan chic, maybe, but passable for the South. One of these days she would have to go visit; she longed to view the plantation house, or wherever it was these cushioned ladies lived, and indulge in a little Carolina luxury, a change from her current reduced circumstances.

It was Thursday night in early September, just ten days to go to the fabled Last Night, and Jessica was even more keyed-up than usual, right in the throes of making it all run smoothly. She had managed to get balcony seats for the Ravenels and Lowell, gold-dust for that special night of all nights. The rest of them, however, including herself, preferred to play it by ear and savour the authentic atmosphere by promenading among the crowds. This summer, for the first time ever, they were planning speakers and a screen in Hyde Park. A far vaster crowd than ever before would be able to listen and join in the festivities. What a pity, thought Jo, that Sebastian would miss it. It was exactly the sort of junket he most loved.

'It will be like the three tenors,' explained Jessica, as they ate. 'Opening up the concert to the masses. Rather a nice thought, don't you think?'

There she goes again, thought Merrily resentfully, *taking more credit than I'm sure she's due*. But Jo caught her eye and gave a sly wink. Jessica's affectations didn't trouble her at all, in fact Jo found she had rather learned to enjoy them.

'Providing it doesn't rain,' she said. 'We must not forget our rain hats.'

It was a pity about the conference but these things did matter and paediatrics was a subject she took seriously. Too many sick and deprived children came into the surgery for her not to realise the significance. After almost four years, the memory of that dying child had faded but still, occasionally, on a sleepless night, the little, lost face would return to haunt her. She would be gone only a couple of days and could just get down from York in time for the concert. She would leave it to Jessica to steer Merrily safely to the Albert Hall. The proceedings could run overtime or the train be late.

'You're sure you'll be all right together?' she asked Merrily privately, as she packed an overnight bag.

'Don't fret, I'll try my best not to murder her,' said Merrily. She had tickets for *Cats* and *Phantom of the Opera* while Jessica was working, and planned to take the Southern belles and possibly also Lowell. She also had a desire to see the Tower of London and maybe even Docklands, which they said was like areas of Manhattan. It wasn't like Merrily to put herself out but, having made the effort to shift her butt this far, she might as well take advantage of it and bone up on a little culture. And, truthfully, Jessica was bearable in small doses; it was only when she started her prancing and posing that she began to get up Merrily's nose.

York was a nicer city than Jo had expected: she was sorry now not to be spending more time there. They stayed on campus in a hall of residence, empty of students as term had not yet started. There were about three hundred delegates, most of them doctors, and she liked the people she encountered on her landing and enjoyed the informal socialising. It did make a change to get away from London. She realised she was developing tunnel vision from too much concentration on the job and not enough breathing space to step back and look around.

Seated at lunch on the final day, she found herself facing a pleasant-looking young woman with sandy, curly hair and a smiling, freckled face. They nodded to each other, then went separately to the buffet table. Something about her seemed oddly familiar and Jo racked her memory in case they had met before. Perhaps at Cambridge? Or in one of her junior hospital jobs.

Once settled back at the table, she took a surreptitious look then leaned a little closer to read the other's name-badge.

'Oh,' said Jo, abruptly ending her subterfuge, startled by what she read: *Geraldine Sutherland*.

The other woman looked at her, surprised, then introduced herself.

'Have we met?'

'I don't think so,' said Jo, still flustered. 'You just remind me of someone. One of my dearest friends, as it happens. Also called Sutherland. What an odd coincidence.'

'Jessie, no doubt,' said the stranger with a smile and Jo's fork practically dropped from her hand in astonishment.

'Now how could you possibly know that?'

'My sister,' said the stranger calmly, reaching across to grab the water jug and fill both their glasses. 'We are often told we look alike, though personally I don't see it.'

She was older than Jessica and less striking, yet with the same fine bones and pallid skin. But it didn't make sense.

'But she's always told us she was an orphan,' Jo blurted out, for once too stunned to think before she spoke. Geraldine remained unruffled.

'That sounds like Jessie,' she said, as she ate her salad. 'Always did consider herself a cut or two above the rest of us. Though I don't think Mummy or Daddy would be amused.' She smiled. She had the same light green eyes and freckles but appeared more composed than the far more jumpy Jessica.

Jo was astounded. She had known Jessica Sutherland now for . . . how long? and thought she was acquainted with most of her innermost secrets. Being an orphan had been so much a part of her stock in trade that it was impossible now to have to rethink her.

'Don't worry,' said Geraldine calmly, crumbling her roll. 'You are not telling me anything I didn't already know.' Her badge proclaimed her a registrar at the Radcliffe Infirmary. She had the peaceful countenance of someone entirely at her ease. 'Poor Jessie always was highly strung. And since the tragedy has been, quite naturally, just a little . . . unhinged. We've done our best. My parents keep an eye out for her but what can you expect? We hoped she'd be over it by now but it seems she is not. Pushing away the family is all part of the syndrome.'

Jo sat transfixed, her game pie forgotten.

'Tragedy?' she said cautiously. *Now* what was she about to hear?

It was Geraldine's turn to look surprised. 'You mean she didn't tell you?' she said. 'About Tom and that frightful accident?'

*　　*　　*

331

'Gracious!' said Merrily, startled. 'You scared the shit out of me.'

She had just returned from a blissful afternoon at Harvey Nichols to find Jessica standing silently on the half-landing balcony, back from the railing, more or less unseen. Jessica turned a stricken face to her, haggard with terror, her eyes bolting in her head.

'There's someone down there,' she said in a hoarse whisper. 'I felt him following me. He won't go away.'

Merrily had a look. The peaceful courtyard, with its mighty elms and Ali Baba tubs of colourful flowers, looked as deserted as it usually did. On this clear, sunny evening it was a haven of serenity, more like Italy or France than busy Fulham.

'Nobody I saw,' she said unfeelingly, far more interested in examining her purchases. She led the way back into the flat and held up a neat little designer number in crisp cerise linen.

'You like? I thought I might wear it tonight.'

But Jessica's attention was back on the courtyard. She knelt on a stool by the window and craned forward but only part of the area could be seen from this height. Slowly Merrily focused on her. She really *was* scared.

'You're not serious? I thought you were kidding. Who the hell is it likely to be and what could he possibly have against you? I'm assuming it *is* a he.'

Jessica moved cautiously away from the window, keeping closely to the wall. She wetted her parched lips before she spoke and her voice, when it came, was the echo of a whisper.

'They've been after me for months and now they know where I am. I'm so scared, I really don't know what to do.' She dug out a tissue and scrubbed at her eyes; when she raised her head, Merrily saw she had been crying.

'Come on, get real.' She took Jessica by the arm. 'This is safe old London on a summer's afternoon. Let's have a cuppa' – she was learning the lingo – 'and then you can tell me all about it.' She lit up a Camel and prepared to be amused but the story Jessica told her set her hair on end.

It started with Tom and their whirlwind romance, first so idyllic, later so fraught. She filled Merrily in on the details, right up to the point where they travelled down to London and Tom had his life-changing meeting with the maestro. She paced the room and wrung her hands. Merrily was impressed.

'I should never have let him go,' said Jessica. 'He was far too young and I too green. If we'd stayed up north we'd still be together. And Tom would be alive.' She gave a great gulping sob but continued while Merrily listened, entranced.

'After they followed us to the West Indies,' she went on, 'they ordered him back to London and tried to break us up. And ever since they've been after me too, so I've had to chop and change and keep moving around, for fear they'll eventually catch up with me. And now they've found me and I'm scared. It was them in the churchyard, I am practically certain of it, and them who did the burglary the other day.'

This couldn't be true, the creature must be raving. Merrily took firm hold of her and tried to calm her down

'There now,' she said, pouring the tea. 'You have to be imagining it, things like that just don't happen.' But she was more sympathetic; Jessica was convincing. 'Who's this "they" anyhow?'

'Richard Stanford Palmer and his manager, Conrad Silver,' gulped Jessica. 'The man has a power complex and would rather destroy than encourage. Years ago he lost a child of his own and ever since he's been hunting down talented youngsters and trying to build them into prodigies like her. He wants to keep them all to himself, he won't allow them lives of their own.'

'And what possibly can they have against you?'

'I know too much,' said Jessica darkly. 'I know they killed him. Sebastian too. And now they're in London and looking for me. I won't be safe till they've gone again but it's almost too late, since they've obviously tracked me down.'

'Don't be so daft,' said Merrily, hugging her. 'I can't believe it can be that serious. And, anyhow, you've got us to protect you now.'

All the way down from York, Jo sat alone in the corner of her carriage, stunned. The train was virtually empty so she had peace in which to ponder and her thoughts traced a merry dance indeed, whirling round and round in her head as the pieces fell slowly into place. At Doncaster there was a long delay, due to signal failure further down the line but, for once, she wasn't impatient. She needed time to absorb what Geraldine had told her, to sort out the facts in this startling new light.

But when, some time later, the train slowed to a snail's pace, she realised she was likely to be late and started to panic. She needed urgently to talk to the rest of the gang, to prime them before the concert began. That was crucial. Jessica and Merrily were making an early start, in order to get good places in the arena before the crowds started to gather. Jo was supposed to meet them at home by six but, at this rate, she would be lucky to get to the concert in time.

At King's Cross she hit the platform running and made a dash for the taxi rank. She needed to get to Fulham to change and dump her bag and was frantic to catch them before they set out. The traffic was lighter than usual, which was a relief, and the driver pulled up outside Elm Park Mansions at a little after seven. In time for Jo to make the concert, just, but too late to intercept the others. She would simply have to move as quickly as she could and hope to locate them in the crush at the Albert Hall.

She needed their support, to talk to both of them, but the urgency was knocked out of her by what happened next. She was just inserting her key in the downstairs lock when she sensed movement behind her and turned in time to see a man silently skulking, apparently watching her from the opposite doorway. Although it was still bright daylight, the doorway was in shadow, and it was only when he bent his head to light a cigarette, that the flare of the lighter illuminated his features. Just for one second but that was enough; enough to set Jo reeling and drive all else from her mind.

For in that swift moment, she recognised the man, glimpsed only momentarily but still fresh in her memory. That glossy, blue-black, almost Eurasian hair, those chiselled cheekbones and dazzling teeth. She had barely met him, yet thought of him a lot. Since New York when Lowell had dropped his bombshell and shown her the photograph.

Dimitri Romanov – but what was he doing here? Of course it was him in the cemetery, she realised that now, and guessed he must now be on the tail of Merrily. But why? She turned to confront him but was already too late. Trailing smoke, he had nonchalantly sauntered away, around the corner to the waiting limo, and out of her sight.

28

Cora Louise was more than satisfied with the discreet ambience of the Connaught Hotel. They sat in the lounge, on low, comfortable chairs, while an elderly waitress in black served them tea from a silver pot. This was genteel living at its ultimate best; not even Louella Petigru would be likely to find fault here. She beamed across at Lowell and settled down to enjoy herself. The concert wasn't until seven-thirty; they had hours to kill until they need start moving. Today Fontaine was beside herself with excitement, bright and pretty and at her most coquettish. She sat with her knees demurely crossed and sparkled at Lowell who was seated beside her. On her wrists and fingers she wore her most spectacular jewels and her flaming hair was a riot of Bond Street perfection.

She was bubbling over with excitement and full of the week they had spent at a stately home.

'They were both such darlin's, the lord and his lady,' she said. 'He was so cute I just itched to take him home and Lady Claire is the world's most wonderful cook. They treated us just like family. We'll definitely be going back there again, won't we, Mama.'

What a long way they'd journeyed to this most consummate of days. Cora Louise was feeling mellow and relaxed. If truth be told, despite their constant travelling, treats like this were growing fewer and rarer and she feared to think how they'd afford them for very much longer. But today was special, with Lowell here with them again, and she wasn't going to let a single gloomy thought spoil the delight of this elegant reunion. She stretched across and handed him the sandwich plate.

'Here, my dear, you could do with a little spoiling.' The poor man looked quite grey with fatigue, thinner and gaunter with hair that was now pure silver. How he must have suffered from the death of his close friend but already the harsh lines about his mouth were softening and a look of sheer affection was in his eyes as he listened to the prattlings of her own beloved daughter.

'Shush now, girl, and let Lowell drink his tea in peace.' What a handsome pair they made, to be sure; even without turning, she could feel they were the focus of the room and not only because of Fontaine's tinkling laughter. If all went well and Cora Louise had her way, there'd be more than just a reunion to celebrate this trip. And most certainly not before it was time.

One thing, though, there were confessions still to be made, secrets to be shared, before she dare risk her daughter's happiness being squandered in the same brutal way as her own. And this was likely to take considerable courage. Cora Louise had waited so long for her daughter's impending nuptials that fear fluttered her pulses at the thought of what she still had to face. But she knew it was vital that she be strong and stick to her fierce resolve. She had shielded Fontaine throughout her life from the harshness and reality of a hostile world. Now was not the time to be holding back; there was far too much at stake not to be telling the truth at last. At least Lowell was a Boston gentleman. She knew in her heart she could trust him.

Vincent had always laughed at Fontaine's loopy enthusiasm and had teased Lowell gently about her obvious infatuation.

'Better watch that one,' he'd been fond of saying, 'or she'll have you hooked before you know what's hit you.'

Lowell had laughed too and brushed it aside. As one of Boston's most eligible bachelors, he was well accustomed to ladies throwing their favours in his direction and, apart from that one long-gone engagement, had become adept at ducking and weaving away from commitment. He was genuinely attached to Fontaine – found her amusing, enjoyed her company and basked in the warmth of her open admiration. She was a handsome woman with decorous manners and an entirely suitable pedigree; in his circles such factors mattered, particularly if he followed his long-time ambition and ran for Congress. An alliance with Fontaine Ravenel would certainly not harm his reputation in Boston society and in some ways it would be a relief to have a presentable wife to squire around and save him the effort of avoiding offending the scores of hopeful women who constantly set their caps at him.

While Vincent was around, such an arrangement had been out of the question but Vincent was dead now and no one in Massachusetts knew about Lowell's secret life. Even his percipient mother still preferred to turn a blind eye to his discreet peccadilloes and continued to nag him about settling down and finally doing something positive about perpetuating the family name. So why not respond to the raw hope he saw so plainly in both sets of Ravenel eyes? The prospect of life without Vincent was dreary indeed. He knew he could never hope to find that degree of love again but it surely wasn't too late to settle at least for companionship.

After Vincent's death, Lowell had gone through his effects and found packets of snapshots of Fontaine in all guises, clearly conserved for some purpose of his own. She was certainly photogenic. With her ivory skin and delicate features, marred only now by a blur of fat and dominated by that striking, hawk-like nose, she nearly always looked magnificent as she laughed and flirted her way through life. Her huge mahogany-coloured eyes, with their doll-like lashes, gave the impression that she was perpetually surprised and, despite her increasing bulk, she was light and dainty on her feet and could still dance the night away like the most agile of debutantes. Yes, she would certainly pass muster. Lowell was aware he could do a lot worse when it came to selecting a bride.

But was it fair? Even through her laughter, he could sense the underlying anxiety and reminded himself what else Vincent had always said; that there was definite instability there, and only just below the surface.

'They are mostly like that in the South,' he had said, unknowingly echoing Sebastian's opinion. 'Steeped in incest and insanity after centuries of inter-breeding and weakening of the bloodlines.'

'You make them sound like horses,' Lowell had laughed.

'Brood-mares, more like,' said Vincent solemnly. 'But surely that's what it's all about?' And he had looked at Lowell innocently with those wicked, fallen-angel's eyes, then punched his shoulder and cracked up laughing at the very notion of him donning respectability and taking a wife just to satisfy his mother. And the State.

Such memories were not improving Lowell's sanguinity so he quickly side-stepped back to the here and now. It was clear that Cora Louise had something important on her mind. He waved to the waitress for a fresh pot of tea and courteously invited his guest to tell her story.

Cora Louise Ravenel was a God-fearing woman who, despite her constant travelling, had seen remarkably little of real life. There was virtually nothing in her past for which she might reproach herself, other than one glaring incident from her youth that she now felt impelled to divulge. If there was any chance at all of Lowell one day becoming her son-in-law, then he had every right to be acquainted with the plain, unvarnished truth. Look how deception had ruined her own life early on; she was determined not to risk such a fate for Fontaine. Cora Louise sat up straighter, took a deep breath and prepared to spill the beans. At least she knew she could rely on Lowell not to judge her too harshly.

Without the slightest doubt it had been a marriage based on real affection. From that moment of crackling intensity, when Gabriel Ravenel's feverish gaze had first rested on the exquisite Cora Louise Bee, you could almost see the electricity in the air, it was that tangible. Heads nodded behind the fans and tongues started to wag in true Charleston fashion as the ladies of the town took stock and began to forecast a match that was faster in the inception than even they might have expected.

Cora Louise could not have been better connected: her father was a direct descendant of the famous Confederate Colonel Bee, while her mother's ancestors bore one of the most illustrious Charleston names of all, Huger, and her great-grandfather, Paul, lay buried beneath the floating Spanish moss in the ancient Huguenot churchyard. Nothing could have been more perfect, an alliance between two such prominent local families, and instantly the cousins and maiden aunts began plying their delicate needles to ensure Cora Louise the most fitting trousseau for such a propitious event.

She was barely eighteen, and as tiny and delicate as a Dresden shepherdess, the day she stepped out of the Georgian house on Meeting Street, with its canopy of Palmetto trees and crepe myrtles, and into an open, horse-drawn carriage for the short drive around the corner to St Michael's Church where her handsome, vulpine bridegroom awaited her, along with half the residents of fashionable Charleston. What a day of rejoicing that had been, to be sure. Cora Louise wore a crinolined dress in finest Chantilly lace, with the Ravenel pearls around her throat and a dusting of diamonds in her hair. She had six debutantes in attendance, among them Louella Petigru, herself newly engaged, and a tiny, velvet-clad Huger pageboy who staggered along in her wake, carrying the wedding rings on a gold-tasselled cushion.

'Don't they make the prettiest picture,' sighed the crowd, and, 'How proud both their families must be, bless their hearts.'

The service was over and the famous bells pealed forth. Bride and groom emerged triumphantly beneath a ceremonial arch of militiamen's crossed swords and a great cheer went up from the worthy citizens of Charleston, welcoming to their hearts two of their most beloved children, worthily united. They ought to have lived happily ever after; all the auspices were there. But in less than a year the dream was shattered and Gabriel Ravenel had ridden out of town.

Cora Louise paused in her narrative and wiped away a little tear.

'He was always a headstrong boy,' she said, 'but oh, so unutterably handsome.'

Unbalanced, too. When, within weeks, his bride gave him the good news, he shared her delight and started to build a crib.

'We'll call him Daniel, after my grandfather,' he told her, 'and he'll grow up to inherit the family fortunes.'

But when Fontaine was first presented to him and he took her in his arms and saw those strange, flared nostrils and the eyes already darkening against the porcelain skin, he gave a great roar like a fatally wounded bull and threw around some china before storming out of the house.

'He never did return,' whispered Cora Louise, her fine lace handkerchief pressed to her mouth. 'Even though I went on my knees to him and swore on the Bible that what he suspected was a lie. Except to collect his belongings and leave me a forwarding address.' She gazed up at Lowell imploringly and he leaned across and lightly touched her hand. Her bright, intelligent eyes were flooding with tears; even after all these years, the shame and humiliation burnt as strong. But he didn't quite understand exactly what she was telling him. He turned to Fontaine for enlightenment.

'He thought I had a touch of the tar-brush,' she explained flatly. 'Said I was a bastard and called Mama a whore.' The splendid nostrils flared with indignation and the mahogany eyes flashed fire. For the first time ever, Lowell saw exactly what she meant. Those striking features he had always found so beguiling did have an African echo about them once you knew. But only when you'd heard the story and had entered the turmoil of a father's tormented mind.

'And then?'

'He turned his back and left us in the shit,' said Fontaine coarsely. 'Up the creek without a paddle with the whole of fashionable Charleston, God rot 'em, laughing and sneering behind our backs.'

Cora Louise was visibly recovering. She tidied away a tiny smear of mascara and a mischievous smile returned to her lips. She leaned across to Lowell confidentially with merriment dancing once more in her eyes. That was one of her most endearing traits, the storm clouds rarely hung around for long. She was bright once more and chirpy as a cricket, bursting to tell him the glorious denouement.

'Joke is,' she said, looking back across the years, 'gal he ran off with and ended up marrying looks a whole lot more suspect than mah beautiful daughter, I can tell you. Stella from Savannah, she was. Ran a beauty parlah. A handsome woman, I'll grant her that, in her youth a dead ringer for Lena Horne, though without the wonky eye. Two sons now whom I've not seen but they do say they have mulatto stamped on 'em as plain as any pikestaff.' She laughed. 'While Fontaine, just look at her, turned out quite lovely. I wouldn't change her for the world, not a single thing about her.'

'Mama!' Fontaine was laughing too, shrugging her shoulders helplessly, pleased and embarrassed both at the same time. She glanced shyly at Lowell to see how he was taking it, but he remained seated calmly in his comfortable chair, as serene and stately and unruffled as always, a staunch and reliable friend. He was touched by the story and the courage of this valiant little woman. He had always loved her and now he admired her too. She was good and kind with the same girlish innocence that must have graced that young bride all those years ago.

'What a terrible story,' he said, thinking how much he disliked the narrowness of the South, even now in the so-called age of enlightenment. Fontaine was magnificent with just a hint of the exotic which only served to enhance her baroque beauty. She'd certainly electrify them back in staid old Boston. He'd give it more consideration, he really would, but his resolution was hardening in the light of what he had just heard.

'Thing is,' added Cora Louise, happily into her story and all of a sudden enjoying it mightily – it was a relief to have finally got it off her chest – 'if anyone has anything in their pedigrees to be ashamed of, it is surely the Ravenels and not the Hugers or Bees. Slave-owners from way back, it's an historical truth, and none of them too particular where they spread their favours. Oh dear me, no. They were forever climbing into their servants' beds. Or so I have always been told.'

'Truly, Mama?' Now even Fontaine looked startled. All those wasted hours spent hating a long-dead ancestor. The things a gal could discover even this late in life.

'I'd have told you sooner only I never felt it quite proper.'

Cora Louise's laughter burst forth. Now that the truth was finally out and she could see that Lowell was intrigued rather than shocked, the whole sordid business shrank suddenly into perspective. This, after all, was the twentieth century, at least in the world beyond Charleston. The witch-hunting season was finally dead; she would learn once more to hold her head up high. She thought of Louella Petigru and her spiteful, small-minded coterie. They might have nothing better to do than gossip about their neighbours but she and her daughter had lives of their own and a future ahead that looked suddenly bright. Lowell was smiling at Fontaine with real fondness as he fished in his pocket for a pen.

'Come along, ladies,' he said briskly as he signed the bill. 'I rather think we ought to get going or we'll risk missing the beginning of the Haydn.'

29

The first dull rumblings of distant thunder stirred the air as Jo joined the milling crowds outside the Albert Hall. The sky, which had for days been a hard, metallic blue, was turning ominously mauve around the edges but anything that would help take the edge off the intense heat could only be a blessing, particularly for this enormous crowd of concert-goers, cheerfully filing into the vast, domed auditorium, waving flags and carrying bunches of balloons. Jo remembered joking about bringing a rainhat; she hoped the storm would be gracious enough to hold off until they were all safely inside. Tough luck, though, on those stalwarts who had chosen to listen to the concert from the park. Still, that degree of fanatic dedication was hardly likely to be bothered by a few spots of summer rain.

She joined the winding queue outside the box office, all the while searching the crowd for Merrily and Jessica. Lowell and the ladies had tickets for the balcony and would surely, by now, be seated there in comfort. Jo was still reeling from her confrontation with Dimitri and the shocking revelation she had heard in York. It was too much to take in all at once. Something bizarre was happening among her friends; suddenly it seemed that not one of them was quite what she had thought. It was all most perplexing; she badly needed to meet up with them in order to straighten out a few things.

Safe in the balcony, overlooking the arena where the exultant promenaders were packing themselves in, Lowell sat silently brooding, thinking of Vincent – this night more than ever – and how much he, especially, would have loved this extravagant ring-ding. On either side of him sat the Ravenel ladies, both fairly purring with contentment, while somewhere down there, in the midst of that dense crush, would be Merrily, Jessica and Jo. Lowell frowned. His mind was still going over and over that startling interview in New York with tonight's famous conductor. It had taken him till now to assimilate properly the shattering implications of all he had been told.

'There they are!' said Fontaine excitedly, plucking at his sleeve and pointing. Right in the centre of the packed audience below, crammed together like sardines, shoulder to shoulder and swaying in unison, stood Merrily in her stylish cerise linen, arm linked with a laughing Jessica in buttercup yellow. Merrily, the assertive New Yorker, was obviously urging her forward towards the front but, for some reason not immediately obvious, Jessica appeared to be holding back. Lowell was intrigued.

'My, it looks mighty hot down there,' said Cora Louise, fanning herself. 'Beats me why those girls would prefer to stand in a sweaty huddle when they could be up here with us.'

'It's all part of the traditional Last Night fever,' explained Lowell, casting around for Jo. 'The culmination of the season's festivities, the night when fireworks can really be expected.' He wondered what was going on between those two; whether Merrily had yet divulged any of what he had told her. He rather hoped she hadn't; this was highly sensitive ground. His legal mind was by nature cautious, the situation potential dynamite.

'Looks fun to me,' said Fontaine wistfully. She glanced around and was torn. Sitting up here, close to Lowell, might in some ways be a dream come true but her adventurous spirit was loath to remain on the sidelines. There was time enough – with luck, a lifetime – for future cosy sessions like this. If down there was where the action was, then that was where she wanted to be.

'I'm going down,' she announced impulsively. 'We'll find y'all later when the music is over.' And she gathered up her purse, tossed her heavy hair and shoved her way back along the row, fighting the crowd to get through.

'Silly girl,' said her mother indulgently. 'These tickets are like gold-dust and now she'll have to stand.' But the bright eyes sparkled as she followed Fontaine's progress and she knew that, in her place, she'd be doing the same.

Jo found them by accident as she battled her way through the tightly pressed crowd, waving their Union Jacks and tossing carnations, while the excitement in the hall grew tenser as they waited for the concert to begin. And suddenly, way in front, there was Merrily, leaping and waving and encouraging her forward, through a wall of cheering promenaders whose ranks looked to be unbreachable.

'Over here!' shouted Merrily, beckoning, and Jo could see

Fontaine fighting to join them too, though Jessica appeared to be somewhat lagging behind. She stuck her bag and programme firmly under her arm and entered the tight scrum whose general good nature parted to allow her through. Only just in time, too. The orchestra was already in place and now their leader was taking his seat, holding his violin and acknowledging the roar of applause. The air was electric with anticipation; this was going to be a stupendous night.

Jo squeezed Merrily's arm when she got there but conversation was out of the question. The promenaders were shouting and stamping their feet and keeping up a stream of badinage with the BBC commentator perched above their heads. Fontaine, still wearing those ridiculous shoes, was fanning herself with her programme while Jessica, tauter than Jo had ever seen her, was now ghostly pale and looked on the point of collapse. Jo sincerely hoped this was not another migraine; this was hardly the time or place. But she knew how much this night meant to her ambitious friend, and sympathised. After all that hard work, her future could depend on it.

Now the whole hall fell silent, then broke again into thunderous applause as Richard Stanford Palmer, the man they had all been waiting for, walked lightly through the orchestra and on to the stage, shaking hands with the leader as he passed. In a white tuxedo, with a red carnation in his buttonhole, he stepped up on to the podium and turned, arms upraised, to acknowledge his ovation.

'My God!' breathed Jo, unable to believe what she was seeing. For the world-famous conductor who now stood before her was none other than her own lost love, the man she knew only as Conrad Silver.

*   *   *

Throughout the magnificence of Haydn's *Te Deum* Jo stood motionless, as if in a trance, while the massed ranks of promenaders around her rocked and swayed to the music. At one point she turned her eyes frantically in search of Jessica but Jessica appeared to have been swallowed by the crowd, so that all she effectively could do, once an element of reason had returned, was clutch Merrily's arm with crazed fingers and hang on to her for dear life.

'What?' mouthed Merrily silently but Jo simply shook her head and returned her dazed stare to her idol above her. Tall, relaxed and unutterably elegant, he held the orchestra together with consummate ease; small, rimless spectacles perched halfway down his nose, longish, sun-streaked hair curving gracefully above his ears. He moved to the stirring music with the grace of a ballet dancer, his whirling baton invisible as he wove a spell in the air with his eloquent hands. The Durer hands, of course. *That's* what Vincent had been telling her. Once he'd followed his trail to Rotterdam and tracked down the ownership of the *Leonore* it had been typical of the man not to let her know outright. What fun he must have been planning to have teasing her, once he made it to London which, of course, he never did. Well, whatever Richard Stanford Palmer was or might have done, tonight he wiped her out. Like the rawest of groupies, Jo stood there and adored him, knowing with certainty that, without him, life could only ever be a pale second best.

The Ruders concerto was quieter so Jo was able to whisper.

'It's Conrad,' she said, 'though I don't know how. Look at him, isn't he wonderful?' His attention was totally on the music; with eyes half-closed and his hair all over the place, he coaxed the unfamiliar Purcell setting out of the players and filled the hall with its resonant sound. Merrily, knowing more than she let on, remained unmoved.

She simply gave the merest of eloquent shrugs. 'Don't bank on it,' was all she would say as she turned her attention back to the music.

Above them, in the balcony, Lowell was watching too, observing Jo's frozen posture and Merrily's apparent non-chalance and the fact that, behind them, Jessica was sur-reptitiously edging herself backwards into the crowd. Only Fontaine appeared to be behaving normally; thrilled with the event, she was swaying with the crowd, a huge beam of happiness on her beautiful, exotic face. He smiled. She was almost a child with her passions and unbridled enthusiasm but he found he loved her all the better for that. Slowly, within his wintry heart, something vital was defrosting. He turned to Cora Louise with a sudden smile and she gripped his hand in understanding.

But there were other, more urgent, matters still to be sorted. There was danger here, in the middle of all these revellers, though Lowell, in possession of most of the salient facts, hadn't yet quite worked it out. Three deaths had still to be accounted for and where did Vincent's ring fit in? In New York he had talked to the cops and the maestro and now he was also making judgements of his own. All of a sudden, he regretted being up here in the balcony; he wished he could be down there in the arena with his girls where at least he would stand a chance of protecting them.

In the interval there was time, at last, to talk, though they didn't leave their places for fear of losing them. The conductor had left the stage with barely a glance down, though the audience had called him back for a second, and then a third, bow. Maybe he really was absorbed in the music or perhaps he couldn't distinguish faces from up there. It was hot as Hades and everyone was perspiring profusely. Outside, in the distance, the thunder was drawing closer and soon, with luck, the rain would begin to fall. There was no sign of Jessica but that was the least of their problems. Jo was bursting to talk to Merrily, to divulge the events of the past few hours. But where on earth should she start?

'It's OK,' said Merrily calmly. 'I confess I knew already he was Palmer.'

'You did?' Jo was startled and knocked quite off-course. 'So how come you didn't tell me?'

Merrily was contrite. She shook her head and squeezed Jo's arm. Confronted with the shock on her best friend's face, she felt like a traitor and had no defence. But Lowell had been adamant after his meeting with the maestro; there were things afoot here that none of them understood. 'Best to be safe,' had been Lowell's instruction and Merrily cared too much for her friend not to abide by caution. In any case, there hadn't really been time; cramped in the Elm Park Mansions flat they had scarcely had a moment alone.

'Lowell found out,' was all she could say. 'After he'd seen Vincent's photo and then met Palmer in the flesh.'

'So why all the secrecy? And where does Dimitri fit in?' The more she thought of it, the more she felt betrayed. 'And who in the world is Conrad Silver?' So many questions still to be resolved. And then she remembered her latest encounter and told Merrily of her glimpse of Dimitri. Merrily stiffened.

'At Elm Park Mansions? You're quite certain it was him?' This was something entirely from outer field; all of a sudden she didn't like it at all. All she could divulge, as she racked her memory, was that Palmer had told Lowell he was on the trail of a killer. Someone had murdered his most talented protégé and the same person or persons had done the same to Sebastian. It might sound far-fetched but the man had been deadly serious; enough so to impress Lowell, who was not easily fooled, and put him and Merrily on their guard.

'That's absurd!' exclaimed Jo, aghast. 'Seb didn't have enemies. It simply makes no sense.'

'And then there's Jessica's story,' said Merrily. 'Though I hardly like to tell it to you now.'

She did, however, as the crowd surged back and had just reached the part about Palmer and his thugs when the hall fell silent and the orchestra leader returned. No more time for whispering now; the rest of the saga would have to wait. Jo drew in a deep, sharp breath as Richard Stanford Palmer returned to the podium, and led the orchestra into a Glinka overture. The heat was oppressive; her dress stuck to her. In a state of thorough confusion, she stood and let the music wash over her. And as she did so, a memory surfaced – of a walk in Chiswick one wintry afternoon and a glorious stranger, immersed in his playing, framed in the window of a Queen Anne house, with the fading sun just gilding his hair. This man. How was it possible she had eclipsed that image? And how could she live the rest of her life without him?

Jessica, meanwhile, was elsewhere in the hall, sick with terror, on the verge of passing out. All summer she had feared this confrontation but somehow ambition had taken the upper hand. In this day and age, she had managed to convince herself, the law would protect her and the truth would finally out. She hadn't yet seen Conrad but sensed his imminent presence; she had moved from the front of the crowd for fear of being spotted by Richard. Now she was glad she had told so much to Merrily; if anything should go wrong, she knew she could rely on her. At least someone she basically trusted knew and Lowell, too, was somewhere in this hall.

Until she saw him again in the flesh, standing above her, tall, bronzed and utterly in command, she had not anticipated such a violent reaction. But now it all came flooding back, the ugliness, the threats, her genuine fear for her safety. What a fool she'd been to dare stand here, in the arena, when up in the gallery she'd have been out of his sight. Jessica felt the beginnings of a migraine coming on and looked around wildly for some means of escape.

They had tracked them down, in their innocent happiness, and rounded them up as ruthlessly as cattle. When it came to music and his own impossible standards, Richard had let fall the mask of mild benevolence and allowed himself to be seen in his true colours: ruthless, icy cold and relentlessly unforgiving. But far more sinister was his evil henchman, Conrad Silver. Just remembering the handsome sneer and those black, malevolent eyes made her shudder. Jessica glanced nervously around the packed auditorium. Somewhere among all these strangers those eyes were undoubtedly watching and when he saw her she knew he was likely to strike. Panic gripped her; she feared she was going to faint.

The tension was mounting as the audience returned to their seats. Lowell, still preoccupied, glanced around at his opulent surroundings, reflecting that the hall must still look much as it had in Victoria's day. He loved its elegant ambience and determined to come here more often. Maybe, next visit, he would even subscribe to a box. One tier lower than the level where they were sitting, the boxes were also filling up, though several remained unoccupied. Private subscriptions, he supposed, on a night when the hall was packed. The selfishness of the super-rich not to share their privilege with the throng.

In the last box of all, a man sat alone, motionless as a statue, his opera glasses trained on the promenaders below. Lowell's glance flicked over him, then returned with slightly more interest. What on earth could be down there that was holding his attention so fixedly? He craned his neck forward but all he could see was the crowd then looked back at the box where the man was now standing up. But the orchestra was assembling and the noise in the hall subsided. The rustling of programmes ceased as the conductor returned to the stand.

Before the music started, two seasoned promenaders solemnly placed a wreath on the bronze bust of Sir Henry Wood and, from that point on, there was no containing them. The hall was packed to bursting with five thousand euphoric enthusiasts while, across the road in Hyde Park and around the world via the television satellite, a further vast audience also listened in. As the end neared and Richard Stanford Palmer led them, inevitably, into a full vocal rendering of *Land of Hope and Glory*, the crowd grew still more boisterous and the hall rained streamers and bunting. Only the lone man remained unmoved, untouched by the euphoria around him.

High on the podium, Palmer was moving like a mad thing, encouraging the orchestra, exhorting them to ever greater heights. And then he turned to include the massed audience and they all linked arms and swayed in unison as they roared forth the words of the stirring traditional song. Jo, gazing upwards, felt his gaze flicker over her and held her breath as he briefly made eye contact. But then his glance had moved on and she saw him look up at the higher tiers and focus on something there. A frown came on to the handsome face as that something broke his concentration. He ran his hand nervously through his long, now sweaty hair but his right arm never stopped moving the baton and the sound of massed voices was in danger of raising the roof.

Next came *Rule, Britannia*, with magnificent vocals from two distinguished sopranos, and then they were coasting into *Jerusalem* and Jo felt her eyes spout tears, as they always did. Two, three encores and the crowd erupted with cheers, then a ripple ran right through the house as the conductor tossed his baton into the air and leapt over the brass rail of the podium and into the crowd.

Run! Jo sensed rather than heard the voice of Jessica from somewhere deep in the throng – or did she imagine it? – so reflexively, without a second's hesitation, that's exactly what she did.

Throughout the Royal Albert Hall, pandemonium reigned. The BBC commentator was, for once, speechless as the conductor dropped out of sight into the crowd, leaving the orchestra floundering until they pulled themselves together and valiantly played the National Anthem unled. Then the serried ranks of promenaders broke and the vast crowd, with one accord, surged towards the several exits, among them Jo, borne along almost against her will. Somewhere ahead of her she caught occasional glimpses of Jessica's yellow dress while from behind, when she dared to pause, came the flash of white of the conductor's formal tuxedo as he rapidly gained ground on her as the audience fell back to let him through.

'Wait, Jo, you've got to hear me out.'

All her instincts were to turn and allow him to catch her; to fall once more into those strong, protective arms she so much missed. But she'd seen the look of pure terror on Jessica's haunted face and remembered clearly Merrily's words of foreboding. *This man*, she told herself sternly, *is not at all what he seems.* He had lied to her consistently, presented himself under a false persona and, if Jessica had told the truth, bullied, threatened and quite possibly killed. And why should Jessica lie? The poor girl was clearly half demented with fright. Something really terrible was about to happen; Jo made a snap decision and shot on after Jessica.

Her progress, though, was impeded, as she got to the outer doors, by a dense mass of sheltering bodies as the storm finally broke and the heavens opened. Great crackles of summer lightning forked across the threatening sky and, it seemed within seconds, Kensington Gore became awash with water. No one with any sense was going to venture out into such a torrent and Jo realised she would have to wait along with the rest. She glanced behind her and saw Palmer closing in, one arm reaching out in an attempt to grab her shoulder, and simultaneously became aware of a whirr of yellow and a door marked 'Private' opening and sharply shutting. As part of the personnel, Jessica knew her way around this building. Instinct told Jo she'd be heading up to the gallery.

'Jo, please listen.' Palmer was almost on to her but the sharp terror on Jessica's face had been enough to convince Jo. Time enough for explanations later, if he had anything convincing to say. Now she was keen only to catch up with Jessica and hear in detail her side of the story which was, she knew, likely to be the true one. Shaking off his hand, she dived for the door and wrenched it open. An ancient Victorian iron staircase opened into darkness above her. Jo allowed the heavy door to slam in his face as she raced on upwards after Jessica's receding footsteps.

30

'Jessica, wait!'

A thinning trickle of promenaders was meandering down the public staircase when Jo pushed open the staff door behind the organ and found herself in the midst of the BBC's lighting equipment. Ahead of her the gallery was deserted but a further staircase led upwards to an outside door and that was the route Jessica must have taken. Jo pressed on. Somewhere behind her Palmer must be gaining fast; there was no time to spare if she wanted to get to Jessica and hear the rest of her story before it was too late.

She exited through a heavy iron door on to a wideish stone walkway, surrounded by a parapet, with the great glass dome of the Albert Hall looming above, lit up dramatically by further streaks of crackling lightning. For one giddy moment, stunned and scared, she leaned against the door, fearing the height and the sudden vast panoramic view, while the rain bombarded her with a fusillade of furious drops. There was still no sign of her friend.

'Jessica?' She had to be up here somewhere but the circular ledge, for as far as she could see, appeared deserted. Then she heard clanging footsteps somewhere above her head and, as another vicious lightning bolt split the sky, saw a narrow cat-ladder just ahead, extending vertically up the side of the building right to the edge of the dome. Taking a great gulp of air in an attempt to still her terror and wishing now she had had more sense than to wear these inadequate thong sandals, Jo took a grip on either side of the narrow ladder and slowly began to climb.

They had to be somewhere, goddammit. Somehow Merrily had managed to lose all three of her companions in the crush and found herself borne along against her will in a festive crowd of merry promenaders, all in party-going mood. At the main exit they were halted by the storm and Merrily knew she was going nowhere, at least till the torrential rain began to ease off. This dress had cost far more than she could afford; she was not going to risk ruining it on its first ever outing, even if it meant hanging around here for hours. Where was everyone, anyhow? She looked out hopefully for some of the others, furious with herself for letting them all slip by.

She knew that Lowell and Cora Louise were upstairs, pigging it in luxury seats in the balcony. Maybe if she headed that way she'd have the luck to meet them as they left. So off she set, up the carpeted stairs, pushing against the flow of people coming down. It would be a damned nuisance if she failed to find them. Plans had been made to meet up after for supper but she didn't have exact details of what they had in mind. Jo, as always, had taken care of that. She reached the grand tier and paused to look around her. The vast auditorium was rapidly emptying and only a few people were left in the corridors.

Ahead of her, leaning against a wall casually smoking, stood a man, alone and apparently waiting. A man in a snazzy, well-cut suit with blue-black hair and a dazzling smile he was directing now at her.

'Merrily.'

'Dimitri!'

'How ya doin', babe?'

She was thunderstruck. He, however, appeared quite unfazed as he slowly exhaled a thin column of smoke and looked her up and down in overt appreciation. It was months since they'd met but, she was shamed to acknowledge, seeing him suddenly like this still delivered the same visceral punch and made her knees go wobbly with desire. She hated him yet still lusted after him too; and what, in hell's name, was he doing here? He was openly laughing at her obvious confusion.

'Are you following me?' Dumb question but it was out before she thought.

'To the ends of the earth.'

'Mr Silver.' A black-tied official appeared and handed him a message on a slip of paper. Merrily gaped; the penny, at last, was beginning to drop.

'Conrad Silver!'

'At your service.' He bowed his head solemnly as he read his message.

'What on earth's going on and why all the play-acting?' Her legendary temper was beginning to revive. Two becoming spots of brilliant colour arose on Merrily's cheeks; it was all she could do not to slug him with her purse.

'Come with me, my dear,' he purred smoothly, grasping her

elbow. 'I have things to do that won't wait but I'll explain on the way down.'

Just in time, she recalled Lowell's warning and snatched away her arm as if she had been stung.

'Up yours, buster,' she growled as she flounced away, then ran like the blazes and lost herself in the crowd.

Outside the wind was growing stronger and Jo's hands were like ice as she grasped the ancient iron. Somewhere behind her a door banged opened and running feet made her climb more urgent. She was scared of slipping, of losing her footing. Of somehow plunging all that dizzying way to the ground. A cold sweat broke over her but there wasn't time now. Jessica needed her; she had to be there for her.

'Jo, for pity's sake, what d'you think you are doing? It's not safe up there and the storm's getting worse.'

Terrified as she was, she turned her head briefly and glimpsed the flash of his white tuxedo as he reached the foot of the ladder.

'Jo!' screamed Jessica, from somewhere above in the darkness. 'He's after me, please don't let him come up.' She could see the glint of Palmer's spectacles as the lightning continued to sputter and rage and the rain grew more insistent. He was standing on the bottom rung, watching her struggle up the vertical ladder.

'Jo, don't be insane!' His concern sounded genuine. 'Come down immediately and we'll try to sort things out. Here, on the ground, where it's not so precarious. Be careful, my darling, or you'll fall.'

His warning certainly had the ring of truth and, for a moment, tugged at her heart-strings. But he'd lied to her once, so why not again? Merrily had warned her and Jessica was in trouble. And Jo was a doctor whose mission it was to preserve life. She gritted her teeth and continued to climb.

'Don't worry, sweetie. Just hang on there and wait for me.' She couldn't see Jessica but knew she was up there somewhere, panicked and, from the way she had looked earlier, very possibly on the verge of passing out. It was essential Jo reach her in time. And there she was, right at the top of the ladder, huddled in terror at the edge of the great sweep of glass, her yellow dress sodden, her hair in rats' tails, shivering so hard Jo could hear her teeth chatter. She stretched out a hand to touch her but Jessica shied away.

'He's right behind you,' she hissed. 'Please don't let him up here. He's a dangerous killer and now he's out to get me. He murdered my Tom.'

And at that precise moment, Jo felt fingers close around her ankle. She screamed in horror and, without pausing to think, lashed out instinctively with her foot and kicked the famous conductor hard in the face. There was a gasp, an expletive and the distant tinkle of glass. He released her ankle abruptly and, when Jo dared to look, stood there, swaying at the top of the ladder, holding his forehead and, bereft of his spectacles, apparently unable to see.

'What I want to know,' said Cora Louise comfortably, now that they were dry and settled, in the plush interior of a famous nearby bistro, 'is what in the world is going on and what y'all are getting so excited about.'

'And where are Jo and Jessica?' chimed in Fontaine, twisting damp corners of her abundant hair and curling them around her fingers to dry. Merrily, luckily, they had encountered along the way and swept her up with them to this pre-arranged meeting spot.

'Don't worry,' Lowell had reassured her. 'It has all been fixed. Jo made the reservations before she went away.'

Now he looked grave. Things had not worked out quite the way he had envisaged. Somehow, in the turmoil at the end of the concert, Jo and Jessica had both gone missing and that was not a good thing. He gazed abstractedly at the winelist and ordered a bottle of Margaux. There was no point in keeping things from them any longer; he had planned, in any case, to have this conversation tonight. He removed his reading glasses and twisted them nervously in his fingers. Then tried to reconstruct what he had learned in New York.

Richard Stanford Palmer had started life as a musical prodigy, playing the piano to concert standard when only seven years old. He had been lucky, or not as the case may be, to be recognised at such an age and his whole early life had been spent in unnatural circumstances, being honed and encouraged to fulfil his destiny so that music had become the main substance of his life. Or so he had explained to Lowell. It had all worked out brilliantly and his success had been entire. By seventeen he was internationally applauded; by twenty-two the youngest conductor ever. Fontaine was growing restless and rustled her menu. Lowell gave her a placatory smile and silently urged her to wait.

He had been thoroughly blessed as he rocketed up the ladder and had completed his happiness by marrying a gifted violinist, from which union had sprung his only child, Jade. And that is when things had begun to turn sour for, by the time she was a toddler and able to pick up a violin, her father was already too celebrated and immersed in world tours to take proper care of her and give her a normal childhood. At least that's what he thought. He had spent, through necessity, so much time away from home that she had grown up not really knowing him and the marriage had started to crack. The overwhelming tragedy of his life had been the day he had come home unannounced to catch his wife on the point of leaving him.

An ugly argument had ensued and she'd snatched the child and just left. Driving too fast along the motorway, with her husband hot in pursuit, she had misjudged a turning and hit the hard shoulder, overturning the car and mortally injuring the child who had died, hours later, in hospital. Everyone looked startled and Fontaine gave a great sob. *Now* what was this he was telling them? Only Merrily remained composed.

Since then the maestro, which is what he had become, had tried to expunge his insupportable guilt by seeking out young talent among his musicians and fostering them as devotedly as any father. What he'd taken from life, he was determined to replace. Such a one had been Tom Hawkyard, an untutored horn player from the North, possibly the most talented natural virtuoso Palmer had ever encountered. Lowell paused. Now they were all staring at him, transfixed.

'Go on,' said Fontaine, no longer fidgeting. 'Put us out of our misery. Then what happened?'

'What happened,' said Lowell thoughtfully, playing with his fork, 'appears to have been Jessica. Which is really, I suppose, what this has all been about.'

'Don't believe a word she says,' said Palmer urgently. 'She's out of her mind and potentially very dangerous.' Jo could just make him out, still outlined against the storm, precariously balanced at the top of the ladder, soaked to the skin and holding on for dear life. Jessica had moved on, crabwise, away from the very edge and up another narrow walkway which led in an arc across the surface of the glass to the centre of the dome. Blindly Jo followed her, trusting now only to instinct.

'He had him killed,' said Jessica, her voice trembling with emotion. 'In order to keep him away from me. We were so happy, so awfully happy. It should have lasted forever, we loved each other so much.' She was climbing down another cat-ladder to a circular grid over the centre of the hall. Though her calves ached and her sandals were insecure, Jo kept on going too. With Palmer guarding the only way down, there was really nothing else she could do.

'Not true,' came Palmer's voice on the wind. Without his glasses, he obviously dared not follow. Knowing he was stranded made Jo feel safer. 'Get her to tell you exactly what happened.'

They were standing huddled together now, on the black Victorian grid which shifted uneasily under their weight like a net of chain-mail. Through the grille, far beneath, Jo could see the lighted arena from which they had listened to the concert. A terrifying wave of vertigo swept over her and, instinctively, she clutched at Jessica for support.

'This can't be safe,' she said in panic but Jessica appeared oblivious.

'He was just like all the others,' she intoned in a voice that had subtly altered. 'Swore he loved me but, when it came to the crunch, was going to put his music first.' She was sobbing again and holding fast to Jo's arm. Jo tried to shake herself free in an attempt to grab the ladder but Jessica stuck fast, as relentless as a limpet, apparently impervious to any danger.

'So she drowned him,' came Palmer's voice again. 'Half-strangled him first and then held him under. Ask her if that's not true.'

The Heimlich Manoeuvre, of course. Another spark of rogue memory flickered in Jo's brain and she saw again clearly two figures entwined, greedily devouring each other on a deserted diving-raft. The one young and lithe, in the briefest of bathers, the other a pale-skinned mermaid with dripping, red-gold hair. What an odd thing memory is, that after all these years it should only surface now.

'He was too immature, he just didn't get it. They'd have taken him over, body and soul, and ruined his life. At least I saved him from that.'

'Like Sebastian?'

Shock caused Jo to draw in a sharp breath and struggle to disengage herself from Jessica's grip. But Jessica proved too strong for her.

'Sebastian was different. He tried to leave me. Said he loved you better. He had it coming.'

'Ask her about the ring.' Palmer's voice sounded calmer and altogether more confident, as if they still had all the time in the world.

'He made a silly fuss about the ring as we were struggling on the balcony. I didn't usually wear it but that night was special. Seb's first concert. It was to bring us both luck.'

Jo recoiled, almost nauseous with horror. But Jessica's thin fingers held on to her like clamps.

'How did Sebastian know it was Vincent's ring?' she asked. 'Surely the two of them never actually met?'

'My point too,' agreed Palmer from the walkway, on to which he had edged for safety. 'They never met but Judge Brooks says the ring was often discussed.' Jo nodded; that was true. Sebastian, the trainee psychiatrist, had always been fascinated by Vincent's murder; for a while it was all they talked about.

Jessica's eyes were steely now as she appeared to be concentrating on the past.

'He accused me of stealing it, can you believe it? I couldn't let him get away with that.' An odd little smile was playing about her mouth, a look both coquettish and unnervingly arch. 'I gave him a shove and it slipped right off my finger. It was always loose. Guess I ought to have got it fixed.'

'And Vincent?' This nightmare was getting worse by the minute. Jo really hated to hear more yet had to know the truth. Jessica's green eyes narrowed. A hard, mean expression now distorted her face. Her nails dug so hard into Jo's flesh that she flinched.

'He laughed at me,' was all she said, as if that was enough.

The grid was most definitely unstable and Palmer too far away to assist. The look in Jessica's eyes was now patently mad; Jo edged away from the slackening fingers and made a sudden grab for the fragile ladder. She, at least, was determined to survive though she realised now that the odds were against her. This crazed woman she had cared for had already killed at least three times.

'No!' shrieked Jessica, making a lunge for her. 'Please don't desert me like all the others. Everyone I have ever loved.'

But Jo was free and rapidly scaling the ladder.

'I'm coming,' she shouted to the marooned Palmer. 'Hang on right there and I'll help you down.'

She covered the narrow walkway over the glass faster than she could ever have believed possible and fell into a pair of strong, familiar arms. Together they watched in silence Jessica's last disastrous move. The storm had abated and the sky was bright with moonlight. Against this background she rose and started to walk, delicately as a tightrope walker, along a narrow rib, right across the old Victorian glass.

'Look out!' screamed Jo but it was already too late. In what seemed like slow motion, she wobbled and fell, bouncing off the shiny, rain-slicked panes as lightly as a ping-pong ball and over the edge into Kensington Gore below.

They sat up there in silence, just listening to the sirens and gazing at each other in wonder and disbelief. Without the trademark glasses he looked younger and more vulnerable but every inch as handsome as when she had first clapped eyes on him.

'At one time,' he admitted, 'I even believed it might be you.' He had tracked down Jessica remorselessly, following up every clue. Tom Hawkyard had been very dear to him, a precious replacement, he had always felt, for the gifted child he had so carelessly lost. 'I knew there was a woman involved and wherever I went, you always seemed to turn up. I couldn't get you out of my mind. And not only because of those strange, odd eyes.'

He kissed her then and she snuggled up against him, dazed and happy to be back with him like this. Some time later she'd ask about Conrad Silver but, right at this moment, there were more important things to do.

'I'll go first,' said Jo gently as she set off down the ladder. Going down was even more horrendous but she was damned if she'd let him know she was scared. One step at a time and she'd get there in the end. There was no longer any need to hurry and she knew he'd be close behind.

'Just follow me and you'll be OK. Trust me,' said Jo.

'With my life,' said Richard Stanford Palmer.

Epilogue

They all filed into Lowell's suite and took their places on chairs and on the bed. Jo, looking radiant, clutched the hand of her handsome conductor while Merrily, on his other side, was similarly transformed by recent happenings. Cora Louise and Fontaine, for their own private reasons, also looked as happy as sandboys. With Richard's assistance, Lowell served the drinks then raised his glass for the customary toasts.

'To absent friends!' he said with the hint of a sigh and they all maintained a second's brief silence for Vincent, whose absence they still so keenly felt. Then Richard rose and raised his own glass.

'To love!' he said, squeezing Jo's hand and looking down at her with eyes that could devour her.

'To the future!' cried Merrily gaily, leaping into the spirit of things, totally rejuvenated by the generosity of this remarkable man. She still didn't quite understand it, this sudden change of affairs and the promise of a new career that would rocket her back to the heights she had always craved.

'It will mean a great deal of travel,' Richard had warned her but he shared her joy at the prospect before her, of touring the world with a celebrity superstar and also spending more time with her closest friend. Jo would like that too; it was partly due to her that he'd had the idea, of harnessing Merrily's impressive skills and stopping Jo being lonely, when, that was, her dedication allowed her to join him. And he needed someone on his team he could trust; recent experience had taught him that lesson.

'I seem to be making a habit of finding jobs for the girls,' he joked as the group hugged Merrily and exulted in her good fortune. Wait till Byron Kaminsky got wind of it!

Jo looked blank and he remembered she didn't know.

'Jessica,' he said apologetically. 'I'm afraid I pulled a little rank and got her that job with the BBC.' They were all staring at him. 'I'd been after her for years,' he explained, 'but never had enough to pin on her that would stick. So when I discovered, through channels of my own, that her main ambition was to work on the Proms, I used a little sleight of hand to encourage her to apply.'

Lowell was intrigued. He was used to things being fixed but hadn't expected it to extend to the world of music.

'So how did you swing it?' asked Jo, impressed, giddy with happiness and barely able to speak.

'Elementary, my dear doctor,' said Richard, stroking her hair. 'I planted a mole who used the force of his personality to inspire her to do the dirty and try to get one over him.'

'The Prat!' chimed in Fontaine, triumphantly.

'The same,' said Richard, grinning. 'Not exactly the brightest of groupies but effective when it came to baiting the trap. She was so intent on elbowing him out of the way, it never occurred to her to look behind her.'

'He was lucky he wasn't more prepossessing,' remarked Cora Louise. 'Else who knows where the poor fellow might have ended up.'

'Belly up on a concrete floor,' said Merrily. 'Now tell us more about Conrad.'

Richard's grin vanished. 'Conrad Silver has been my concert manager for years, based in Beverly Hills where he runs a pretty mean outfit, organising concerts and representing a privileged handful of stars, one of whom is me. He is loyal and effective and fiercely tenacious and has, I have to hand it to him, done wondrous things for my career. But he is inclined to go over the top and sometimes can't control himself.'

He looked at Merrily apologetically and she winced. Despite her new-found optimism, she still smarted at the way she had been treated and, deep down, languished for the rat she had once thought a prince.

'I'm sorry about that,' said Richard sheepishly, 'but it seemed a good idea at the time.'

They'd been hot on the scent of Tom Hawkyard's murderer but, although they'd known there was a woman in the case, had not yet narrowed the field to Jessica. Jo had been one of their suspects, though, purely through happenstance as it turned out. So that when they ran into her at the Mill Reef Club, and Merrily had caught Conrad's eye, it had seemed too good an opportunity to miss.

'Dance with her,' Richard had suggested and Conrad, ever ready for an adventure, had leapt deftly into his role. As always, of course, he had gone too far, had donned that absurd alias and taken Merrily for a ride that was way beyond the call of duty.

'And entirely unprofessional,' frowned Richard, 'which is one of the reasons I have had to let him go.'

'So where's the bastard now?' growled Merrily, fierce on the surface yet still secretly hoping. 'And how come you confused my friend here by impersonating him?'

'Back in LA, grounded for a while,' said Richard, dealing with the easier part of the question first. 'Doing a hundred hours community service for some tax discrepancies that recently came to light. He won't be troubling you again, I assure you, not for a year or so at least. Maybe longer, if the State has its way. They're also looking into some drugs-related charges.'

It was the drugs thing, explained Richard, that had finally got to him and provoked that dramatic leap into the audience at the Albert Hall.

'Not my usual style, I assure you,' he said with a grin. 'But when I spotted him with his eyes glued to the arena, I knew he was stalking someone and couldn't risk taking any more chances.' He looked at Jo. 'I knew he was dangerous and getting out of control. There'd been incidents before, on the road, which we'd had to hush up. It was only a matter of time before scandal hit the papers and I certainly wasn't going to allow that.' He took Jo's hand and gazed at her fondly. 'Then he trashed your flat and that was it.'

'And the impersonation?' Merrily was relentless. Richard had the grace to look a shade uncomfortable.

'It started quite simply as a misunderstanding,' he said. 'I needed something to write on and my manager, as always, provided his card. After that, once I realised you thought I was him, it still seemed easier to go along with it. One of the burdens of celebrity, I'm afraid.' He turned and shrugged and Jo smiled up at him and squeezed his hand. *Does he deserve her?* wondered Merrily then decided that, on the whole, perhaps he did.

'One thing I'd like to know,' said Lowell. 'When did this all start, the Jessica business?'

'December nineteen ninety-two,' said Richard promptly. 'The day you arrived in Antigua, in fact.'

'When we heard about the Englishman drowning.' Fontaine looked puzzled. 'But Jessica wasn't even there then. I distinctly remember Vincent bringing her in at least three days later.'

'Ah,' said Lowell, finding the missing piece. 'But she was on the island, just not in our hotel.' Marjorie Barlow had commented on the wind-burn; crafty devil, she was simply covering up. Fontaine shuddered, what a close shave they had all had, but her mother was kinder and less inclined to lay blame.

'Poor child,' she said softly, with the hint of a quaver. 'All she ever really wanted, I do believe, was a little unconditional love.'

'And now,' said Lowell, resuming his role of host. 'Everyone have a top-up and then we'll go down to dinner.'